MARIJUANA GIRL

It's the striptease in the gymnas
from school right before gradua
But the dean is not amused. It's

love and attention in all the wrong places. Her parents have been
bouncing her from relative to relative all her life while they travel
around the world. At least she has Tony. Or did. When Joyce takes
a job at the local newspaper and starts seeing her boss Frank, Tony
blows up and deserts her. But that's okay because Frank takes her
into the city and introduces her to the world of jazz musicians, jive
talk and marijuana. It's all happening so fast for Joyce—and all
she really wants is to be loved.

CALL SOUTH 3300: ASK FOR MOLLY!

Slade Martin is a womanizer and a heavy drinker, but he's the
shining star of the sales department at All-Channel TV. His job is
to sell sets, so when he meets Ann Frank, he immediately corrals
her into helping him land the biggest client at the convention,
Mortimer Kane. How she accomplishes this task is her own
business. But Ann has a secret of her own. Besides working for
All-Channel, she is also a high class prostitute working for Molly,
the local madam. Unaware of this, Slade falls for Ann in a big
way. Ann would like nothing more than to fall for Slade, too, but
the feeling just isn't there. Instead, she's in love with Eric, who
only uses her for her money—if only he weren't so good in bed.

THE SEX CURE

Justin Riley has to admit that his troubles always have something
to do with women. What he really wants is someone who believes
in him, who believes he's the best doctor on earth. Someone
young, eager and exciting. There's Betty, pregnant with his child
and suffering a botched abortion; Misty, a failure at marriage but
not sex; and unattainable Marge Miles. His wife Olivia is quick to
point out that her money and father's influence got him where he
is. But Justin is tired of pretending—pretending to love the women
he just wants to sleep with, pretending that his marriage is
respectable and good when he knows deep down that he is nothing
but a liar and a cheat. A man ruled by sex… and fear.

A TRIO OF BEACON BOOKS:

Marijuana Girl
by N. R. de Mexico

Call South 3300:
Ask for Molly!
by Orrie Hitt

The Sex Cure
by Elaine Dorian

Stark House Press • Eureka California
www.starkhousepress.com

A TRIO OF BEACON BOOKS: MARIJUANA GIRL / CALL SOUTH 3300: ASK FOR MOLLY! / THE SEX CURE

Published by Stark House Press
1315 H Street
Eureka, CA 95501
griffinskye3@sbcglobal.net
www.starkhousepress.com

MARIJUANA GIRL
Originally published by Uni-Books and copyright ©1951 by Universal Publishing and Distributing
Corporation. Republished by Beacon Books, 1960

CALL SOUTH 3300: ASK FOR MOLLY!
Originally published by Beacon Books and copyright ©1958 by Universal Publishing and Distributing
Corporation.

THE SEX CURE
Originally published by Beacon Books and copyright ©1962 by Universal Publishing and Distributing
Corporation.

Introduction copyright ©2019 by Jeff Vorzimmer
Proofreading by David Rachels

ISBN-13: 978-1-944520-89-2

Book design by ¡caliente!design, Austin, Texas

First Stark House Press Edition: September 2019

Introduction
Jeff Vorzimmer

You are holding in your hands over a thousand dollars in books. That's about what it would cost you to buy the original Beacon editions of the three books contained herein. Although original Beacon books have become very collectible over the last several years, it's not the only reason these three have become highly prized collectibles.

As any collector will tell you, it's a combination of factors that drives up the price of a collectible paperback. These factors include not only scarcity, but books on certain (previously) taboo subjects (drugs, homosexuality, etc.), first editions, self-published editions, signed copies, books with covers illustrated by popular artists, books with an interesting back story or written by authors with a cult following—especially written under a pseudonym. Usually a book becomes highly collectible because of a combination of these factors.

Certainly that is the case with all three books included here, which makes them more valuable than other Beacon books. Sometimes, though, it's not always apparent what drives up the price of a book. For example, Orrie Hitt has become a bit of a cult author over the last ten years, with many of his books rising in demand and—subsequently—in price. But why would *Call South 3300: Ask for Molly!* command a price of $120? It could be that the print run of that book was less than those of other Beacon Hitt titles, or the fact that it's received better reviews than some of the other 150-plus books he wrote. It might even be due, in part, to the book being featured in Gary Lovisi's *Dames, Dolls and Delinquents: A Collector's Guide to Sexy Pulp Fiction*.

A recent survey of Amazon, eBay and AbeBooks has revealed some astounding prices for Beacon Books. Here is a list of the top fifteen:

Lust Is a Woman	Charles Willeford	$550
The Sex Cure	Elaine Dorian	$500
Marijuana Girl	N. R. De Mexico	$450
High Priest of California/Wild Wives	Charles Willeford	$300
Honey Gal	Charles Willeford	$300
Pick-Up	Charles Willeford	$275
She Got What She Wanted	Orrie Hitt	$221
Flesh	Philip José Farmer	$203
A Woman a Day	Philip José Farmer	$203
This Too Is Love	Tom Vail	$125
Call South 3300: Ask For Molly!	Orrie Hitt	$120
The Woman Waster	Richard Orth	$111

The Third Sex	Artemis Smith	$100
His Neighbor's Wife	Peter Rabe	$100
Queer Patterns	Kay Addams	$100

As you can see by the list, the most collectible Beacon books are the four that Charles Willeford wrote. They are acknowledged classics and some of the best books to appear under the imprint. But there are also three books by Orrie Hitt on the list, one under his pseudonym Kay Addams, which he reserved for lesbian-interest titles. Hitt has become the second most-collected of the Beacon book authors after Willeford.

Also on the list are two books of what Beacon called "adult science fiction," Philip José Farmer's *Flesh* and *A Woman a Day*. In fact, all of Beacon Books fall into one of only three categories: adult fiction, adult crime fiction and adult science fiction. Willeford's novels are examples of the adult crime fiction, as are most of the novels of Orrie Hitt, although the crime in Hitt's novels was, more often than not, white-collar crime and a few without any crime at all.

What the three categories have in common is the designation "adult," which can be read as "erotic." Designating them as "erotic" in the 1950s would have gotten them seized by the U. S. Postal Service. There were many ruses Beacon used to downplay the sex contained within the covers of its books. One favorite tactic was to tout the books as exposés of the corruption within certain industries. After reading many Beacon books you come away with the impression that no business is immune from dishonest practices and sexual misconduct. Here is a sampling of cover blurbs:

A COMPELLING NOVEL THAT STRIPS BARE
THE BEAUTY CONTEST RACKET
(*Affairs of a Beauty Queen*)

A CANDID NOVEL THAT TAKES YOU BEHIND THE SCENES
AT THOSE SALES CONVENTIONS!
(*Call South 3300: Ask for Molly!*)

RIPS THE MASK FROM DOCTORS
WHO MIX WOMEN AND MEDICINE
(*The Sex Cure*)

BOLDLY TAKES YOU BEHIND THE SCENES AT A SWANK RESORT
CLUB WHERE UNUSUAL PARTIES WERE
PART OF THE SOCIAL PROGRAM
(*Private Club*)

NEVER WAS THERE SO OUTSPOKEN A NOVEL AS THIS ... TELLING
THE PLAIN, UNCENSORED TRUTH ABOUT TEEN-AGE ADDICTS—AND
THEIR SEARCH FOR THRILLS
(*Marijuana Girl*)

WHAT REALLY HAPPENS IN THE SWANK, ULTRA-FASHIONABLE
SUBURBS OF A BIG CITY? THE ANSWERS IN THIS BOLD, SLASHING
NOVEL WILL SHOCK—FASCINATE—AND OUTRAGE YOU!
(*Sexurbia County*)

WHY DO SOME GIRLS WITH LITTLE SUCCEED—AND OTHERS WHO
ARE GIFTED FAIL? THIS SHOCKING, HARD-HITTING NOVEL WILL GIVE
YOU THE ANSWER
(*The Casting Couch*)

A SCATHING ATTACK ON THE EVILS OF OFF-CAMPUS HOUSING—
AND CO-EDS OBLIGED TO LIVE IN DANGEROUS PROXIMITY
(*Girl's Dormitory*)

Beacon Books were to mainstream fiction what country music is to pop music concerning, as they do, the real-life struggles of the working class—divorce, adultery, incest, crime and poverty.

Beacon Books was started in 1954 by publisher Arnold E. Abramson as a mass-market paperback successor to the digest-size Uni-Books, which was the first venture into a line of books by Abramson's company Universal Publishing and Distribution, a publisher of special-interest magazines such as *The Family Handyman Magazine* and sports magazines *Ski* and *Golf*.

Uni-Books started the trend of salacious covers and titles that was carried on in the Beacon line, which would republish some of the Uni-Books, most notably *Marijuana Girl*.

Some of the authors that started with Universal's Uni-Book line who later went on to publish Beacon titles included Orrie Hitt, Harry Whittington, Peggy Gaddis, Evans Wall, Jack Woodford and John B. Thompson. Beacon would add to that roster authors such as Peter Rabe, Charles Willeford, Lawrence Block (as Sheldon Lord), Charles Runyon (as Mark West), John Jakes, Michael Avallone, Seymour Shubin, Richard Geis, Ovid Demaris, Hal Ellson, Robert Turner, Lee Richards, Joel Townsley Rogers, Dean Owens (as Hodge Evens and as Dean McCoy), Philip José Farmer, Brian Aldiss, A. E. van Vogt, C. M. Kornbluth (as Cyril Judd) and Robert Silverberg (as L. T. Woodward)

In its first three years, Beacon published a title a month, but by 1961, the year Universal went public, they were publishing eight titles a month and had over 450 titles in print with combined book and magazine sales of over 13 million copies.

Marijuana Girl

Originally published as a digest-size Uni-Book in 1951, *Marijuana Girl* by N. R. de Mexico, it was later published by Beacon in 1960. Until fairly recently the identity of its author N. R. de Mexico had been a bit of a mystery. That changed about ten years ago, when Kim Bragg, the son of the author, came forward to claim, after reading much speculation as to the identity of N. R. de Mexico, that it was the pseudonym of his father, Robert Campbell Bragg.

With a name behind the pseudonym it was fairly easy uncovering corroborating evidence. The Rosetta Stone that linked Robert Bragg to the name of N. R. de Mexico appeared as early as 1976 as a casual mention in, of all places, a scholarly journal. An article in the *Southern Folklore Quarterly*, Volume 40, titled "Bawdy Monologues and Rhymed Recitations" by folklorist Gershon Legman, contains the following brief mention:

> The most extreme statement of this kind is a recitation called variously "A Girl's Prayer," "The Yeomanette," and other titles, first recorded in the scarce erotic miscellany, *Cleopatra's Scrapbook* ('Blue Grass, Kentucky' [Wheeling, W.Va.?] 1928: copy, Kinsey Library) p. 53. This begins romantically, *"Put your arms around me, darling,"* and so forth, each stanza becoming more and more passionate, though never omitting the "darling" — in deference to the presumed female character of the speaker — until it ends in a blaze of castratory *(vagina dentata)* passion, after the orgasm: *"Break it off and let it stay!"* Other texts of this recitation are longer and much heightened in their eroticism, in one case by a man known to me. The pornography and "fantasy"-fiction writer, N. R. de Mexico (Robert Bragg, who is not the man just referred to, and who was born in New Jersey), was accustomed to deliver this piece at mixed parties.

In retrospect it's easy to see how Robert Bragg fell into such obscurity that no one was able to identify him previously as de Mexico. He always used the pseudonym, not only as a writer, but also as an editor for publications such as *Suspense Magazine*.

Another major contributing factor to his falling into obscurity was the fact that he died young, dropping dead of a heart attack at the age of 36 in a Greenwich Village grocery store.

ROBERT C. BRAGG

NEW YORK—Robert C. Bragg, 36, of 224 Sullivan Street, died here Saturday. He was the husband of Mrs. Gerry Bragg and the son of Capt. Amos and Marion C. Tilton, Shelter Cove, Toms River, N. J.

Other survivors are a son, Kim, and a brother, A. Richard Tilton, USMC, Washington.

Mr. Bragg was born in Newton, Mass. He lived in Plainfield, N.J., for several years, and here for the past 10 years. He was a writer.

Arrangements are in charge of Anderson and Campbell Funeral Home, Toms River.

Asbury Park Press, Feb. 15, 1955

Just a year after *Marijuana Girl* was published it was clear that Bragg would not have wanted the attention that being identified as N. R. de Mexico would have brought him. In May of 1952, a congressional committee was convened to probe the paperback, magazine, and comic business to determine the extent of "immoral, obscene or otherwise offensive matter" or "improper emphasis on crime, violence and corruption."

Marijuana Girl was one of the books it singled out as a book of particular corrupting influence in its "Report of the Select Committee on Current Pornographic Materials":

"Other paper-bound books dwell at length on narcotics and in such a way as to present inducements for susceptible readers to become addicts out of sheer curiosity. As an example of how this subject is handled by current books, one need only read *Marijuana Girl*, by N. R. de Mexico. A more appropriate title would be: 'A Manual of Instructions for Potential Narcotic Addicts.' It even has a glossary of the jargon used by dope peddlers and their customers. . . . Even the evil effects of drug addiction are made to appear not so very unattractive by artful manipulation of the imagination. While the analysis of this book has been directed chiefly to its narcotic phase, that should not be construed as implying that it is not replete with lewdness and vulgarity."

Unlike other books and films of the 30s, 40s and 50s on drug use, *Marijuana Girl* wasn't a harrowing melodramatic account of the evils of marijuana. In fact, it downplayed the harmful effects. The following passage is a good example:

> Nobody in all of history had ever been hurt by marijuana, at least to Frank's way of thinking. There were traps to the stuff, of course, as nobody knew better than Frank: psychological traps, the traps of getting to depend on the stuff to fill psychological needs—the way a person might get to depend too much on liquor or the movies. But there was all sorts of medical evidence to prove the stuff itself was harmless and non-habit-forming and that all the things usually said against it were no more than the meaningless nonsense of ignorance.

The 1951 Uni-Book Edition

What we have in *Marijuana Girl* is an attempt by Robert Bragg to portray, in an even-handed way, the effects of marijuana. Something that was virtually unheard of in 1951. On the other hand it doesn't downplay the ultimate, potential danger of its use. More on this cannot be said without giving away too much of the book.

In *Marijuana Girl* we have the trifecta of circumstances surrounding a novel that will contribute to the value of the book as a collector's item and has pushed the price up to $450 for the Beacon edition and as much as $700 for the Uni-Book edition.

An interesting back story is, of course, one of many factors that can make a book more valuable as a collector's item, and *Marijuana Girl* has two of them.

Call South 3300: Ask for Molly!

Orrie Hitt's *Call South 3300* is a good example of his fiction. The only crime committed within its pages are extortion and prostitution. The sex in it isn't explicit—this *was* 1958—nor all that erotic. If you read Orrie Hitt, you don't read him for the sex.

Only four Beacon Books of Orrie Hitt's qualify to be listed in Allen J. Hubin's definitive bibliography on the genre, *Crime Fiction IV*: *Four Women, Hot Cargo, Ladies' Man* and *Untamed Lust.* Yet, in almost every book of his, some sort of crime is committed.

No single author on the Beacon roster represented the ethos of that line of books more than Orrie Hitt. If Beacon put forth their books as exposés of various industries, revealing the seamier sides, Hitt was able to provide a steady flow of books about such businesses as used car sales, siding, television manufacturing, burlesque, modeling, hotels, resorts, hospitals, nudist camps, carnivals, insurance sales, unions and so on.

Since most of Orrie Hitt's books for Beacon precede the court victories of the late 50s/early 60s, which made explicit sex permissible in books, they cannot be classified as erotica. What would condemn Orrie Hitt to obscurity for so many years was the fact that his books fell into the crack between the genres of crime and erotica.

As Beacon B101, Orrie Hitt's novel *She Got What She Wanted* was the first title in that line. He would go on to write over 60 more titles for Beacon under his own name and under the pseudonym Kay Addams.

At the peak of his career, from 1958 to 1961, Hitt was averaging over 17 books a year. Beacon Books itself would go from publishing a book a month in its early years to over 100 a year by 1962.

Of course, an author can't keep up that kind of output without eventually burning out. By 1963, Hitt's output slowed down and he turned out fewer titles each year until 1965 when the machine that was Orrie Hitt came to a grinding halt. He didn't publish anything in 1965 and only sporadically after that until 1970.

By late summer of 1975 he was dead of cancer at the age of 58. He had written over 140 books in his lifetime.

It would be more than a decade into the next century before Orrie Hitt would be rediscovered. It was a rediscovery made possible by the advent of the digital age. The internet made it much easier to track down copies of Hitt's books through outlets such as Amazon, AbeBooks and eBay.

Another big factor that made the rediscovery of Orrie Hitt possible was the advent of the ebook. Beginning in early 2012, ebook versions of Hitt's titles started appearing on Amazon. By May there were 18 titles available all for $4.99 or less and, of course, could be downloaded immediately.

The Sex Cure

Elaine Dorian was the pseudonym behind which Isabel Moore hid while writing novels not-so-loosely based on the residents of Cooperstown, a small town in upstate New York to which she had moved to be with her youngest daughter, Elaine.

Previous to moving to Cooperstown, Isabel Moore had been working in New York as an editor for *Photoplay* magazine. Her ex-husband, from whom she had split in the mid-40s, was also a writer, as was her oldest daughter, Pamela.

While still a student at Barnard College her daughter Pamela had written her first novel to much critical acclaim in 1956. At the time publishers had been searching for the American equivalent of French author Françoise Sagan who, by then, had had two bestsellers in the states with *Bonjour Tristesse* and *A Certain Smile.* Pamela Moore's novel *Chocolates for Breakfast* seemed to be the answer.

The Sex Cure was one of eight novels that Isabel Moore would publish with Beacon Books in 1962, the year after moving to Cooperstown. The characters in the novel were all based on real people who lived in Cooperstown, which was fictionalized as Ridgefield Corners.

Apparently the likeness of the characters in the novel to real people was such that they—and, of course, other residents—could easily identify themselves. Libel suits were threatened. In one instance even the name of a character differed from that of the actual resident on whom it was based by only one letter.

If it wasn't clear from the description of the character of Jane Dieterle who she was based on, the name was a dead giveaway. The very real *June* Dieterle filed a libel suit two months after the publication of the book on December 12, 1962, asking for $600,000 in damages (the equivalent of $5 million in 2019).

As the press got wind of the lawsuit, news stories appeared that likened Cooperstown to a real-life Peyton Place. The people of the town were incensed and threatened Isabel Moore. On Halloween of 1962, Moore's house was defaced with spray paint.

Book Incenses Cooperstown

★ ★ ★   ★ ★ ★

Author Paid Off with Unsolicited Paint Job

COOPERSTOWN ⑭—Obscene words and threats a foot high have been painted on the outside of the home of paperback novelist Isabel Moore because her novel "The Sex Cure" deals with Cooperstown.

"I think the town revealed itself as a sick town. The people like to hate," Mrs. Moore said when she learned of the paint job done Halloween night in this history-packed village.

• • •

MRS. MOORE, who used the pen name Elaine Dorian for the book, was staying with relatives. Police said they had been warned that something would happen to the novelist or her house.

"That book shook the town up real well," Police Chief William Ross said.

Mrs. Moore had made no secret of the fact that she was the author. She called the short novel a behind-the-scenes look at Cooperstown and the lives and passions of the upper strata—"a sort of Glimmer-glass version of Peyton Place."

"It sounded like Cooperstown and it was supposed to," she told reporters. "This is the last of the feudalistic towns in America."

The police chief said the lettering, on all four sides of her house, indicated that three or four different persons had done it.

• • •

MRS. MOORE, 47, moved to this usually placid community of 2,500 recently to be near a married daughter. She says she has been writing successfully for 24 years.

Police said town feeling against her had been rising ever since "The Sex Cure" was published last month.

Cooperstown is named for James Fenimore Cooper, who used this locale as the setting for his novels on pioneer and Indian adventures.

The village is on the shore of Otsego Lake, and Cooper referred to the lake as "Glimmerglass." Mrs. Moore appropriated the term in mentioning the novel Peyton Place, by Grace Metalious, which described extra-marital relations in a small New England town.

Mrs. Isabel Moore

Elmira Star-Gazette, Nov. 2, 1962

The trial was scheduled to begin March 16, 1964, but Moore's lawyers pleaded with the judge to have the trial moved out of the county for fear they wouldn't get a fair trial in Cooperstown. On May 18, 1964, the motion to move the trial was granted and ordered to be moved to Cortland, 70 miles away from Cooperstown.

During the delay caused by the trial being moved to Cortland, Isabel's oldest daughter, Pamela, committed suicide in her apartment in Brooklyn Heights on June 7, 1964, at the age of 26. In a suicide not unlike Ernest Hemingway's, to whom she referred in the last pages of her diary, she shot herself with a rifle while her nine-month-old slept in the next room. The comparisons were no longer to Françoise Sagan, but to Sylvia Plath, who had taken her own life the year before.

On November 28, 1964, it was announced that the libel case had been settled out of court for an undisclosed amount. Ultimately there had been more drama surrounding the publication of the book itself and subsequent libel suit, than there had been on the pages of the book itself.

The character of Jane Dieterle is only a minor character in *The Sex Cure*, but the only one guilty of a crime—that of performing illegal abortions. But the real-life June Dieterle didn't sue over being outed as an abortionist but for the damage to the other half of her business—daycare. In the novel Jane Dieterle routinely administers hydro-chlorate to sedate the children for whom she cared, often leaving them unattended.

With a back story like that, is it any wonder that *The Sex Cure* is a collectible paperback!

Sources:

Asbury Park Press, Feb. 15, 1955, Pg 2

Binghamton Press & Sun-Bulletin, Mar. 8, 1964, Pg. 3A

Binghamton Press & Sun-Bulletin, May 18, 1964, Pg. 3

Binghamton Press & Sun-Bulletin, Jun. 9, 1964, Pg. 3

Binghamton Press & Sun-Bulletin, Nov. 28, 1964, Pg. 9

Elmira Star-Gazette, Nov. 2, 1962

Report of the Select Committee on Current Pornographic Materials, House of Representatives, Eighty-second Congress, Pursuant to H. Res. 596, a Resolution Creating a Select Committee to Conduct a Study and Investigation of Current Pornographic Materials U. S. Government Printing Office, 1952

Crider, Bill Allen, editor, *Mass Market Publishing in America*, G. K. Hall, 1982

Davis, Kenneth C., *Two-Bit Culture: The Paperbacking of America*, Houghton Mifflin, 1984

O'Brien, Geoffrey, *Hardboiled America*, Van Nostrand Reinhold Company, 1981

The Los Angeles Times, June 9, 1964, Pg. 13

Nedelkoff, Robert, *"Pamela Moore + 40," The Baffler Magazine*, Issue 10, 1997

Oneonta Star, Jan. 14, 1964, Pg. 3

Oneonta Star, Mar. 13, 1964, Pg. 3

Oneonta Star, Jun. 9, 1964, Pg. 3

Oneonta Star, Nov. 30, 1964, Pg. 3

June Dieterle, Plaintiff, v. Universal Publishing and Distributing Corporation et al. Defendants, Supreme Court, Special Term, Otsego County. April 15, 1963

Rochester Democrat and Chronicle, May 19, 1964, Pg. 6A

The Troy Record, November 3, 1962

MARIJUANA GIRL

N. R. de MEXICO

To Yelena—without whose cooperation
I would have been better off.

Part One

THE GRASS

But should I love, get, tell, till I were old
I should not find that hidden mystery
Oh, 'tis imposture all:
And as no chemic yet the Elixir got....

John Donne

1 • Reflection

"Hubba, hubba," the long thin boy with the unruly hair said, as she brushed past him in the high school corridor. He stopped and turned to watch her as she walked, her dark hair falling to her white-sweatered shoulders, her books held in her folded arms so they squared the heavy roundness of her breasts, her wine-red corduroy skirt a little smooth from sitting, clinging to her hips and buttocks, and her crepe-soled shoes whispering on the highly waxed floor. There was something adult, almost regal, in her walk.

Joyce flung back over her shoulder, "Hi, Tony." She was pleasantly aware of him, carrying herself even a trifle more erectly, so that her breasts molded her sweater into sharper relief as she swung sharp left through the door marked DEAN.

The office of the Dean of Paugwasset High School had been an afterthought of the board of education of that suburban Long Island community. It had emerged, during additions to the building, as a vaguely triangular alcove growing off a corridor, in which Dean Iris Shay and her secretary, Miss Ellsworth, occupied cramped space.

Joyce, with experience born of custom, halted at Miss Ellsworth's desk first, waiting politely in front of it as though Dean Shay's desk were not a scant three feet away. The girl was a little frightened, now, but trying hard not to let it show.

Miss Ellsworth, rather young for a school secretary, looked up sympathetically. She tried to smile reassuringly as she said.

"Miss Shay has been expecting you, Joyce?"

Joyce smiled back, somewhat feebly, and stepped the three paces which brought her to the older woman's desk. Miss Shay turned from the ruled-off schedules that lay on the green blotter; her white hair and bleached blue eyes staring through black-rimmed spectacles, lent her a semblance of cold harshness she did not really possess.

"Sit down, *Miss* Taylor," the dean said. Joyce felt the tremor in her stomach increasing. Whether a student were addressed by her first name or as "Miss" was an accurate index of the dean's attitude. She put down her books on a corner of the desk and seated herself in the hard wooden chair beside it, holding herself rigid and erect under the older woman's scrutiny.

After a moment the dean returned to her schedules, calmly adding up a column of figures before saying, "Miss Ellsworth, would you give me Miss Taylor's record, please?"

The old witch; Joyce thought, feeling the fright growing as she sat waiting for whatever was going to happen. Behind her, atop a shelf of books, she heard the cruelly regular ticking of a pendulum clock that had once been presented to Dean Shay and which, Joyce knew from other sessions in this office, bore the inscription: *To Iris Shay, our beloved mentor, from the Class of 1943.* She had an impulse, swiftly crushed, to pick up her books from the desk and throw them recklessly at the clock.

"Now, Miss Taylor," the dean said when Joyce's record card was given her, "I'm sure you know why you're here." Joyce said nothing. "How old are you, Miss Taylor?"

"It's right there on the record card."

The dean grimly compressed her lips. "Ah, yes. Just turned seventeen and you're a senior."

"Can I help it if I'm smart?"

"Miss Taylor," the dean said, controlling herself with an effort, "we have two thousand students in this school. Obviously, it is impossible for us to watch all students all the time. But with a school population of two thousand—of both sexes—it is essential that we maintain some kind of discipline. I'm sure you agree with this, Miss Taylor?"

Joyce vouchsafed a nod.

"Thank you. I had hoped you would." The dean paused and at Miss Ellsworth. "Terry," she said, "would you mind going to Mr. Mercer's office and asking him for—ah—for the freshman class list for nineteen-forty-seven?"

Ellsworth, taking the hint, hastily picked up a newspaper lying on the radiator beside her desk and scuttled through the door, closing it quietly behind her.

"Now, look here, Joyce," Dean Shay said, "I don't want to make this seem like a courtroom, but you're in serious trouble."

"So I gather." The tremor in Joyce's stomach seemed to reach out and seize her knees.

"Here at Paugwasset, we rely on seniors to discipline themselves for violations of the school rules. The honor system, you know," the dean continued sarcastically. "We permit seniors to write their own absence excuses, for example. I'm reminding you of all this because I think you're an exceptionally clever girl—"

"Dean Shay," Joyce said, managing to muster a tone of bored annoyance, "just what is the trouble?"

"Don't act cute with me, young lady," the dean said. "You're not old enough for it and you're not big enough for it. You know what I'm talking about. I've already spoken to your instructors about you … That's why you weren't called in yesterday. I wanted a little time to think this over."

"That's not what I mean," Joyce insisted. "I have a right to be accused of something, instead of just having you go at me like this." She could feel a fine edge of hysteria rising within her.

"If you insist," the dean said.

"I do," Joyce said. "I can't think of any school rules that I've broken of which you have any knowledge."

"You show a fine candor, Joyce, and your argument would do you a lot of credit if you happened to be a lawyer. Unfortunately, we are running a school and not a court of higher jurisdiction. Our purpose here is to train people to live in an adult world. We try to teach not just mathematics or history, but a self-discipline which will make our graduates capable of handling themselves in the community. We expect you to conform not just to the school rules, but to the rules of good taste, and that exhibition of yours in the auditorium yesterday was—well, hardly in good taste!"

"Oh." Joyce said, "that."

"Yes, young lady. That! I know you're going to argue this is limply the prudery of an old maid. Well, maybe I am an old maid. But I firmly assure you that there isn't a high school in the country, and probably in the world, which would tolerate having a student get up on the auditorium stage and—ah—begin to—ah—shed garments. Frankly, I think the study class watching your little performance was as much at fault as you were. We've let the seniors use the auditorium for study periods without any teacher being present because we thought we could depend upon seniors to show self-discipline. Evidently we were wrong. If one of the teachers—no, I won't tell you which one—hadn't just happened to look in unintentionally we would never have known what was going on."

Joyce held her rigid posture in the chair. "Don't you think it would have been fairer," she said, holding on to herself to keep her voice from breaking, clutching at the strange, adult dignity she could sometimes keep in time of stress—"Don't you think it would have been fairer if the teacher that saw me had kept her mouth shut."

"Truthfully, Joyce, I don't know. I can't tell you what I would have done myself. I might have done what that teacher did—it was a man, by the way—or I might have spoken to you personally. I don't know. But this teacher went to Mr. Mercer, and spoke to several other teachers. Naturally, the fact that this is public information leaves me no alternative …"

2 • Reaction

Joyce stepped out of the side door of the school into a long narrow yard where two hundred feet of bicycle racks paralleled a cinder sprint track. She stood for a moment on the stone steps, worn by generations of scuffing feet, letting her mind go on by itself. Joyce, this is a difficult thing to say, but I believe you need psychiatric help… *Old Iris.* A talent for doubtful limericks does not suffice to earn good grades in English. *The witch.* The physical is important, young lady, but not the only thing in life. I can't prevent you from experimentation—I understand most of you girls, nowadays, have your own theories about that kind of thing—but I can prevent you from carrying on inside the school. *Filthy-minded old maid* …

Then she discovered herself standing still, and set her feet in motion. Ruth Scott was waiting for her at the street gate. Ruth was shaped like the familiar potato sack, and had honey-colored blonde hair and blue eyes constantly wide with shock at ideas too big for her small mind.

"What happened?" Ruth demanded.

"She kicked me out."

"Out of school!"

"That's right."

"Oh, how *could* she?"

"She did."

"What will you tell your aunt?"

"I won't."

"But, Joy, you'll have to."

"Why?"

"Because what will she think when she finds out you're not going to school?"

"She won't."

"How can you keep her from finding out?"

"I'll just leave the house in the morning and come back at night."

"Aren't you afraid of what will happen if she finds out?"

"She won't. That's all."

"But, what happened? What did Dean Shay say?" demanded Ruth.

"She told me they wouldn't even bring a thing like this before the Senior Court, and I'd have to bring my father in before they would let me come back to school. I told her my family was in Europe, and she said, well, somebody would have to come in to see them. I said I wouldn't bring anybody in, and old Iris said, I'm really very sorry to have to tell you this, but I'm afraid you will have to remain suspended until you bring in either your parents or your guardian." She mocked the dean's accents.

"Are you going to write your folks?"

"No. I'm going to get a job. The same as I had last summer, if I can fix it. I'll be a copy-girl on the Daily Courier." Joyce pointed over Ruth's plump shoulder. "Hey, isn't that Tony's car? Let's get him to take us for a ride!"

Ruth almost ran toward the convertible parked halfway down the block. But Joyce walked slowly with her odd adult grace.

"Want to drive us home?" Ruth asked as she reached the car.

The dark-haired boy in the front seat, slowly disentangled his much involved limbs and straightened himself up in the seat; looking at Ruth with a steady, appraising gaze of his brown eyes. "I might," he said. "Where's Joy?"

"She's coming."

"All right. Get in back." He kicked at the door handle and the door swung open. Ruth scrambled into the rear seat, and when Joyce reached the car she got in and seated herself calmly in front, drawing her skirts tight about her legs.

"Take Ruth home first," she said. "I want to talk to you."

There was a loose-jointed ease about Anthony Thrine that lent his every movement a feline flexibility that also contained something of beauty, and his manner was as easy as his movements. He had the assurance and poise of absolute security—his father was the largest stockholder in the Farmers and Mechanics Trust company of Paugwasset. He was not the president of the senior class, but he could have been. He was not the editor of the student weekly, because he had refused the job as ill-suited to his indolent nature. His grades were high in the subjects that attracted him, and barely passing in the ones that didn't. He had been going, in a tentatively steady way, with Joyce since the beginning of the senior year. He had not been the first of the student body to get a drivers license, but he was the first to own his own car.

His driving was faultless—but in the California manner. He started the car with much tossing of road-shoulder gravel, and took the corners of the narrow tree-lined streets in a squeal of tires. He stopped the car in a long slither before Ruth's house and had the door open before the momentum had ceased.

Ruth got out and closed the door behind her, then hung on it for a moment "Joy," she said hesitantly, "hadn't you ought to talk to your aunt?"

"What for? She'll only nag."

"But don't you want to graduate?"

"I don't give a damn," Joyce said. She tossed her hair. "Come on, Tony. Take me out to Chester's. I need a drink."

Chester's was a roadhouse that led a sheltered existence off the main highway about three miles outside of Paugwasset. Its income traced almost exclusively to the fact that the line of demarcation between the ages at which high school students may drink or not drink is unapparent to the naked eye, so small is the visible difference between seventeen-year-olds and eighteen-year-olds. Once its dance floor had been the rendezvous of the respectable middle-class citizens who directed businesses in New York and lived in Paugwasset—the upper middle class which kept accounts at Tiffany's, cruisers at Manhasset and lady friends in Greenwich Village.

But somehow this adult trade had waned, to be replaced with, first, a collegiate set—the sons of the middle-class, down for the summer from Harvard, Yale and Princeton, down from M.I.T. and in from Chicago. By a subtle contamination these had given place to their younger brothers and sisters, the near-collegians, who attended high schools in Paugwasset and Glen Cove and Mineola, until at length weekly or semi-weekly intoxication at Chester's had become as essential to social prestige in the senior class as the use of Dad's car on a Saturday night.

The place boasted a high raftered ceiling, a long, much-mirrored bar. A juke-box stood near a dais which, on Friday and Saturday evenings, supported a good hot trio. The upper panes of the windows were of stained glass which, with the ceiling rafters, gave a vaguely cathedralesque atmosphere to the gaudy whole. And, in a way, Chester's *was* a cathedral. It was a religious edifice in which youth might worship, by imitation, the adulthood so soon to come.

Friendly voices greeted Tony and Joyce as they entered. Chester said, "Hiyah, folks. What's your pleasure?" He was too good a businessman to say, "Kids." You saved that for the older generation.

Tom Houlihan raised a languid hand from his rum-and-coke for a gesture of welcome. Harry Reingold said, "How're things?" Sandra Hart winked at Joyce and said, "Chin up, old man." Mickey Kramer, in one of the booths with a boy just a shade too young for her, pointedly disregarded Joyce and nodded brusquely to Tony before turning back to her escort and her Scotch.

Tony pulled out the table so that Joyce could slide into the booth, but himself strode long-legged to the bar. Joyce watched him without really seeing. With her fingernail she gouged shapes into the cork coaster on the table. Old Iris was like her aunt! No attempt to understand the justification that might explain the act. There had been no point, even, in attempting to tell why she had given that silly little exhibition there on the auditorium stage, because old Iris in her prudery would never have been able to understand. Oh, there was a reason—or there had been. A clear, sensible reason. But now, thinking about it, it was also clear that the reason was something old Iris should have understood from talking to Joyce's teachers. Maybe Iris did understand, but just couldn't condone. Because the real reason, and Joyce knew it well enough, was a compulsion for defiance. Just as the biology paper she had written had been a defiance. They had asked for a general study of a disease. Joyce picked venereal infection. All right, so she was a "bad" girl. A defiant girl.

But the injustice in her punishment, she felt, was that defiance was no crime. Why, lots of famous heroes had been—well, just defiant. Even her mother and father, it seemed to Joyce, were pretty defiant when someone was stepping on their toes …

She suddenly fell into reverie.

She tried to remember when Mom and Dad had not been off somewhere, and the recollection was reaching for memories of rare days in long years.

Tony came back to the table, slopping daiquiris at every step. He sat down.

"All right, Joy," he took her hand. "Tell me all about it."

"There's nothing to tell," she said. "I just need a drink."

"Quit kidding. Iris had you on the carpet for the strip act, didn't she."

"Um-hunh. She kicked me out."

"She couldn't. All right, they had to do something to you. After all, that was a pretty raw stunt you pulled. It might have been okay at a party, or something, out in the high school auditorium. I mean, that's pretty raw stuff. But she couldn't kick you out just like that. You've only got another month to graduation."

"That's what she did."

"Can't your folks do anything?"

"What do you mean do anything? They don't even know I'm alive."

"Can't you send them a cable or something? Maybe if you radioed them they'd come back. My old man wouldn't let the school get away with anything like that."

"Listen, all my family ever does for me is leave me lying around with whatever relatives they can find who'll take me. It's been going on like that since I was five—ever since Dad got to be president of Intercontinental."

"You don't mean that kind of stuff."

"The hell I don't. Every darned thing in the world comes ahead of me with those two. The year I was five they went to Mexico, As soon as I was old enough they sent me to a private school, and then left me there summers while they went off to Washington or Texas or China or Brazil or almost anywhere I wasn't. First they could leave me with grandpa and grandma, and then, later on after they died, with my aunt. Anyway, they always found some place to leave me where they wouldn't have to be bothered. And even when they were here they never paid any attention to me—unless I did something really wrong. Once I ran away from a school in Boston. That was two years ago, just before I came back to Paugwasset. You can bet they paid attention then, came tearing in from Chicago by plane." Joyce grinned, as though their frenzied arrival made a pleasant memory. "After that, for about a month, I was a real big deal. There was nothing good enough for me—until they forgot, and dumped me on Aunt Priscilla, who only stays at the house with me because Daddy gives her so much money to do it."

She broke off, shaking her head, so that her hair swung heavily on her shoulders.

"Can I have another, Tony?"

He rose obediently and went to the bar where Chester mixed a second set of daiquiris. She thought, maybe Mom and Daddy would come back if they knew what had happened. But, no. They were in Europe for the summer, and they would, instead, cable Aunt Priscilla to go to the dean and straighten everything out—and Aunt Priscilla would, too, but her nagging would be beyond endurance; she would be reminding Joyce of it every day, needling her, preaching …

Tony set the fresh glass before her and squeezed into the booth. Somebody had encouraged the juke-box with nickels, and a sex-in-a-highchair voice was whispering, "… Just a little lovin', honey, would do a lot for me …"

On the floor Sandy Hart and Harry Reingold, his six feet tremendously mismatched with her five, were dancing with determined irrelevance to the music.

The May afternoon sun had slipped behind a tree, casting a deep shadow on the stained glass windows, and darkening the room to a warm, intimate mood. Joyce's cocktail filled her mouth and throat with a raw distaste, but her body was becoming warm, and the tense feeling in her abdomen was subsiding and Tony was so good and sweet and wonderful, listening like this to her.

"I thought I would go down to the Courier and get the job this summer," she said, "and then if I'm working they can't say I'm no good, can they?"

"Who?" Tony wanted to know.

"Anybody. Daddy or Mom. Aunt Priscilla or dirty old Iris."

"Whoever said you were no good?"

"Everybody. They all do. You will, too, after a while."

"Why should I, Joy?"

She was a little drunk, now. She knew it. She could feel it. And it was such a wonderful feeling. "Because I'm bad. Because I do crazy things just to get into trouble. Because I got up there and started taking off my clothes in front of everybody. Tony, am I pretty?"

"Of course, honeybun."

"That's the first time. The very first time."

"The first time you—uh—took things off?"

"No. I don't mean that. I mean it's the first time you ever called me honeybun. Tony, you're very sweet to me." She could feel tears of earnestness coming into her eyes. "That's the first time *anybody* called me honeybun—except once Daddy did, after they found me when I ran away."

Just a little self-consciously, because he too was feeling the warm, singing flow of the liquor, Tony put his arm around Joyce's shoulder and drew her close to him, "You'll always be a honeybun to me."

He bent closer and kissed her cheek. She let her head fall back on his shoulder, and her face looked up at his. Her lips were a little slack, slightly parted and moist and glistening. Her eyes sparkled. He bent and kissed her wet lips, letting his tongue caress the pink flesh.

Suddenly he pulled free, a little frightened at the ardor with which her lips answered his. "Let's have another drink," he said.

"Not now, darling. Kiss me again."

"First another drink," Very firm and adult, though his heart was pounding and his breathing seemed to swell him to the bursting point.

Joyce watched him crossing the floor, aware of his tension as of her own. Something inside her kept saying, honeybun, honeybun, honeybun, over and over, as though it were especially important, and she had a confused recollection of her father, holding her close in his arms as he had after they had found her when she ran away, and saying to her, "Poor little honeybun. Poor little baby."

Honeybun. There was a song like that. *Having too much fun—with honeybun.* What's Tony doing with that drink? What's that drink doing with me? Me baby honeybun, Daddy's gone away for fun … No. My baby bunting, Tony's gone a-hunting. Gone to get a glass of gin to dip his baby bunting in … What kind of nonsense? Pull yourself together, Joyce—you're a big girl now and Tony loves you and you don't need your Daddy …

Tony was coming across the floor now, unsteadily attempting to keep the daiquiris intact in their glasses.

Joyce slid out of the booth. Got to help Tony carry the glasses to dip his baby bunting … What's wrong with the darned feet? Silly feet, dopey little feet.

Funny about feet, funny about bunny, funny about Tony. Everything was suddenly very funny. Tony and his glasses. Iris Shay and her spectacles. Men seldom made passes at Iris Shay. But they would make passes at Joyce, because men loved Joyce. Funny—ha-ha. Tony had reached the table and was carefully sliding the glasses across.

"Tony," Joyce said, standing there trying to control her feet. "Tony," she said urgently.

"What's the trouble, honeybun?"

"That's it. That's what I wanted you to say. You love your honeybun?"

"I think so," Tony said. "But you'll have to wait till I sit down. I'm concentrating on these daiquiris."

"Never mind. That's all I wanted to hear." She pulled herself very erect, and with a supreme effort seized herself by the arm and escorted herself back to the table. "Let's drink a toast."

"What kind of toast?" Tony had a sudden, somewhat owlish dignity.

"A toast to Tony and his honeybun."

"I dig that," Tony said, "Here's to honeybun." They drank quickly, and the flavor of the liquor was suddenly mild, going down almost like water.

"Don't you think we ought to have another?" Tony inquired.

"I kind of think you've had enough," a voice said, and they looked up to find Chester standing over the table. "Maybe it would be better if the next couple drinks were coffee? Hunh, folks?"

"Were we getting noisy?" Tony asked, very innocently.

"Well, just a mite," Chester said. "Let's put it like this. You're not as lit as you think you are, but you're a little more lit than you ought to be."

"Thank you, Chester," Joyce said, graciously, struggling to slip out of the booth again. "We knew we could depend upon you to keep an eye on us."

"Anytime at all, Joyce," Chester said, "You and Tony are two of my favorite people. And Tony has to drive you back to town. I like my favorite people to get back okay."

"Check," Tony said. He took Joyce's arm. "Well, s'long Chester. Be seein' you."

There was a little difficulty getting the car turned around, but, once on the road, Tony found the machine amazingly responsive to his slightest whim.

The late afternoon sun was warm on their flushed faces, and the wind caught at Joyce's dark hair. She moved closer to Tony on the seat of the convertible, ducking her head to slip it under his right arm.

"Tony?"

"Yes, baby?"

"You love your honeybun?"

"Yup. Intensely."

"Then kiss me."

"Not while I'm driving."

"Then stop driving."

A side road turned off at right-angles to the dirt thoroughfare over which the convertible was bumping. Tony swung the car into it. Suddenly they were in deep woods. The waning sun cast a golden light on the pale spring greens of the trees, and a swift brook gurgled over its stony bed beside the road. Tony halted the car.

Joyce said, "I feel so free and light." She got out of the car and ran to the little brook. In a moment Tony came and stood beside her, putting his arm about her. She turned to him, suddenly and pressed her lips up to his.

"Tony," she said. "Let's go wading."

"Okay," Quickly he slipped his sleeveless sweater over his head, and quickly shed his shoes and socks, rolled up his trousers. Joyce's shoes and stockings fell at her feet. For a moment she stood there, a strange golden-haired wood nymph in a white sweater and red corduroy skirt.

He came close to her. Then suddenly, his arms went about her, crushing her against him, crushing her lips to his lips.

Then she pulled her mouth free. "Honey," she said hoarsely, her voice urgent and almost fierce.

"Not here," Tony said. "Not now."

"Why, Tony?"

3 • Shock

Anthony Wayne Thrine, registered owner of New York State motor vehicle number 6N83-215, director under trusteeship of the Farmers and Mechanics Trust of Paugwasset, beneficiary of Freedom Mutual Life Insurance policy number L-615357-M and insured under policy number L-615369-V, former Eagle Scout (annual membership card now four months expired), retired president of the Paugwasset High School Dramatic Society and Senior in the student body of that academy of secondary education, was a seriously upset eighteen-year-old. A morbid fear had been growing in him for hours, and now had reached a pitch where even that source of interminable wonder, the easy, flowing motion of his car, had lost its joy.

He had been unable to reach Joyce all day, though he had telephoned her aunt right after classes, and repeatedly during the afternoon. He had called Ruth too and she had, with her passion for vicarious excitement, immediately begun to worry at fever pitch.

It was almost seven now, and he had called the Taylor house again only a few minutes before. Still no word of Joyce.

He swung his car into the gravel turnaround his father had had installed in the back yard and leaped over the door without bothering to open it—simply because leaping over the door was more difficult than the more ordinary procedure. He was close to the steps of the back porch when a voice caught him in mid-stride. "Tony!" It was his mother. "Tony, you just put that car right in the garage. Don't you dare leave it there in the driveway."

He stopped and called upward to a window. "I'm going to use it right after dinner, Mom."

"I said put that car away."

"Oh, all right. Did Joyce call me?"

Satisfied, the maternal voice lost its shrill pitch, and floated down sympathetically in the suburban quiet. "No. Nobody called."

Unhappily, Tony backed the convertible into the garage and went into the house. The cook, who was also the laundress, said, "Better get washed up, Tony." He didn't answer her, but climbed the back stairs to his father's room, where he used the bedside telephone to call Joyce's aunt.

"Has Joyce come in yet ... Yes, it's me again ... No, I just wanted to know if you'd heard from her ... Well, we had a sort of date after school ... Is she supposed to come home for dinner? ... Well, I'm home now, so if you do hear from her could you ask her to call me ... Thank you ... Goodbye."

He got undressed for his shower, thinking about Joyce; about her slender body, about the soft smoothness of her lips. He found himself naked, staring at the cluttered top of his dresser. It was a strange litter—a photo of his and Joyce's heads, slightly out of focus; a pocket game the object of which was to guide four little balls into a central aperture; a left-over radio tube from the last repair job on his portable; a pair of broken pliers; a silver-backed military brush set, deeply scored with the initials he had himself imposed with a nailfile; an ink bottle; a locket that belonged to Joyce; a pair of cheap binoculars; an ink-stained doily; a retired hunting knife; miscellaneous phonograph needles; a solid geometry textbook; a cartoon book picked up on the expedition he and Joyce had made to the burlesque show in Union City, New Jersey, which had strangely provided the basis for Joyce's expulsion from Paugwasset High; a key-ring with numerous unidentifiable keys and, finally, a button-covered beanie left over from some remote era like an archaeological relic of a forgotten civilization.

He raced through his shower, dressed quickly and came down to find his parents already seated at the table.

"You're a little late this evening, Tony," John Thrine said, mildly critical. He personally made a fetish of promptitude.

"I was trying to hunt down Joyce Taylor." Tony tried unsuccessfully to smile. "She was supposed to meet me this afternoon." He set about his soup with great protective vigor. What was the matter with Joyce? Where was she? What was she doing? Didn't she know he'd be worried about her? She had been terribly silent on the ride home, last night ...

It hadn't been very good. None of it had been good. You had both been frightened and unsure and worried, and Joy had screamed that once, and then, after you'd stopped in front of the house, she'd talked about her father—in a way that didn't quite make sense, talking as though her father were to blame for her being kicked out of school.

Tony couldn't figure that part out. After all, she was the one who had got up from her seat in the auditorium and gone up on the stage. Of course, there had been some kidding and horseplay going on before that, but nobody had thought anything about it when she'd got up. And then, suddenly, there she was on the stage, walking back and forth in long strides that stretched out the flare of her light dress, and everybody was watching her. After a moment or so, she had caught the mood perfectly—exactly like the girls in that burlesque show in Union City.

Suddenly she had deftly done something with a zipper, so that with each stride one slim, nylon-clad leg poked into view almost to the thigh. Then, faster and faster, she had whirled in a wild dance.

He remembered how the infection had suddenly caught up the other kids. How they had applauded and whistled, stamping feet to give her a throbbing rhythm for her dancing. Then she had begun a mock "grind", weaving and contorting her body! No one had seen the teacher watching from the back of the auditorium. The whole huge auditorium rang with yelling.

Then unexpectedly Harry Reingold was up on the platform calling, "Come on kids, break it up. You want old pussyfoot in here? Come on, break it up!" And Ruth Scott, tubby little Ruth, was pulling Joyce offstage. Then, as silence descended once more, and the students went back to their books, you had caught a sound from the rear of the auditorium and turned to see a door swinging closed. And you had known, then, that Joyce was in for it ...

"Tony! What on earth is the matter with you?" Tony looked up at his mother. "What ails you, Tony?" His father put in. "Have you been drinking?"

"I just don't feel so good. I don't think I want anything to eat now. Excuse me, Mom? Dad?" He deserted the table and went into the living room, where he tossed himself upon the couch. This hadn't been the way he'd expected it to happen at all. He had always thought that the first time— well, there would be an exaltation, as well as a tremendous feeling of having achieved adulthood. And it wasn't like that. Not a bit like that. Instead he was terrified, feeling as guilty as though he had stolen money. He was frightened because Joyce had not called, because he had not been able to find her. Supposing she had—well, maybe not that. But you never knew. She had been a little drunk yesterday, and now perhaps she regretted so much that she had been driven to ... to what? How could you think like that? But after all, wasn't Joyce different? Didn't she have those funny moods, where she did odd defiant things. And if Joy had ... done something like that, it would be his fault, because he, Tony Thrine, should have had more self-control!

He remembered his father saying: "Tony, the most important thing you must learn in the process of growing up is to exercise self-control." How long ago had the old man said that? A year? Two years? Anyway, it didn't matter, because when the time came that was just what he hadn't done. And now Joyce? What had happened to her? What would happen? Would she— uh—become interested in other boys? Rumor suggested that this was inevitable. But he didn't want her to. He wanted her for himself. She belonged to him. She was his girl ...

The telephone rang, faintly, as though troubled with timidity. He leaped up from the couch and started toward it, calling, "I'll get it, Dad."

He snatched the instrument from the hall stand. "Hello?"

"Tony?"

"Joyce? I've been going out of my mind. What happened to you?"

"Oh, don't be like that, Tony."

"I've been calling and calling your aunt!"

"How could you be so stupid? I told you not to call there. Do you want her to find out about me?"

All the pent-up worry and fear in his mind turned to anger. "You promised to meet me right after classes. I waited over an hour for you."

"Maybe I didn't feel like meeting you. Maybe I had something more important to do."

"More important! Listen to me, damn you. After last night …"

"Last night," her voice was cold, "doesn't mean you own me. I had things to do today, and I couldn't spend the afternoon thinking about some silly boy …"

"Joyce," he said, filled with a cold rage, "do me a favor. Drop dead!" He slammed the receiver into place and started back to the living room.

Then, suddenly frightened by his own anger, his own presumption, he ran back to the phone and hastily dialed Joyce's number. Her aunt picked up the phone. "Hello?"

"Hello, this is Tony. Let me speak to Joyce, please?"

"Tony? She's not here. She just called and said she wouldn't be home for dinner; that she was meeting you."

"Did she say where she was calling from?"

"No. Is something the matter?"

"No. Nothing." He started to put the telephone down, then raised it again. "I just got something mixed up. Thanks very much." He hung up. For a long moment he stood there, hating himself for his stupidity, for his meaningless anger. But she must be downtown somewhere. Maybe he could find her. He went to the doorway of the dining room. His father and mother were still sitting at the table. The crystal chandelier over the table cast little glints of light on their faces.

"I'm going out," he said. "Maybe to a movie or something." He went through the butler's pantry and the kitchen and out to the garage, started his car and was passing into the driveway when he heard the telephone ringing again.

He stopped, got out of the car and ran into the house, reaching the hallway just in time to hear his mother say, "No, Joyce. He just said he was going out and he just went out the driveway this minute … Wait, here he is now. Joyce? Joyce? Oh …" She put the receiver in its cradle, and turned to Tony. "You just missed her. She hung up."

He went back out to his car, got in, and drove through the elm-shadowed streets in the gathering dusk. There was a great lump of self-pity in his throat. It was mixed with anger at himself, at Joyce, at his mother—meaningless anger at them—and a very reasonable anger at the sequence of events.

He drove down Howard Street, braking sharply at the traffic lights, and racing the engine to leap forward as they changed. She must be somewhere downtown. Everything was on Front Street—everything and everybody.

He turned at the corner of Howard and Front. The traffic was heavy. It was Friday evening and the shops were open and people were downtown for the movies. He had to wheel slowly through the jam. Just as he reached Park Avenue, he saw Joyce standing on the curb about to cross. Her slender figure drew his eye like a magnet, and he felt a wave of affection for her. He called to her—though he was on the other side of the street. "Joy! Joy!" She turned, looking about without spotting him. Then she said something to the man standing beside her. He nodded his head and smiled. Together they started across the street, the man—an older man—taking her arm.

"Joy!" Tony screamed again, but the wild honking of blocked cars behind him drowned his voice. Desperately he tried to pull the car close to the curb and get out, but a traffic policeman blew his whistle and the cars behind him honked louder.

He started up, perforce, and drove down the block, at last finding an opening in which he parked. Then he ran along Front Street, panting with anger and disappointment and jealousy. Hs ran all the way along Front as far as Howard, but there was no sign of Joyce.

4 • Frustration

For long moments after Tony had slammed the receiver on the hook, Joyce stood with the earpiece still dangling from her hand. It had been so important to tell him, so necessary, so vital to share her good news with someone who loved her. It would have been like going to her father—who was not around to be gone to, who was never around to be gone to. She replaced the telephone instrument. She felt unduly disturbed without knowing exactly why. Yet she had some inkling of it; knew she was terribly frustrated at not having reached Tony, talked to him, rejoiced at the news with him.

The whole purpose of getting the job was defeated. What did it mean if there was no one to understand its importance, no one to take pride in her? But Tony hadn't even allowed her to tell him the good news, hadn't even allowed her to say there was good news. He acted as though he owned her—as though she must always do his bidding, and if he told her to meet him after school then that was what she had to do—and what right had he to demand that?

And then she thought: But I did promise to meet him, and he does love me. Doesn't he? He's supposed to love me. That's what giving yourself to a man means, isn't it? When you sleep with him you love him, don't you? And that makes him love you, too? Doesn't it?

There had to be someone to love you—really love you, want you, possess you, the way your parents were supposed to. And sex was just love, wasn't it? It was love carried to the nth degree. Then she thought about last night, trying to understand herself, trying to get some kind of grip on the fleeting impressions which had shot through her mind, leaving quickly fading traces like fast-falling stars. She thought about the strength with which Tony had carried her to the car, the tenderness of his embrace yet the impassioned need implicit in it—a need no less urgent than her own—the

terrible, terrible need to be cherished, to be protected within a warm shield
of affection.

You couldn't let Tony misunderstand about this afternoon. You had to
put him straight, and then he would come and hold you in his arms and
understand and kiss you and tell you how wonderful you were.

She pressed down on the hook of the phone, heard the coin collected,
inserted another and dialed Tony's number. There was a busy signal.

She tried again a moment later. Still busy. Now the importance of
reaching Tony had assumed the dimensions of panic. She had to reach him.
Had to. She tried her own number. "Hello, Aunt Priscilla? … Has Tony
called? … Just now … I'll be home later … Bye." Then, feverishly, she
dialed Tony's.

"No, Joyce. He was here for a while, but said he was going out. He left
just this minute."

Joyce said, "Thanks," and let the receiver fall on the hook. He hadn't
waited, hadn't wanted her enough to wait for her to call him back. She
couldn't hold anyone. Not her parents, who didn't care enough about her to
stay with her or take her along with them. Not Tony. Not anyone. Everything
was such a mess. Anybody had to be important to somebody. Anybody was
worth *something.*

She opened the door of the booth, feeling the tears welling up in her
eyes, and tense agony in her knees and stomach. She had counted so much
on Tony's love, on giving herself as the means for assuring love.

She realized, then, that she hadn't eaten since morning. Getting the job
on the Courier had been so exciting, and the instructions for working so
wonderful, and the immediacy of obtaining the job so surprising that the
idea of food had vanished entirely from her mind.

She went to the lunch counter across from the telephone booth and
ordered a sandwich and milk.

She was trying to reconcile her vast appetite with her emotional anguish
when a voice beside her said, "Joyce?"

She swung around on her stool. "Oh, hello, Mr. Burdette. Gee, I didn't
expect to see any more of you today."

Burdette was the city editor of the Courier. He was young—thirty-one—
for the job, since most of the men over whom he held dominion were his
seniors. But the staff was a homegrown product and Burdette had been lured
from the hustle and bustle of a huge Manhattan daily by an advertisement
in Printer's Ink that promised "fine future and rapid advancement to the
right man." Moreover the canyons of concrete and the dying lawns of
Central Park had never satisfied an earthy passion within him that cried out
for greenery and small homes and suburbia.

He had brought with him to Paugwasset his wife, a small son, a passion
for jazz amounting to a religion (which he kept reverently concealed from

Vail Erwin, his managing editor and immediate supervisor, who believed there should be no religions before the First Church of Christ Scientist). He had also brought an automobile which would have been legally outlawed fifty miles to the west where Jersey state laws protect the citizens from mayhem on the highway and, finally, he also brought the cult of the weed—marijuana.

He was conscious of no wrongdoing in indulging himself in a smoke now and then, though in Paugwasset he kept its use secret from everyone but Janice, his understanding wife. She knew that it was an almost inescapable part of his background, a product of formative years spent largely in the company of musicians, entertainers and others who took "tea" smoking as much for granted as others take tobacco smoking. She knew also that Frank took pride in the fact that he could take the stuff or leave it alone, deliberately resorting to it on occasion for the pleasure it gave him, rather than smoking it willy-nilly by virtue of habit or addiction.

Certainly it did not interfere with Frank's home or his life. But sometimes, as now, he found himself lonely for the highways and byways of New York. As he often pointed out to Janice, whom he had married some years ago in a sudden fit of domesticity, suburbia was fine for commuters who could leave it every morning and return every evening, but it was damned dull if you had to stay there all day long. His heart was in Harlem, and Jimmy Ryan's, and Nick's, and Eddie Condon's. His heart was on Fifty-second Street where small bands and trios and quintets were writing history in marijuana smoke and music. His heart was in these places—and Janice at the moment was away for a week before going to Maine for the summer, where she would take Frank, Jr. to be admired by his maternal grandparents.

This was an annual event, and one to which Frank Burdette could never fully accustom himself. There was something unsound about the idea that toward the end of May, as spring was turning to full summer, his wife packed up herself and her off-spring and went away for three months. As the summer grew and reached its full height he had always, so far, managed to become adjusted to the idea, and even to enjoy it. Nothing, for example, compelled him to sleep at home of nights—or to spend his evenings alone, for that matter. But the first week or so of this annual departure, which reminded him of salmon heading for their spawning grounds, left him with a feeling of tremendous loneliness.

He had been headed, this particular evening, for a quick snack in the Cozy Luncheonette at the corner of Front and Park. Afterward he would reach a decision: whether to go home and read, go to a movie, or drive into Jamaica and take the subway to Manhattan where something was bound to turn up.

It was in the midst of this storm of indecision, this triple-horned dilemma that he saw Joyce.

He said, "How do you like being back on the job this year?"

"Very much," Joyce said. Her face was grave and serious, but registered pleasure, too. Yet, there was a faint redness around her dark eyes and Burdette decided she had been crying. "It's different from last year, though, now that Mr. Harrigan is gone. He was so nice—"

"Well, I'm not exactly Harrigan, but I hope we'll get along well."

"Oh, we will, Mr. Burdette. I'm sure we will,"

"Are you going to stay with us this time, or are you going back to school next year?"

"I'm through with school now, Mr. Burdette."

"Look, honey," Frank said, "Don't call me Mister. I'm not that old. My name is Frank."

Joyce blushed. "All right, Frank."

"I thought you lived in town. How come you're eating down here?"

"No special reason. I just didn't feel like going home."

"Meeting your boyfriend?"

For a moment that bothered Joyce. What had happened to Tony? Then she said, "No. I hadn't really made up my mind what I would do."

"Let's move over to a table, shall we?"

"Why not?"

She fascinated him. Frank kept trying to remember that this was only a high school kid—or anyway, just finished with high school. But she was beautiful, and it would have been impossible for him to tell her age. Her dark eyes were steady and wise-seeming. Her hair was a little long for the current fashion, and suggested the softness of immaturity, but her dress— a sleeveless brown shantung with a deep V neckline that bared the first swelling roundness of her breasts, and smoothly shaped her body down to the longish, full skirt—was conservative enough for the most adult tastes. He was not the sort of man who referred to attractive girls as "a dish," but if he had been he would have.

Frank had a theory that all girls are beautiful, provided they're young enough. But he had to admit that Joyce had peculiar individuality in her good looks, rendering her unique, putting her in a class by herself. He had trouble keeping himself from staring. After a while, feeling around for a conversational base, he found jazz. There were names to talk about in common, though she had never met the names, never seen them, knew them only from records. There were Art Hodes, Max Kaminsky, Peanuts Hucko, Bud Freeman, Sol Yaged, and the older names, more magical through tradition, Muggsy Spanier, Louis Prima, the old Goodman group, Jimmie Lunceford—names to conjure with. And there were names to be sneered at—names like George Shearing and Nat Cole, deserters from the higher art; names that were too esoteric, names that had deserted the old tradition of fine jazz for music that was beyond them both, names like Gillespie, Parker.

He learned, to his inutterable surprise, that there was a hotbed of Dixieland growing on a sideroad, and the hotbed was called Chester's. She offered to go there with him sometime.

He said, "What about tonight?"

She thought of Tony. Could Tony be there? Now, at this very hour?

He went on, "We can drop by my house and pick up the car and drive out—unless you have something else planned."

And she thought of the triumph of meeting Tony, after his rejection of her, meeting him with an adult and snubbing him. And that would have been all right, but there was something wrong with taking Mr. Burdette—Frank—into a group of kids, something mismatched about it, something that would have detracted from the adult role she meant to play.

"No," she said. "I didn't have any plans, but I'd just as soon not go out to Chester's tonight. Can't we make it another time?"

"Of course," Frank said, wondering why he had asked her in the first place. After all, attractive or not, she was just a kid. And it had been a mistake to ask her to go anywhere with him. Supposing they should be seen? After all, it was a small town, and he was a married man, and this girl, how old could she be? Seventeen? Eighteen? Nineteen? Anyway, just a kid. And he was the respectable city editor of the local newspaper, circulation 13,570. City editors just didn't go out with copy girls!

They finished eating and somehow, mixed in with everything else, he managed to ask her, "How old are you, Joyce?"

"Nineteen." She was proud of the speed of her response.

Then, without meaning to, he found himself inviting her to come into New York with him to visit a very special little haunt of his. A Greenwich Village night club, where he knew all the musicians and they were doing something special with Dixieland—not like bop—but adding to it without destroying it.

And Joyce said, "Gee, that sounds nice. I'll 'phone my aunt and tell her I won't be back until late." She got up and went to the booth.

He watched her as she walked, seeing the slender body, the easy grace of movement, and telling himself, after all, women are supposed to be more mature than men. You don't think of a nineteen-year-old as a kid. Not a girl. Even the state laws recognized that an eighteen-year-old girl could marry without consent.

He watched her in the telephone booth. She was poised and assured as she talked into the 'phone—not like someone asking permission to go somewhere, but someone saying, "I'll be home a little late. Don't wait up for me."

And he thought—dammit, I'm making a fool of myself. But when she came back to the table, smiling and pleased with herself, he suddenly didn't care.

5 • Intoxication

The name of the night club known as The Golden Horn was not a reference to the oriental pleasures of Byzantium in the Near East, but bespoke instead the brazen blare of the hot trumpet. Left over from an era when Greenwich Village was still a sinkhole of prohibition iniquity, it had none of the gaudy trimmings of the more modern night spots on Eighth Street. But its dance floor was equally microscopic, its lighting equally concealed.

The chairs and tables ran fanwise in a semi-circle from a small dais and gave an uninterrupted view of six sweating colored musicians. There were no fairies, few intoxicated tourists, and little conversation.

The Golden Horn was a serious establishment, without funny business or sidelines. People who came to the Horn came to drink and listen to the jazz when it was hot.

The air-conditioning was insufficient, the seats wire-backed and hard to the touch of spine or buttock. But the music was the best. Here, from time to time, came Sidney Bechet, Louis Armstrong and other greats of native American music. Here had played such supermen as the immortal Bix Beiderbecke. Here was the temple of a noble art.

Here they came to attend to the important business of drinking, smoking and listening to music.

In taxis and afoot, by bus, subway and private car, they came to have their pulses speeded by the hammering rhythms, their minds diverted by a spectacular run of guitar or piano—to have their attention caught, breathless, by glittering arpeggios.

Here, too, came Frank and Joyce.

Frank parked his middle-aged car on Broadway, empty and deserted at that hour of the night, and led the way into a dim sidestreet where yellow neon formed the outline of a trumpet; and green neon spelled out the name. There was no doorman, but a sidewalk awning shielded a cavernous, artificial stone entrance to a flight of stairs leading down. Sounds poured, in immodest fury, from the opening. Frank took Joyce's arm as they went down the steps. It was a flattering gesture, for her—Tony would never have thought of it. She said, "I'm not really dressed for this."

Frank said, "Nobody ever is."

Inside the lower door it was dim and cool. The dangling chandeliers were dimmed and brilliant amber spotlights, in the corners of the room, caught the brass flare of the trumpet with which a tall, lean, good-looking colored man sporting a tiny black mustache, was desperately trying to blow off the ceiling.

They stood there for a moment, taking in the silhouetted figures of men and women, strangely hushed and silent, leaning on tables in tense attention to the music. A waiter in black trousers and white shirt came over to them, "Good evening, Mr. Burdette." The accent was Italian.

"Hi, Louie. Got a table for me?"

"Of course, Mr. Burdette." He led the way to an empty table near the dais.

It pleased Joyce that Frank was known here. They sat down at the table and ordered drinks, and then Joyce tried to sort out the confusion of her senses. The music seemed, at first, almost, too loud to be distinguishable. A microphone, before the tall trumpeter, caught up the sound and carried it to twin loudspeakers mounted in the corners of the dais, making it louder still. The flaring spotlights seemed blinding on the white linen suits of the six musicians. The dark figures in the room behind their table seemed totally blacked out, so dark and silent were they. Almost, it seemed, she and Frank sat alone in a darkened room with only the musicians before them.

It was an intimate atmosphere, despite the numbers of people in the room.

Then other things began to come to her, as her mind became accustomed to the din. The hushed roar of an air-conditioning unit, the clink of glasses, the soft lights behind the bar in the rear of the room, strange cartoon-like murals on the walls—and over all, an odd smell that clung to everything and damped down the atmosphere.

It smelled, a little, like burning hay—old hay. But there was something else in the odor that made it different. It was a touch of sweetness that made the odor nearly pleasant—as though it were going to be a pleasant smell but had never quite achieved it and had stayed an unpleasant smell.

She asked Frank, "Do you smell something burning?"

"No, honey." He sniffed. "Smells fine to me."

After a while she gave it up and concentrated on the music. "That's Jerry Best on the horn," Frank said. "Man on drums is Phil Schuyler. Piano is Don Willis. Clarinet, Frankie White, and the bass is Nutsie Burke. I don't know the other guy."

Joyce said, "Oh," with the proper reverence.

At first the music meant nothing, but then it began to come on her. It was hard, nervous music, underlaid with an exciting rhythm that first touched her lightly and then began to sink in, deeper and deeper, until it touched her pulse.

She looked at Frank sitting beside her, thinking, I didn't even know him until this afternoon, and now he seems so familiar, so close, so nice. He had put on the horn-rimmed glasses he wore in the office. She liked them. They aged his face, a little, but gave him an air of masculine authority. He looked a little like Ronald Colman playing a college professor—or something like that. His hair, she saw, receded a little from his forehead, giving him a widow's peak that added an exotic touch to his features. She watched his fingers, long and square-tipped, tapping out the beat of the music, and wondered how it would feel to have those hands touching her.

But that was silly, of course. He was an older man, and how could he be interested in a kid. He was just taking you out tonight because he had nothing else to do. And yet, there was a thing she could feel about him—a sort of strength that grew out of his being older, and having an important job, and being a big man in Paugwasset. She started to compare him with Tony, but changed her mind. She didn't want to think about Tony, because she felt that she was doing something wrong to Tony by being here.

Abruptly the music came to an end. Jerry Best put down his horn and drew the microphone close to him. "Now, just take it easy, folks. Give us a few minutes to replace all that air we been blowing and we'll be right back."

Something clicked in the loudspeakers, and the musicians began to leave the stand.

Joyce saw that Frank had risen from his chair. "Hey! Jerry," he called. "Over here."

The lean negro turned, looking about, and then came toward them. "Hiya, man!" he said, thrusting out his hand. He called to the pianist, "Hey, Don. Dig this."

Wilson came over, his brown face and white teeth lit with a smile. "Frankie," Jerry said, "Where you been, man. Had us near flippin'. You get out there in the stix and we don't hear a word. Who's the chick?"

"Don, Jerry, this is Joyce Taylor. She works on my paper."

"Newspaper gal, hunh?" Wilson said. "Gimme five." He shook hands. It startled Joyce a little, seeing the big brown hand close around her small, white one. She had never touched a negro before, and was somewhat shocked that she felt no difference.

"Sit down for a while," Frank said. "Have a drink with us."

"No man. We want to light up."

"So get on in here!"

"Naw. It ain't cool here. Well cut on outside, C'mon with us. Louie'll hold your table."

Joyce said, "It seems cooler in here than outside?"

Frank laughed. "Not like that, Joyce. What he means is it isn't safe in here. All right, Jerry. We'll ask Louie to save the table."

Joyce followed the three men up the flight of stairs to the street. Frank said, "Where shall we go?"

"Over in the square," Jerry said. "Right over in front of NYU. Nobody bothers you there."

Joyce was puzzled. "What does he mean?" she asked Frank. "I don't understand a word he's saying."

"It's jive-talk. Musician's language. It's a sort of a short-hand talking," he said.

Frank was walking on one side of Joyce and Jerry on the other. Suddenly, shockingly, Jerry put his arm around her shoulder. It was so startling that she almost threw it off. Then she caught herself in time. Frank didn't seem to object and it must be all right. But …

"It's like this," Jerry said. "Musicians like to make all their noise with whatever they blow. Like you get kind of so you don't want to talk with words. So you make everything real simple for yourself? You dig?"

"I don't quite see …"

"Well, you don't have to look around for words you want. Like, I want to say, you like this? so I say, you dig it?" He hesitated. Then, to Frank he said, "Tell her, man," as though the burden of word-finding had been too much for him.

Frank asked, "You understood, didn't you?"

Joyce nodded her head. But that wasn't what she had meant. "Safe … Nobody bothers you … Light up …" But she was ashamed to ask any more questions, ashamed to reveal her ignorance.

The hulking buildings of the university towered dark and blank above them as they entered the bench-lined paths of Washington Square, and the greenery formed a dark tunnel over their heads. Don said, "Ain't Ginger over by the fountain?"

"Yeah," Jerry said. He took his arm from Joyce's shoulder. "You met my new chick, Frankie?"

"I think so. Ginger? Sure. Hey, Jerry, what happened to Bang Morley?"

"My old sax? Out!"

"Why? He was the greatest."

"Got on horse. I don't want nobody on hard stuff. Man that's dangerous. Junkie in the band with all that gauge around? Not for me."

"How's the new guy?"

"He ain't in the same groove. Got a different style like. But I dig him a lot more than Bang and all the time having to worry while he'd shoot the stuff. Man, I like to keep things cool." A girl, sitting on the concrete rim of the big central fountain stood up end came toward them, "Hiya, Ginger."

He went over to her and put his arm around her waist. Ginger had a light, almost golden skin, that glowed in the street lights. Joyce thought she was the most beautiful woman she had ever seen—for a colored girl. Then, after a moment, she amended that in her thoughts. Frank didn't think of people as colored or white, and—well, maybe she shouldn't. And, besides, Ginger was more beautiful than anyone she had ever seen.

They crossed the great open space of Broadway and sat down on a bench in the shadows of the trees.

Jerry pulled a cigarette case from his pocket, opened it and handed it to Ginger, who took one. Then he passed it to Frank. "Going to turn on, man?"

"Why not?" Frank took a cigarette and held it up to his mouth. Joyce thought it looked a little thinner than cigarettes ordinarily did. Don took one and passed the case back to Jerry.

"What about your chick?" Jerry asked. "Don't you want to light her up?"

"I'll have one," Joyce said.

"Wait a minute," Frank said, as Jerry started to pass the case. "You know what that is?"

"No. I—you mean …" Newspaper stories of jazz musicians floated through her mind. "Is it marijuana?" Her shocked voice startled them all to laughter.

Jerry said, "That's right, honey. That's the grass. It's the greatest."

Frank said, "Hey. Take it easy, Jerry."

"What's the matter, Frank? Will it hurt me?"

"No, honey. It won't hurt you. You haven't had any?"

"No. But …" It was important that she fit in. Maybe Frank wouldn't like her, if she refused. Maybe he would feel she was too young for him to take out. And suddenly it was desperately important that Frank should feel well-disposed toward her. Now, with Tony gone, there was no one. And besides she wanted to do what Frank was doing—to bring herself closer to Frank. "No," she said. "But I'd like to try it. May I have one?"

Jerry looked at Frank questioningly. "It can't hurt her," he said. "Never did anybody harm."

"I know," Frank said, "But …" He hesitated. "All right."

Jerry held out the case, and she drew one of the cigarettes from under the band. It was thinner than a regular cigarette. One end had a tiny, spiral twist, designed to hold the marijuana inside the thin paper roll. The other end was flattened, until only the paper remained. She started to put the spiraled end in her mouth.

"Not like that, honey. Watch me," Jerry said. He put the flattened end in his mouth, lighted the spiral with a quick touch of a match and without drawing on it When the tip was clearly aglow he drew the cigarette from his mouth. "Pinch a hole in one corner of the flat end with your nails—like this, and then press on the edge of the flat part so it makes a little hole." She followed his instructions carefully.

"Now, don't put the stick in your mouth. Make a mouth like whistling, and breathe in, holding it just in front of your lips." She did that, too, drawing in heavily. Suddenly the strong sweet odor, like burning hay, filled her throat and lungs.

"Don't cough, Joyce," Frank said. "The next puff wont seem so rough."

She drew again on the stick, more lightly, this time.

"Solid," Jerry said.

She took the stick down from her mouth. "What'll it do to me?"

"Maybe nothing," Frank said. "Some people it doesn't do anything to."

"But what's it like when it does do something?"

"There's only one thing charge does for you, honey," Jerry said. "It makes you feel good. That's all. Just good," He turned to Ginger. "This grass is great. The best. I dig it."

Joyce took two more drags on the stick, watching the little amber fire creep upward on the thin roll. The strange odor and unpleasant taste were gone now. It felt almost as though she were drawing very cold air into her chest. But nothing was happening. She said it. "Nothing's happening."

"Maybe it won't," Frank said, discouragingly.

"Will I do anything funny—I mean silly?"

"Of course not," Frank said. "It's not like liquor. You don't lose control or anything."

She drew again, still aware that it had no effect, then let her hand hang down holding the tiny cigarette. Suddenly she became aware of the night beauty of Washington Square Park. The cross atop the Judson church, glowing against the deep blue of the sky caught her eye, and the streetlamps against the facade of the arch. Each was a detail worth infinite attention. There was a faint, warm haze lying low against the ground, lending the whole park an atmosphere of unreality. Beyond the Square the lighted windows of a row of tall apartment buildings had a crystalline clarity—so clear were they that even from where she sat, nearly a sixth of a mile away, she could see well into the rooms, see the people moving about, see what they were doing.

It was as though every window of those huge apartment buildings were a stage on which a special performance was taking place for her benefit. Even the sky was richer and more velvety ease. How strangely wonderful and lovelier than any she had seen before, with deep-glowing blue stars—all warm and close and friendly—peering down at her. "God!" she said. "It's beautiful here." Then she remembered the stick and drew on it again. She turned to Frank, "But nothing's happening."

"Are you kidding?" he said.

"No."

"Look around again. Here. Lean back against me." He put his arm around her shoulders as she sat on the bench and drew her close to him. Her skin was suddenly tremendously sensitive. She felt that she could count the individual strands of the wool in his sports jacket where it touched her shoulders. The warm breeze, more like July than May, caressed her skin, touched her instep, her toes, her ankles—slipped lithe fingers of air over her calves, fluttered her skirt and drifted upward over her thighs, passing over her stomach and chest like a sensual caress. Her body felt weightless, and her mind at complete rest.

Jerry said, "We got to get back for the next set, folks. You coming?"

Frank said, "We'll be along in a while."

"See you," Don said, and the three went off together. Joyce was hardly aware of their going, watching them as they walked through the archway of light formed by the trees. All they had become was part of the absolute, inutterable beauty of the park.

The important thing, though, was the feeling inside her—the wonderful, wonderful feeling. Now, as never before in her life, she felt safe, protected by Frank's arm about her. She snuggled closer against him, and his arm tightened responsively. It was like—like being in Daddy's arms, protected and safe and warm.

She turned, suddenly, and kissed Frank full on the lips.

6 • Compulsion

"What time did you get in last night …"

The sharp voice tore at the lovely fabric of the dream, shredding it into smoky tissues.

"Did you hear me, Joyce Taylor? What time did you get in?"

Slowly, with deliberate insolence, Joyce let herself come awake. She stretched luxuriously and yawned, half-rising on the bed to lend herself greater ease. The covers fell away from her; and there was another, immediate shrill outcry.

"Why aren't you wearing your nightgown?"

"Aunt Priscilla, can't you leave me alone?"

"What is the matter with you, Joyce. You've been acting like a maniac, and you've had that Thrine boy nearly frantic—calling me at one o'clock in the morning …"

"Oh! Tony."

"Yes, Tony," her aunt said.

"What did he say?" Joyce demanded, suddenly frightened.

"He didn't say anything. He just wanted to know if you had come home."

"What time is it?"

"Eight o'clock. Now tell me, what time did you get in last night?"

"Aunt Priscilla, I don't have the faintest idea. Does that satisfy you? Now I've got to get up." She started to scramble from the bed.

"Don't you dare get out of that bed. I'll get your robe for you. What will the neighbors think?"

"As far as I can see they won't think anything, since they can't see in. All right, give me the robe. I've got to hurry."

"And for what, may I ask?"

"I have an appointment for a summer job, and I have to be there at nine o'clock."

"Oh!" Priscilla Taylor was faintly mollified. "And how do you expect to hold a job if you keep this kind of hours."

"Don't worry," Joyce said. "I'll hold it all right." She was a little proud of the promptitude with which she had come up with this particular lie. Now it occurred to her that she could admit to working afternoons and Saturdays for the Courier preliminary to the end of the school year.

She showered and dressed as quickly as she could, coming downstairs to find her aunt sitting opposite the place on the table where Estelle had arranged her breakfast.

"I don't want any breakfast," Joyce said. "Just a cup of coffee."

"You sit right down and eat your breakfast," Priscilla said.

"All right." The fact was that she was almost starving. She remembered the huge meal she had eaten with Frank and Jerry and Ginger in the early morning before driving back to Paugwasset, and wondered if marijuana could have given her this voracious appetite.

After a while Priscilla said, "Do you or do you not intend to tell me where you were last night?"

"Oh, Aunt Priscilla, why carry on this way?"

"Have you been drinking?"

"No."

"Don't lie to me!"

"I don't care whether I do or not. But I wasn't drinking. You know I don't drink. You'd think from the way you talk I'd been doing something terrible, smoking marijuana or something." She suppressed the laugh that bubbled up inside her. The fact was that she felt particularly well this morning.

"I wouldn't put it past you," Priscilla said. "Well, if you won't tell me I'll just have to talk to that Thrine boy."

"Oh, all right. I had a fight with Tony yesterday so I went into New York last night with a couple of kids. We went to a late show at the Paramount."

"How did you go in?"

"Drove!" Her voice shrilled her impatience.

"Who with?"

"Charlie Case, if you must know—and his sister."

"Doesn't he have a junior license?"

"I don't know."

"Well, I'm sure he does, and he's not allowed to drive in New York."

"All right. Now I have to go." She rose from the table.

"Well," her aunt was weakening, "All right. But if you stay out like that again I'll just have to write and tell your father."

She caught the bus on the corner.

Frank Burdette came out of the front door of his house on Randolph Road wondering why he felt so much like a sinner. After all, looking back on it, he hadn't done anything wrong. What was there wrong with taking a girl to a night club. Nothing. And the marijuana? Nobody in all of history had ever been hurt by marijuana, at least to Frank's way of thinking. There were traps to the stuff, of course, as nobody knew better than Frank: psychological traps, the traps of getting to depend on the stuff to fill psychological needs—the way a person might get to depend too much on liquor or the movies. But there was all sorts of medical evidence to prove the stuff itself was harmless and non-habit-forming and that all the things usually said against it were no more than the meaningless nonsense of ignorance. Take the investigation once sponsored by New York's Mayor La Guardia, and that Academy of Medicine report ... Oh, anyway, anyway, that wasn't it. Not the grass.

No. The trouble was the girl. Something about her touched him and held him. And *that* could assume the proportions of tragedy. After all, she was just a kid. A beautiful kid, with a body like a dream and a mind that maybe threw off sparks like Einstein on a hot night—but a kid. He turned the key in the lock and went down the steps.

Still, there was something about the way she cuddled up close to you, as though she trusted you—depended upon you for protection—that kind of caught at your heart and made you feel strong and wonderful. But you were a married man. You couldn't let this kind of stuff go to your head.

No. The solution was to have nothing to do with her. But she was working on the Courier. Could you keep the relationship on a nice impersonal basis?

Of course, you could fire her. But that would be a rotten trick. After all, she worked there last year for Harrigan and she did a good job, and yesterday she'd shown she could continue to do one. There was no legitimate reason for canning her; besides, it wasn't her fault if Frank found her attractive.

He waved good morning to George Gernert who was watering his front lawn, and a second later to George Jr. who was watering a corner of the lawn right through his romper.

He called, "Hey George! Junior's sprung a leak?"

And George called back, "Not again! That's the third time this morning."

That was the way to handle things, Frank decided, throwing back his shoulders and inhaling the fine air of early summer on Long Island. Just be firm and responsible and careful and friendly. Never let it get beyond being friendly, because that would be a terrible mistake.

All right, now. That was settled. And here came the bus. Frank stepped out from the curb and the bus pulled up. He got aboard, deposited his money in the receptacle and headed toward the seats. There was only one empty seat and—by heaven.

Oh, well. You couldn't make yourself look ridiculous and stand when the only empty seat was the one next to her. Frank sat down. "Good morning, Mr. Burdette."

"Not mister—remember?"

"Frank!"

"Lunch with me today?"

7 • Conflict

Tony swung the car around the corner and braked to a stop on Randolph Road in front of Burdette's house. He turned to Joyce on the seat beside him. She was leaning forward, adjusting her hair against wind-damage with the aid of the rear-view mirror.

"I don't see what you want to come here for," he said. "And I don't see any reason for dragging me along. Why should the city editor of the paper invite a copy girl to his house? After all, they're older people."

"If you don't want to come," Joyce said between clenched teeth that held a bobby-pin, "nobody's twisting your arm."

That caught Tony enough off base so that he lied. "Of course I want to," he said. "I want to spend a little time with you now and then. After all, I've hardly seen you this week."

His real purpose in coming had been to dissuade her. But now he allowed her to urge him out of the car.

Joyce said, "How do I look?"

She was a little worried about this. Frank had asked her to come tonight specifically to meet his wife, and it was not exactly the kind of thing she could approach easily. It brought to mind, somehow, one of those rare times when her parents had been at home. Her mother and father had planned to take her to New York. Mr. Taylor had driven downtown alone in the morning, and had then come home to pick them up. Joyce came out to meet the car and said—for some reason she had, by now, forgotten—"Daddy, Mother's not coming. She said for us to go ahead." And they drove off together.

She could not understand why this recollection kept to mind as they approached the front door. Unless it was because Frank had invited her to go to New York with him—although it might be better if she didn't mention it tonight. Since then, she had only had that one lunch with him during the week.

As they mounted the steps, Tony suddenly took fright. "Look, why don't you just go in alone. I'll only be bored with old people like them. I'm going. You go ahead and stay here." He released her arm and turned to go back down.

"Tony!" Joyce hissed. "Don't you dare. You come right back here."

She seized his elbow and pulled him along with her. Janice Burdette opened the door to the bell. She stood slender and blonde, with an alert look about her blue eyes, and a set of features to which animation and intelligence lent a beauty beyond features themselves. She said, "Hello, Joyce. You are Joyce, aren't you? Of course. Frank said you would be here this evening, and I'm afraid it's my fault that Junior isn't in bed yet. Come on in, and I'll whisk him off to dreamland."

In the middle of the living room floor a small boy, a very small boy with his little finger deeply intruded into his mouth, eyed the newcomers with a critical expression. He was standing a little straddle-legged, and the trap door of his pajama dangled open. Janice caught him up in her arms.

"You just sit down here, and Frank'll be right in. Frank! Frank! Company! Would you like a drink? Of course you would. I'll have Frank make you one while I stuff the by-product into his bed." She fled from the room trailing a wake of friendliness just as Frank came in.

Frank studied Tony Thrine as he performed the ritual of drink-making and strove, simultaneously, to keep up a flow of light, meaningless conversation. This was, of course, the cure that he needed. Once it was done—once this evening was over—he would see Joyce in her true perspective and she would see him. That was why he had insisted she bring Tony. Generation would belong to generation. Age to Age. And this would clearly point up the difference.

He counted on Janice to fall in with his plan—perhaps not knowingly but still to fall in with it. Her maturity would fit together with his, like matched parts of a whole, while Tony and Joyce would naturally go together. And then he would be rid of his obsessive interest in this—this kid.

Tony was a good-looking boy. You had to give him that. His dark hair was unruly, but not untidy. And at first, what seemed an entirely disjointed array of arms and legs and trunk on the divan became, on closer observation, a figure of graceful, feline ease—of total relaxation that could, catlike, instantly spring to action.

Then the most appalling thought struck Frank. He wondered if Tony had—that is, had known Joyce intimately, as a lover. After all, they were the right age for it. Nineteen, Joyce was. How old was Tony? Frank asked him.

"Eighteen," Tony said. "I'm just a year older than Joyce. We have the same birthday."

It was like a stick of dynamite going off in his brain, and Frank almost spilled the brace of highballs he was carrying over to the pair on the couch. Seventeen! Holy cow! And here he had almost … No. Hadn't thought of it for a second. Not a second. He rattled away furiously to conceal his shock. "You know, you two can get passes to anything you like. Movies. Even the major league ball games. After all, Joyce is a full-fledged newspaperwoman now." And then, "Where are you going to college, Tony?" Then, "I wanted to go to Harvard, too, when I was a kid." When I was a kid! Holy jumping Jesus! Look, Ma, I'm spinning.

The pressure had eased a little when Janice came back downstairs. She led the talk into feminine channels: clothes, travel, her trip to Maine on which she would leave tomorrow, how very easy was knitting once you got down to it, the latest rumor from Hollywood. It was amazing how easily Joyce and Janice got together. And yet, Frank thought he detected a certain tightness, as in the feeling-out thrusts of fencers, or the cautious sniffing of two suspicious dogs. But Janice was good. Really good. She could get along with anybody.

Like with Jerry. He remembered the first time Janice had met Jerry. He had always known Jerry—before high school, even. But Janice had never met a Negro socially before, and he could imagine her New England background really getting in the way the first time. But she had fallen right in the groove. Not a word about the tea, even. You expected these upcountry girls from Maine and places like that to be real prudish. But once he and Jerry had explained about it, she'd fallen right in. Once she got it straight that it wasn't even as bad for you as liquor—well, now she was a regular old viper, like anybody else. That was the difference between Janice and other girls …

Other girls? Hadn't Joyce taken it the same way. But Joyce was only a kid and he was thirty-one—and what the hell was he thinking about!

Janice said, "How do you feel about working on newspapers? Frank says you worked for the Courier last summer too, so I guess you must have made up your mind by now. Do you think you want to make a career of it?"

"I've been thinking about it," she said. "I guess I'm still a little young to get steamed up about it, but I'd like to work on newspapers for a while and then somehow get on a big magazine like Seventeen or Harper's Bazaar."

"I used to work for the Bazaar," Janice said. "I was an editorial assistant there. That's how I met Frank. We were both assigned to cover some demonstration of a new laundry machine. They always serve drinks at these press previews, and we both got a little tight and then he insisted on

dragging me to some place in Harlem where he knew all the jazz musicians
…"

Good old Janice, Frank thought. Consciously or unconsciously. She
knew what she had to do, and was doing it.

He tried to get some kind of conversation going with Tony, but soon
gave up. There was such an undercurrent of hostility, at least on Tony's part,
that nothing could get started.

Then he heard Janice beginning something else, and a sensation of
apprehension threaded up into his mind.

"Frank has covered some pretty big stories. Once he even made a hero
of himself. The firemen—this was in Brooklyn—had been working on a
tenement blaze and all the reporters—they get fire-line cards so they can
get close enough to see and take pictures—the reporters were pretty close
up to the building. A wall was about to come down, and everyone was being
ordered to stand back, when Frank saw this child standing in the doorway
of the wall that was going to crash. He yelled, 'C'mere, kid,' and started to
run toward the child, but the kid was too frightened to do anything, and he
had to go all the way up under that dangerous wall and grab the kid out of
the doorway and start running back. He had just gotten out of the danger
zone when the wall crashed down. He wouldn't write the story about
himself—but the other reporters did, and it was in all the papers. But let me
tell you something—That was the phoniest false modesty I ever saw,
because he bragged to me about it for a week afterward …"

"I did not," Frank said. And everybody laughed. There was a sudden
easing of the tension. Then Janice said, "Frank, why don't you show Joyce
some of those stories. You've got them all in the scrapbooks upstairs, and
I'll take Tony out in the garden. It's just beginning to be nice, Tony. I made
Frank put the furniture out there while I was away, and you'll find it lovely
and cool. I never saw a June like this. Why there are already fireflies in the
yard, but no mosquitoes yet …"

This was the apprehension. This was what Frank had been fearing. He
said, "No, Janice. She doesn't want to see those scrapbooks."

"Oh, but I do, Fra—M—Frank."

"Oh, come off it, now," Janice said. "Don't be such a phoney. Everybody
knows you're dying to show them."

"I'd like to see them, too." Tony said—for obvious reasons.

"No you don't, young man," Janice said. "Who's going to keep me
company in the yard? Besides, they wouldn't mean anything to non-
newspaper people. You come along with me."

It was clear, Frank thought, how Janice's mind was working. She had
sensed the trouble, taken steps to treat it, and now wanted them to be
together so that the last vestiges could be swept away. But she was hurrying

things too much. He didn't want to be alone with Joyce. Just didn't want to be alone with her yet. But what could he do now?

"All right. Joyce, come upstairs with me so I can show you what a big shot I am."

Tony and Janice carried their drinks out through the dining room and kitchen into the back yard. Frank watched Joyce climbing the stairs ahead of him. She caught the full skirt of her light dress high on one thigh so that it would not interfere with her feet. The gesture charmingly shaped her figure under the light fabric.

"The books are in the bedroom—to the left." he said. His throat felt tight and dry. His voice came almost as a whisper. "Careful. Don't wake Junior."

In the bedroom she sat down on the spread, leaning back on her arms. Her skirt spread out fan-wise on the tufted chenille. Her attitude emphasized the freshness of her youth.

He thought: Cut it out, Frank! Stop it! Get control of yourself, man.

Through the open, screened window overlooking the yard and the garden came the murmur of voices, Janice's and Tony's, blended with the tinkle of the little concrete fountain full of goldfish that Frank had, himself, installed last fall.

There was a vanity, on one side of the room, cluttered with the miscellaneous appurtenances of feminine charm: bottles of cream, ointments, nail polish; a jar full of bobby-pins; brushes, combs, a silver-backed mirror engraved with the initials JB; there were nail-buffers, emery boards, scissors, a single fastener from a garter belt, eye-shadow boxes, tweezers, a compact and hosts of other items.

Facing the vanity, but across the room, stood a bureau, with the male equivalents of these beauty aids—lotions, hair tonic, after-shave talc—the array perhaps a little neater because Janice was committed to restoring order to whatever chaos Frank might create, but felt no such responsibility toward her own things.

And against the wall, between the two windows that looked out on the back yard, hunched a desk—a very wreck of a desk, teetering on spindling legs of oak which supported a bookshelf before reaching up to maintain the inclined face of the drop-leaf and the frame. The shelf was loaded down with scrapbooks.

Tensely, insistently, Frank bent down and picked up three, bringing them back to where Joyce was seated on the bed. He seated himself next to her and opened one book across their two laps.

His voice trembling, his grip on himself slipping, he tried to tell her the story behind each yellowed clipping.

Suddenly Joyce turned to him, looking up at him with her great somber eyes. "Frank," she whispered, the faint sound of her voice merging with those from the window. "Frank, do you love me?"

He bent, quickly, and kissed her lightly on the forehead, feeling his whole body trembling. But he said, "Of course I do, honey. Now, this story began when …"

"No, Frank. I mean, really."

His mind cast about frantically, but all control was gone now. There was nothing to seize upon which could protect him from his own burning hunger. The books fell to the floor as he caught her to him and felt the response of her warm, excited lips. She trembled against him, and her fingers dug deep into the flesh of his back.

Something, very like fire, seemed to be consuming them …

8 • Substitution

For Joyce the romance with Frank had always the added poignancy of impending tragedy.

The first blow fell that same night—the night she shared ecstasy with Frank, while Frank's wife and Tony talked together in the garden below.

The rest of the evening had gone off, somehow, in a state of continuing tension. Tony was hurt and angry because Joyce had deserted him. Frank was tormented by his own guilt—faced with the horrifying realization that he had against his will succumbed to a girl only a little more than half his age. Janice, her plans all made to depart for Maine with the baby the following morning, was openly bewildered at the tensions of the others, and still more bewildered by a psychic unease, that told her something had gone dreadfully wrong.

But the real blow came later, when Tony and Joyce had muttered "good nights" and "thank yous" to Frank and Janice in the doorway of the little house on Randolph Road, and had gone out to the parked car at the curb.

They got in and Tony, jaw grimly set, started the motor.

"It was fun, wasn't it?" Joyce said. It wasn't what she meant. She meant glorious, wonderful, tremendous. But these were not words she could say. A man loved her, wanted her—would protect her. Frank was strong and able and adult. He was already a father, the very symbol of adulthood. He was successful, mature.

Tony said nothing.

"What's the matter with you?" she demanded.

He put the car in motion, driving down Randolph Road like a man escaping demons. At Central Avenue he forced the rebellious vehicle around the curve with a mad squealing of tires on the macadam.

After that, the convertible shot through the moonlit darkness, a thunderbolt of whistling winds and whirring motor in the silence of the night. Past the big, silent houses on Central Avenue, past the recurring streetlamps, past the end of the macadam where the street became a highway and turned to concrete paving, past the new development in South Paugwasset.

"Tony!" she said. "Where are you taking me?" In the dim lights from the dashboard, his face was brewing a storm of violence. "Answer me!" Still the car sped on. "Tony, you stop this car right this minute."

No answer.

"If you don't let me out of this car, I'll … I'll …" Sudden hysteria gripped her. She caught at the doorhandle, pressed downward and tried to force it open against the flying wind-stream. Tony reached over with one hand, not taking his eyes from the road, and caught her wrist with steely fingers, pulling her back into the car. Then he reached past her and pulled the door to full latch. After that, as though nothing had interrupted him, he drove forward into the night, faster and faster, until the whipping airstream lashed Joyce's unfastened hair down in stinging blows against her face. Suddenly she dropped her face into her hands, and sobs jerked at her shoulders.

"What are you doing, Tony?" she wailed. "Please, Tony."

Then he stopped the car, pulling it up sharply like a horse that is forced to rear, on the shoulder of the road.

The silence, after the roaring of wind and motor, was poignant, almost unbearable. Then, one by one, the night-sounds of the country insistently made themselves heard. Crickets in the tall grass that bordered the highway. A nightbird "hooooo-ed" in the distance, and somewhere ahead a late train on the Long Island railroad clicked its electric way over an untidy roadbed. Water gurgled faintly through a culvert, and leaves, lightly displaced in the gentle breeze, rustled softly.

Tony drew a pack of cigarettes from his pocket, offered it to Joyce and, when she refused, lit one for himself.

The girl stared at his grim face, she was frightened. Tony was never like this.

"Joyce," he said, suddenly, "are you in love with Burdette?"

She stalled, "What?"

"I asked if you are in love with—with that editor?"

"Don't be silly." Was that the right tone? Should she have said: Don't be ridiculous? Or: What are you talking about?

"He's a lot older than you are, Joyce." He wasn't saying it flatly. His voice was flat, but something underlay the flatness, as though he were keeping, by a tremendous effort, from breaking into sobs.

"Oh, stop talking like a child."

"I'm your age, Joy. If I'm a child, so are you."

"Girls mature earlier than boys."

"I've heard that before. It all depends on which girls, what boys."

"You'd better stop this nonsense and take me home."

"No, Joy. This is too important for us to just shrug off. If I find out that you're—you know I saw you last Friday with Frank."

"I don't care what you saw, and don't you dare threaten me."

"I'm not threatening you, Joy; I'm just telling you what I'm going to do if things turn out the way I suspect."

"You are absolutely the stupidest boy I've ever met."

"Keep it calm, Joy. We're not fighting. We're just clearing up some confusion."

Desperately she wished that Frank were here. Frank was a man, full-grown and protective. Strong, wise. He loved her and would defend her from—from this kid who had rejected her when she had needed him. She forgot that it was she who had really done the rejecting. "Well, let's clear it up then," She felt so much older and stronger than Tony.

"I don't know how you feel about it, but after last week, I feel that you belong to me, and it's up to me to look out for you. If you broke off with me for some other kid, that'd be all right. I wouldn't be happy about it, and I'd probably make a big fuss, but it wouldn't be wrong—like this is."

"What on earth are you talking about?"

"I'm talking about Frank, and you know damned well I am. Joyce, you're too young to get involved with an older man, like that. He's married. He's got a wife and kid. Can't you get it through your stupid head that you'll ruin your life with that guy. Even if he loves you, he doesn't want to love you. He's—oh, hell, I don't know what he is, but he's not for you. And if I find out you're going too far with him—I'll tell your aunt. You know what she'll do."

Then the idea came to her. She forced her voice to a calm. "Tony, you know better than what you're saying." There was only one way to convince him. And, for one blinding moment, she saw herself as a martyr, sacrificing herself at the stake for her love.

She moved closer to Tony. "I'll show you who I love, Tony." She had to do something. If her aunt found out about Frank, she'd probably have him arrested, have him run out of town. She put her lips to Tony's and kissed him.

Frank and Janice went to bed that night like two strangers who, by chance, have been forced together into a shipboard stateroom. Janice was troubled because of something she could not bring into the forefront of her consciousness. She knew that something had happened which threatened her; knew too that some part of her had understood it fully and was weighing it; taking measures for her protection from it—she knew, too, that whatever had happened had lowered a veil of estrangement between herself and her husband. But what, exactly, it was that had happened she did not know, could not let herself guess.

But Frank's problem was far greater. He *knew* what had happened. Worse still, he knew that it would happen again and again. He loved Janice. She was his wife, the mother of his child, a capable, wonderful person on whom he could depend for everything he needed. But something about this strange kid, this seventeen-year-old *femme fatale,* had caught him in a terrible grip.

She was beautiful, intelligent, sensuous—but that wasn't quite it. Nor was it the tense, passionate excitement she roused in him. That, too, was mere seasoning for the dish. No. There was something else she gave him, something not quite healthy—not for either of them. A kind of unquestioning obedience. A slavish devotion to his orders and desires which flattered him and made of him more than he was, but which at the same time gave him virtually an incestuous feeling, like that of, say, a father over-affectionate with his daughter.

He looked across the room at Janice, brushing her soft, ash-blonde hair before the mirror. He couldn't let such a thing happen again. It must never happen again. What did a man want out of life more than Janice gave. All right, she had moods. All right, she had a mind of her own—and could raise utter hell with it, too. But he and Janice were two parts of the same whole—perfectly matched, perfectly mated. He wished she were not leaving tomorrow to be gone for the whole summer.

She was wearing a pale, transparent gown of green nylon or silk, or something, and the soft light of the small lamp on her vanity outlined the lovely shape of her legs. He thought, how can you get excited over any woman but her, lovely Janice, his Janice.

"Janice," he said softly. "Honey." She did not turn and he could not see her face. What was she thinking? Did she know? "Baby," he said. "Turn out the light and come here."

There was a click, and he saw her pale figure coming to him across the room in the faint, leaf-spotted moonlight seeping through the window.

Then she was in his arms, her lips parted and pressed to his, and he tasted the salt of her tears.

Joyce undressed slowly, her whole body aching with exhaustion. Her dress she let fall to the floor. Her arms hurt. She looked in the mirror. Her shoulders and neck and upper arms felt bruised, but they showed no marks. She stretched the rubber waistband of her panties, let them drop to her feet, stepped out with one foot and with the other kicked them onto a chair. Her hair was wild with the slip stream of the convertible and she had no energy left to brush it. She went to the bathroom and washed away the lipstick smears around her mouth—but nothing could wash away the smear inside her. She started to the closet for her nightgown, thought of the vast energy that would require, and turned back to the bed, pulled down the sheet and single blanket and slipped in.

What's the matter with me?

She pressed the convenient switch that turned off the light over the bed and tried to settle herself for sleep.

Why did I do it?

She fluffed up the pillows and shifted her head, then turned and tried the other way, but there was no rest in her.

She thought, how could you do such a thing? How could anybody let themselves get like that? What was wrong with a person who behaved like that? What was it old Iris had said, "… you need psychiatric help …" Was that it? Was she crazy?

She remembered things in school. Defiance. That had been the thing. Why did she have to write a shocking paper when everyone else was satisfied with things like measles and virus pneumonia? Why had she insisted on smoking in the school corridors between classes? After all, she hadn't actually needed a smoke. Why had she tried that idiotic dance during the auditorium study period? That was so stupid, so meaningless, so ridiculous except as defiance. Or was defiance the whole story? Wasn't it also something else, almost as if you were courting disaster, searching for trouble, demanding punishment?

And the afternoon, just one day over a week ago, right after Dean Shay had kicked you out of school—what had happened that you *had* to tempt Tony so disgracefully? Supposing you got—got yourself with child? Was that it? Was that the trouble you were courting this time? Or was there still something else?

She remembered it another way, then. There had to be someone. You had to belong to someone, be someone's property, so they would take care of you and keep you safe, because people did take care of the things that belonged to them, didn't they?

And then, when Tony was so angry, why shouldn't you have gone out with Mr.—with Frank. And everything had been so wonderful—the fine, safe feeling, the protected feeling of being with a grown man.

But tonight—first one and then the other. Betrayer. Delilah. First betraying Tony with Frank, and then Frank with Tony. Awful—but just wonderful, wonderful, the feeling of being loved. And two loves were better than one.

Now she belonged to two men, but it was horrible. No, wonderful. No …

Tony drove his car into the garage, switched off the lights and climbed out closing the garage doors behind him. The moonlight cast long shadows over the lawn, making it look vast and deep and mysterious, and the huge darkened house where his father and mother lay sleeping loomed like a castle out of a fairy tale. He walked over to the grape arbor and seated himself on the long bench that ran the length of it.

There was something wrong with Joyce—something he would have to figure out. Maybe, if he were to write to her parents—but no, you couldn't do that. There was honor among kids. You couldn't betray that.

And for a while—he took out a cigarette and lit it—he had thought she was getting herself into trouble with that Frank Burdette. No. Nothing like that could happen. Frank was too nice a guy. And he had a wife and kid, and that kind of thing just didn't happen. Besides, he knew better now—after the way she had demonstrated, in the car, her ardent regard for him.

Still, it was too bad Joyce couldn't graduate. After all, what could her aunt do to her? Nothing. She'd just yell a little and then go to the school, and yell some more, and then Joyce would be back in and she'd graduate. Why couldn't she face the consequence of what she'd done? But then, there was always something a little funny about Joyce. Not that it made any difference with him, Tony.

You had to take the bad with the good in another person, and things couldn't always be your way.

Then he indulged himself in a moment of tender dreaming about Joyce—about the fact that she was his girl and everything was going to be all right.

He tossed away his cigarette, then, seeing the spark still glowing on the lawn, got up from the bench and stepped on the butt. Then he went into the house.

9 • Flight

Even the single crisis Joyce had feared she easily managed to evade by a quick fabrication. She had been terrified that her aunt would insist on attending the graduation exercises. But her aunt's interest was not really that deep. When Joyce told Priscilla that she had decided not to participate in the commencement exercises, the older woman had been more than pleased at the assurance she would not have to cope with that additional burden.

Priscilla Taylor was not a lazy woman, but a tired one. The comfortable income her brother provided in return for her care of Joyce was not enough to make up for the life which had somehow slipped by her, but it did ease the struggle to maintain the struggle. Once Priscilla Taylor had harbored a desire to have a life of her own, a husband of her own, a home of her own.

Now, the money provided by her brother was an excuse for abandoning the desire, and she had reached the age where she had convinced herself that she preferred things as they were.

Joyce never understood this mechanism—but she regarded its effects as all to the good.

At the Courier she had progressed. At first tentatively, and later because it had proved practical, Frank had given her minor assignments to fulfill. Once, when Lew Myron had 'phoned in sick, he had sent her in Lew's stead to cover a meeting of the Community Welfare Society, and her tense anxiety to satisfy had resulted in a more than routine story on the normally tedious.

Then he tried her on day police court. She had covered the routine arraignments with the elaborate attention to detail of a proceedings-reporter for the Congressional Record, and the enthusiasm for color of a *Time*-staffer.

So Frank gave her a raise, and told her she could call herself a reporter—although copy traffic was still her proper province.

As the summer wore on, Frank took her repeatedly to the Golden Horn, to the Stuyvesant Ball Room where the greatest of Dixieland musicians held forth weekly in the best New Orleans tradition, to Jimmy Ryan's, to Birdland, to the Three Deuces, to all the places where he was known by the musicians as a connoisseur of jazz. He introduced her to players, famous and infamous, and took a strange pride in the way she took to them and their music, and the way they took to her.

Cautiously, for fear of the police and not for fear of any other consequences, he further taught her the use of marijuana. Solemnly he steered her away from the junkies, users of heroin and cocaine, and solemnly explained the perils of those drugs with a "hook."

"Look," he told her one night when she asked why he regarded marijuana as so right, heroin as so wrong, "heroin has a hook. It's a narcotic. If you take it once you only need a little tiny bit to get high, and it'll give you a lift that takes you right through the ceiling. But the next time you come around it won't do the same thing for you unless you take a little bit more, and, every time you use it if you go at it regularly, you've got to keep adding to the dose. Pretty soon you need two capsules, then three, then five, just to get your regular kick. All right, that might not do any harm. But, suppose you take three caps or five for several days running. One morning you wake up and find you're clean. You can't put your hands on any. Suddenly you get into a panic, because you've got to have it. You chase all over hell and gone looking for it and you don't find it. After a while that panic wears off. Then you get it again, and you're more cautious. You get enough for a longer stretch, and you hoard it carefully. When you come to the end of that supply you're desperate. You'll sell your soul for more. You can't eat. You can't think. You can't do anything but hunt for heroin." He looked at her. "Remember Bang Morley?"

Joyce shook her head.

"Well, Bang was one of the greatest sax men that ever lived. He used to be with Jerry Best. He could do things with a sax that would curl your hair. He started off sniffing heroin—inhaling it up through his nose through a rolled up dollar bill from a little card where he'd spill the powder. At first that was all right. Made him feel like the king of the band. Then it began to get him. He couldn't play as well. His mind was always taken up with where he could get more of the stuff. Jerry offered to pay for a cure for him, but he wouldn't take the cure. He was too much bound up in the stuff. He stopped showing up for work and finally Jerry had to fire him. Yesterday I read in the News that he took a flying jump off the Empire State Building."

Joyce said, "Oh," with a quick little indrawn breath of horror. Then she said, "You're just playing games, Frank. Isn't marijuana just as bad?"

Frank shook his head. "As far as anybody has ever been able to tell, marijuana can't hurt a fly. I don't say it's good. It isn't. Anybody who needs marijuana, or liquor or anything else, such as coffee or cigarettes, to get along in the world—well, there's something wrong with that guy. But marijuana doesn't have a hook. If you can't get it—okay, you can't get it. You wish you had it, then you forget about it. You never lose control of yourself in tea, the way you do, for example in liquor. It doesn't load you down. It doesn't damage your body or your brain. I told you—the New York Academy of Medicine once checked up on that. But good for you? No, it isn't good for you. I know a lot of people who try it and don't like it. The significant thing is, they are always people I'd call mentally healthy. They're the really sane people I know …"

Joyce learned about other things from Frank. He introduced her to classical music, explaining that the channel through which it could be approached was the same channel which led to jazz—good jazz. He brought her to books, to Chinese food, to modern painting. He introduced her to long, rambling, conversational walks through the byways of Manhattan. He showed her Harlem and the Williamsburg Bridge. He took her to Coney Island and the Lewisohn Stadium. Together they saw ball games, went for a moonlight swim at Jones Beach.

And in time Joyce learned that Frank was jealous of Tony …

One day he said, "Joy? Every once in a while I see you with that kid Tony Thrine. Do you still go out with him?"

"Sometimes. Don't you like him?"

"Oh, sure. Nice kid. But he drives like a maniac."

"Don't be silly, Frank. Tony's a terrific driver."

"You know best," he said. "But I don't care much for the way he cuts through traffic. He's going to get himself in a sling one of these days."

"Frank, you aren't jealous are you?"

"Don't be dopey, kid. I'm never jealous of anybody. But I wish you wouldn't ride around with him in that car so much."

"But I don't ride with him much. I hardly ever go out with him."

"Aw, forget it." Then, after a moment, he said, "Joy, do you have to wear that dress?"

"What's wrong with it?"

"Nothing. Nothing at all."

"Then why did you mention it?"

"Because I hate to see you wearing things in poor taste."

"What are you talking about, Frank. I've worn this lots of times and you never said anything."

"I know. But it's cheap looking. You look like a small town brat trying to look like a loose woman. Don't wear it again when you're going out with me."

And by his anger she understood that he was not put out about the dress, but about Tony.

Joyce was seeing Tony, all right. Sometimes once a week, sometimes twice. If she had asked herself why, she would have said it was because every once in a while she wanted to get out with somebody her own age— somebody who wasn't constantly teaching her things and forcing her to be older than she was.

But she was being pretty intimate with Tony as well. Not always. Not very often. But sometimes. He lacked Frank's maturity, sophistication, sensual tenderness; but his fumbling excitement was sometimes more edifying to Joyce's soul. She could not tell exactly why or how, or what made it that way, but Tony was very important to her. She told herself that she was being sweet to him only to prevent him from suspecting Frank, from spilling the beans to her aunt who would cause trouble for Frank.

But in her heart she realized that she wanted Tony to love her, just as she wanted Frank to love her. She wanted love, love above all—the certainty of male affection.

After a time she became inured to the subtle tensions, the two-way stretch of the problem. She settled into the calm of being the beloved of two men as though it were as normal as corn flakes for breakfast.

Then, in mid-August, the final blow fell …

Frank left his house, that morning, at peace with the world and with himself. Even the burning heat of the August sun, glaring on the black macadam, could not interfere with the great calm that lay on his soul. The Managing Editor, old Force Dutney, had increased his salary and he was, this afternoon, to collect his first paycheck. Moreover, an article which he had written on tea-smoking had been accepted, the day before, by Esquire Magazine.

God was in his familiar heaven, and Frank Burdette was getting along just fine.

Then he met the postman.

"Hi, Mr. Burdette," the little gray man said. "Don't have much for you this morning. Just this one letter here. Guess it's from your wife."

"Thanks, Mr. Main," Frank said. "Beautiful day, isn't it?"

"'Sall right if you're in an air-conditioned office, I guess," Mr. Main said, thereby revealing the smallness of his soul and his inability to appreciate the glories of nature. "But, as a carrier of the mail, I kind of prefer autumn. Well, see you tomorrow." He hitched the bag a little higher on his shoulder and plodded up the street.

Frank turned the letter over, as though something new could be revealed by Janice's familiar script on the envelope, then put it in his pocket. He would read it in the office. Nothing should be permitted to distract him from the loveliness of nature this fine August morning.

He did not get to the letter until just before lunch. Then he opened it read the first few lines, put it down, rose to close the ever-open door of his office, and returned to the neat, tight script.

My dearest fuzzyhead:

I can see from your few letters that you are terribly unhappy, and I wish with all my heart that I knew some way to help you.

This has happened before, I know. But never like this. I knew, even before I went away, that it was a mistake for me to go.

It's very hard for me to write this—because it means admitting it to myself as well. But I did see it before I left, and your letters say it over and over again between the lines, even if they don't say it overtly. I'm only putting it down like this so you'll know I understand the facts—not just know them. It's very important, my darling, that you see the difference between understanding and knowing.

You've been having an affair with that lovely little Taylor girl. I don't blame you for it. Every year I go off like this and leave you alone with no one to keep you company and I guess—like it says in the old saying—a man isn't made of wood. I could say that I don't mind, but it wouldn't be true. The thought of you intimate with another girl makes me frantically jealous. Fortunately, for me, I don't really know this in the literal sense. It just kind of comes to me from what you write in your letters. And she is very beautiful. It's like putting two and two together and then saying, well, I won't add them up so I only suspect they make four.

I wouldn't write you like this if it were just for the affair you're having. You've had these summer affairs before. But there is something else. You're probably concealing it from yourself, but you're terribly unhappy without her, and jealous and angry with yourself. That shows in your letters, too. And if you let yourself get more deeply entangled in the emotional problems this thing is making for you, you'll become so involved with the Taylor girl that I'll never get you back.

I don't like to threaten you, my darling. And this isn't really a threat, because I'm so sure of the outcome. But, my darling, you must decide now, before things become worse. You are supposed to come up here the eighteenth anyway, so let's make that the time for decision—a sort of cutting-day for the Gordian knot.

Don't come here, my darling, unless you have finished off this affair. Please don't come. And if you don't come, then I'll know that it's all over and that it has been wonderful being married to you, but that we had to break it off.

And, if you do come, I shan't say a word to you. Not a word, my darling. But I'll know that you love just me …

P.S. Junior slobbered on the letter. He means he loves you, too.

Joyce met Tony at the corner of Second Street and Madison. She had intended to go with Frank to New York, that evening. But all day long he had been in a strange, tense mood. At noon she had seen him close the door of his office, a thing he never did ordinarily, and he had kept it closed until late in the afternoon.

She had been supposed to have lunch with Frank, but he did not open the office door, did not come out, as he ordinarily would, to ask if she was ready. Finally she had gone by herself. About four o'clock he came to her desk.

"Listen, Joy," he said. "Something's come up, and I won't be able to make it tonight. There's something I have to get straightened out here." And that was when she decided to telephone Tony.

"Want to take me out tonight?"

"Why not? Don't I always?"

"So pick me up at the corner of Madison and Second at six o'clock, Okay?" Tony's car was parked on Madison, just above where it narrowed for the underpass beneath the Long Island Railroad bridge.

She waved at him as soon as she saw him, his spidery legs mysteriously entangled in the steering wheel, his arms stretched back behind his head as he reclined in luxurious ease against the leather seat cushions.

"Hi, lazy," she said.

"Saving up my energy for school," he said. "It's been decided. I'm not going to Harvard at all. I'm registered at NYU. Went in to town this morning to get signed up."

"Good," Joy said. Not really meaning anything special.

"Any particular place you want to go?" Tony asked, as he started the car.

"I got eyes for some sea-food."

"What kind of an expression is that? I've got eyes for some sea-food?"

"It's musicians' talk," Joyce explained. "Jive-talk. All the cats dig it. You mean you ain't hip, man?"

"Cut it out."

"What do you mean, cut it out? I'll talk as I please."

"Not with me, you won't," Tony said. "And another thing, why did you tell me to meet you at the corner of Second and Madison? What's the matter with in front of the Courier building? You do still work there, don't you?"

"Of course I do."

"Then …?"

"Well …" She stumbled. "I—I had something I had to see about at the corner of Second and Madison."

"Something important at the ice house, of course …" His voice was loaded with sarcasm.

"As a matter of fact, it was. I had to see a Mister—Mister Pelley there. It was about an—an Elks meeting."

"Quit lying to me, Joy."

"Don't you dare call me a liar, Tony Thrine. If you ever say that again I'll …"

"Just what will you do, Joy?"

"I'll never see you again."

"All right. Now I'll tell you a few things. The reason you didn't want to meet me in front of the Courier building is because you didn't want Frank to see you riding off with me. And the reason you didn't want him to is because you've been lying to him just the way you've lied to me. And if you've been lying to him about going out with me, then you've been lying about how—how close we are. And if you've been lying about that, you've been lying because you were close with him and you couldn't let him find out about anybody else—just like you couldn't let me. Is that true?"

"How can you talk like that?"

"How could I not have before? That's the real question. There're a couple other deductions I can make, too. I'm just a kid. Joy, but I'm a smart kid, and you aren't so darned brainy you can put it over on me all the time."

"But it's not true, Tony. I swear it's not."

"All right. There's a simple way to test it. We'll drive to Mr. City Editor Burdette's house, and we'll walk in, and I'll ask him."

"You can't."

"Of course I can."

"Think how it would embarrass me."

"I am thinking. And that's just what we're going to do. You've been putting it over on both of us, and I'm not going to stand for it any more. Either we see Burdette, or I know I'm right and it's all over between us. How about it?"

For long minutes Joyce sat silent on the seat of the moving car.

"You can't decide. All right." He swung the car into a street "We'll go to Burdette's."

"No, Tony!" Joyce was crying.

"Don't give me that sob-stuff, Joy. What's it going to be? Will you admit it, or do we go there."

"All right. I admit it. Now take me home."

Tony said nothing. Grimly he drove through the tree-lined streets, all golden and shadow-striped in the setting sun, grimly stopped the car before the Taylor house, set back from the street among its landscaped lawns.

Joyce got out of the car without a word, and stepped across the grass island to the sidewalk. Then she turned to look at Tony. "I hate you," she said, and started to run across the lawn.

"Joy!" Suddenly he could forgive her anything. She half-halted. "Joy!" Then his anger got the better of him. "Go to hell," he said. He jerked the car into low gear and, racing the engine, took off.

It was not until the following evening that she had an opportunity to talk to Frank. He stopped by her desk in the morning. "Want to come to the house tonight?"

"Of course." She smiled up at him.

"Good kid," he said, patting her hand, and went on to his office.

That evening they rode uptown together on the bus, but Frank said nothing. Something strange and intangible seemed to have come between them, and it frightened her. She needed Frank, now, needed him desperately.

When they reached the house Frank unlocked the door and let her pass into the hallway. "Let's go out in the kitchen and get something to eat."

"No, Frank. Not yet." She came up close to him, her face tilted up to his. "Frank, darling," she said, her voice husky. "I want you."

Suddenly, almost angrily, he caught her in his arms, crushing her to him. He lifted her in his arms and carried her up the stairs.

Afterwards, she told him.

"I had to be good to him, Frank. Honest I did. He would have told my aunt, and would have—I don't know what she would and you know what he would have done."

"It's all right, honey. I understand." He kissed her tear-streaked face.

The envelope was lying on her desk when she arrived at the Courier next day, and the door of Frank's office was closed. It was addressed to Miss Joyce Taylor, in a handwriting she recognized from memos and notations on copy.

She looked about her to see if anyone was watching. But the scattering of people in the office were bowed over their typewriters, each with its continuous roll of yellow copy paper mounted on the back, or closely attending to the long strips of manila paper on which they were marking the strange hieroglyphs of the copyreader.

She opened the letter and read it through, then read it through again. It was the same, both times—a short, typewritten note.

Joyce:

I have gone to Maine to spend two weeks with Janice and Junior. When I come back, I hope we will both have forgotten the things that happened this summer. Please do not misunderstand me. You are a wonderful person—far too good for me, in fact. But Janice needs me and, in a funny way, I guess I need her.

Go back to Tony. He's a fine boy, and he does love you, no matter how angry he may be now.

Don't quit the paper. You're going to make a terrific newspaper woman. And by the time I get back, you'll see, this whole thing will have worked itself out.

So long,
Frank

That night Joyce packed her things in the stillness of her bedroom. In the morning she waited until her aunt had left the house to go shopping. Then she called a cab, went to the bank where she had deposited her earnings from the Courier, and withdrew all her money while the cab waited. Then she went to the station and caught the 11:20 for New York.

Part Two

THE HORSE

With phantoms and unprofitable strife,
And in mad trance, strike with our spirit's knife
Invulnerable nothings....

Percy Bysshe Shelley

Joyce went to see Jerry Best as a last resort.

She had thought about it a long time—perhaps an hour or so during each of five or six evenings—before she actually got on the subway and rode downtown to Washington Square.

For a while, before that, she had been able to kid herself that things were going very well. For anyone else but Joyce Taylor, in fact, they would have going well indeed. But the desperate forces that drove her demanded something beyond the simple successes of employment, food and a place to live.

She had spent almost no money at all during the summer of work on the Courier, and it had not been hard to get a job—theoretically an editorial job—before her reserves ran out. She was, officially, an assistant editor on the *Machine Tool Journal*, a publication devoting itself to internal grinders, lathes and other subtle mechanisms of the early atomic age. Behind her official title she concealed the fact that she was one of four employees of the publisher, the others being a myopic baldhead with the entirely surprising name of Eugene Tip, the editor; a stenographer named Myra Feldman, who lived in Brooklyn and had designs on a genuine dentist; and an advertising manager-cum-bookkeeper who hid behind the pseudonym Chauncey Scott Arvin, and was altogether too glorious a person for the *Machine Tool Journal*.

Her duties were multitudinous and tedious, requiring only a minimum of intelligence—that is, just a trifle more than that possessed by Miss Feldman whose perfunctory performance of them before had necessitated hiring Joyce. She was in charge of mailing out cards inducing manufacturers to provide information on new products, in charge also of the measurement of type, the production of cuts, the reading of galley proofs, and the fetching of innumerable containers of coffee for Eugene Tip—who took his eminent position with great seriousness.

Her salary had been thirty-five dollars a week, and within a month had climbed to forty-five, to the scandalized amazement of Miss Feldman who, after two years of unremitting indolence, was earning only forty.

Thus, in things material, Joyce was a success. But Joyce had conceived of glittering Manhattan as a gay round of night clubs and orchids, an orgy of parties and diaphanous nightgowns, and in this direction she had failed miserably. Mistakenly assuming that she needed, above all things, freedom, she had rented a furnished room instead of going to a girls' residence hotel. She understood that YWCAs and the like prohibited male companionship, and failed to apprehend that acquaintance with women often is requisite to acquaintance with men …

For men were what Joyce needed.

She had been thinking about Jerry and Don and Ginger and the boys in the band for a long time—but not thinking of seeing them. An unconscious residue of prejudice—which even the months with Frank had not entirely overcome—would not allow her to think of herself as a girl whose only friends in all the great city of New York were colored.

But as September turned to October, and October to November, it became more and more clear to her that she must, must, must make human contacts other than with the trio of gay souls who produced the *Machine Tool Journal*. The mad round of cinema palaces had now so far palled that she could summon no shadow of sympathetic passion for Gary Grant or Van Johnson, Bing Crosby or Montgomery Clift. No longer could she identify with Elizabeth Taylor or Olivia de Havilland, and she had never liked Frank Sinatra in the first place.

When she finally decided to go see Jerry, the problem became one of finding a reason. It could not be admitted that she wanted to see them just because she wanted to see them. She never for an instant believed that her own personality was sufficient to engage their attention. There had to be an excuse—and the excuse was, of course, the fine thing that she had first discovered with them: the green grass that grew greener where music dwelt.

It was a Friday evening when the impulse finally came that sent her into the hurrying subway, through the rushing tunnels, and out into the piercing winds that swept through the street canyon in which was the Golden Horn. It was almost like a homecoming.

Louie, the Italian waiter recognized her immediately. "Good evening, Miss Taylor. Anyone meeting you?"

"Not tonight, Louie," as though she were an habitué. "I just thought I'd drop in and see Jerry and the boys."

"I'll get you a table right up front," Louie said. "Let me just chase those people over there. Haven't seen you or Mr. Burdette in the longest time." The dark-trousered, white-shirted figure glided through the gloom to a front table where a mildly intoxicated trio were giving a minimum of attention to the music and a maximum to the liquor.

After a moment she saw the three, two girls and a man, get up to move to another table, and then Louie came and led her up to the vacated table only a few feet from where Jerry Best's glittering trumpet was juggling a melody with skill and grace and passion. His face was intense, dedicated, rapt as it always was when he took a riff. But Don, filling in rhythm at the piano, saw her and winked. Then, when the sax took over the melody and Jerry took his trumpet down from his lips, Don reached out and touched Jerry's arm and pointed to Joyce.

Jerry saluted her with a loose, graceful gesture, pointed her out to Louie and then tapped himself on the chest, a gesture that clearly meant put everything on my bill.

Suddenly Joyce was aware that she was the focus of attention in the room. Who, she imagined them saying, is that girl up front? They made some other people move to give her a table. Who is she?

And even this mistaken flattery went to Joyce's head like wine. A homecoming. A welcome.

She felt reinstated in her own respect.

Then, as the piece ended, Jerry pulled the microphone to him, and in a voice that was half a whisper, said, "We got a special request from a charming young lady who ain't even requested it yet. So the next number we're going to play is for Miss Joyce Taylor, a very special friend of ours, and it's going to be them Royal Garden Blues."

When the set ended Jerry left the stand and came directly to her table. "Come on out back with us. Ginger's out there. Louie'll hold the table for you," and she followed him through the narrow passageway that led through the kitchen and into the dressing room that was also the office of the club's owner, a man named Michell.

Ginger, in a strapless gown of gold lame pulled high to expose her shapely legs, perched on the corner of a desk. She said, "Hi, Joy! We really been missing you and Frank, kid." And the others came over in genuine pleasure.

Joyce felt her throat constricting with sentiment, and moisture gathering in her eyes.

"Ginger's making it with us, now," Jerry said. "Best damn blues-shoutin' you ever heard, and she don't weigh a pound over a hundred and ten." Ginger nodded happily. "But where the hell you been?"

"Living in town for about three months now," Joyce said.

"And you ain't even come around to see us? Man, you're flippin'!" Jerry expressed complete disavowal of such insanity. "And what ails Frank? He drop dead or something?"

"I haven't seen Frank for months," Joyce said.

"Gee, that's a drag." Then, with an agile tact, "Ginger's got a spot now, and I want you to dig her. Go on, take it Don. I'll sit with Joy at her table."

He led the way outside and they sat down. After a moment Don came out and went to the piano, feeling out a slow introduction.

They didn't give Ginger a spotlight, and she didn't need the microphone in the small room. She just came out and walked on the little space of dance floor carrying a chair. She plunked the chair down and sat down on it, not playing it for sex or anything. Then, as expressionless as, and with the folded hands of a little girl paying strict attention to a Sunday school lesson, she sang St. James Infirmary so it ripped great chunks out of your heart. She had a full contralto voice, with a low range that was almost a moan, but that could become as raw and sharp and edged as a slide trombone, and she made the words really hurt. Then she did other things—ordinary things, the kind of stuff everybody did; things like *Georgia on my Mind* and *Lover*

Man and *If I Can't Sell It, Goin' Sit On It*—and each one came out like something new and strange.

Afterward, when Ginger had left the floor, Jerry asked her. "What happened between you and Frank? Something I can fix?"

"No," Joyce said. "Nothing like that. After all, he is married, and it couldn't last forever. In the long run it had to be Janice."

"She's a fine chick." Jerry said. "The greatest. I dig her."

"The funny part is," Joyce said, "I dig her, too, Jerry. But I couldn't go on seeing him and working with him every day after that. So when it happened I came to New York ... Let me tell you the truth, Jerry. First I was going to come down here and tell you I just wanted to see you to make a contact for some charge, but that wasn't really it. I don't know anybody in New York. I'm absolutely alone here and I don't want to let anybody know where I am, but I did want to see some people I know, and have somebody to talk to and everything." She felt the tears coming.

Jerry put his arm around her shoulder, right there in front of all the people in the club, and gave her a firm squeeze. "Cool, Joy. I dig you. Listen, after we get through here we're going up town tonight. After-hours place on hundred 'n twenty-eighth. Got a session all set up. We got plenty of pot and I'll lay some on you before we cut out to keep you straight anyhow, but we'd like you to make it with us ..."

"Hold on, man," Joyce said, suddenly smiling. "I don't dig you? What's pot?"

"That good, green Mexican grass," Jerry said. He chuckled—a sound as musical as his trumpet playing it sweet. "Going to have a jam session uptown and we'd like you came along."

"Cool," Joyce said. "The coolest."

"Solid. See you after the next set. We'll all get on a little out back."

11 • Transference

Things might have been all right if it hadn't been for Christmas. And they might still have been all right if, just at the beginning of December, Jerry Best's band hadn't gotten the telegram.

Joyce had fallen right in with Ginger and the boys in the band. All day long she would work like a machine tool for the *Journal,* and at night she would come downtown and have dinner in some Village spot, where it wasn't unusual for seven colored people to be seen together with a white girl, and go over to the Golden Horn, and Joy would hang around until about eleven or twelve o'clock and then go home to bed.

On Mondays, when the club was closed, she would spend the evenings with Jerry and Ginger in an apartment the dark-skinned girl had on West Twelfth Street, and somehow the marijuana would take the edge off the loneliness she felt when she saw how close Jerry and Ginger were.

The part that amazed her about them was that they seemed so glad to have her around, so willing to introduce her to their friends, so anxious to help her in anything she wanted to do.

It was more Jerry than Ginger who showed this concern for her future, because Ginger was, at bottom, an easy-going sort, given to immense indolences and occasional moods; but Jerry was a different cut—a strong, sure individual who knew where he was going, and was going there through the only channels he could find.

One evening, after they had been playing off some phonograph records on Ginger's changer, and while that talkative mood of the weed was still on them, Jerry asked, "Are you going to stick with that machine shop for keeps?"

"I don't know," Joyce said. "I hadn't thought about it."

"Well, you ought to quit," Jerry said. "That right, Gin?"

"Sure, man," Ginger said. "That place is the most uncool for you. You'll wind up so hung you'll flip. My dig is them cats up there got you working so you got no time for just plain grooving yourself."

"She means …" Jerry started to say.

"I know what she means, Jerry," Joyce said. "But I don't know what to do about it. It's funny with me, I never felt till just about now that I really fit in anywhere. That's something you and Gin did for me. Made me feel—right in there. I never felt it before, I goofed off in school, because I couldn't really feel I was worth anybody paying any attention to because—well, nobody in my own family felt I was worth paying attention to. You know what I mean?"

"Yes, I know," Jerry said. "Maybe I know it better than you think. You kind of get to know these things automatically when you're colored. But you can't just let yourself go, honey. You got to get in there and push. Like, I like music. Music is the greatest with me. Sometimes I dig if they took away music from me I wouldn't be nothing, but when I set off I didn't plan to be a musician. Music was like something I was going to keep for me. That was how I was going to get my kicks. But my real dig was—I was going to be a doctor.

"All the time I was in high school I worked nights as a musician. That's where I got to know Frank, when I was in high school. When we both were. Then we got out and Frank went to college and I was going to take a premedical course, see. I had the loot all saved up. I made enough gold out of music so I could pay my way. But I wanted to do it the right way. No second-rate, all-colored medical schools for me. I was after the best and I had the loot to pay my way—and I couldn't get in. Not medical school, and not even the pre-meds that I wanted.

"So one day I sat down with me and I figured it out. If you're colored there are ways to get to the top. With the breaks I could make it as a doctor—but I just didn't happen to get the breaks. And the other way was, like, entertainment. You see what colored people make the real money. They're boxers, actors, singers, writers, and musicians. One or two others break out, sometimes. But they're the freaks. Like Ralph Bunche at the U.N., and a couple of scientists and people like that. But what I had to do was—like I don't have any talent for words, and I never was specially handy with my fists—so I like stuck to the thing where I had already got a ways."

It was the first time Joyce had ever heard Jerry talk about himself. "I didn't know that," she said. "I thought you always wanted to be a musician."

"Oh. I did. But the big deal was I was going to be a doctor. Once I made up my mind though, I forgot about the other and got right in there with the blowing."

"Does all right, too," Gin said. "He's right in there with the best." She leaned over from where she sat beside him on the divan and kissed his ear.

"All right. It's cool for me. I dig it. But you got to do what you dig doing. You can't make it doing something you don't like. Way I see it, you ain't awful cool with those machine tool cats. They sound awful square."

"You wouldn't exactly call them hip." Joyce admitted wryly, thinking of Eugene Tip and his colleagues.

"So whyn't you skin an eye. Look around, honey. There's other ways of making the loot. I don't mean another kind of work. Frank said you were great for this kind of stuff; but you ought to get on like a magazine like, say, Look or something; you dig? A real magazine."

Joyce went home that night feeling that things were right. Gin and Jerry were looking out for her. You could feel safe with people like that, people who had your best interests in mind. It was the kind of thing that made you feel wanted. You could go to their house and sit down and turn on the jive, get just a little high and really feel in there. She caught herself thinking in jive, and laughed gaily to herself, making a middle-aged woman facing her in the subway give her a disapproving frown. Then she thought, maybe colored people were the real people, the right people. Maybe that was the way to live …

It was a hard thing for him to do, and Tony wasn't quite sure he could manage it, even when he was standing in the hallway where Estelle, the Taylor's maid-of-all-work, had left him when she went to find Priscilla Taylor. You can always make some excuse, he thought, and beat it out of here. So then he tried to think up an excuse, such as Mom sent me over to see if I could borrow a cup of sugar.

But when Priscilla Taylor came into the hallway, all Tony could think of to say was, "Miss Taylor, where's Joyce?"

The questions caught the woman completely off guard. Yet it struck her like a blow that she had always known would have to come.

Priscilla said, "Come in the other room, Tony. Leave your coat there on the seat."

He followed her into the living room. The room was immaculate and fussy. Victorian chairs confronted battery-driven electric clocks under glass domes, and annoying antimacassars and tidies cluttered the chair arms and table surfaces.

"Sit down, please," the woman said.

"Thanks, but I can't stay," Tony said. "I just wanted to know where I could reach Joyce?"

"I don't know, Tony." Suddenly she dabbed at her eyes with the handkerchief she held crumpled in one hand. "I haven't heard from her since she left."

"Well, where was she going?"

"I don't know, Tony. I don't know what to do." Her voice broke completely. "I don't know anything about that girl. How could she go away like that and not even suggest where she was going?"

"You mean she just went away like that, without even saying where she was going?"

"I've been so distraught, Tony. You can't imagine how this has upset me."

"Let me get this straight, Miss Taylor. Joy just went away and didn't say where she was going. Is that what happened?"

"Yes."

"Well what did you do about it?"

"What could I do?"

"What does Mr. Taylor say?"

"He doesn't know yet."

"You mean you haven't told them that Joy's gone?"

"I couldn't, Tony. I just couldn't. How could I write them over there in Europe that their daughter has run off? Heaven only knows where the girl has gone."

"What about the police? What do they say?"

"I didn't talk to the police."

"Look, Miss Taylor, I don't like to tell you your business, but you'd better call Mr. Taylor, wherever he is, right this minute. Did Joy leave a note or anything?"

"Yes. She left me a note. She just said that she was going away, and wouldn't be coming back. She said I wouldn't hear from her anyway, so that there was no reason for me to worry about her. That's all she said."

"You better start placing that call. It takes a long time to put a call through to Europe. Where are they now?"

"In Rome. My brother's arranging a contract there. But how can I call them? At first I thought she'd be back in a day or so. How can a young girl like that go out on her own? I knew she'd be back. And then time went by, and—and then I just couldn't. I can't."

"This happened in August, Miss Taylor. They have a missing persons bureau, the police, I mean. You call them first and then—No. I have a better idea. Let me see what I can do. I'll be back later." He went into the hallway and snatched his coat from the bench. On the porch he stood for a moment looking at the December rain and planning his movements. Then he ran across the lawn, cutting across backyards until he reached the Thrine garage. He opened the doors and backed his car out into the turnaround. For a moment he stopped there. "What if—?" But he decided there were no what-ifs, and drove on out, swinging into Central Avenue and keeping straight until he reached Randolph Road.

They had been building up to Christmas for weeks now—all three of them. All four, really, because Don Wilson, the pianist was in on this deal. The tree was purchased and mounted, and stood in the cool of the paved backyard behind the brownstone house on Twelfth Street.

It was a time of conspiracies and counter-conspiracies. Out of small sums, quietly conserved, Joyce had bought a tape recording unit for Jerry, a watch for Don, and a fine string of cultured pearls for Ginger.

She knew that Jerry had ordered a car for Ginger, because she had been with him when he had made the down-payment, and she knew that Ginger had laid out a fortune for uniformly bound Bach scores which Jerry had been studying lately.

Don had inquired of her whether she thought it would be all right if he gave Ginger lingerie and, when this scheme was rejected, had settled on a vast vase of costly perfume.

There remained only a week now till Christmas, and Joyce was working on a complex scheme of small presents to be stuffed in stockings by the useless fireplace.

With Ginger she had just returned from an expedition to secure a final miscellany of small gifts, that particular Saturday afternoon, when the doorbell rang long and loud—as though whoever were below could not wait patiently for admission, but intended to deafen them into an immediate response.

Joyce said, "Stick everything under the couch. I'll buzz downstairs." She went to the kitchen and pressed the door release. The ringing stopped, then she ran back to the hallway and, leaving the chain on, swung the door inward. Jerry came up the stairs three at a time.

He said, "Let me in, Joy." His face was hard and angry.

When she released the door-chain he brushed past her. She followed him into the living room. Ginger was still bent over, stuffing things under the couch when Joyce reached the doorway. She saw Jerry stalk across the room, stop behind Ginger, draw back his foot and kick her squarely.

Ginger toppled to the floor, then quickly twisted around to look up at Jerry.

"What's the matter with you, man?" she said.

"Got a present for you, honey. Man left this with me. Man named Roy Mallon. Roy Mallon the pusher." He tossed a small, manila-wrapped package no bigger than a ring box on the couch.

"What you talking about?" Ginger's voice was shrill and whining.

"I told you once, I want no junkies with my band. I got no time for junkies. I want nobody from my band going to any hospital, and I don't want to get hung up on no narcotics rap. Bad enough there's a law against charge. But charge ain't got no hook, and I think it's a good thing, a fine thing. But this—nobody's going to have it around me."

"Jerry!" Ginger got to her feet and came toward him.

"Get away from me. I got a few words to say. I don't know how bad hooked you are. I seen—I saw them little marks on your arms, but I couldn't believe you'd shoot it. I thought they were just blackheads or pimples or something. I tried to convince myself and I let it pass. But no more. We got a wire from a Miami place, a big place. We're taking it. But you ain't coming along. I got a replacement for the band and I asked Bob Mitchell to let us go to Miami. It's only for two weeks, through Christmas and New Year's. He said it would be okay. So then, when I found out about you buying horse from that pusher—then I called Bob and told him you were staying. So that's all right. But when I come back if you're still on that stuff, girl, that's the end." He turned and walked out, without a word to Joyce. It was as though Joyce's whole world had exploded before her very eyes.

The dark girl stood for long seconds, just as Jerry had left her, unmoving until the slamming of the downstairs door came up through the walls. Then she ran into the bedroom and banged the door behind her. For a while Joyce could hear her sobbing. Then, after a time, the sobbing stopped.

Joyce thought, I'll wait a little longer and then I'll give her some coffee. She went to the kitchen and ran water into the pot.

Frank led Tony into the living room, trying to choke down the fear that had caught at him as he saw the boy's face framed in the doorway. When he had opened the door he had started to say, "What's the matter, Tony?" Then, hearing Janice behind him, he had laid his finger on his lips and, turning to Janice, had said, "Could you excuse us a few minutes, Jan?" And she had gone up the stairs, looking pale and terrified.

He said nothing, waiting for Tony to speak.

"I just want to know where Joy is, Mr. Burdette."

"Frank," Frank said, automatically. Then, "Don't you know?"

"Of course I don't. I wouldn't be asking if I did."

"I haven't seen her." The fright wag growing. What had happened to the kid? Had she been hurt?

"When was the last time you saw her?" Tony demanded.

"Not since the summer. What's the trouble?"

"Neither has anybody else."

"Sit down," Frank said. He dropped into a chair and extended a cigarette to the boy from a crumpled pack on the coffee table. "Let's get this straight now. I haven't seen her at all since she left the paper last summer. Sit down, fella." Tony sat down. Frank picked up the table lighter and fired both cigarettes.

"Now," he said, dragging deeply at the cigarette, "you tell me what happened and I'll tell you." Frank was getting some control of himself now.

"I had a fight with Joy just before she left. It was about you. Then, after that, we broke off. A few days later I noticed she was never around. See, I didn't really want to break off. I just thought that if I sort of blew up, well, it might bring her to her senses. Anyway, I called up a couple of times. Kind of disguised my voice so nobody would recognize it and asked for her. The maid, Estelle, said she'd gone out of town. And then, another time, she said, Miss Joyce has gone away. Nobody knows where. I let it go and let it go. But—but I couldn't get it out of my mind. I mean, Joy is very important to me. I know I'm still not of age and all that, but …"

Frank said, "I know what you mean." Then he said, "I think we could both do with a drink, don't you?" He said, "Where …?" Then he said, "Let's have the drink first." He went to the sideboard in the dining room and brought out a bottle and two glasses, placing them on the coffee table before the two chairs, and then poured out two stiff shots, all the time searching desperately for a way to begin.

Then he said, "I did have an affair with Joyce last summer. I know how that hurts you, but it's a thing we've got to get clear. And maybe I'm to blame for her going away. So we need to know that, too. What about her aunt— what's her name? Priscilla?"

"Her aunt only knows that Joy went away a few days after we had the quarrel. I don't know exactly when. She left a note that said not to try to find her. I didn't find out about it until just tonight. I thought—I thought you might know. I don't know. I thought you might have her in New York somewhere, or something."

"I don't," Frank said.

"Do you have any idea …?"

"Not any. Has her aunt notified—oh, but of course she has."

"No. She hasn't. That's just it. I don't know what's happened to her. I don't know, even, if she's alive. I don't know what to do."

They talked for a long time, and after a while Janice came down and talked, too.

"Mostly," Janice said, "I don't think either of you were to blame. A lot of the blame belongs to the aunt. But it's hard to blame her, really, either. The ones really to blame are Joyce's parents. Somebody's got to notify them, of course. But I don't think it will help much. The only real thing anybody can do about Joyce is wait ..."

12 • Narcosis

After Joyce made the coffee, she set the pot on a tray with cups and saucers and spoons, and got some cookies from a box in the cupboard. These she arranged on a plate for maximum attractiveness. Then she laid out the cream and sugar, and carried the whole tray to the bedroom door. She listened for a moment and then tried the door. It was locked.

She knocked, gently, and then louder.

Ginger said, "Wait a second, honey." She heard Ginger getting up, heard the sound of a drawer being shut, and then the door opened. She carried in the tray, and Ginger watched her setting it down on the little night-table beside the bed.

"I thought you might like a little coffee or something." Joyce said.

She looked at the dark girl who stood there, her hand still on the knob of the door as though opening it had somehow frozen her to silence. In the light of the dim ceiling fixture Ginger's face looked strange, and there was something odd about her dark brown eyes that Joy couldn't quite place.

After a second the dark girl moved. "Gee, that's awful sweet of you, honey. That's the very sweetest. An' I hope you won't be awful mad if I don't drink the coffee right away, on account of I'm just a little upset to my stomach."

"No, Gin. Of course not. Is there anything I can get for you?"

"No, honey. Except you can sit down here with me."

That was when it really struck Joy—when she sat down on the bed beside Ginger and took the dark hand in her light one. It was as though Jerry had suddenly destroyed her home, ripping it out from under her. She thought of the things it was going to mean. No Christmas. No tree. No presents. No being together. No more evenings in the Golden Horn. No more lighting up together in the comfortable evenings, and no more going out together in the afternoons. No more feeling of safety—of being protected by the tall, handsome colored man with the small mustache; no more having a place to come home to, because it wouldn't be quite the same with just Ginger there. Her stomach seemed to be quivering with the idea, and her head ached with it.

Then Ginger said, "You heard what the man said?"

Joyce nodded, holding back the tears.

"He's wrong, Joyce. This time the man is wrong."

"What do you mean?"

"What's so different about gauge and the white stuff? Nothing. You don't see him knocking off the gauge. He never put gauge down. Only reason he's so down on horse is on account of his old man."

"What do you mean?"

"What I say. His old man got on horse when Jerry was a kid. He didn't get on like a sensible guy. Not like I do. Not like other people. He used it till it was using him—till he was carrying a monkey bigger than he was."

"Who? What monkey?"

"Jerry's father. He had a bad habit. He was a real junkie. Used to get himself committed to the Government hospital for the cure, just so he could get the habit down small enough so he could afford to start all over again."

"Is that why Jerry's so down on it?"

"That's right. When he was a kid his old man used to sometimes send him out to make the contact for him. Finally they had a real hassle about it, when Jerry was in high school, and he left home."

"What's it like, Ginger?"

"It's like gauge—only a great big kick, like it takes you right through the ceiling. You get so high. You can really dig this kick." Then Joyce knew what she was going to do. She thought, I've got to find out so I'll know what to do about Ginger. And there was something else, too, that she thought. It was something fleeting, that made fleeting sense. If I know what it is, she thought, then I can tell Jerry about it and he'll come back, because we've got to get him back. Ginger and I do. She said, "Gin?"

"What's the matter, honey?"

"I want to try that stuff."

"Oh, no, honey. You don't want to get on that kick."

"Yes I do, Gin."

It went on like that, back and forth for a few minutes. Then Ginger went to the bureau drawer and took out the little packet Jerry had thrown on the couch. She opened it, unfastening the brown paper secured with scotch tape. Inside were a series of little packets, made of waxed paper and fastened with the tape. Each measured about one-and-a-half inches square. Carefully Ginger removed the tape from the packet and spread it out flat.

"Get yourself a dollar bill," Ginger said. Joyce went to her pocket book in the other room, thinking it was funny that Ginger wanted her to pay for it. When she came back, she saw that Ginger had split the little pile of powder on the wax paper into two tiny piles. Joyce thought, where's the needle? She had seen the needle when the drawer was opened. "Give me the bill, honey," Ginger said. She took the rectangle of paper and rolled it into a tiny tube—tight, so that the opening down the center was smaller than the thickness of a toothpick.

"You do it like this," she said. She put the waxed paper with its burden of white powder on the edge of the bureau, then inserted the dollar bill tube into one nostril and bent down. Holding the other nostril, she inhaled deeply through the tube, sucking up the white powder through the tube like a vacuum cleaner tucking cigarette ash from a rug. In a moment she had disposed of the one half of the white powder. Then she rose to her feet, still inhaling at the dollar bill. When she had taken the bill from her nostril she held both nostrils for a moment, as though to keep from sneezing, batting her eyes rapidly.

"You make like that, Joy, honey," she said.

Joyce followed the same detailed procedure, holding her nostrils when she had done. The inside of her nose felt strange, a funny, cool tingling. It wasn't like tea, this stuff.

Suddenly she heard Ginger rushing from the room and saw her run to the bathroom. Then she heard the dark girl being sick—and in a moment knew why and followed her.

She vomited, strangely without effort, and then was s-o-o-o-o happy.

The pain of Jerry's going had vanished, and a million reasons why it was a good thing came swiftly flowing into her mind. How could he not understand about this? How could he be against this? What was a "hook" compared to this? Where was marijuana when you could get like this?

Why, you could do anything, make anything, be anything. There was nothing impossible. If it were cloudy, you could make the sun shine. This was really grooving. This was being right at the top.

She followed Ginger into the living room and sat down. You could do anything, except that it was so wonderful not to do anything—just to think and feel the fine sensation of blood rushing through your veins, and hear the thoughts ticking off inside your head, and follow the thoughts as they dashed swiftly about the room, thinking things out for themselves.

After a while she said, "Ginger? Isn't the light pretty bright?" And Ginger got up, very slowly, and turned it off. Then the peace and beauty was suddenly perfect.

The great thing about it was, it was so mental. Everything was so mental, now. You could go back and relive every wonderful moment of your life, skipping all the bad parts and all the little things that had gone wrong at the time. And you could live them better than you had before, because now there was only pleasure and nothing but pleasure.

Ginger had turned on the radio, and the little dial light in the corner of the room became a friendly, protective eye. Then out came music—visible music, music that darted about the room in little blue bolts of lighting, in little colors of sound. It came so slowly, now—so much more slowly than with gauge—that every separate note had time to be counted in its individual vibrations and colors, and to develop an overlay of meanings on meanings on meanings.

Joyce let herself sink deeper into the soft armchair that felt like caressing paternal arms clasped about her body—that seemed to pick her up and carry her, like a little girl, with kisses, to bed ...

13 • Tolerance

The answer to the cable that Priscilla had decided to send instead of
making a telephone call—perhaps because it deferred the evil day of
having to hear her brother's angry voice—came the following morning. It
read:

> CAN CONCLUDE BUSINESS HERE IN TWO MORE DAYS
> THEN WILL TAKE PLANE LANDING AT IDLEWILD
> THURSDAY NITE—EDWARD

She thought, you're in a great hurry about your own daughter, aren't
you, Edward. But then she remembered how slowly she herself had hurried
…

Christmas got by, somehow, and so did New Year's. Joyce spent both
holidays with Ginger at the Golden Horn, where a mixed band of somewhat
indifferent skill played under a white leader who served mainly to provide a
background for Ginger's easy talent. Then, before Jerry came back with his
anger and his storms, Ginger had a new offer from a mid-town club—a big
club with a big all-colored show. And after that things began to roll faster
and faster for Ginger. There were record dates and radio shows and guest
appearances.

Joyce meanwhile, was learning a new language. The language of the
heroin user was deeper and more occult than that of the "viper", as was
determined by the relative illegality of the narcotic heroin compared to the
intoxicant, marijuana. *Sniffing* and *popping* replaced *blowing* and *lighting
up* or *turning on,* though the latter two might on occasion be used
interchangeably with the former. Then there was *shooting it* and
mainlining it—when you drove deep into a vein with a hypodermic needle
and a solution of the white powder. There was nothing comparable to that
in marijuana. But you got high on the big charge. You hit the horse, and
when the stuff was real gone, you, sometimes blew your top.

You had to be careful with it. You couldn't let the habit get out of hand.
A three cap habit, now, that was bad, because when you started making it
with three capsules, you could get in deeper, and when it got up to six caps,
suddenly, one day, you were liable to wake up all of a sudden carrying the
monkey on your shoulders.

That was what they called it when it had you—when you really felt the
hook. That was when you had to go out and get it, no matter what.

It didn't get like that with Joyce for a long time, and the time seemed
even longer because there was so much happening in it.

After a while Ginger had shown her about the needle and taught her
how to shoot the white stuff, because the other way, sniffing it, was so
wasteful.

There was no money problem, because Ginger was making all the money in the world. It came rolling in, faster and faster, and you could find her voice calling to you from juke boxes, chanting at you from radios, shouting out those blues from the doorways of bars and from the windows of apartment houses, from televisions.

Then the spring began to roll in from somewhere in the Southland— but it was hard to notice the spring when there was so much happening in the little apartment on Twelfth Street.

Joyce had made some sort of peace, too, with Eugene Tip and his machine-tooled colleagues. That is, the job no longer appalled her as it had. And it was great not to be bugged just because the job was something you could do with your eyes shut.

Mr. Tip, though, was not quite as reconciled as Joyce, It seemed to be his absurd opinion that sometimes she was doing the job with her eyes shut. And it was things like that which sometimes put you to a great strain making it to work in the morning.

Things like that ...

Jerry knew as soon as he got back. He knew when Ginger never called, never came to see him, never dropped in at the Golden Horn.

He talked about it with Don. He said, "I'm putting gauge down, Don."

"Why, man? Ain't nothing wrong with gauge."

"I know. But you got to put things down once in a while. You got to put them down so you keep being sure who's boss. Like liquor. Even cigarettes. You got to keep in the habit of being on top of things."

"No point quitting till you get beat," Don said.

"No, just running out of charge doesn't prove anything. You have to put it down when you got it. I know a couple of cats, three-four of them, that are really hooked with charge."

"But you can't get hooked."

"Not the way you can with hops or junk. Not with your body. But you can get mentally hooked, like with any kind of a crutch. You get so the way you feel happy is with grass, not with yourself. I know a cat's making maybe forty bucks a week, which is real beat loot, and he spends about twelve of it for gauge. He just lost the habit of balling without his hay. If he runs out, he can get along. But he'll go for it the first chance he gets. And it comes before most other things. Not like horse. Not before food. But it comes right after food for this cat. I don't like to owe that much to anything. Look at Ginger, man."

"Gin's doing all right. She's really grooving."

"It ain't the ball she tells herself it is. She's not really grooving. She got on that hemp crutch and walked with it so long and so hard that she got used to having a crutch stronger than her legs were. Then, when it got real hard going there, then she had to go try a bigger crutch. I know that chick, man. I got eyes for her—but not with the junk. Part that really bugs me, though, is that little chick, Joyce. She's a flipped chick. She's got a real trouble there. I only know a little about it, like her parents dumped her on her aunt, man. But nobody can make that, man.

"You got to be bugged in a way to get into any of these grooves. Big bug or little bug, you got to have a bug to turn on with anything. And Joy's got a big bug, like the kind that really throws you. And being around like that with Gin, she's digging that white stuff, and it scares me."

Don said, "You done what you could, man."

"Not everything, Don. I could of straightened her out, made things come out for her. I don't feel good with myself about that chick."

"Come on, man. Get that horn, man. Let's turn on a little jive here."

"Look, Mr. Taylor," the Chief told him, after a particularly virulent outburst of abuse, "You really can't expect a helluva lot from us. When you wait half a year to tell the police your daughter is missing, we're kind of in the position of someone who comes so late to the show he can't tell what it's all about. We've put out an eight-state missing persons alarm. The New York bureau has broadcast descriptions of the girl, but you can't count on that. Besides, she's not a criminal. She's eighteen years old now, and you can't even make her come back if she doesn't want to. Maybe she got married? You can't tell."

"Look," Taylor said, "I don't want any excuses. I don't want any stories. All I want is for you to find my daughter."

"I haven't lost any daughters, Mr. Taylor. She went—all on her own. From how I can make this thing out, you never gave a damn about her until she took off on her own. My pitch on this thing is, you and your wife got no more than was coming to you. You don't just dump a kid on relatives and let it go at that, Mr. Taylor. I'm trying to find your daughter—but I'm not doing it for you or your wife or anybody else. I'm doing it because I have to—because it's my job. The way I feel about it, she's probably a lot happier where she is …"

14 • Trauma

The cops came one fine warm spring night, and snatched Ginger right out of her dressing-room at the Hot Club. It was really the pusher they were after, a man named Gonzalez, a dark little Puerto Rican with thin, hollow cheeks and great, deep-sunken eyes, but they followed him to Ginger's dressing room and they watched them make the deal through the keyhole, so they took her along too, because it was a good idea, now and then, to make an example of somebody well known—and who better than a black singer?

It happened just before Joyce got there. They had found Gonzalez with some other little packets in his pockets, and they found the stuff where Ginger had pushed it in the drawer when they burst open the door. They found it there with the needle and the flattened-out spoon and the matches, and the little vial with a pierced rubber top that she used for loading the needle. They found everything they needed, right there in those few seconds.

And then Joyce came. She knocked at the door, and one of the cops—a federal man with no uniform—pulled it open.

She saw Ginger standing there, between two men, and there was a little dark cat, with manacles on his wrists. And then Ginger put on her act.

"What the hell do you want?" she demanded.

"Gin …"

"What right have you got to come busting into my dressing room? You, copper, get that kid out of there. You think I want everybody to know about this? Isn't it bad enough you pinch me without making a public performance of it. Get her out of here."

Then one of the cops came to the door. He was a big guy, and his voice wasn't mean at all. He just said, "G'wan. Beat it, kid. Beat it out of here."

And that was the last time Joyce saw Ginger.

Joyce woke up the next morning with the monkey …

Jerry did what he could. He saw Ginger, and he got her a lawyer, and he raised the bail for her with the money he had planned to spend for her Christmas car. But they were really out to make an example of her, so his offers to finance her in a private hospital didn't impress the United States Commissioner. She waived trial and was sent to the United States Public Health Service Hospital for the full cure.

Joyce hadn't felt the hook before. But now it was in there, turning and twisting. She got out of bed, that morning, feeling there was something wrong with her. Her mouth tasted dry and fuzzy, and water wouldn't make it go away. She kept yawning; great gaping yawns that went on and on and on. Her hands trembled, and her legs were rubbery and uncertain. Her stomach kept twitching as though it were trying to detach itself from her flesh and just flatten out there inside her.

Her eyes kept watering and watering and watering, so that her vision blurred, and there was no getting them clear, and her nose felt runny, but faster and harder and looser than with a cold.

At first, not knowing what it was, she couldn't place it. She was just sick. That was the thing. The flu, maybe. But it wasn't the flu, because there was something you wanted—something you had to have. Something you couldn't wait another second for.

Then she knew what it was, and she went to the drawer where she kept the needle and the stuff. She could hardly steer her trembling fingers as she brought out the spoon with its handle bent straight so that it would hold the cup part without spilling. There were only two capsules. That wasn't going to be enough. But it would have to do for the moment. She spilled one capsule into the spoon, thought hard for a second, and then dumped in the other feeling her hands endangering the whole project.

She went to the washbowl and got out the eyedropper from the little medicine chest, and half-filled it with water from the warm tap. Then she squeezed the water from the dropper into the spoon. With shaking hands she lit a match and then picked up the spoon, holding the match under the cup and counting off the long frightful seconds until it boiled. Another match, and the boiling water dissolved the white crystals, and then it was ready. She set the spoon down and took the eyedropper and sucked it clean and dry, then she took a little pellet of cotton from the toothache kit that stood on the bureau and squeezed it into the mouth of the eye-dropper, leaving just a little tail free to pull it out with later on.

From the closet she got a belt, and doubled it through the buckle, then, slipping it over her left arm just above the elbow, jerked it tight, liking the pain because it took her mind from the great, gaping yawns that swept her again and again. She stuffed the belt under itself in a hitch so it would stay tight, then bent the arm and tightened the muscles until the veins stood out in ridges against the pale skin.

Then, because she had been too hurried, she made herself go calmly. With her cramped left arm she held the eyedropper. Then, like a laboratory technician, inserted the hollow point of the depressed hypodermic through the cotton in the tip of the dropper and into the body, then, slowly, cautiously, pulled outward on the piston.

When all the liquid had been withdrawn from the dropper, she laid it down, and took the bit of cotton from it and threw it into the washbowl in the corner. Then she held the needle, point upward, and depressed the piston, driving the fluid up into the hollow point, until just one tiny drop formed at the open point.

The swollen veins now stood out clearly. She selected a spot free of old pits, and fiercely rammed it into the vein, then slowly depressed the piston— down, down, down, all the way, then withdrew it a little, seeing the winy blood spurting up into the cylinder behind the glass piston. She allowed the blood to flush out the cylinder and then returned it to the vein with the needle Then she pulled the needle out and lay down on the bed.

In two singing seconds the yawning ceased, the shimmering tears ceased to flow in her eyes, her pulse settled to tranquility, and her stomach stopped flapping at the walls of her abdomen.

But it was not enough. There was nothing for later—nothing for the monkey. She would have to get a fix.

She knew the contacts, but now it was a question of money. Ginger had always had all the money in the world. Ginger had always paid the fix man. She looked in her pocketbook. She had only five dollars. That would get her two, maybe three caps, Not even a deck. Not enough. Not even enough for today, and what about tomorrow?

She tried to think about Ginger. Ginger in jail. Ginger going to prison. Wasn't that what they did to you? Put you in prison? But she couldn't think about her. Couldn't even take time to think about how Ginger had got her out of it—pushed her out before the police had understood what was happening. How could you think about a thing like that when this was going on, this terrible gnawing anxiety?

Joyce knew that if she had what she needed for today, five more caps, maybe, the anxiety would be gone, and she would be calm and able to function, able to do something about getting more. But now what?

Then she thought about the office and Mr. Tip. What time was it? Eight-thirty. She was due in at nine o'clock. And now Tip loomed in her mind like a great wonderful figure. The boss. The boss had to take care of his employees. That was what a boss was for.

She'd tell him—something, anything. She went out into the morning not seeing the spring sunlight, not seeing the sprouting green of the park, because all there was to think about was the terrible yearning that was coming, the great need that only money could answer.

She stood in front of Tip's desk feeling helpless and small and incompetent. He kept her standing, like that, only his bald head turned to her, and his myopic lenses closely focused on the paper that lay on the green blotter.

Joyce said, "Mr. Tip?" very tentatively.

"Yes?" He did not look up.

"I have to have some money, Mr. Tip. I don't feel well this morning and I have to go to the doctor. I wondered if I could get a small advance ..."

He looked up at her. "Miss Taylor," he said, "your work hasn't been very satisfactory lately. I meant to tell you on Friday, but I missed you when you left. It's too bad you had to come in this morning, and I really regret the waste of your time."

"What do you mean?" It was so hard to concentrate, so hard to follow. The little nerves were tingling again, demanding, wanting, needing.

"Don't you understand?" as though there couldn't be any misunderstanding.

"No, Mr. Tip. I just wanted a small advance."

"Miss Taylor, you are discharged, as of Friday. I will be glad to supply satisfactory references if you need them." The head was down again.

All right. This was one kind of answer. She'd get the money now, anyway, and something would come up before that ran out. Two weeks salary was—ninety, less ... "Where do I get my check?"

"What check, Miss Taylor?" The question seemed genuinely to interest him. He raised his head, and peered at her through the thick glasses.

"My two weeks."

"There is no check, Miss Taylor. We don't make a practice of paying unnecessary amounts." The head went down again. There was nothing left to do but go.

Joyce found Roy Mallon sitting, as always, on the rim of the circular fountain in the middle of Washington Square. Roy, this joyous May morning, was a happy man. He had just made a stick deal with a cat from Brooklyn, and the loot would make it a ball for him for at least a week. That gauge deal was worth a hundred to him, and he had his own comfortable stash of white stuff in his pad.

Roy tended to look down a little on the vipers—but not too much. After all, they were customers, and he did have stuff. He adjusted his sunglasses and let himself lean back against one of the gargoyle figures, feeling the charge circulating through his veins.

Vaguely he saw Joyce as she came toward him from the Fifth Avenue bus. A nice chick. Friend of Jerry's and Ginger. Too bad about Ginger. They must have been on to Gonzalez for a long time to come like that.

Joyce came up and stood in front of him. She said, softly, so as not to alarm the women whose children were racing and sprawling about the empty basin of the fountain, "Look, man, I got to get a fix."

"I got a little," Roy said. "Eight a deck. Real gone. Eighteen percent."

"I can't make that," Joy said. "I'm beat. I got no loot."

"Gee, that's a drag." Roy said. "I'd fix you up, but you dig what's with my connection. It's all gold in front. I got to lay it out, and then get it back."

"Listen, Roy. I got to have that stuff. I'll get gold for you tomorrow, but I got to have a fix right now. I got to have enough to carry me the whole day and tonight."

He didn't feel sympathy. He just felt good, and this was no time to stop feeling good. You couldn't let a thing like this drag you; not when you felt so gone, so really sent. And the kid was getting hysterical. She knew where you lived. You had to do something.

"Joyce," Roy said, his sallow tanned face reflecting what sympathy it could, "I got six decks in a stash, right around here. I don't know when I'll get more. I may even have to find a fix man myself tomorrow. But I'll lay half of it on you."

"Great!" Joyce said. "The end! You saved my life, man."

"I dig," Roy said. "I'll make it back here in fifteen minutes. Now, don't cut out, now."

"I won't man. And I'll have the loot for you tomorrow …"

15 • Insecurity

That was the morning when Tony saw Joyce. He had just come out of New York University Commons, and was walking slowly across Washington

Square Park toward the subway. He had left his car in Jamaica and come in on the Eighth Avenue subway that morning, and now he was undetermined whether to go back out to Jamaica and pick it up before his afternoon class began, or whether to go up to the Griddle on Eighth Street and just hang around.

Then he saw her. She was standing at the edge of the big fountain among a clutter of loungers and women airing their children, talking to a deeply tanned man wearing sunglasses who might have been, and probably was, a race track tout.

He saw the man hand her something which she put in her handbag. He was still on the other side of the broad thoroughfare that bisects the Square—and still not quite sure. She was more slender than he remembered her, and a little better dressed. For a moment or so he just stood there, trying to be sure before crossing the street to approach her. Then she left the tanned man and walked toward a Fifth Avenue bus. The walk was what made him sure. The even, unhurried pace, with something approaching a regal dignity.

He started to run across the street but a line of traffic halted him for a moment. When it had passed he started across again, but Joyce had disappeared and the bus had started.

She was on the bus. He knew that, and ran after it, yelling after the driver. But the bus caught the lights and was gone up past the arch before he could reach it.

He remembered the number of the bus and looked for a cab, but it took nearly two minutes, and when he had located one and followed the bus, they were unable to catch up through the heavy traffic until it had passed Forty-second Street. Then he clambered aboard the bus and looked on both decks. But Joyce was gone.

He went to see Frank Burdette that evening and told him about seeing Joyce. Frank said, "I don't see that it helps us much, except that we at least know she's alive and all right." Somehow it didn't occur to Tony to communicate his news to the Taylors—so he didn't.

Joyce sat in the bar with a drink on the table in front of her, because she couldn't think of anything else that she wanted to do. She didn't much want the drink, but it gave her an excuse for sitting.

She was full of a sort of quiet desperation, realizing that tomorrow or the day after, whenever the two remaining decks of the white powder ran out, she was going to be through.

She had been able to get the three decks from Roy today by something that lay, in Roy's estimate, halfway between blackmail and sympathy, but that was really more the former than the latter. She knew that the pusher had said he had only the six decks of the stuff. That though, was to keep her from turning herself in to a hospital and then telling who supplied her in pique because he had refused her. Now, though, with official notice that he had no more of the stuff—even if it weren't true—she could hardly blame him for failing to supply her without payment.

And there was no chance of paying for any. She looked at her pocketbook. There was still a little more than four dollars left in her purse. She thought of Jerry Best. But he wasn't at the Golden Horn anymore. He was playing somewhere out of town, she didn't even know where. Maybe she could find out where he was—from an agent, or Down Beat or something. But Jerry was down on junkies—real down. She pictured him giving her the quick brush-off once he found out about her.

Then a man came and sat down at the table opposite her. "Hello, honey," he said. "You look lonesome."

He was young, a little over-dressed with lemon yellow tie and a dark shirt, but his face was pleasant, and having someone to talk to was suddenly vital. She had dinner with him and, at the end of the evening, took him to her room.

When she awoke in the morning he was gone, but on the dresser was a twenty-dollar bill that had not been there the night before. The money relieved all of her panic and some of her guilt. And by the end of the week her indoctrination into the profession was complete.

16 • Integration

The worst were the mornings because you woke up in the mornings with the feeling you had done something particularly awful the night before—though you could not quite remember it clearly. You wondered if it was the horse that made forgetfulness, or shame for your actions.

Joyce's first recollections, in that hour of the early afternoon that had become morning for her, always had to do with men, except on one or two rare occasions when there had been a woman somewhere in the evening's confusion. That had happened, too.

But, by and large, Joyce's "Johns" were little different from other men. The things they demanded from Joyce, that they could not demand from their wives or mistresses, were as much because they were paying her as because they wanted those things to happen. And the demands were more often self-imposed than coming from the men themselves. "Johns" were surprisingly undemanding—more giving, in fact, than taking!

But each demand seemed, to Joyce, only like a fresh degradation—like one more step down into the abyss into which her life teemed continually to be descending.

The problem of the "fix" seemed almost providential relief from those morning thoughts—those matutinal despairs. The remembered feeling and the taste of heroin did not come immediately when she awoke. Those first moments were dedicated to black despair. Then—next—came the thought to be seized upon, to be clung to, to be emotionally rebuilt into a problem that obliterated all other problems. The problem was: How be assured of a sufficient supply of the stuff to ward off the dire moment when you were out—beat?

You could concentrate on that, once you got around to it in your mind. You could concentrate on it while you had that special taste in your mouth, while your hands had that light sensation, while all the little nerves under your skin seemed to itch for the fine feeling of a charge. And if you kept concentrated on that one fear, all the others somehow would become pressed down—would sink out of sight. Still, with practice, the fear of being without had come to be reinforced with all the other fears until it was a ceaseless thing, and the pleasure was gone from the charge itself. The "mainline" shot was only the relief that permitted you to go in search of the next shot.

Sometimes, as this morning, Joyce looked at herself in the mirror and wondered that there were no marks or signs to indicate what went on behind the facade of flesh. She looked at her body, searching for the scars of her disintegration, and the body was firm and rounded and beautiful—as virginal as before so many hands had fondled it, molded it, compelled it into variant male-factions.

Then she went to the telephone and tried to reach Roy Mallon, looking at her watch and knowing that it was almost deliberate that she was trying at a time when he could not possibly be at home.

It felt almost as though she didn't want to reach him, as if she wanted to hear the phone ringing unanswered in that basement apartment on West 21st Street where he lived. Now and again she let herself think about that—as though she were preserving the urgency of the "fix" problem so that, all through the long evening it might press on her mind, and distract her from present reality.

When the phone had buzzed enough, and all hope had long since vanished, she dressed and made herself up. Suspants and Maidenform, Halfmoon and Arts & Ends, Bonwit's and Lord & Taylor, Chen Yu and Helena Rubenstein, Andrew Geller and Barra, John Frederics and Ohrbach's. Then a dash of perfume from Saks, a scarf from Peck & Peck, a pocketbook from Hermes. She could tell from which of her "Johns" each of them had come.

Then she went out to meet Eric.

Eric Tanger was waiting for Joyce in the bar near Madison and Fifty-third. He stood there looking exactly what he was—a man, youngish, balding, well dressed in a flashy sporting manner—a successful sharp businessman of thirty-five who some day hoped to grow out of the garment district.

Joyce said, "Hi, baby," then stepped back a little to admire him. "Very sharp," she said. "Very sharp, indeed." She flicked highly imaginary ashes from his lapels, and slipped her arm into his.

"How," Eric said, "would you like to go for a walk in the park this beautiful afternoon."

Joyce pouted. "Oh, Eric! My feet!"

"Just a stroll, my little trollop. Nothing to louse up those shapely gams. Incidentally," Eric said, "you're rather well turned out yourself this afternoon. Shall we try the Tavern on the Green?" It went like that, most of the time, with Eric. Underneath, she knew, Eric and Edsel and Marty, and John and Pelvin and Lee, were after the somewhat standardized offerings of harlotry. But on the surface they were willing to go along with her self-protective fiction that these were love affairs.

As they crossed Fifth Avenue and entered the Park they came into the full afternoon sunshine and Joyce put on sunglasses. Eric waited until they were safely in the park before he unhooked her arm from his and swung her around to face him. "Take off those glasses!" he said.

"What for?"

"Never mind, just take them off."

Reluctantly she lifted the green lenses from her eyes, blinking at the brilliant sunlight. The pupils were dilated, and seemed almost opaque.

Eric's voice was suddenly harsh. "I thought I told you I didn't want to see you when you were on that stuff."

She stood there, completely miserable, unable to say a word.

"Joy, you're no good this way. Not to me. Not to yourself. Not to anybody or anything."

She could feel the words, and the meaning of the words. But the misery was not because of the words. It was because he was dragging her—bringing her down. But the horse, singing in her blood, that could be a shield. She could let the words flow by without hurting, never really hurting, never really meaning anything, only this kind of words brought you down, down, down.

"Joy! I don't see you as just another goddamned tart. You're smart. You're on the ball. You could get out of this if you wanted to. All you have to do is try."

The words hammered against her face.

"You're not paying any attention. You're not listening. You go into this filthy dope and turn yourself off like a radio. What's the matter with you, kid?"

Joyce didn't say anything. There was nothing to say. The words had no meaning.

"Can't you see you're just going in a circle? You think I don't know what's going on with you? You think I don't see that you hate what you're doing, and you take this—this filth to hide behind while you're doing it?

But can't you—haven't you enough intelligence left to see that it works the other way, too? That all you do this hustling for is to buy the rotten crap you take to hide from yourself that you're hustling? Oy! Talk about vicious circles!" Then, louder, "Joy! Do you hear me?"

"I can hear you," Joyce said. There were other things she wanted to say. But she couldn't say them because—because Eric had the money to buy her; because she had to have that money.

"Can't you turn yourself in?" he demanded. "Can't you go to a hospital and get off this stuff?"

Then whatever it was that was guarding her broke. Suddenly the utter agony of living descended upon her, and tears streamed down her cheeks. All she could say was, "Eric, leave me alone. Leave me alone. Stop it!"

Angrily then he reached in his pocket and pulled out a wallet.

He opened it and snatched out bills. "All right. That's what I'll do. Here's your goddamned money." He almost threw the bills at her. "Take it and go to hell. I don't want to see you. I don't even want to smell you—you disgusting little tramp."

And then he was walking away. It was the second time it had happened like that ...

Frank had walked home in the pleasant May evening, disdaining the crowded bus. He heard the telephone ringing as he came up the steps of the front porch and, from upstairs, he heard Janice's voice. It said, "Oh, damn!"

He called, "I'll get it, Jan," and stepped into the hallway where be snatched up the receiver.

"Frank," the telephone said, "That you, man?"

"Jerry! Where are you?"

"I'm at the station, man. You want to drive downtown and meet me someplace?"

"Why meet you? Come on up here." Then, realizing the thoughtfulness that had prompted Jerry, he said, "Don't be a dope, Jerry. Grab a cab and get up here for dinner."

"It ain't just that," Jerry said. "I can't talk about this to front of Jan. It's about that old chick of yours, Joyce."

"Yes you can, Jerry. Do you know where she Is? How is she? Jan knows all about it."

"All right," Jerry said. "I'll make it on out there in a few minutes."

Jerry told them about it over dinner.

"I guess it was a lot my fault," he said. "But I was so damned mad at Ginger I didn't even think what it might do to Joyce, leaving her with Gin like that. Then, when Gin told me that Joyce was on the stuff, I guess I was so busy trying to swing things for Ginger that I just plain forgot about the kid."

Janice said, "The poor thing."

Jerry said, "You're really cool about this Jan. I dig that." Janice smiled, not really happily.

He went on. "After I left the Golden Horn I been working mostly out of town—so of course you haven't been seeing me around—and she hasn't been either, even if she wanted to.

"Anyway, this particular Friday night Don Wilson and I were both in on the session at the Stuyvesant Ballroom, and Joyce came up to see me. She was with a real drug cat—an ofay, the worst, the kind of guy who goes out with pros, but flips his wig when he sees the chick he's with talking to a colored cat. She didn't like this cat, much … Sorry, Jan. This man she was with was like a real low type. The kind of guy who goes out with—well, prostitutes, but won't …"

"Jerry" Jan said, "I dig you, man."

"Anyway, she said he wanted her to do things she just couldn't. I laid some gold on her. I only had fifty with me; and then I got her address. I know she doesn't dig going with men, but it seems the only way she can find the loot to buy the stuff …"

"Jerry," Frank said, "I've got to telephone somebody. Can you excuse me a minute."

"Solid, man."

He went to the telephone in the hall and thumbed through the little book on the stand, then dialed quickly, nervously pulling the dial back round after each numeral.

"Hello. May I speak to Tony, please? … Thanks … Tony? … This is Frank—Frank Burdette. Get over here. Get over here quick … We've found her, but I don't know how long we can keep her … Good … See you." He hung up and returned to the diningroom.

After Jerry had gone, Tony and Frank talked it out.

"It wouldn't do any real good if it was me," Frank said. "It's you who must go to her. I've got to explain to you about Joyce a little. Don't get the idea that Janice would interfere with my doing it—if it would help. But the trouble is, it wouldn't. It would work quicker, it's true. But it wouldn't get her off the heroin, and it wouldn't stick. So don't think I'm ducking out of what's really my job. I'm responsible for this. But the cure lies with you, not with me. So it's got to be up to you."

"I don't get it," Tony said. "You're older than I am. You know more than I do. Why can't you do it better than me."

"Look, Tony, before I got into the newspaper racket, I wanted to be a psychoanalyst. It was the big parlor kick in those days to be a psychoanalyst, and I was all for it. I was a psych major in college, and I was set to go on with it, too. Then I got into newspapers, and I liked it and I stayed. But there are certain things you learn about people that sort of stick with you. When you establish a certain habit as a kid—oh, like Junior's getting the habit of not eating—it somehow gets built into your personality, and without knowing it, you more or less keep repeating variations of the habit all through your life. Sometimes the habit can be broken while you're still a kid. Sometimes it can be diverted, or changed into another habit when you're older. That's the kind of habit Joyce has, and we've got to break it."

"I still don't understand," Tony said. "She has a drug habit. She never had that before."

"That's right. I forgot to mention something else. Sometimes people will substitute a worse habit for another kind they've had a long time. I'll try and show you what I mean. Joy's parents began leaving her alone and dumping her off on relatives when she was very small. They kept on like that, right up till now, going off and leaving her, putting her in schools where they wouldn't have to be bothered with her. It didn't take Joyce long to get the idea that they didn't want her. It made her feel that she wasn't good enough for them to want. So she got a habit of thinking of herself as not good enough to be wanted. That's one of her habits. Do you see it?"

"Yes," Tony said, dragging the word a little.

"It shows up in several ways. She had to give people things to make sure they would want her and value her. I don't know what she gave Ruth Scott. Probably brains, because Joyce has them, and from what she told me about Ruth, Ruth doesn't. The thing with you, that first time, was typical. She gave herself to you, because she thought that sex was something you could give that would make people value you. She tried to give the same thing to the whole senior class the time she did a strip-dance in the study class. When she did it, what she was saying to herself was, 'I've got something they want. I'm valuable.' And the person she was trying to convince of this was herself."

"But why couldn't she do that in other ways," Tony said, "like other people do?"

"Well, we know a couple of reasons. Joyce managed to get her parent's attention a few times in her life. And when she did, they acted for a while as though she were valuable. She ran away from school, and when they found her they made a big fuss about her. She told me about that. Did she tell you?"

"Un-hunh," Tony said. "She did."

"That, and other, similar experiences, started another habit in Joyce. If you got in trouble, the way this other habit ran in her mind, it made people pay attention to you. So, that's what she did. She went out of her way to get in trouble."

"She did that, all right," Tony said. "She was always doing things in school to put her in hot water."

"Yes. But always with the hope of getting attention from her parents—the people who couldn't be bothered with her. I've got habits like that, too. So have you. You could probably notice mine, and I could notice yours. But neither of us can see his own. Joyce too. She isn't aware of these habits. But she has them. In psychology these would be called insecurity conflicts. But there's something else, too. Part of the urge to get into trouble is to punish her parents, because she's really angry with them for rejecting her. And that's another habit that she's carried over into her life with other people besides her parents. You were angry with her one day because she missed a date with you. So she punished you. She went out with me. And, from her habit point of view, she managed to get in trouble with me. She smoked marijuana that night for the first time. She did what her mind and emotions thought of as 'wrong things'—getting in trouble. That was because she wanted you. She has still another habit. Her parents failed to love and protect her. So she developed a habit of looking for love and protection— looking even harder than anyone else does—because we all do that. When she found love, any kind of love, she habitually tried to make a parent, a father, for herself out of the person who loved her. And the better the role fitted, the better she liked it She tried it first with you. Then, when you were angry with her, she tried me. I was older. I actually was a father. That was good. She could fit the pattern that she wanted on me more easily than on you. I was free enough of my parents—because I didn't have any around— to make a father figure for her, better than you could. Do you get all this?"

"Yeah," Tony said, a shade of surprise in his voice. "It sort of makes sense."

"Didn't you expect it to?"

"Not at first. But now it does. It was like that with Jerry and Ginger? They sort of were parents for her, too? Right?"

"That's it. Now the narcotics come into the picture. When Jerry broke up with Ginger, the shock was suddenly more than she could take. She needed something to cushion it—the way people have a drink when they're upset. For Joyce, heroin was really no different than marijuana—but it was stronger. Marijuana won't let you forget your troubles, unless they're very minor ones. But heroin will. So it was easy for her to go along with Ginger. Ginger was protecting her. Ginger was a kind of mother. She would see that nothing bad happened. But when the police took Ginger away, then she had to lean on the heroin itself. The heroin made her able to forget how desperately she needed love. The heroin let her feel good enough for herself. In a way the final step, her turning to prostitution to get the money for the heroin, was the same sort of thing. Every time a man paid her for love, he convinced her that she was worth something. Do you understand that, too?"

"Yes. I get it. But a lot of these things go on at the same time. They kind of overlap. Several habits push her at once. Is that it?"

"That's right. Now I'm one of these bad habits with her. I fit her role of a father figure too well. Jan—my wife—wouldn't object to my seeing Joy if it would save her from heroin. But I can only supply a temporary remedy. The real remedy isn't there anyway. She's a grown girl. She doesn't really want a father. She really wants a lover—a man of her own. And that's where you fit in, and I don't. Dig?"

Tony grinned. "I dig. The normal-er it is, the better. And the thing I've got to do is convince her I really love her—no matter what, but more when she's good than when she's bad."

"That's right. And it's slow. It won't happen right away. There's one other thing, too. I don't think—I'm not sure of this—but I don't think that Joyce is a full-fledged heroin addict. Not yet. Not in the physiological sense. From what Jerry could find out from one of the men who sells her heroin, she isn't taking enough for that. It hasn't been long enough for her to need that much. But if it goes on longer, then she will need it." He stood up. "If you want anything from me, any time, I'll do what's necessary."

Tony got up to go. "I'll keep in touch," he said. He was suddenly very adult.

17 • Resolution

She was asleep when the telephone rang. Asleep, but not undressed. Her skirt had worked up around her waist, and her blouse was open and the bra unfastened at the back. Her shoes lay on the chenille coverlet beside her feet, and she had unhooked her nylons from their panty supporter so they had fallen around her slender ankles to give them an elephantine look. The lipstick had smeared about her mouth, and made a gory display on the rumpled pillow case. Her coat lay on the floor where it had fallen when she came in, and there deep grooves from the wrinkled cloth pressed into the soft flesh of her cheeks. She had a damaged soiled look as she dragged herself up from sleep and stumbled toward the clattering instrument.

She held the open blouse together as she bent to the phone, though there was no one to see.

"Hello?" Her voice was soggy and hoarse.

"Joy? Is that you Joy?"

"Who's this?" Her head ached and there was a fierce pressure in her chest.

"Tony, Joy. It's Tony. Tony Thrine."

Her mind refused to take in the words.

"Tony! Joy. Don't you know who I am? Honeybun, what's the matter?"

She didn't answer. Her nerves crawled under her skin, and there was a fierce itching.

"Can't you hear me?"

"I hear you."

"Joy, I've got to see you."

"Look," Joy said. "I can't talk now. Call me back in an hour." She dropped the phone into its cradle and dragged her wretched body to the bureau, yanking open the drawer. Her hands shook with a fierce ague as she spilled the capsule into the bent spoon, and then were so uncontrollable that the white powder fell to the floor.

Frantically, as though her very life depended upon it, she scraped it up with a torn fragment of paper, disregarding the dust and lint that clung to the precious particles.

Then, in an easy routine that was complicated by the unmanageability of her hands, she followed the ritual formula of the junkie, slipping the needle into the scarred vein, and sucking the blood up again and again to flush out the last vital drop.

Then, with a great sigh, she sank into the worn armchair, letting her body relax against the shabby fabric, feeling herself come alive in one great tidal wave of relief.

After a few minutes the phone call floated, like disembodied words without meaning, into her mind. She tried to attach meanings to them, with little hooks that slipped from the letters and slid away before the whole thing could be decoded. Then, by and by, the meanings began to stick. "Tony." "Honeybun." "I've got to see you."

And with the meanings came panic. Not Tony! Never Tony! He must never see this.

She couldn't remember what she had said, she couldn't recall what she had told him. It was so ordinary to say, "I'll meet you in the bar at Fifty-second and Sixth in half and hour." Was that what she had told Tony? How did he know where she was? Had he traced her? Was he outside the front door of the house, waiting in case she came out? Had she left such an easy trail? What if he came in, now, and found her like this?

Joyce got to her feet and went over to the mirror. The fabric wrinkles had gone from her face, but the thinness had given it an artificial maturity, shearing off the roundness of youth, molding the young skin to the bone structure.

Joyce saw nothing of that, only the wild hair, the mussed and gaping blouse, the slipped bra, the smeared cosmetics, the deep-shadowed eyes.

Got to get out of here. Got to leave before Tony finds me. Hit the road, tart!

She pulled the blouse from her shoulders and dropped it on the floor, then reached behind her and hooked the band of the bra. She went to the washbowl and scrubbed frenziedly at her face with a damp cloth. An irritated color rose sullenly to her cheeks. Got to get out of here.

She went to the closet to look for a dress—and the phone rang again. For a long time—seven or eight rings—she stood it, and then she went and picked up the instrument. "Hello."

"Hiya, honeybun." Tony's voice was tense, as though the enthusiasm he injected into it was costly and hard gained.

"Hello, Tony. How are you?" That was the attitude. Friendly. Cool. Polite.

"I'm fine. How is everything with you?"

The conversation was becoming more strained. Already. Joyce said, "How is everybody in Paugwasset?"

"Look, baby," Tony said. "I didn't call to talk to you about everybody back home. I want to see you. I didn't want to bust in on you, or anything. But can't we meet somewhere?"

And suddenly she wanted nothing else. It would be, almost, like—she didn't know what it would be like. But it would be wonderful. "All right, Tony. Where shall we meet?"

"Down here. In the Village?"

No. It must be, now, on neutral ground. Somewhere she had not been. Under other circumstances. She was silent, thinking.

"Or anywhere else. It doesn't matter," Tony said.

They met in a cafeteria on Lexington Avenue, where the continual tidal flow of people assured a paradoxical privacy. He was waiting for her when she came in, watched her walking across the table-littered floor, saw her looking about for him from behind dark green glasses, and finally caught her eye.

She came over and sat down at the table, letting the coat slip from her shoulders onto the chair back.

Tony knew enough about clothing to see that this was a different Joyce. She looked older in a way that he could not define. She made him seem almost kiddish.

For a moment neither of them said anything. Then Tony reached over and took her hand. "Joy, I've been trying so hard to find you—all this time."

"I didn't really want to be found," Joyce said. "How did you find out about me? Through Jerry?"

"Uh-hunh. He saw you at the Stuyvesant, wherever that is, and then he came out to see Frank, and Frank called me over and—well, here I am. I saw you once on the street. In Washington Square. You went uptown on a bus and I tried to follow you in a cab, but I lost you."

"How is Frank?" Joyce asked.

"All right." He had managed to keep that one under control, though it had plucked a chord of jealousy.

Joyce reassured him. "Don't look like that," she said. "He's a wonderful guy, but—not for me."

"What about us?"

"What do you mean, us?"

"I mean I want to see you. I want to be with you."

"Easy does it, baby," Joyce said. "You don't know about me anymore. I'm not Joyce Taylor from Paugwasset any more, I'm somebody else."

"Oh, stop it, honeybun. You just think you're different."

"Aren't people what they think they are?"

"Not if what they think is wrong."

"Look, Tony," Joyce said, "I'm not a good local talent any more. I've changed. And if you don't know about it, Jerry can tell you. Even Frank can. They know what happened. Especially Jerry. I'm bad, now. I'm different." There was a sort of a pleasure for Joyce in hearing the words coming out of her mouth—in hearing herself say these things. "You don't know what's happened to me. You don't know how I live. What I am. What I do."

"Yes, I do." He said it softly, not trying to keep the injury from showing in his face. "I know about the whole thing. About your—work. About the dope. I know all about you."

Then, because some inner feeling told him that it was the thing to do, he searched out the past in his mind and brought it up and drew it all there, in words, at the little table in the cafeteria. About Paugwasset, and boats, movies, and the Senior play in which they had appeared together. About Chester's and about Harry Reingold going to N.Y.U. with Tony. And then— more cautiously—about how Joyce's parents had come back from Europe, and how they were looking for her, and how he and Frank, with Jerry's information, had decided that whether they should be told, or not, was something for Joyce, herself to decide.

Then he said, "Honeybun, you've got to come back home. We all want you to come back. Honest."

It was as though he had pierced some kind of armor in which she had been girded. He saw she was crying and held out a handkerchief to her. She shook her head. Then she stood up. "I have to go, now," she said. "I can't stay any longer."

He didn't try to hold her. "When can I see you again?"

"I don't know. Where can I call you?"

He tried desperately to think of some place where he could be reached. But the N.Y.U. student is a transient in the Village. There is no center of communication. Frantically he searched his mind. There had to be some place, and it was clear that she didn't want him to call her. He didn't know why it was important for her that it be this way—that she call him and not he call her—but some intuition told him that it was.

Then he thought of a little craft shop on West Fourth Street. He would arrange it there, and then see them once a day. Maybe pay them something to take messages for him. He told her the name of the place, and then, because he wanted to be sure, went to a phone booth and looked up the number.

"All right," Joyce said. "I'll remember." And he watched her as she went out through the wheeling door into the hurrying avenue.

Tony saw Frank again. They sat in the livingroom of Burdette's house and drank rye with beer chasers, and Tony felt adultness coming into him as they talked—and as the soft tentacles of intoxication reached up into his mind.

"I don't know, Frank," he said. "I couldn't seem to reach her. It was like meeting somebody you haven't seen in a long time and you're still anxious to talk to them, but things have changed so much with them that everything you say has lost any kind of meaning. I couldn't even see her face, really, on account of those sunglasses."

"Sunglasses?"

"She even wore them indoors."

"She was high when you talked to her, then."

"How do you know?"

"Well, it wouldn't be surprising, anyway. The first thing that would happen when she knew she was going to meet you would be for her to get on, because she'd be afraid to face you unprotected. I imagine that for that one time, at least, it was a good thing. Because if she hadn't she would probably have run away, and hidden, and we'd never find her again."

"But what do I do?"

"Nothing."

"I've got to do something."

"Don't press her. Don't call her. Try not even to think about her. Just make sure that you get any message she does leave for you. And no matter what happens, meet her exactly when and where she tells you to. Understand?"

"Okay. I hope you know what I'm doing. I don't."

Tony waited.

Joyce went to see a doctor, somewhere in this period. She didn't expect him to be much help, and he wasn't. He recommended the substitution of ordinary sedation. Barbiturates. And gradual reduction of dosage with heroin. Even more strongly he recommended commitment to a private hospital, where all this would be seen to by medical authorities. And, as a last alternative, he suggested voluntary entrance in the U.S. Public Health Service Hospital in Lexington, Kentucky.

Joyce knew that much herself.

She tried the ex-junkies of her acquaintance. They knew more. "You got to make it cold turkey. There's no other way. You stop. You quit. The end. You can't make it otherwise. You can't cut down. You'll flip. You'll flip anyway. But you get it done."

And then there were the "Johns." She still needed the money, as she always had. Day after day, always money. Money to get straight. Money for food. Money for clothes. Always money.

She was making up her mind. You had to make up your mind. Even Roy Mallon told her, "Nothing does it, Joy, without you make up your mind.

When you do, it's licked. You got to kick it—cold turkey. No tapering. No messing. Cold turkey."

But she didn't believe them. She cut it out for one day. Two days. And the third day she had to hit it again. And the next day was a postponement of stopping. And so was the next.

She wanted to call Tony. Sometimes in the morning, she lay on the sweat-damp sheets thinking of Tony, thinking how he was no farther from her than the telephone sitting there on the small table against the wall. She thought about that. And then she thought about the "Johns." Good guys, too. A little rigid. A little frightened—even of Joyce. Feeling guilty whenever they saw her, and, at the same time, wanting her, even wanting the fright and guilt of being with her. Not like Eric. With Eric it was love—of a sort—and braggadocio. He wanted to be able to talk about her. He wanted to be able to tell his friends how he had cured a bad girl of drugs, how he had made her over. He felt, somehow, that it would make for prestige. And then he would think to himself that, having done this, he had possession of her.

And that had to be avoided, too. Because of Tony.

Always Tony. And if she saw Tony again, it was the end of the "Johns." It had to be, because, even now, the thought of them and their possession of her—her ceaseless seduction of them—made the mornings harder, made the need for horse greater, made it that much harder ever to call Tony.

And then, one day, she did.

She met him in the cafeteria at N.Y.U., that second time. She was wearing sunglasses, and when she took them off her eyes looked like hard little balls, as though nothing were getting through them to her mind.

He kept telling her, "Joy, I love you. I really do. But you've got to get off this damned habit of yours."

It was all right when he didn't press. She could talk about getting off heroin, then. But if he tried to force her, tried to insist, she hardened up. That day she said, "Why should I? I'm no good to anybody. Not to anybody. I'm what they call a fallen woman. Really, that's what I am. A no good, down and out, rotten harlot." Her voice rose, and he had to take her out of the cafeteria. And then she said, "See, you're ashamed of me, aren't you?"

Tony shook his head.

She said, "Yes, you are. And you're right." Then she ran away from him, and it was another week before he saw her again.

When he did, she looked ill. Her eyes were sunken, and she seemed to have a cold. She kept yawning and sighing as he spoke to her.

He said, "Joy, you look sick. Let me take you to a doctor."

She shook her head. "No. I didn't have enough today. I—I took less. I'm trying to cut down."

He bent over and kissed her. Suddenly she was clinging to him, crying wildly. She said, "Help me, Tony. Just help me."

"I'll help," he said. "I'll always help."

That was when he knew she would make it.

But it was a long time before Joyce knew it, too. He tried to induce her to go back to Paugwasset with him, but she shook her head. "Not till I'm out of it, Tony." And the next time he saw her the sunglasses were back in place.

But the time came when she asked him to go home—to her room—with her.

The little room was stuffy and dingy and stark. Clothes were draped over the chairbacks, and the bed was a rumpled mess of blankets. He said, "Honeybun," softly, "can't you move to another place?"

Joyce said, "That's the thousandth time," smiling.

"The thousandth time I've asked you to move? No it isn't."

"Stupid! The thousandth time you've said honeybun. I'm keeping track."

They went down the ramp side by side, hand in hand, as people should who are deeply in love. It was a hot day, in mid-July, and the people on the platform, waiting for the red Long Island cars to open their doors, held coats on their arms.

Joyce said, "It feels awfully funny to know that home is so near. I always thought of it—all the time—as being somewhere way off, as far away as Europe." Tony squeezed her hand.

"Look," she said. "Well, I'll be darned. There's old Iris, up there. Dean Shay."

Tony looked. "Don't let her bother you."

"She doesn't," Joyce said, a little surprised.

"Look, honeybun," Tony said, "there's something I've got to ask you."

"What?"

"Will you marry me after I finish college?"

Joyce just nodded her head, and he kissed her. Hard. Right there on the platform.

The doors of the red train opened, and they scrambled for seats.

As the train slid through the tunnel under the East River, Tony said, "You won't be bothered about your parents any more, will you, honey?"

"I don't think so."

Then a voice from the aisle said, "Miss Taylor …?" A sort of imperative question.

Joyce looked up. Dean Shay was leaning over the edge of the seat, swaying with the movement of the train. Joyce said, "Hello, Miss Shay."

The dean smiled, a little embarrassed. "I've been trying to get in touch with you for some time. It's lucky I found you like this. I just wanted to tell you that on sober second thought Mr. Mercer and I decided last fall that—well, that you needn't repeat your senior year if you wanted to go on to college. We decided that you could be allowed to take a special examination.

It wouldn't be exactly fair to let things go all to pot over that one little incident."

Joyce smiled up at her. "They didn't, Miss Shay. I just thought they did."

THE END

A GLOSSARY OF JIVE

Jive-talk is both a code-speech for the protection of its users, and a sort of spoken shorthand for a group of people whom psychologists would call "non-verbal." The adoption of "jive" as a criminal argot by the narcotics community is, in reality, the piracy of an established speech form for use as a verbal concealment code.

"Jive," in this use, was taken over from musicians who developed it to simplify their verbal problems. For the musician, this simplified speech makes possible, in a total vocabulary of only a few hundred words, a delicate pattern of facile communication in which only approximate word meanings are required.

Thus each "jive" word carries a vast load of multiple meanings. The particular value of a word, in any given sentence, is entirely dependent on the context.

Typical of the whole patois is the word "jive." In its original usage, "jive" meant a particular type of hot music. But it has come by evolution to mean: Marijuana, nonsense ("Don't give me any of that jive!"), sex, joy, heroin, and also lends a name to the jargon itself. As a verb it means: to dance, to smoke marijuana, to be happy, to distort facts, to make music, to get high, etc. etc.

The vocabulary given here is incomplete, and applies only to the jargon as it is used in this book.

N. R. DE MEXICO

ball—to have a good time, to enjoy; as "to have a ball".
beat—out of supply (of money or drugs).
beat for—lacking.
beat loot—poor pay, small money.
best, the—very nice, pleasant
big deal—the main transaction or thing; also, a large purchase of drugs or marijuana.
blow—to play an instrument (any instrument).
bug—to make crazy, to drive insane.
bugged—emotionally disturbed.

cap—capsule (of heroin).
carry a monkey—to be addicted; to require a heavy dosage of a narcotic.
cat—person, particularly a person who knows music or frequents musical circles.
charge—marijuana (in general); also, a single shot of heroin.
charged—high on marijuana or narcotics.
chick—girl; woman.
clean—with no supply (of marijuana or narcotics).

cold turkey—to be abruptly and permanently deprived of drugs; as "a cold turkey cure".

connection—a person with a source of supply (of drugs).

contact—a source of supply (of drugs).

cool—relaxed, happy, safe, comfortable, good, pleasant.

cure—usually, gradual or progressive deprivation of a narcotic.

cut on out—leave, depart.

cut out—to leave.

deck—a measured quantity of narcotic.

dig—to understand, see, follow (as a conversation), like, enjoy; also, attitude; also, line of business.

drag—a discomfort; an unpleasantness; to make uncomfortable or unpleasant; to be an unpleasant person.

drug cat—an unpleasant person.

end, the—wonderful! terrific!

fall in—fit in with the group.

fall out—to leave.

five, give me—shake hands (five fingers).

fix-man—a narcotics pusher.

fix—a supply of narcotics.

flip—to lose emotional control; a disturbed person.

flipped—emotionally disturbed; more rarely, insane.

flip your wig—go crazy.

gauge—marijuana.

get off—to quit the use of drugs.

get on—to get high.

get straight—secure a supply of marijuana, narcotics or money.

gold—money.

gold in front—payment in advance.

gone—powerful, as "This is real gone gauge." Also, happy.

goofball—narcotic pill; also, an unbalanced person.

goof off—blunder.

grass—marijuana.

great—nice; okay.

greatest—very nice; pretty good.

groove—to enjoy oneself; also, solid, legitimate, as "He's in the groove." Also, spirit, mood or style, as "that Dixieland groove".

habit—addiction; also, degree of addiction, as "a three-cap habit," "a five-cap habit."

hard stuff—any of the narcotic drugs, as distinguished from marijuana.

hassle—fight, argument

have eyes—to want, desire, as "I got eyes for that chick." Also, to be in love with.

hay—marijuana.

hemp—marijuana.

high—intoxicated.

high on lush—intoxicated on liquor rather than drugs.

hip—in the know.

hook—in a narcotics addict, the physiological requirement which compels him to return again and again to the drug.

horse—heroin.

hot—passionate, as to "play (music) hot"; compare Italian classical music terminology, *con fuoco* ... *i.e,* with fire.

hung up—in a state of depression; unable to function.

hustler—harlot

in the groove—exactly right (from the fitting of a needle into a phonograph record track.

in there—participating; meeting social or musical demands.

jam—to improvise.

jam session—see: session.

jive—music, marijuana, etc., etc.

john—client of a hustler.

joy-pop—injection of heroin beneath skin (rather than into vein).

junky—heroin addict.

kick—the emotional state accompanying being high; any strongly pleasurable emotional state.

kick a habit—to break a habit: specifically, the drug habit.

lay on—to give some of, as "I'm going to lay a stick on you."

light up—get high.

lift—sensation or state of being high.

loot—money.

mainline—injection of heroin into a vein.

make it—to achieve a goal; to get along (in a given situation).

Mexican grass—imported marijuana.

narcotics rap—jail sentence for possession of narcotics.

O—an ounce of marijuana.
ofay—Negro word for unliked white people.
on—high; also, addicted.
O-Z—an ounce of marijuana.

pad—home or apartment.
pot—marijuana.
pro—hustler.
pusher—drug or marijuana seller.
put down—to reject; refuse.

riff—solo musical passage, often improvised.

set—group of musical numbers played by orchestra between rests.
sent—made happy.
session—group gathering of musicians to play, particularly to improvise.
sharp—fashionable in a flashy manner; also shrewd, clever.
shoot—inject (heroin) with hypodermic needle.
shoot it—inject heroin with hypodermic needle.
skin-pop—same as joy-pop; also, accidentally missing vein while injecting
    heroin.
sniff—to take heroin by inhalation through nostril.
solid—Understood! (As it were, "the connection between us is solid.")
square—bourgeois, conventional, provincial, stupid, ill-informed, not hip.
stash—concealed supply of drugs; to conceal.
stick—marijuana cigarette.
stick deal—sale of pre-manufactured marijuana cigarettes, as
    distinguished from sale of marijuana in bulk.
straight—supplied; stocked up.
stuff—marijuana, heroin, cocaine.

through the ceiling—very high.
turn off—to become sober; to come down from a "high".
turn on—to smoke marijuana; to take narcotics.

uncool—dangerous, unpleasant, uncomfortable, unsatisfactory.

weed—marijuana.
white stuff—heroin; cocaine.

Call South 3300: Ask for Molly!

Orrie Hitt

PART ONE

1

Slade Martin rode the elevator to the fourth floor, got off and unhurriedly walked down the long, narrow hall in the direction of Cyrus Willouby's office. A slick little blonde from Accounting, her hips tightly encased in a narrow skirt, emerged and preceded him through the hall. Appreciatively, his eyes followed her movements until, just before reaching the end of the hall, she turned in at the little girl's room.

Slade smiled and pushed open the door to Willouby's outer office. They had some nice numbers around All-Channel TV, that was for sure. No matter where you looked, along the huge assembly lines on the first and second floors or in the offices, there were some nice ones.

"Hi, chicken," he said to the redhead who guarded the entrance to Willouby's inner sanctum. "How's your reception lately?"

"Lousy," the girl replied, her lips unsmiling. "Especially channel six. You come in on that, Slade."

Slade nodded. He always offered the same greeting and she always gave the same answer. Only once, months before, had it been different. He'd taken her to dinner, bought a few drinks and they'd gone up to his bachelor apartment in the West End section. There had been no resistance on her part when he'd taken her to bed but there had been no fun in it, either. She had been colder than a block of ice in a snow storm.

"Baby," he said now, "don't hate me. I gave you my very best."

"Oh, shut up."

"And what I haven't got you just don't find around any more."

"Don't brag," she told him, buffing her nails. "You can't keep all of us happy."

Slade laughed. He knew that almost everybody in the building said he was the biggest woman chaser in North Hope, that there was hardly a girl who worked for All-Channel who hadn't willingly or otherwise crawled between his sheets. But this wasn't true, at least the last part of it wasn't. There were some—not many, maybe, but some—he wouldn't touch with a nine foot pole on the end of a twenty-foot rope. And he hadn't forced any of them. At twenty-eight he was tall, dark, good looking and he had been lucky. No, he hadn't forced any of them. If it ever came to that, the first one he would force would be that Ann Frank from Promotion. She was a blonde dream.

"The genius in?" Slade wanted to know.

"Do I have to tell you?" The redhead glanced at her wrist watch. "You've only kept him waiting twenty minutes already."

"Waiting's good for the soul."

"Not his soul. Or his temper. He thinks his sales manager should hop like a trained dog."

"He hops for me," Slade said. "On one foot at a time."

The redhead was unimpressed. "How else can you do it?" she inquired, returning to her nails.

"Oh, you're sharp," Slade assured her. "Sharp as the focus on an All-Channel TV set—our new Wonder World set, that is." He bent low over her desk, spoke softly. "Lady, you haven't lived until you've seen our Wonder World set. No more up and down lines, no more crazy pictures. Why, lady, we bring the studio right into your living room. It's so real when you get up to go to the kitchen, or wherever else you have to go, you'll stumble over the props, bump into the cameras and—"

"Slade." The redhead was laughing now. "Slade, you're nuts."

"You can say that again," Slade said. "Or I wouldn't be here."

The big, dark door behind the redhead's desk opened and Willouby stuck his head out. Willouby had a forty-five year old skull, completely bald, and a round, large face which, at the moment, was inclined to be red.

"Slade!" Willouby screamed as though he had just gotten his hand caught in a meat grinder. "Where have you been? Man, you're late!"

"I'm not late," Slade said easily. "I got here today, didn't I?"

Willouby swung the door open wide and gestured with a fat hand.

"Get in here," he said. "Let's get this over with. You've made me late for golf as it is."

"By all means," Slade said, moving forward, "don't mess up your golf."

Slade entered the office and Willouby slammed the door shut. It made a nice comfortable sound as it closed, a rich sound. The sound of the door matched the thick carpet on the floor, the dark green walls, the long polished desk and the expensive leather furniture.

"Why do you have to be late?" Willouby demanded, sitting down behind the desk.

"I guess it's because I take my time."

"Don't be flip."

"I'm not flip. I'm the only sales manager in the television industry who hasn't got an ulcer. I don't want an ulcer. I like to drink, I like to play. How can I enjoy life if I'm a sick man?"

Willouby blinked his dark eyes and stared at Slade.

"Sometimes I don't understand you," he said.

"Nor I you."

"Let's not argue. Have you seen the new models?"

"I've seen them."

"What do you think?"

"I think you're going broke."

He expected Willouby to leap up from his chair but the older man didn't respond quite that way. His face simply drained of all color and his eyes blinked faster.

"Why do you say that?"

"Because you've been playing too much golf."

"You don't make sense."

"I do make sense." Slade found a cigarette and lit it. "Every time Engineering wants to find you, you're out on the golf course. If Promotion needs an okay from you, you're out on the golf course. Hell, I don't even look for you anymore. I know where you are. On the golf course. Either it ought to be winter around here all the time, so you couldn't play, or you ought to install a telephone in your golf bag." Slade thought about his suggestions and rejected one. "No, not winter all the time. You go to Florida in the winter. That's even worse. They got golf courses down there by the pound."

Willouby leaned forward. "Now see here—"

"No, you see here. You listen to me, Cyrus." Whenever Slade was upset or angry he called Willouby by his first name. "You listen good and I'll tell you a story. Once there was a fine old man by the name of Daniel Willouby. He was a pioneer and with practically his two hands he built one of the most successful television manufacturing companies in the country. He made money, lots of money, and then he died. The business was left to his son, a man who knew nothing about television, a man who felt that the world was just one big golf ball to knock around. And what happened? Engineering lost interest, Promotion lost interest, Sales lost interest—and the public lost interest. The same old models, with only a few modifications, were put out year after year. Gross and net profits began to slide off. The assembly lines grew shorter, smaller, but did that interfere with this man's golf? It did like hell."

"Look, Slade—"

"Let me finish. In spite of this, Sales was supposed to set new records, get new dealers and distributors. Advertising was supposed to put All-Channel right on top of the heap."

"Things will be different," Willouby promised. "The automatic tuning on the new models—"

"A half a dozen other firms have had it for two years," Slade said. "What's so new about it?"

"Well, then, our new dials."

Slade shook his head. "Movable sets are even older than that." He felt anger seize him again. "Don't you ever do anything but play golf and drink whizzers? Don't you ever look at a competitor's set?"

"I'm satisfied to look at All-Channel," Willouby said.

"You're satisfied. That's the trouble. The parade has passed us. The parade is so far ahead of us that you can't hear the music anymore. Take a look at sales—that'll tell you. Do you think I like a drop in sales? Hell, Cyrus, I work on an over-ride."

"What do you suggest?"

"Give up golf and take some interest in things around here."

"But I like golf."

"All right, then put somebody in here who doesn't, somebody who knows the television field."

"Who, for instance?"

"Me, for instance."

Willouby smiled. "I thought you would say that."

"So? What else did you expect me to say? I know the television business. I learned it from your father and anybody who learned from your father learned his job well. I know what you need, and what has to be done."

Willouby placed an unlighted cigar in his mouth.

"You tell me what has to be done," he said. "You're so smart."

Slade stubbed out his cigarette. "It's the easiest thing I ever did in my life," he said, "telling you what has to be done. We have to give the public something different, something new. We could have done it this year, or last, but it's too late for that now. We've got an improved chassis, maybe, but we've got the same old cabinets and we're going to have to hump our backs to unload them."

"Go on."

"We could have brought out a line of color cabinets. You know—match the interior of your home and all that stuff. Sure, some people wouldn't want the colored numbers but it would focus attention on us. And remember, a lot of folks buy the pretty ribbon on the package, not what's inside the box. We could have had a triangular cabinet, one that would fit into a corner and save space in a small room. That idea, by the way, came up to you from Engineering but you were too busy trying to get a hole in one." Slade laughed. "There's only one place where I know you can get—"

"Don't be filthy, Slade."

"If it gets my point across to you, I will. I have to make you see what's happening, things you have to see but which you refuse to recognize."

"You're quite a psychologist."

"Don't try to be superior with me," Slade said, annoyed. "Just because nobody else around here has the guts to tell you off doesn't mean that I won't."

Willouby held a match to the cigar and puffed a cloud of smoke toward the ceiling.

"That's why I sent for you, Slade," he said. "Because you've got guts."

"I'll bet."

"No, I mean it." Willouby was thoughtful for a long moment. "You're right, Slade. Things are rough. We've got to do something."

"I told you. Give up golf."

Willouby waved the suggestion aside. "No, not that. Hell, I play golf mostly because I don't know what's going on around here, anyway. What good is it for me to sit behind this desk? I never took any interest in the business when my father was alive and I've got even less now."

"You want to make money, don't you?"

"Well, yes, that."

"You borrowed money from the bank last year."

"How do you know?"

"I heard." Slade grinned. "Go out and borrow some more, a bundle. Scrap these monsters we're turning out now. Postpone our show at the hotel for a few months. Put Engineering on the double and feed hot stuff to Promotion. Turn out some real hot models that'll set them back on their ears. That's all you have to do."

Willouby held up his hand. "I couldn't do that. The bank—well, they won't let me have another dime."

"What!"

"That's why I called you up here today. The show is next week and the new models aren't all that they should be. Even I know that. It makes me sick when I think of—well, what's the use? I've analyzed the whole thing, and the answer lies in Sales. Sales has to pull us out of it."

Slade's face became serious. "Are you out of your mind?"

"No. What else is left? The stuff is made, or being made, and it's inventory. We've got to sell it. It's up to Sales. Up to you."

"Thanks," Slade said. "For nothing."

"You put on a good show and I'll make it up to you."

"That's what the promoter said to the guy who jumped out of a plane without a parachute."

Willouby arose from behind his desk and came around it to slap Slade upon the shoulder.

"Come on, boy, you can do it!"

"Sure," Slade said. "I can do it. All I have to do is get a big order from Kane and the rest will follow like sheep. The only hitch is to get the order from Kane."

"Show him the chassis."

Slade dug for a fresh cigarette. "I might better show him the chassis on a blonde. If I could catch him in the act, with his mind scrambled, I might get him to sign."

"That might be an idea," Willouby said. "Get a woman for him."

Slade considered the possibility. Kane was a big man, rough, and from the middle west. He was a heavy drinker and he had a strong personality.

He dominated every show. If Kane bought, everybody else did. If Kane didn't buy, nobody did.

"I'll sleep on it," Slade said. "A blonde might be just what he needs."

Willouby smiled, pleased that he had contributed something to the conversation.

"I'm sure you don't need one," Willouby said.

"Who? Me? I can always use a blonde."

Slade stayed a few minutes longer, discussing some unimportant details about the show to be held in the grand ballroom of the Hotel Temple the following week. It was to be a big affair, he said, and he expected more than four hundred dealers and distributors. It would be expensive, but if they had any luck at all it would be worth the investment.

He rode the elevator down to the third floor and sauntered along the hall toward his own office. Again he did not hurry. Who wanted to hurry? Hurrying was for suckers who didn't know where they were going or what they would do after they got there. Slade knew where he was going and what he was going to do. He was going into his office, forget about work for the rest of the day, and make that little Betty holler for more.

Still, he was worried. He was worried about All-Channel and that show and himself. He guessed that was only normal. All-Channel, whether he admitted it or not, was an important part of his life. He had been with them six years now, starting as a salesman and working himself up under the old man to be sales manager. He drew a good salary, lived comfortably and drove a new car. Nobody in his right mind would want a thing like that to crack apart. It could, easily. And it would if he couldn't wear down Kane and the rest of those monkeys who would be at the show. You had to get television sets into dealer show rooms before you could sell them to the public.

All-Channel was the biggest industry in the city of North Hope, population slightly in excess of twenty thousand. Twelve hundred people worked at All-Channel. This wasn't as many as there had been—at one time almost two thousand had been employed by the company—but it was a lot. Twelve hundred jobs meant that nearly twelve hundred families depended on what he did and how he did it. The responsibility, when he looked at it that way, was a little frightening.

Slade was seldom serious but for a moment he let down the bars and he felt the fear creep in. Not only did these twelve hundred people count on Willouby and him, but his own job was at stake, too. And you didn't pick up a three hundred dollar a week job, plus overrides, off the ground. He knew plenty of other sales managers who worked with bigger firms for less money. The prospect of that happening wasn't a pleasant one for him.

He entered his office through the back way. It was a small office, not air conditioned, and there were papers and charts scattered all over the place.

The windows facing the street were open and he could hear the trucks and cars down below and, from the building itself, the whine of machines along the assembly line on the next floor.

He looked at the leather settee and smiled. The settee was empty but it wouldn't be that way long. Betty filled it nicely, but not too much, and there was always room for both of them.

"Hi, honey," he said, flipping on the intercom. "Get those letters done yet?"

"Which ones?" a throaty female voice asked him.

"The ones I didn't dictate yet."

"You're a card," the voice said, laughing. "A real card."

Slade felt a twinge of tension at the sound of anticipation in her voice. He removed his coat and threw it across the back of a chair. In almost the same motion, he opened his necktie and shirt.

"You alone, Betty?"

"Yes."

"Well, come on in." He chuckled and made a kissing sound into the intercom. "And better remember the boy scout motto."

"Oh, you!"

Slade found a bottle of rye in the bottom drawer of the desk and took a long drink. A guy his age, he decided, shouldn't have so much responsibility. A guy under thirty should have just one thing on his mind. After thirty it was all right to think of something else and settle down with the one regular girl who might be a wife. Until then, though . . .

The door opened and closed and Betty stood in front of the desk. Even before he looked up he could smell her perfume and sense the woman-odor of her that wasn't perfume at all.

"The slave comes to her master," Betty announced. "And, for your information, I hung a 'Preparing to Be Prepared' sign on the door. That way people will know we're busy in here."

Slade corked the bottle and put it back in the drawer. Drinking was the only vice Betty didn't have. She said the others were much more fun.

"I hate working Friday afternoons," Slade said. "Don't you?"

"I hate working any afternoon. Or any morning, for that matter."

"Yeah. You've sure got a point."

Betty had more than one point. But that went without saying. Why else would Slade bother with her?

"I wish you'd get it air conditioned in here," Betty said.

"So do I."

Betty had dark hair, a small, oval face and generous dark eyes. Her lips were always brilliant red and if she used lipstick it was the kind that didn't come off. Further down, where he had been looking before, he could see the taut line of her pink underwear. Below that was her flat little belly, bare beneath the blouse, flowing down, with the just the hint of a bulge past the navel, to flaring hips and firmly contoured thighs.

"It makes it pretty hot in here for me to do my work," Betty said. "Air conditioning would be better."

That was one thing about Betty—she didn't pull any punches. She knew that she couldn't type worth a damn, or take dictation without making a hundred mistakes, or earn her salary any other way except flat on her back. She served, in plain language, as office sex. Without her—or someone like her—the white collar would probably strangle.

"Well, Friday's payday," Slade said, coming around the desk. "That's something."

"And you're out to collect?"

"I'm out to collect."

There were never any formalities for them. What they had was sex, plain sex, and they both recognized it for what it was. He simply took her in his arms, put his lips to her mouth, and pushed her toward the settee.

She had a good mouth, a wet, soft mouth, and when she was in the mood she could really make it wild.

"Baby," Slade sighed.

She was in the mood. Her mouth opened and her tongue became a spear of probing flame.

"Don't mess up my clothes," she told him.

"I won't."

Their lips locked together and his hands became alive, moving, touching her, making her tremble.

His lips ground against her mouth, seeking her tongue, finding it, retreating and then returning to find it again.

"You must be in a hurry, baby."

"I am. I want to catch the early bus."

He kissed her on the lobe of one ear, then down along the smooth fines of her neck.

"You will," he promised.

But she didn't.

She wanted him just as badly as he needed her.

"I love you," she whispered, fiercely.

He kissed her. "You could get fired for that, baby."

"No," she told him. "Someday, Slade, you're going to need somebody to love you."

He wondered, vaguely, if he ever would.

2

Ann Frank promised herself dozens of times that she would never go down to Molly's again but later, right after the fifth of the month when the rent was due, she found herself hailing a cab and giving the driver the familiar River Street address. Not that she worked in Molly's house any more. She didn't. She just picked up her calls there.

Right and wrong, Ann decided, had very little to do with it. Who was to say what was right or wrong, anyway? She hadn't seen two people yet who could agree on the subject. Certainly her mother hadn't and her father hadn't. They'd had vastly different ideas about a lot of things.

"It's all right for you to go out with boys," her father had said. "But you have them come here to the house and meet you. None of this around the corner stuff for Pete Frank's daughter."

Then the boy would come to the house, ring the bell and her mother would answer the door.

"I don't want Ann going to any dances," her mother would say to the boy. "You two kiddies just sit down in the living room and watch television. But not that comedy show. It isn't—nice. The jokes sometimes aren't for young people."

How could a girl figure a deal like that? For gosh sakes, how could anybody make sense out of it?

Well, Ann had figured it out when was seventeen. She just didn't bring the boys home anymore. She told her mother that she was going to the movies with the girls—and she went down to the corner and met the boys.

The first boy had been Jerry, a tall, lanky youth who played on the high school basketball team. She had gone to a party with him—her mother thought it was a bridal shower for a friend—and she had taken three or four drinks of wine. Afterward, out in the car, she had felt wonderfully warm and lazy and when his mouth touched her lips she didn't fight back. But when his one hand began going where no one's hand had touched before, and the other hand started doing funny things to her, she had begged him not to do anything else. She had struggled against him, afraid, but she had been unable to prevent it. Then, in a moment of frenzy, it had seemed as though she had never lived before, never been a whole person, never enjoyed a satisfaction which was beyond all understanding.

During that summer she had lived for those stolen moments with Jerry—in his car, behind the bushes along the beach, even once in somebody's porch swing. She couldn't get enough of him or enough of this unfamiliar excitement to fill the new hunger in her body.

She began to look down on the so-called nice girls who blushingly kidded about sex. They were fools. They didn't know what they were missing. Oh, golly, golly, it was so good.

And then in September, on Labor Day, Jerry had been killed in that horrible automobile accident, a smash-up which had left him so crushed and broken they hadn't even permitted his casket to be opened. She had cried terribly, both at the funeral and in the secret misery of her bedroom. She had loved him, so she thought. But after the funeral some of the gang who had known Jerry had gotten together, down at the beach, talking about the tragedy, and there had been some beer. She didn't have to be home early that night and she had drunk a lot of the beer. The shadows of the night had been long and thick over the beach, the weather warm, and somebody had kissed her. She felt traitorous, as though she were betraying Jerry, but the flame had spread from her lips all through her body. There had been a brief struggle there under the trees and then she had learned that it didn't have to be Jerry at all, that it could be almost any man.

She never forgot that night, and since that time no one man had ever been important to her. During her last year in high school it had been for fun, for the sheer physical pleasure of it, but then her mother and father found out.

Her father, suspecting that she wasn't visiting a girl friend, had followed her. He caught her in the arms of a boy on the River Road.

"What have I done to deserve this?" her mother had wailed. "To think that we—"

"She's a slut!" Pete Frank had bellowed. "A cheap, no-good slut."

"Frank! What a horrible thing to say!"

"It's true. True! I shined my light on them. And there she was with this fellow and—"

"Stop! I don't want to hear it!"

"They were pretty damned busy, Martha. And do you know what he said to me? 'Turn out your light, you old bastard, and get out of here.' That's what he said, Martha. He said it to me. Her father!"

"You should have killed him, Frank."

"No, Martha. Not him. He is a man. It's not his fault. He couldn't have had her there without her consent. She's our daughter, Martha, but she's no good. She's a young chippy. There are many of them in this city. But that's our daughter. That's worse."

The next day, while her father was at work and her mother was telling her tale of woe to a neighbor, Ann left home.

Her first job was in a cosmetic factory, working on an assembly line. The line she was assigned to bottled liquid rouge and she was given the task of screwing on the caps. The metal caps were small and rough and at the end of the second day her hands and fingers were so sore that she could hardly eat.

"To hell with this," one of the girls on the line had said. "I know a better way to make a buck."

"I wish I knew," Ann confessed.

The girl laughed. "With your looks, honey, it wouldn't be hard to find out." The remark made the girl laugh all the more. "Well, anyhow—you'd sure as hell find out."

That night after work, following the ride downtown on the bus, the girl had told Ann what it was all about. Molly Ford, the county's leading madam, needed girls for her house. Young girls. Pretty girls. Girls who were willing to give themselves for money.

"I'd never do that," Ann said.

"No? Well, maybe you'll change your mind. Here's her address, in case you ever do."

The next day when Ann reported for work at the factory she found the place shut down. A long line of pickets paraded before the high, iron fence, many of them carrying large white cards. You were a sucker, a dirty scab, if you crossed the picket line. Few tried it. They got their hair pulled and their shins kicked if they did.

For a week Ann existed on buns and coffee, going out to the factory each morning and returning on the next bus when she saw the strike was still in progress. On the eighth day she didn't make the trip. She didn't have the money.

"You poor thing," Molly said when she opened the door, "you must be broke."

"I am."

Ann made her first call that night, to a big house in the East End section, and she made more money in an hour than she had made at the factory for a week.

She could not remember the man, his name, what he looked like, anything about him. He was like all the other men who had followed him— just a face, a body and an elemental need.

She made a lot of money with Molly but she spent it incredibly fast. The apartment was expensive, she bought clothes by the pound and she ate only the best food in the finest restaurants. She tipped well for what she wanted and headwaiters and doormen fell in love with her.

During this time, through a girl friend, she managed to keep track of her family. Her father had started drinking, often missing several days from his work, and her mother had taken a job checking in a grocery store. She felt sorry for them, regretted what she had done, but made no effort to help them. She knew that they would not want her help, would refuse to accept it, and that any offer she might make would only make the situation worse.

She did not drink. Many of them who bought her body for a few minutes of pleasure insisted that she drink with them but she always refused. She came to them for one purpose, one purpose only, and this she delivered on the line.

And, still, she felt nothing, nothing from any of them. She was a hollow shell that was examined, purchased, and used. Her body ached with desire, crying out for fulfillment, twisting with an inner agony that sought but which could find no satisfaction.

In the end, she was like almost all the others, looking for a man, wanting a man for what he was. But in one way she was different than the others: she wouldn't pick up a man off the streets and, if necessary, pay him to give her what she craved. The man she sought was young, strong, fairly tall and handsome, and he should have a good job. He should be the type who could, in the swift violence of his embrace, bring her a measure of self-respect and physical freedom.

One night, in Hermes Restaurant, she saw him. He was standing at the bar, laughing at a joke which the bartender had just told.

"Who is he?" Ann asked her waiter.

"The gentleman at the end of the bar?"

"Yes."

"Slade Martin. A very nice man."

"He looks like a movie actor."

"Guess he does. He's sales manager of All-Channel TV."

Ann was familiar with the company, since it was the largest industry in North Hope, employing almost twice as many people as the railroad. The huge brick buildings in the South Bend section of the city, not far from the river and the railroad, were both impressive and clean.

"It must be a big job," she said.

"It is. A very big job."

She wondered if Slade Martin were married but rejected the idea of asking the waiter, afraid that the waiter would only relay the matter of her curiosity to the man at the bar. And this, at the moment, would spoil her plans. She didn't want to look like she was chasing him. She wanted to make Slade Martin chase her.

Two nights later she saw him at the bar again, this time with a stunning redhead. She tried to determine if the girl wore any rings on her left hand but the light was so dim in the bar she couldn't tell. The next night, however, he was back at the bar with a different girl and she heaved a sign of relief! Either he wasn't married or, if he was, he wasn't working at it.

She stayed there so long that night, just watching him, that she didn't show up at Molly's or even check in by phone. It proved to be the luckiest night of her life. Molly was picked up by the police along with half a dozen of her girls, including the girl who had worked in the cosmetic factory with Ann.

A week later Ann saw Molly on the street, near the corner of Fifth and Elm.

"The crazy bastards," Molly complained, "they always get these ideas just before election. Next time I'm going to take two weeks off and they can beat their tom-toms on somebody else's head."

"Then you're closed down?"

"Closed down? Don't be silly! For a month, maybe, but no more than that. The cops have gotten some publicity, the politicians can holler and everybody's happy. By Christmas we'll be rolling along as strong as ever. Get in touch with me around then."

The next day Ann took the bus down to All-Channel TV and applied for a job. The big money was gone, at least for a while, and she had to pay her bills.

"We can use you in Promotion," Personnel told her after she'd completed her tests. "As a typist. You start at fifty-seven fifty a week. Forty hours, Saturdays off. If you work on Saturday it's time and a half."

Somehow, by cutting down on meals and walking back and forth to work, she had managed to hang on to the apartment. At Christmas, though, when the plant shut down for a week—she'd been with the firm only a short time and she wasn't entitled to any vacation pay—she'd found herself in trouble.

"I've got a call for you," Molly said, when Ann phoned. "This man knows you from before and he won't take anybody else. The Carlson, room four-fourteen. I told him it would be two bills for all night if I could get in touch with you, and he said he'd do a little better than that. God, baby, I'm glad you're back!"

But she only went that one night and not again until next month when the rent and some other things came due.

"Holy hell," Molly said, "you can't make a living that way, baby."

"Well, I've got a job, too."

"A job? I never took you for a sucker."

Her work at All-Channel wasn't hard and it wasn't easy, either. The worst part of it was being bored to death with the constant rattle of typewriters in the office, the inane chatter of the girls about boy friends and husbands and babies. Quite a few of the girls had husbands and babies and those who didn't were out for both.

"I'll tell him we got caught, that I'm pregnant," one girl said, referring to the recent lack of interest by her boy friend. "That'll make his hair droop down."

The best part of it was that Slade Martin was in and out of Promotion a great deal. As sales manager he was tied up very closely with Advertising and Promotion but she often heard him say that Promotion was the most important of the two.

"You get us a free plug in a national mag, kiddies, and I'll buy you all a box of candy. Anybody can buy space but it takes some cozy doing to get it for free."

Ann's desk was right near the door and sometimes when he came in he would stop and speak to her. He did that with all of the girls. But whenever he spoke to Ann she found herself feeling the same way she had the first night she saw him in Hermes Restaurant.

He was always respectful to her, usually a little distant, and she couldn't quite understand it. He had the reputation of taking any female to bed who didn't fight too hard. And not many of them fought. He was, most of the girls thought, a desirable representative of the male animal.

Ann had done much to try to attract his attention. She wore skirts that were two sizes too small and thin woolen sweaters that were equally snug. She stopped wearing bras, and sometimes when he was near her desk she bent over to pick up a piece of deliberately dropped paper from the floor. Several times she noticed him looking down inside the big, gaping V of her sweater but whenever she caught him at it he turned away, quickly. The fact that he seemed to be interested and yet unwilling nearly drove her out of her mind.

Somehow, she had to have Slade Martin.

And somehow, in some way, she would get him.

Now as she stood before the mirror in her apartment she thought of him in a desperate, helpless way that screamed for an answer. Yes, somehow she would. Somehow, she must.

She looked at herself in the mirror.

She was naked, gloriously naked, wonderfully alive, ready to accept and return his love.

Her glance traveled to the long, soft, beautiful blonde hair that tumbled downward to her shoulders, molding her face in a framework the color of white beach sand under a hot sun.

Her eyes were blue, as blue as the blue crayons she used to use in school and beneath the curving eyebrows they were a sea of soft warmth and mysterious invitation.

Her nose was small but just the right size, turned up a little yet not too much. An inquisitive nose, a saucy nose, the kind men liked to peck at with their lips. A nose that was never shiny, whether she powdered it or not. This superb quality was true of the rest of her face, too; she could go for days without the use of cosmetics and still be as beautiful. Her skin was pink-white and it retained the same velvet softness even when exposed to the hazards of sun and wind. She was lucky, she thought; her skin matched so well with the red, oval pout of her generous lips; lips that were always wet, always parted just enough to reveal the white, even line of her teeth.

Beautiful, men said. Lovely, men said. She hoped so. She didn't want to be just one thing; she wanted to be all things.

Ann ran her hands down her body, and smiled.

Oh, take me, Slade, she thought. Oh, take me, hold me, want me and love me. Yes, love me. Love me with all of your body, all of your soul, all of your wonderful, masculine love. Oh, love me, love me . . .

Her hands moved down her body again, touching the flaming flatness of her stomach, caressing the provocative, womanly flare of her hips. Going lower to her thighs, neither hard nor soft, neither big nor small, and then down to the long, tapering lines of her legs.

These are your legs, Slade, she thought; these smooth, perfectly formed legs belong to you. These are yours to own, to know, to possess.

Suddenly, without wanting to, she began to cry. The tears filled her eyes and rolled down across her face. Nervously, she brushed them aside. She was being a fool, an utter, stupid fool. Slade Martin didn't know she existed. Or if he did, he didn't care.

Slade, she thought miserably; oh, Slade!

And then she sank to the bed, sobbing.

Slade was the man for her.

She had to have him.

And wanting him like this, like an ache after a dream, was a little slice of hell.

3

Slade felt miserable but that wasn't anything unusual; on Saturday mornings he always felt miserable.

Friday night, he thought; Friday night is the worst night in the week. You start drinking early, before dinner, and you're lucky if you eat anything at all. You get to drinking and talking, and after a while the only appetite you've got left is to fun it up with some jane. So you find the jane and what happens? You drink more, a lot more, and pretty soon the whole world is filled with a dense fog that has neither identity nor meaning. Maybe you get what you started out after and maybe you don't, but it actually makes very little difference whether you do or you don't. Your mind retains the fog and you never remember it, anyway.

He turned his head, looking at the face of the girl on the pillow beside him. It must have been a lousy night. He hadn't called on Molly for a girl in so long he couldn't remember when.

The girl was small, dark and, in the relaxation of sleep, inclined to be pretty. Not beautiful. Just pretty.

He got out of bed without waking her. He tried to remember if he had paid her but he supposed he had. This stuff was cash on the line and you didn't get past the first button on credit. He wondered, without much caring, how much she had cost him. Enough, that was for sure. More than enough when he considered that he should have been able to have any of a dozen women for nothing.

He showered, shaved, and dressed in slacks and polo shirt. He never dressed formally on Saturday although he went down to the office and often had his busiest day. All of the offices were shut down on Saturday, the assembly lines halted for the week end, and he could work without the usual distractions. Not only that, but he would have the weekly activity reports of the salesmen in the field and, not infrequently, orders from dealers and distributors. On Saturday he sat down at his desk, figured out just how bad the past week had been and tried to determine just how awful the coming week would be. It was getting so he could do both with his eyes shut. Sales had been sliding downhill faster than a sled on ice.

"Good morning," the girl said from the bed, yawning sleepily. She made a distasteful sound with her lips. "Where on earth did you get that liquor you had last night."

"I don't know. Was it that bad?"

"It was pretty terrible."

Slade stood in front of the mirror and tied his tie. He didn't bother looking at the girl. Now that it was morning and he had spent the money he began to resent her.

"I must have been hard up last night," he said, trying to hurt her.

She laughed, her pretty face awake suddenly.

Slade found a ten in his wallet and dropped it on top of the dresser.

"For you," he said, moving across the room. "Just make sure the door is closed on the way out."

"You work Saturdays?"

"Yeah. Why?"

"I was just thinking."

He glanced at the girl now. She sat up in the bed, the sheet down across her hips.

"Don't think," he told her. "It'll ruin your mind."

He left the apartment, took the elevator to the main floor and walked around the building to the garage. His head ached mildly and the bright sunlight nearly blinded him. It was even worse when he stepped into the darkness of the garage.

A few minutes later he drove downtown. The car felt good beneath him, big and solid. It was a new Chrysler, their biggest and most powerful model, and you could bust your neck just by tromping down on it. Between the stop lights he teased the quietly running engine, feeding it gas with short, measured jabs of his right foot. Someday, or some night, he would take the thing out on the highway and see what it could really do. What if he did get a ticket? He could afford it, couldn't he?

There was a diner on Main, near the corner of Melrose, and he stopped for breakfast. Sometimes he went there and sometimes he didn't. The little brunette behind the counter had intrigued him once but now she annoyed him. He had taken her out one night, bought a few drinks and then taken her home to bed. She had stayed with him all night. Neither of them got any sleep—she was an insatiable little slut. She had been frantic and demanding, saying that she wanted to have a baby, and asking to stay with him forever and ever. Later, she had made a nuisance of herself, calling him at the office every day and at home at night, until finally he'd called her a cheap little tramp and hurt her feelings. But the incident had really secretly pleased him, though it hadn't been the first time a girl had felt like that about him. He often wondered what he'd do if he ever found a girl he couldn't satisfy or, even worse, a girl who wouldn't let him try.

He sat down at the counter and the fat little man who owned the place came down to wait on him.

"Bacon and eggs," Slade said. "Over light."

While he was drinking his coffee he noticed that the girl wasn't anywhere around and when he had an opportunity he asked the man about her.

"Susie?"

"I guess that's her name."

The owner shook his head. "Crazy little piece of yard goods," he said. "Single as the day she was born and yet she kept saying that she wanted to go and get herself a baby. I told her if she didn't look out she'd be on her way to having a nest of kittens. She is. She went out with my dishwasher and he cleaned her silverware for her."

"She so big she can't work?"

"Naw. Not yet. It's just that in the morning she gets sick and she can't stand the sight or the smell of food. But in the afternoon she's okay. In the afternoon she comes on and you wouldn't know there's a thing wrong with her, the way she works."

"What about the dishwasher?"

"Oh, him. He's already married."

"Cripes."

"That's what I say. How do you figure some of these people, anyway?"

After breakfast Slade drove down to the hotel and checked on the ballroom and the reservations. The ballroom was almost ready, with tables and chairs set up for the salesmen, and some of the All-Channel sets had already been moved in. He refused to look at the sets, deciding that he would see more than enough of them during the coming week.

Reservations, the desk told him, were heavy and they expected about three hundred, possibly more, for the wing-ding. It made Slade feel good to know there would be so many. And somehow it made him feel a little inferior, too. It would be three hundred to one and he had to get a bundle of orders out of those clowns. If he could only nail Kane . . .

He rode down to the factory and parked the Chrysler in the spot reserved for him near the main entrance. On Saturday the parking lot was deserted, a bare strip of asphalt stretching down toward the river.

Inside the building he walked along the first floor, smelling the odors of lacquer and metal shavings, seeing the hundreds of chassis and cabinets in the process of being assembled. Realizing that he would be responsible for the sale of every one of these sets gave him a feeling of power, but the sense of responsibility made his guts tighten just a little. If he couldn't sell them, that lot out there would remain empty and these hundreds of machines would stand idle. And he didn't know how he was going to do it. He just didn't know.

You could, he told himself, sell garbage if you put it up in a fancy box and tied a red ribbon around it. But if you left it in a pile you couldn't give it away in exchange for sour apples. And that's what they were doing at All-Channel, letting it pile up.

He cursed Willouby and he cursed Engineering and he cursed the whole stinking mess. Willouby should drop dead and be buried on the golf course, with a whizzer in one hand and a hole-in-one flag planted over his skull. And that guy in Engineering, that simpering Thomas fellow—he ought to drop dead too, and be buried alongside Willouby. They'd make a good pair. Neither one of them had any guts or any vision.

Still cursing he walked upstairs to his office and ripped open his mail. It was even worse than he expected and he broke out into a cold sweat. Damn that Chadco and their remote control switch. Why hadn't All-Channel come out with something like that? Sure—the controls were expensive, but they were added to the price of the set in a package deal, and the suckers who bought them didn't know left from right. The public was made up of suckers, that's what it was. The suckers sat around in big, sloppy chairs, drinking beer, and playing with the automatic control. Ma, give me Channel Six. Pa, flip 'er to Channel Two. Shut the thing off. Turn it on. Don't move. Go to six. Go to four. Go to hell. Start it. Stop it. But don't move, you big, fat, lazy slob. Just sit still and make her work.

Hell!

He sat down behind the desk. It was incredible. Two days work would fill the week's orders. More and more would go into inventory and the inventory was getting bigger every day. He hated to think about it, hated to think about what would happen if he failed. And he would fail unless he could nail Kane. Make Kane buy and the rest of them would buy. Load them up so that they wouldn't have enough money, or enough floor space, for a competitive brand. But how did you do that? They would be shopping and, actually, he had nothing to sell.

Hell, he thought; oh, hell!

He left the office and moved along the hall, trying to think, trying to figure it out. He was almost past Promotion before he realized that somebody was working in there, running a typewriter. Jefferies? No, not Jefferies. Jefferies was too lazy to work more than three days a week and, besides, he had friends in New York who invited him down every weekend. No, not Jefferies. Somebody else who didn't know any better.

He turned around, returned to Promotion and stepped inside.

"Oh, hi," he said.

Most of the girls he called chicken but this one he didn't dare call chicken. There was something regal about this dolly, something that disturbed him deeply and kept him in a state of perpetual awe.

"Hello, Mr. Martin."

"Overtime?"

"No, not exactly. But I was working on this yesterday and I didn't get it out. I thought I should. Have you seen it?"

"Seen what?"

"The picture."

He was glad of the excuse to get close to her. He liked the smell of her perfume, the shine of the overhead light against her hair. And he liked that white sweater, the one that buttoned down the front, with the two top buttons undone. He was willing to bet his last chance at selling an All-Channel set that every bit of what was underneath belonged to Ann Frank.

"Not bad," he said.

He glanced only briefly at the picture of the girl standing alongside an All-Channel Hurricane Model 74, "the set that defies all weather and atmospheric conditions." Most of his attention was directed to the top of the sweater and the start of the warm, deep hollow between her breasts.

"Mr. Jefferies thought we might hit *Tomorrow* with it."

"He's nuts," Slade said. "That's the biggest Sunday weekly in the country."

"Well, he says you shoot big and you're lucky if you hit small."

"He's got something there."

"And he says that sex will sell almost anything."

"You call that sex? She's dressed, isn't she? And anyway, her face has about as much expression as a burlap bag."

"Well," Ann said, "I'm trying, Mr. Martin. I can't do any more than that."

"Oh, I'm not blaming you. It's that crazy Jefferies. He must smoke a dreamy brand of cigarettes."

She typed a few words and stopped.

"You know something?" she said. "He is funny sometimes. I never thought of it until now, Mr. Martin."

"I wish you wouldn't call me Mr. Martin. Everybody calls me Slade, Miss Frank."

Her face colored slightly.

"I'm Ann," she said, banging at the keys again.

He watched her work. Every time she punched one of the keys that sweater looked like it was going to ride down lower. But it didn't. It just stayed right there, clinging and almost plastered to her body.

His eyes lowered and found the long, trim thigh, the nylon encased legs that were pulled back under the chair.

Sweat crawled along his belly and he felt his breathing becoming more rapid.

"Ann."

"Yes—Slade?"

"How would you like to make some real money for yourself?"

She looked up from the typewriter, her hands still resting on the keyboard.

"I'd love that. Any girl would."

Quickly, he outlined his plan to her. The more he talked the better it sounded. Why hadn't he thought of it before?

"Look," he said, "we can pull most of the girls out of Promotion and use them at the show next week. You know, sort of mix with the men and laugh it up."

"We would get paid extra for that?"

"Well, a little. I could clear it with Accounting and Jefferies is no problem. He'll go along with anything that would put him in good with Willouby and this will. But that isn't what I had in mind—not for you. We've got one big buyer coming in, a very big buyer by the name of Kane. He's rough and tough but I've got an idea the woman touch would weaken him. Your job would be to stick with the guy, encourage him to buy and, in general, promote the welfare of the company."

"Yes?"

He looked down into those wide blue eyes, at the wet, red lips and, of course, straight at those two mounds that lifted up under the sweater. At the moment, there was only one idea that seemed good to him.

"Yes, Slade?"

He ran his tongue across his lips. "What I was saying, if we can belt him with a good order, break the ice, the rest will be easy. It'll be your job to work on him, soften him up, slow him down for the kill. I don't know just how you'll do it, or if you can. But it's worth a try. The models we've got this year, anything is worth a try."

She smiled up at him. Her teeth were white, perfect, and his head began to throb.

"I'm listening," she reminded him.

"I'll make *a deal* with you," he said. "You work the sales convention next week, bending Kane's ear, and you'll not only get your salary, plus expenses, but I'll guarantee you a buck for every set that he orders. How does that sound?"

"I don't know. How many sets does he usually buy?"

"There's no set amount. Some years a lot, other years a little, but he sets the pattern for the whole works. To give you an idea, I could pick up the telephone and get an order for five hundred sets without even having him come here. Anything above that is gravy. He could go to a thousand sets, or fifteen hundred, or two thousand and never bat an eye. That's what we have to shoot for—the top. I've never used a girl on him before so I don't have any idea how it'll work. I do know, though, that he wouldn't go for a tramp. It has to be somebody fresh and young like you, somebody—well, nice. You know. Nice face, nice figure. Class."

Again she colored. "Thank you, Slade."

"No. I mean it." Then, "Will you do it?"

"I'll try. What harm can come from trying?"

He grinned. "I like your spirit."

She laughed. "Mr. Jefferies says that sex will sell anything. We'll see if he's right."

Slade turned at the door.

"If sex will sell TV sets," he said, looking directly at her, "we've got a two thousand unit order already."

"I hope so, Slade."

"I hope so, too." He paused, pleased with the way she had accepted his somewhat blunt remark. "Say," he said, "I've got a wonderful idea. Why don't we have dinner together tonight and talk about it some more?"

"Well—"

"Unless you have something else to do."

"No," she said, playing with the keys on the typewriter, "I don't have anything else to do."

"Then?"

She seemed to be making up her mind, as though she didn't trust him or something. He wished, in that second, that he hadn't played around with so many women, that he didn't have such a lousy reputation.

"All right," she agreed, finally, "you can pick me up at my place around seven."

He was surprised that she mentioned such a good address; it was even better than his own.

"Okay," he said, unable to keep the excitement out of his voice. "At seven."

Whistling, he started along the hall. His steps were sharper, quicker than they had been a few minutes before. He tried to think about Kane, how they would handle him, and the thousands of TV sets he had to sell somehow. But, still whistling, he gave up on the whole effort as just a bad job. He could think, right then, of only one thing.

He had to get himself a sample of that stuff back there in Promotion.

He sure did.

And he would.

Even if he had to steal it.

4

Ann dressed carefully for her date with Slade Martin. She was nervous and at times her hands shook so badly she thought she would never be ready on time. After three attempts she finally got the bra strap hooked and then she discovered it was twisted.

"Oh, damn!" she murmured.

She was being foolish, like a teenager getting all frilled up for her first date. Of the hundreds of men she had known there had been many of them more important than Slade, far richer; men who were accepted as pillars in the community. She should be calm and collected. She shouldn't be upset. But she couldn't help it.

Maybe she shouldn't go to all this trouble, putting on a bra and panties. Slade was supposed to be a heller with the women and they said around the office that all he needed was five minutes of a girl's time and he could make her so happy she couldn't see straight for hours.

She hooked the bra, properly this time, and stepped into the black lace panties, a pair which were very thin and filmy and which clung to her white skin like the shadows of night creeping across new-fallen snow.

Can't make things too easy, she thought as she smiled at her reflection in the mirror. If you did that you felt like you were just giving yourself away. And that wouldn't do, not at all, for Slade Martin.

She examined her face in the mirror, decided there was little she could do to improve it—well, just a touch of lipstick, maybe—and then turned to the closet, hunting for a dress.

The gray was no good, the gray didn't do anything for her. Spending forty-five dollars on that thing had been a waste of money. And she hated black. Black was for old ladies and funerals. She pushed that dress aside.

Red. That was it, the red one. Not the red one with the pleats down the front and the side, but the red one that was like a sheath. What was it Molly had said about that dress? Bawdyhouse red, Molly had said. Bawdy red on the most beautiful girl in the city. But that wasn't so. It was Molly's crude way of trying to say something nice.

She crossed the room and stood before the mirror, holding the red dress next to her body. It was a warm red, the color of a dying fire, and it complimented the white-blonde of her hair, contrasted sharply with the sea-blue of her eyes. Yes, this was the dress to wear. This was the one that would show him everything she had.

She dressed hurriedly and then lingered once again before the mirror. The neck of the dress was low, but not too low; just low enough to excite the interest of the male, revealing a tiny hint of the bold, deep hollow between her breasts. She swung to the side, twisting her head, and looked at her body's profile. Below the upper soft outline her stomach was small, a narrow band of flesh, and below that, where the dress became a red skin over her body, the small of her back swept away into the wonderfully rounded mounds above her stalk-slim legs and pleasantly heavy thighs.

Briefly, as she sometimes did when she stood like this, her hands went to the flatness of her stomach, holding it. She had been lucky, very lucky. Someday, she felt, she would not be so lucky. Someday there would be a man, a man she could fully enjoy, and later, when she was alone and afraid, her stomach would get bigger and bigger. The fear of this thing happening, a fear which never lasted more than a few moments, brought about a larger, more haunting fear. What would she do if she ever found herself like that? What could she do? Unless she was in love with the man and the man returned that love.

Love. This was the thing that bothered her most. What was love? Was it something that she had once and lost, something which she couldn't remember? Had it died when Jerry died in that frightful wreck? Or had it lived and died the night her father found her with that boy on the river road? Or perhaps it hadn't died at all. Perhaps, until now, it had never lived for her.

What she felt for Slade Martin—was this love? Wanting him, needing him, burning up inside at the mere thought of him—was this love? It might be. It could be. She had never felt this way about a man before. She had never looked at a man and really wanted him, really needed him. Yes, this could be love. Or—don't think of this, she told herself; don't ever, ever think of it—it could be something even less than nothing. It could be nothing more than a thing two animals might share.

The buzzer at the door sounded and she whirled away from the mirror. She was stupid to torture herself this way. Tonight, this night, was a night she had wanted for a long, long time. She should be happy and free and gay. She should, as advised by an old song, count her blessings and not her troubles.

She crossed the living room and, smiling, opened the door. He stood there in the hall, looking at her, his eyes widening slightly as his glance went up and down, caressing every curve, every secret hollow.

He whistled. "Lady," he said, grinning, "you have just blinded me."

She laughed. "Don't worry," she said. "You'll get your eyesight back."

"Maybe I will. But that guy Kane won't, not if you wear that dress. You wear that dress, and you smile the way you're smiling now, and he'll order more All-Channel sets than we can turn out in six months."

She picked up her pocketbook from an end table and joined him in the hall. She was flushed and blazing inwardly, but outwardly she was calm.

"You overestimate the power of a woman, Slade."

"Of a woman, maybe. But of sex, no. Jefferies is right when he says that sex is the greatest moving force in this world. It is."

"With everybody?"

"Everybody. Me, included." He took her arm and led her toward the elevator. "Especially me."

She didn't want to appear obvious, to let him know how much she wanted him, so she gently removed her arm from his hand.

"I know," she said as he pushed the elevator button. "So I've heard."

"They say a lot of things around the factory."

"Enough."

"They say I'd chase anything in skirts."

"Or out of skirts."

They both laughed and the elevator door slid open. All the way down to the ground floor she felt his eyes on her, drinking in her lines, taking the dress off, putting it back on. She wondered about what he thought he saw and she wondered, too, if it were as good or better than the real article.

He suggested dinner at a small, intimate restaurant in Riverdale and they drove over there in his Chrysler. Part of the trip passed through the countryside. Huge, rolling farms were on either side, and the evening voices of the river and the hills were all around them.

"Some night I'm coming out here with this crate, lay her down and let her run," Slade said. "I'll bet she can go fast enough to bust the speedometer."

"Don't try it with me, please."

"You don't like do travel fast?"

"Not in a car."

"Any other way?"

"Some other ways, yes."

They were given a table at the rear of the restaurant, near a block of French windows that overlooked a small pond. Longnecked swans moved up and down the calm surface of the water.

"Drink, Ann?"

"I don't drink."

A money-maker, Molly said, never drank, or if she drank, she drank in private. Keep your head, Molly said. Keep your head clear and your imagination going.

"Mind if I do?"

"Oh, no. Go ahead."

Slade, she soon discovered, was a heavy drinker. He drank all through dinner and later, as they still sat there talking, he told the waiter to have the shots of rye doubled.

"Saturday night," Slade said. "You let your hair down on Saturday night. Saturday night you can get sick as a dog, potted as a house plant, and on Sunday you can sleep it off."

"Maybe it's the tension."

He nodded. "It could be. I know one thing: this next week had better be a ringer or Willouby can mortgage his golf clubs and we can all look for other jobs."

Ann was shocked. She had thought that All-Channel was such a big company, doing so well. Why, you saw their ads in all the big magazines.

"Is it that bad?"

Slade emptied his glass without even stopping and motioned for the waiter again.

"Why do you think I asked you to help us? Willouby suggested it and I've gone along with it, because there isn't anything else. I don't know if it'll work or not but it's worth giving it a whirl. Personally, I doubt if Kane will be swayed so easily. He doesn't strike me as the type. Yet, you never know. By some stroke of luck, and your good looks, we may be able to pull this one out of the fire. If we don't, if the convention flops, you'll see a mass lay-off. You can't build television sets unless you sell them. The deck just isn't stacked that way."

"What do I do?"

In between drinks he outlined the campaign. Kane and the others would be arriving late the next day, or early Monday morning.

"There won't be any sales meeting Monday but there will be a dinner Monday night. Dinner and drinks. I'll introduce you to Kane and you can go to the dinner with him. I know you can't help making a good impression on him, but give it just a little extra. Get yourself in solid. Then the next day, and Wednesday, the last day, stick with him. Talk up the company and every set on the floor. Hell, I don't know. Frankly, I've never been mixed up in anything like this before. I don't know what you should or shouldn't do. Just act natural and be polite to him. What else can you do?"

"I get the idea," Ann said. "Don't worry about it. I'll do the best I can."

"I'm sure you will."

It was late when they left the restaurant and Slade staggered just a little as they reached the car.

"Dammit," he said, "I shouldn't have made such a pig of myself."

"Can you drive?"

He thought about that. "Sure, I can drive, but I'd rather not. Why don't you take the wheel?"

Although the big car handled beautifully, she wasn't used to power brakes and power steering and she drove slowly. The night slid by on either side and the farms which she had seen earlier in the evening were merely dark shadows against the skyline.

"Know why I asked you to drive, Ann?"

They were part way to North Hope, along the flat stretch of highway which skirted the river. To the right, and a short distance away, the river lay like a silver thread under the light from the moon.

"I guess because you'd been drinking."

"That's half right."

"Half right?"

"Yes. I can drink a lot and still manage this car. I can drink more than a lot and still stay on my feet. But I can't drink even a little bit, Ann, or even not at all, and not think you're the most beautiful girl in the world."

Her throat tightened, her mouth got dry, and for a second the mist in her eyes made it impossible for her to see the road.

"That's nice of you to say, Slade," she told him, huskily. "Even though it isn't true."

"It is true!"

"How many times have you said the same thing before?"

"Never."

"Are you sure?"

"Look," he said, lighting a cigarette—she noticed that his hand actually trembled. "I've got a bad name with the girls. I know that. Maybe I deserve it and maybe I don't, but that isn't the point. The point is I looked at you that first time—you were just sitting there at your desk, typing—and I told myself here's the prettiest girl you've ever seen, Martin. She's beautiful and she's nice and she's all of the things you ever looked for. But don't spoil it. Don't be a damned fool and spoil it."

"Slade," she said, and looked at him.

"No. Let me finish. That's one thing about drinking—it gives you some courage, it gives you some guts. I couldn't say this if I was dead sober, not in a million years. I could think it but I couldn't say it. Know what I mean? Have you ever felt anything, and not been able to put it into words?"

"Yes."

"Then you know how it is, you know how I feel. I look at you—Ann, don't get sore at me. I don't think you will—you're not that kind—and I can't afford to have you get mad at me. What I told you about Kane was true. Somehow, somehow, I've got to get a big order from him. I need your help. I can't have you getting mad at me. But—look, Ann. Look. There are times when a guy has to be himself, when he has to say all of the things that are inside. I like you, Ann. I've liked you right from the start. You're beautiful and wonderful and all of the things a man could ask for. Maybe— Ann, maybe it's something else. I don't know. I've never felt quite this way before. Never. Not about anybody."

She didn't know what to say. This was the sweetest thing a man had ever said to her, the words she had waited to hear, and now that it was true, now that he had said them, or almost said them, she was so filled inside with warmth that she couldn't speak.

"That's why I didn't want to drive. I knew I would ruin it if I did. Down the highway a little distance there's a road that goes to the right, down along the river. I knew I'd turn the car down there, Ann. I knew I would spoil it if I drove. I've been there with other girls. I'm not afraid to say it. I'm not ashamed. But Ann, I didn't want to do anything wrong."

He's good, she thought; he's good and fine. He isn't anything like what they say he is. He's good and fine. Involuntarily, she reached out and touched him on the arm.

"You're nice," she whispered.

Up ahead, just coming into view of the headlights, she could see the narrow road that led down to the river.

"I wanted to tell you all this," Slade said, flipping his cigarette outside. "I wanted you to make up your own mind. Ann, you can drive down there if you want."

No, she decided; no, she mustn't do that. As much as she wanted him, she would be wise not to let him know. There was always time for that later on. Yes, there was always time.

"Slade." The sound of his name was like a touch of heaven against her lips, the promise of wonders that she had never fully felt before. "Slade."

She turned in at the road.

"Baby," Slade whispered. "Oh, baby!"

She parked the Chrysler at the end of the road, under some trees and near the edge of the river.

"I love you," Slade said, as he reached for the ignition key. "I think I love you very much."

She went into his arms. She felt the strength of his arms as they encircled her, the glorious warmth of his body as she pressed against him.

"Kiss me!" she begged. "Oh, kiss me hard!"

And then he kissed her, his lips on her mouth, moving, hurting, teasing. She locked her fingers in his hair, forcing his head down. Her lips moved against his and her mouth parted as her tongue reached out, seeking, seeking, seeking.

"Baby!"

Again and again she kissed him, driving him wild. But inside her body she could find nothing, feel nothing. It was almost as though he were any man, one of a thousand men, and her lips were doing this because that was what they were paid to do.

"You're crying!"

She didn't want to hurt him, didn't want to let him know. Her own hurt was enough for both of them. She couldn't take this away from him.

"Maybe it's because I—I'm so—happy."

His hands were on her now, finding her, trying to make her body live. She closed her eyes, fighting back the tears, and she clung to him, shaking in false ecstasy.

"Oh, please!" she cried out. "Please!"

But it was no use, it was no good. The hands which moved over her and caressed her body could have been any of a hundred pair of hands. The hands went lower, lower, the pressure of his lips became greater, and still nothing changed. Within her she was cold, as though something priceless had been dissipated, even as though it had never been born.

"Slade!"

"I love you, baby! I love you!"

Later, as he drove toward town, he kept one arm around her, holding her close.

"I meant it," Slade said, gently. "I love you."

The tears were no longer in her eyes but they were buried way down deep, stinging, aching, filling her with pain. He had been good to her, so good, and it had meant nothing to her. It was almost worse than having sold herself. She had given herself to him and she had nothing to show for it.

"You can forget about Kane if you want to," he said. "I'll get by some way."

"No," she said, taking a deep breath. "Let's leave it the way we planned. I'll take care of Mr. Kane."

An she would. If she couldn't return Slade's love, if she couldn't be a whole woman, there was one thing she could do for him. She could make Kane wish he had never heard of All-Channel TV or a place called North Hope. Yes, she could do that. It was the very least she could do.

After this tragic experience with Slade she wouldn't ever feel a thing again.

No, not a thing.

5

On Sunday afternoon Ann took a cab uptown to visit her family. She didn't know why she was going or what would happen after she got there. It was crazy.

"You mind if I make this run for myself?" the cab driver wanted to know.

"I don't care."

"Supper money," the driver explained. "You've gotta eat, don't you?"

"Yes."

The cab driver was wrong. You didn't have to eat. She hadn't eaten all day long. Just the thought of food made her feel ill.

I'm sick, she thought; I'm sick inside. Something's wrong with me. Something terrible and awful is wrong with me.

She wanted to forget about those moments with Slade Martin along the river road and yet, she had to remember them, too. Moments which should have been wonderful, beautiful; moments, now that she recalled them, which had been even less than if she had sold herself.

I'm sick, she thought.

Something's wrong with me.

I'm dying inside.

Dying.

Or already dead.

"You live up here?" the driver wanted to know.

"No. But I used to."

Used to, she thought. That's where she had been born and raised, where she had seen the dirty kids playing in the streets and where she had heard the filthy stories that the girls either repeated or made up.

Corny jokes.

Lousy jokes.

But for some reason she remembered them now; she remembered a lot of things. She recalled looking out of her bedroom window one night and seeing the boy from next door down there in the alley, caught in the rays of the street light, doing what he was doing. The sight had repelled her, but she nevertheless watched him with a curious and awe-filled fascination. She had never seen a boy, not like that, and the thought of being with a boy herself for the first time made her tremble. She hadn't been able to sleep that night, and in the morning she had been late for school.

"I saw a boy last night," she told an older girl the next day. "And he looked funny."

Then she tried her best to tell the girl what he had been doing. The older girl had finally laughed.

"You'd better pull down your shades when you get undressed at night," she told Ann. "You don't want the poor guy to go out of his mind, do you?"

Ann had pulled her shades down every night after that. But a month later there wasn't any need for precaution. The boy next door had been arrested for raping a high school senior and had been sent away to a reform school.

"He didn't have to go and do that," the girl said afterward. "Not on my front porch, where the folks could hear. All he had to do was ask me nice and there wouldn't have been all that trouble."

Just before graduation time the girl had been kicked out of school for taking some students into the movie projection booth over the auditorium and letting them form a line.

Yes, she remembered these things and she remembered others. But she remembered Jerry mostly. Their first time, his clumsiness and his gentleness, and how he had ruined his new sport coat because his sweat made the dye of his shirt run and soak through.

Perhaps that had been love; the first love and the only love she would ever know. Last night had not been love. Last night had been the same as before, the same as it would have been with any man.

She hadn't slept at all, not a bit. She had been awake all night, all morning, thinking, thinking, thinking. She had wanted him so terribly, so desperately, and it hadn't meant a thing. Less than nothing, if that was possible.

The tires of the cab hissed on the pavement, rumbled over the uneven brick patches left by the gas company.

Maybe she was trying to run away from reality, from herself. Maybe none of this since she had left home had been real. Maybe she ought to come back home and live, be satisfied with what she had.

It was the only reason she was making the trip. She either had to find herself now or lose herself forever. Something inside said that, kept telling her that. She was like a man hanging onto the edge of a cliff by his fingertips, a man who struggled to climb back to the safety of the earth. Either she was going back or she was going down.

Down? That was a laugh. How many times had she gone down? Being what "nicer" people referred to as a call girl was going down about as far as you could go. All the way down.

But you could come back, you could change. People did it every day. She had read about prostitutes who had become good wives, good mothers, good people. Perhaps they became good because they understood the bad better than anybody else, because they could see a mistake a mile off before it was made. Perhaps that was why. She didn't know. But somehow she had to find out. She had to find out now, right now, today, or she'd go out of her mind.

Everything had started there, at home. All of it had started there and might end there. Again she didn't know. It wouldn't end unless she found something real; that much she knew. Something real there in the home, something to cling to, something to want beyond anything else.

She could quit her job at All-Channel and she could forget about Slade. She could forget about Slade and Molly and all of the others. She could forget about wanting nice clothes and a nice apartment and stop living like a beautiful fish in a glass bowl. She could move back home, get a job nearby, and pay rent to her parents. In this way, she could salvage something of herself and she could help them as they had helped her. It was right. It was the sensible thing to do. It was what normal people did after they tried to find something and couldn't or after they lost what they did have.

"I don't know this part of town so good," the driver said. "Where do I turn?"

"The next block."

The houses were run down, in need of paint, and even on Sunday the smell of fish lingered in the air. A lot of the people who lived in the area went shopping on Saturday night but stopped in at one of the bars before they made it to the store. By the time they finished drinking the grocery stores were either closed or they were out of money and then, early on Sunday morning, the men would hike down to the river and catch chubs or rock bass or, if the day were cloudy, possibly some catfish.

"This is a rough neighborhood," the driver said, making the turn.

"It only looks that way."

Actually, most of the people who lived in the section were pretty honest and pretty decent. They worked for low wages, that was true, and they had very few really nice things, but the majority tried to live like decent people. They were caught in a web of unfortunate circumstance.

"Which house, girlie?"

"The gray one."

She was surprised to note that her father hadn't painted the green shutters hanging on either side of the windows. Every year he painted the shutters and the trim. Paint the trim and the shutters, he said, and it made the rest of the house look neat and clean.

"Two bucks," the driver said. The meter had been turned off all the way uptown. "Two bucks, if it's all right with you."

The ride was worth about a dollar and a half but she didn't argue. She gave the driver two ones and a fifty cent tip. A couple of kids on the other side of the street gawked at the cab. A cab on the street was a rarity, reserved mostly for funerals, weddings or extreme emergencies. Riding in a cab was like sending a telegram or making a long distance phone call; you only did it when there was nothing left for you to do. If somebody received or made a long distance telephone call, or sent or received a telegram, everyone along the street knew about it in a matter of minutes. When the Norton boy had been killed in the service, and the government had sent a wire of sympathy, half of the neighbors had been crowding into the tiny apartment hardly before the mother had had a chance to break down and cry.

"Here's my card," the cab driver said. "You need another lift and you call me, huh? I won't keep you waiting none."

As soon as the cab drifted down the street she dropped the card by the side of a broken wine bottle and turned toward the house.

The porch, she noticed, also needed painting. That too was unusual. Her father generally painted the porches twice a year, using cheap paint that didn't last long but which looked nice when it was new and fresh.

The oilcloth cover was on the porch swing and as she passed it she saw that the cover was caked with dust. This was even more surprising. Her father and mother liked the swing and they would sit out there for hours in the evening, talking and watching the people move along the street.

She pulled open the screen door and the hinges squealed. That wasn't typical of her father, either, putting up with noisy hinges. Not only that but there was a hole in the screen above the center brace, big enough to shove your arm through.

Inside the house she was assailed by a series of odors that ranged all the way from stale wine to fresh tobacco smoke. She could smell the onions cooking in the kitchen and she could smell the dirt that was deep and thick in the worn hall rug.

"That you, Mrs. Scamper?" Martha Frank's voice drifted from the kitchen. "I'm back here, trying to make a pie out of my imagination."

The Scampers lived next door on the right, and Scamper worked for the railroad as a brakeman. It was said that Scamper had a woman at either end of his run in addition to his wife, and one in the middle. Mrs. Scamper was always trying to borrow flour, or eggs, or something else which she had no intention of returning.

"No, Ma. It's me."

A dead silence filled the house.

"I said it's me, Ma. Ann."

"I heard you."

Her mother came out of the kitchen and stood at the end of the hall. Wearily she pushed a strand of loose hair away from her face and smoothed out the apron with the palms of her hands.

"What are you doing here?"

"It's been a long time," Ann said.

"It could've been longer."

A big emptiness filled Ann. "Aren't you glad to see me?"

Martha Frank merely stared at her daughter. She made no move to go to Ann and Ann made no move to go to her. They merely stood there, staring at each other as though they were strangers from two different worlds.

"Aren't you glad to see me, Ma?" The emptiness got bigger, burning at her insides, driving hot tears up into her eyes.

"'Course I am," her mother said, finally. "But it's what your father will say if he comes in here and finds you. He's apt to say or do almost anything. You don't know him anymore, Ann. He's changed."

"Where is he now?"

"Out in the back yard, digging fish worms. So's he can go fishing. So's we can eat. Isn't that funny, though? Me working in a grocery store and he has to go down to the river to catch our meat."

"But why?"

"Because I charged so much at the grocery store that they won't even let me work on the cash register any more. They put me on the vegetable counter and they said if I don't pay it up out of my pay, a little every week, they'll fire me and sue me for it."

"Oh, Ma!"

Her mother shook her head. "You got no idea what he's been like since you left. None at all. All he can think about is that you're our only child and that you're no good. I don't know. I just don't know. He broods and broods and then he drinks. He don't go to work half of the time and he won't do anything around the house. He just says that the world is crazy and you're no good and that everything's gone wrong. I put up with it and I try to help him but it's beyond me. I used to think there wasn't anything I couldn't do, but this is one thing that I can't. I don't know how to cure him, or fight him, or anything. It's awful."

Ann moved down the hall to her mother. She wanted to put her arms around her mother's shoulders, to kiss the tiredness of her face away, but she did neither. She remembered, with a strange touch of guilt, that her mother had never been very affectionate. Just a peck with her lips on the cheek, a touch of her hands, and that was all. She had never kissed her mother on the mouth. She had never thought about it much before and it was odd that it should seem so important now.

"I want to help," Ann said.

"There's nothing you can do. There's nothing I can do. He has to do it by himself or it won't be done at all."

"I thought of moving back home."

Worry crept into Martha Frank's eyes.

"Aren't you doing well? Are you out of work?"

"No, I'm not out of work. And I'm doing well. It's only that—"

"Ann, please. No. It would never be all right, not with him the way he is. It would be nothing but fight, fight, fight. It's bad enough this way. I couldn't stand any more."

"But—"

"No, Ann. You don't understand. Your father isn't the man he was when you left. He's bitter, hurt. He wouldn't let you back in here if you came up the steps on your hands and knees. He—he's heard things."

"What things?"

"The boy who was in the car with you that night, the boy that caused all the trouble—what was his name?"

"Eric."

"Well, Eric. He knows a man who works where your father works. A man who isn't very good, who doesn't take care of his family."

"Yes?"

"He told this man—this Eric did—that he went down there with you that night because you wanted him to go. He said you asked him to do what he was doing when your father came up."

"Damn him, he lied!"

Martha Frank nodded. "I think he lied, too. I think he lied—about that. But your father was there and he saw you and—Ann, you don't know how he felt. I don't know. We can't understand. We're women and we know that—that these things happen. But a man doesn't. A man always blames the girl. If a man goes out with a girl and she gets pregnant, to hear him talk, it's her fault. Men don't like to take that kind of blame. Men are stupid."

Her mother raved on and on. Her father was drinking, drinking all the time, wine and beer, and the only wrong thing he hadn't done so far was hit his wife. But, Martha said, one of these days he would get around to that.

"One of these days he'll clip me good," she said. "I know he will. I feel it. He blames me because of what you did. And he'll never stop blaming me. One of these times when he's drinking he's just going to haul off. I'll leave him after that, Ann. I will. I couldn't stand him doing a thing like that to me."

The house, everything, sickened Ann. This was her fault, every bit of it. Once they had been happy, nice people, and then she had let her body run wild. In that second she hated her body. She hated herself, inside and out. The hate was there, burning, because she had done something and now, no matter what she did, she couldn't change it.

"I'm sorry, Ma."

"I'm sorry, too. I'm sorry for your father and for you and for me and for all of us." She laughed a little, nervously, and her voice thickened. "But it don't do no good to be sorry, Ann. Being sorry don't help. All you can do is try to do right and let it go at that."

"Ma," Ann said, suddenly, "how much do you owe that grocery store where you work?"

"Almost sixty dollars. I make forty dollars a week and they want me to pay back ten of it. It'll take me six weeks that way and in the meantime we have to—"

"Ma," Ann said. "Ma, I'll give you the money." She opened her purse and fumbled inside. She had seventy-two dollars but, she thought viciously, she could always get more just by calling Molly. "Ma, I'll give you the money and then you can straighten it up. And I'll send you some every week. I honestly will."

Martha Frank's hand remained at her sides.

"You have to live, too, Ann."

"That's all right. I'm doing well."

"You must be."

"I make over a hundred dollars a week," Ann lied.

"You do!"

"I'm a typist."

"That's a lot of money for a typist, isn't it?"

"It is for a regular typist. But I'm a special typist, they call it. I type important things."

"I see. Sort of secret."

"Sort of."

"Well." Martha Frank rubbed her hands against her apron again and slowly patted the sides of her face. "Well," she said.

"Here, Ma."

"I oughtn't to take it. He'd raise the Old Ned if he knew."

"He doesn't have to know. And I could send you the money each week to the store. He won't know where it comes from and if he drinks the way you say he does he won't care."

"I guess you could, at that."

"Here, Ma."

Reluctantly, her mother accepted the money.

"What's the name of the store?"

"Goldie's Market. It's down on the corner."

"Beechurst and Waymart?"

"Yes."

"I'll send it there, then."

"You're a good girl," her mother said. "An awful good girl." Anger crowded her words together. "Dam him, anyway, if he'd only—"

"Never mind, Ma. It's all right."

"But you don't know how I feel. You're my daughter."

"I know," Ann said, softly. "Because I am your daughter."

She stayed only a few minutes after that. There was no sense to hanging around and feeling sorry about things or getting into a fight with her father. No good could come of it. Just misery. And she had enough of that. Her mother had enough of it, too. She could tell that when her mother walked with her to the front door, the money still clutched in between her fingers, her face drawn in tight lines that spoke of an inner, pressing agony.

"I'll call you at the store sometime," Ann said, fingering the hole in the screen door. "Maybe we can meet downtown sometime."

"I couldn't get away," her mother replied, shaking her head. "All I do is run to the store, work and come back home to see about your father."

Ann shrugged. "I'll send the money to the store. Every week. Every week I'll send it, Ma."

"You're a good girl," Mrs. Frank said.

Ann said nothing. She pushed the screen door open and stepped outside. "Goodbye, Ma."

"Goodbye, Ann. I'm—sorry."

As she walked down the steps she felt like crying. It was almost as though she had left something behind, something slightly tarnished but good, something that she was exchanging for even less than she had had before.

She walked to the corner and waited hopefully for a cab. To get a bus you had to walk ten blocks East and they were long blocks. She didn't feel like walking. She felt weak in the knees and for some reason even her feet ached. Plainly, she felt miserable.

A cab came along but it was loaded with passengers and it kept right on going. The tires made a funny, hollow sound on the brick. Another cab moved down the street but that, too, had passengers and it continued to roll downtown.

Damn, she thought. Damn! She had been a fool to come out here, to even think that she could pick up the pieces again. You could never pick them up. You smashed something and it stayed smashed. Oh, you could put it together with glue but it wouldn't stand up. It would always fall apart.

She felt better about things, though. She wasn't turning her back on anything. And she could help her mother. She could send money to her every week. That would be something good, something decent. She could cling to that when there wasn't anything else.

A car slid to a stop at the curb and the driver leaned across the seat toward her.

"Hello, baby," he said, smiling. "You going somewhere?"

It was Eric.

"Hello, Eric."

"You going somewhere?" he asked again.

"Downtown. To the North Shore."

He whistled. "Getting exclusive, huh?"

"Well, I live there."

"Get in."

He pushed the door open and she hesitated only a moment. There was a chance, just a chance that she could reason with him. If he'd tell the truth about that night, if he'd be honest about it, why . . .

"Thanks, Eric," she said, smiling. "I'm glad you came along."

She got in and slammed the door and he put the car in gear. The bricks rumbled underneath as the car shot forward. At the next intersection he turned left instead of continuing on down the boulevard.

The road left, she knew, led up into the mountains and to the resort colony at Crystal Lake. It was in the opposite direction from the North Shore along the river front.

"You're going wrong," she told him.

He glanced at her and grinned. "You're the one who's wrong," he said. "I'm doing this the right way. And for nothing."

Ann wondered what he meant.

6

Crystal Lake was one of those places maintained by the rich and patronized by the poor. The rich had big houses and fancy boats and long, low cars and the poor sneaked in along the smooth roads, crept into the bushes or behind the trees and did what the rich did in fancy bedrooms. Or maybe the rich, upon occasion, used the bushes, too. Nobody seemed to know and nobody seemed to care. Everybody got what they wanted when they went to Crystal Lake and that was the important thing.

"Eric," Ann said, provoked with herself now for having gotten into the car with him, "why are you driving up here?"

"Two reasons. And you get two guesses."

"To talk?"

"That's one of them."

"It better be the only one," she said. She wouldn't do anything else if he was the last man in the world and she was dying with the need of it. She still remembered that night along the river road and the shame she had felt when that light had burst into her eyes. She recalled having looked down, trying to shield her eyes, seeing the whiteness of her own thighs, the brownness of his hands, poised there. Then the hands had moved, not caring about the light or anything, and he had cursed. "And, anyway, I wanted to talk to you," she added. "I'm glad you came along, Eric. I really am."

The woods slid by on either side. Up ahead Crystal Lake looked pale and blue in the late afternoon sun.

"I ain't seen you in a long time," Eric said. "Not to talk to, anyway."

"No, not since that night."

"Boy, that was hell, wasn't it?"

"It sure was," Ann agreed.

"Like getting hiccups in the middle of class graduation."

Ann glanced at him. Something inside her during that second hated Eric. Lowen, wasn't that his last name? Yes. Lowen. Well, she hated him regardless what his name was.

"Eric," she said, slowly, "I have to talk to you."

"Yeah?"

"You know a man who works with my father, don't you?"

"I didn't know he was working much any more."

"Well, when he is working."

Eric nodded and slowed the car as they approached the lake. They drifted down a slight hill and when they got to the bottom he took a grassy wood road to the right. She had the feeling, from the way he drove, that he had been there before. About fifty yards in he brought the car to a halt. They were completely shielded from view by anyone on the lake or on the shore road.

"That must be Craver," he said. "Will Craver. He lives a couple of houses away from where I live. Young guy, maybe thirty. Nice fellow only he drinks like a fool." Eric laughed and played with the ignition key. "My old man blames him for getting me started. But the old man blames him wrong. I got my start in the cellar, on a jug of dandelion wine. You ever have homemade wine?"

"No."

"I've got a bottle of blackberry under the seat. It's good."

"I don't want any."

Erich reached for a cigarette and lit one. She could smell the sulphur from the match and it wasn't any worse than his sweat. She could also smell the heat that washed out of the woods and filled the car. She began to wish that she hadn't come.

"You told this man Craver something about me. And he told my father. Something that wasn't true."

"I did?"

"Yes. You told him I wanted to go down to the river road with you that night, Eric. That's not true and you know it isn't. It makes me sound like a—well—"

"Go on."

"You know. I don't have to say it."

"You hadn't ought to mind saying it."

Ann's eyes flashed. "Just what do you mean by that?"

"You know what I mean." He bent down, reached back under the seat and brought forth the bottle of wine. It was almost full. He removed the cork and took a long drink. "I gotta draw you pictures? Cripes!"

From the direction of the lake she heard a shout and then laughter. Somebody, she thought bitterly, was having a good time. Why did things have to be like this for her?

"It was just one of those things, Eric," she said, patiently. "It just happened. You didn't have to exaggerate. It happened and that was enough."

He took another drink from the wine bottle.

"Sure you don't want some?"

"No."

"Well, suit yourself."

"I am."

"I didn't exaggerate none."

"Ma says you did. She says you told this man that I wanted you to take me down there."

"Well, didn't you?"

"No. I just didn't argue with you, that's all. But I didn't ask."

Eric slouched down in the seat and placed the bottle between them.

"You knew what you were doing," he said. "You asked for just what you got."

"Eric!"

"What'd we do that night? Before we went down to the river road? You remember?"

She tried to but she couldn't. She could recall getting in his car, the same one in which she was now sitting, and going somewhere with him, first.

"We stopped at the drive-in."

She nodded.

"Yes," she said. "I remember."

"I don't know what the picture was, though. Do you?"

"No."

"I wouldn't think so. You were pretty hot that night. If it hadn't been for those people next to us and the windows being down we wouldn't have waited until we got to the damned river road."

She looked at him, briefly, and then away. He was rotten inside; filthy. Even though she was what she was—and he had no way of knowing that—she was entitled to some respect.

"You ruined everything for me at home," she told him. "You and your big mouth. You told this man who works with my father and the man told my father. I didn't even dare see him today. That's how bad it is."

"I'm sorry," Eric said, but he didn't sound sorry. "I got to drinking one night and I shot my mouth off. Somehow, Craver got to talking about it, wanting to know if I'd made any time with you and if you were any good. And I said yes, I'd made my time with you and that you were plenty good." He reached for the bottle, raised it and held it poised inches away from his mouth. "Hell, you know how guys are. You get a few drinks and you get to talking. You say things that aren't so, or things that you don't mean, but you don't do it to cause any trouble. Craver's got a big mouth. He must've gotten tanked and then blabbed to your old man."

"Nothing happened that night," Ann reminded Eric. "It almost did, but it didn't. I don't have to tell you that."

Eric nodded as he drank from the bottle.

"That light did it," he said. "That was just like getting doused with cold water in the middle of the winter."

"Then you should have told the truth."

"What's the difference whether I told the truth or not? Your old man sure as hell thought I'd had my fun. And I was—until he came along. He ruined it, that's all." Eric made a face. "Jeeze, to hear you talk you'd think everything was a big surprise to you. That's just a fat lie. Remember what happened while we was watching the movie? You remember that?"

"Stop talking about it."

"But you said you wanted to talk."

"Not about that. About something else."

"What, for instance?"

"You started some of this trouble, Eric. You told Craver these things and then he told my father. Now I want you to tell him the truth. I want you to tell him that I was just a kid and that I was mixed-up and that you—well, that you didn't, that's all. Maybe this Craver will tell my father and then he won't be so sore any more."

"I could tell him about this afternoon," Eric offered.

"This afternoon doesn't mean anything."

"Not yet. But it will. It will, baby. You see if it don't."

Once more she looked at him. There was a hardness about his mouth, almost a sneer, that lifted into his dark eyes. Why hadn't she noticed this before? She once thought him—no, she hadn't, either. She hadn't thought of him as anything except what he was. A slob. A slob who didn't know when to keep his mouth shut.

"Don't get your hopes up," she said, reverting to the fierceness of the girls in Molly's house. "This afternoon is just a waste of time for you, Eric."

"Is it? I don't think so."

"Well, I know differently."

He drank some more of the wine. "We'll see how much you know," he said. Then, turning to smile at her, "Do you know where River Street is?"

"Yes, I know where it is."

"You're honest about that, anyway." He held the bottle in both hands, rolling it from side to side and sloshing the red liquid around. The wine made a strange, hollow sound, like water spilling over a dam and landing on a cave of rocks. "What about Molly Ford? Do you know Molly Ford?"

Something cold and sharp filled her stomach. The sharpness, the pain, crept up her throat and held her tongue almost rigid.

"Molly Ford!"

"Yeah," Eric drawled. "Redlight Molly, that's what they call her. Redlight Molly, who controls the best string of girls in the county."

She closed her eyes, trying to fight down the feeling inside. He knew something, that much was obvious. He wasn't just guessing. He knew something.

She was afraid to think about what it might be.

"Why, no, I—"

"Don't lie, Ann."

"I'm not lying," she flung at him.

"You are lying, baby. I know. I saw you there."

How long, she suddenly wondered, had he been looking for her on the streets, hunting her? And she had made it so easy for him. She'd just stood there on the corner, waiting for a cab, and when he'd come along she'd gotten into the car with him.

She opened her pocketbook and reached for the package of cigarettes.

Ann was not afraid, not at all. This was too familiar. She smiled a little as she noted that her hands did not tremble. She lit the cigarette and inhaled the smoke. The smoke went down easily, filling her lungs.

She knew what he wanted, and that was no different from what most men wanted. It wasn't at all the same as it had been with Slade Martin. With Slade she had been looking for something wonderful and she hadn't found it. Her body, she thought now, had dried up in Slade's arms. She had tried so hard, so desperately, and there had only been the emptiness of defeat. At home she had tried again, seeking to capture something elusive and vague, but she had failed that time, too. Both had seemed important at the time, vitally important, but as she sat beside Eric now and thought about them it was almost as though they hadn't happened at all. She was what she was and there was no use trying to change it. Even given the opportunity, she suspected she might not want to change it.

"I don't believe you," she told Eric, blowing a ribbon of smoke out of the window. "I think you're the one who's lying. I don't think you've ever been to Molly's and you certainly didn't see me there if you were."

"I was at Molly's, all right," he insisted.

"Maybe you were. But you didn't see me."

"And I saw you."

"Go on."

He found the cork and jammed it in the neck of the bottle. He smiled, a little and held the wine bottle up to the light.

"You drink too much for your age," Ann said.

In disgust he shoved the bottle back under the seat.

"I'm nineteen," he said.

"Big deal. I'll send you a card."

"Now you're getting nasty."

"Well, I don't like being up here with you. And I don't like you, Eric. You might as well know that."

"I don't care whether you do or not," he said. He turned toward her and placed his right arm over the back of the seat. "I saw you down at Molly's," he said. "I saw you come in and I saw you go out."

"You're lying, Eric."

"No, I'm not lying. It was last year, just before Christmas. Kidder Altman—you don't know him, I don't guess. His first name is Marv but we call him Kidder, because he's always horsing around. He lives up on Lincoln Place, not near the railroad tracks but way up on the hill. His old man has lots of dough and he had this Christmas club check so we went out to jazz up the town."

"This is all very interesting," Ann said. "Someday, when you have the time, you should sit down and write a book about it."

"You don't have to be so snotty. You got nothin' to be snotty about. Nothin'!"

"All right."

"There were three of us that night and we rode around, drinking a little here and there and having a ball. Then we went down to Molly's. You know how it is in Molly's."

"You're telling it," she reminded him.

"Sure. I'm telling it. I've been waiting months just to tell you what I know."

"I can bet."

"Like I say, we went down to Molly's. We went inside and after you go inside there's a big room on the right, off the hall, where the girls come down and you look at them and you make up our mind which one you want. There were four girls there that night, in the room, and they were all sort of nice. I'd settled on a blonde, a little thing that kept dragging her dress up over her hips, teasing, when I looked out into the hall and I saw you come in. You went straight back, past the opening, and you were gone a couple of minutes. Then you came out again, talking to Molly this time, and she must have walked to the front door with you. Anyway, when Molly came into the room I went up to her and I said how much and she said you weren't house stuff. I had a few bucks on me and Kidder had this bundle so I asked her again how much. She said a hundred dollars, maybe a little more, and that I had to supply the hotel room. But she said I couldn't that night because you'd just gone out on a call and that you'd be busy." Eric paused.

"That's when I saw you in Molly's. That how I saw you in Molly's, baby. You ain't going to lie now and say that you weren't there, are you."

She could have told Eric to go to hell, that he was mistaken, but the fact that she was worth a hundred dollars or more, and that he'd never seen that much money at one time in his whole life gave her a superior feeling. She was a protsie, maybe, a girl who sold herself for the green stuff, but she was a lot better than he was any day of the week.

"So where does that leave you?" she wanted to know. "You haven't got any hundred dollars."

"It leaves me right here with you."

"A lot of good it's doing you."

His arm moved down the seat and rested on her shoulder.

"I've got news for you," he said. "It's going to do me plenty of good. I'm going to get my ashes hauled but not for no hundred bucks. I'm going to get them hauled for free."

Ann hated to hear a man talk like that. The words and what they implied brought everything out into the open. And she didn't want things in the open. She wanted them in the dark, where she couldn't see them, where she could forget they ever existed.

"Shut up," she said.

"No, not me. You. You shut up, baby. You listen to me like you never listened before. I could have told Craver about this and he'd have told your old man, or I could have gone to your old man and told him myself. I could have told your old man, right out, that you're even out selling. I could have told either one of them that, but I didn't. I didn't tell anybody. I just kept it to myself, even from the guys I was with that night, and I made up my mind that some day I would collect." He hesitated and the tips of his fingers traced a little line along one of her shoulders, going down, stopping just at the top of her blouse. "And today is the day."

"You must be out of your mind," she said, tightly.

"No, you're the one who's crazy if you think you can turn me down and get away with it. Hell, you refuse me and I'll go right to your old man. You can bet your last pair of panties on that."

She reached up and pushed his hand away.

"My father already thinks the worst of me." she said. "A little more won't make it any better or any worse."

"What about your mother?"

His hand returned to the top of her blouse and this time she didn't push his hand away. She didn't want her mother to know the truth. Her mother, for some reason, still believed in her; it was the one thing that she couldn't destroy.

"What are you after, Eric?" It was a silly question, a stupid question, but it was the only one she could think of at the moment.

"You," he said and his hand, going lower, added emphasis to his statement.

She was numb.

"Just this once?"

"Only once."

"You promise?"

"I promise."

He was lying. She knew that he was lying.

Some girls, she knew, kept men for their own individual pleasure. They paid the men's rent, bought them clothes, and had their fun with them when they were off duty. It gave them a feeling of superiority they could find no other way, a feeling of ownership; it provided one small part to their lives which they could control. Others were not so lucky. Others were blackmailed for money, for sex, for a thousand and one different reasons. So far, she had been lucky. She had been part of none of this.

But now she was.

Now there was a man who held something over her, a man who could do her harm. It was a terrible, helpless feeling but one which could get only more terrible and helpless if she refused to face it.

"Where?" she wanted to know.

"Here. Why do you think I drove up here to the lake?"

"In the open?"

"It isn't open. There're trees and bushes all around. Nobody can see in here."

"How do you know?"

"I tried it once."

"Peeking?"

"Not exactly. There was this girl I was going with and she came up here with another guy. I tried to watch them but I couldn't. You can't see a thing from the road or the lake. You have to get close and if you get close you make a lot of noise coming through the woods. Nobody can bother us here."

"What about the girl?"

"She got herself pregnant." His fingers fumbled with the top of Ann's blouse. "I saw her the other day and she's as big as a house."

"Married?"

"Married! Who'd want to marry that? She don't even know herself who the father is."

"Maybe you are."

"Not me. I was careful with her. Her old man's on the police force." Eric laughed. "Can you imagine that? Her old man's on the police force and while he's running around telling other kids to break it up his own daughter's out getting herself fixed up."

"It isn't very funny."

"You ought to know," Eric said. "You've been exposed enough." His hand moved slightly down. Her glance lowered and she saw his hand shake. "Exposed—that's a good word, baby. I want to see you exposed all the way down."

She sighed and gently pushed his hand away. She could fight and argue with him but it would only prolong the situation. And she didn't want to prolong it. Now that she knew what she had to do she wanted to do it and get it over with. The quicker he had his fun the quicker she could get back to town and forget about him.

"How old are you, Eric?" She was smiling at him now, contemptuously, trying to make him feel small and mean "Nineteen?"

"Going on twenty."

"Well, be prepared to grow up," she said. "And in a hurry."

He watched her with a small smile on his face.

"Close your eyes," she said.

He closed his eyes.

"Keep them closed."

In a few moments she said. "Now you can look."

He opened his eyes. His lips twisted, relaxed, then twisted again.

"Oh, cripes!" he whispered.

Everything went wrong after that. Everything. Nothing went the way she had planned it.

"You're beautiful," he said, as his lips sought her. "I never knew a girl could be so beautiful!"

"Eric!"

"Most girls aren't pretty without their clothes on." His voice was muffled, far away. "But you are. You are!"

And then things really went wrong.

She had planned on making him feel beneath her, but the pressure of his mouth on her lips began to lift her, lift her. She felt herself going up and up and up and then in a surging moment of passion of being flung down.

"Eric!"

His lips had the fire of hot, tormenting flames, the darting tip of his tongue the wonderful, wonderful promises of the unknown.

"Oh, Eric!"

And now her arms were around his neck, holding him tight. Her whole body sought to hold him tight. She was sharply aware of the touch of his hands, of their secret explorations, and every movement of them caressed a dormant, yearning need that flowered within her.

"You're wild!" he whispered. "Wild!"

And then, the way a ship would be torn loose from its moorings in the midst of a furious, raging storm, she surrendered to him. In a moment mixed with violence and tenderness she belonged to him completely, finally and gloriously. She accepted his love, all of his love, asking for more, receiving more, begging for more.

Later, she pulled his head down and kissed him hard on the mouth.

"Love me?" she wanted to know.

"I'm crazy about you," he confessed, his lips moving against her mouth. "Crazy about you."

"Would you do anything for me?"

"Anything!"

"You're sweet," she murmured.

"It's a funny world," he said. "A few minutes ago I think you hated me."

"I think I did, too."

"But you don't now?"

"You know better than that."

He kissed her and held her very close.

"Can I see you again, Ann?"

"You know you can."

"Whenever I want to?"

"Whenever we can."

"What do you mean by that?"

"I don't know," she replied. "I'm not sure."

But she knew. She was a prostitute and she had found her man. Maybe she didn't love him the way they wrote about love in books, but she loved him—and for a deeper and more necessary reason. He could awaken in her the fire that burned, the fire that other men extinguished. He could fan the flames which would drive her out of her mind if they should die.

"I'll call you," he said as he started the car. "I'll call you every day until you let me see you again."

She said nothing as they drove toward town. There was nothing to say. She had found one man who belonged to her.

Right or wrong, it was a lot better than having no one, better than being alone.

7

Slade was sick of the staff meeting even before it started. As usual, Willouby was late—probably he was arguing with somebody about his golf game—and Thomas from Engineering had called to say that he would be delayed a few minutes because of some urgent correspondence. The only one who had been on time had been scheduled in his office for eleven. Fifteen Jefferies, all out for coffee. Slade couldn't stand him. Jefferies was an old woman who thought that Promotion was only slightly less important than the Congress of the United States.

"Damn," Slade said. He looked at the clock on his desk, the one that was supposed to resemble the master's wheel on a ship. It was eleven-fifteen and the meeting had been scheduled in his office for eleven. Fifteen minutes shot and nothing done. The whole morning shot and nothing done. "Damn," he said again.

Monday, he thought, was always a bad day anyway. Monday was the day when you remembered the drinks you'd had over the weekend, trying to fit all of the pieces of the puzzle together.

He thought about that new girl, the one from Promotion, and then he grinned.

She had been the best.

The very best.

You could take Betty and those girls from Molly's, or any of the others he had known, shake them up in a bag and they'd all come out with the same emotions. False, maybe desperate and responsive for an instant, but false, anyhow. But not that Ann Frank. Not her. She had it. She had it plenty, with enough left over for two dames.

The intercom hummed and he reached for the switch.

"Yeah, Betty."

"Mr. Jefferies just called and he wanted to know if you said three containers of coffee, or four."

"I told him five. One for you."

"Thank you, Slade."

"You're welcome."

He cut off the intercom and he began to curse. That was the trouble with this place—nobody had sense enough to make an independent decision. When it got so bad that a guy couldn't make up his mind about how much coffee to buy it was rough.

To hell with them, he thought; to hell with the crazy, crazy fools. No, he thought again, not to hell with them. At three hundred bucks a week, plus over-rides—that last was a laugh—you couldn't afford to say to hell with anybody. Three hundred bucks a week was a lot of money, fifteen grand-plus per year, and fifteen grand could buy a lot of clothes, a new car and a lot of women. It could buy a raft of all three and more besides.

He looked at his watch. Eleven-twenty. Eleven-twenty and, as they said in Advertising, all was well.

What was he griping about? So everybody was late, the entire thing was screwed up. So what? So he had to pull the whole convention out of the fire by himself, that was so what. He had to do it or there wouldn't be any chestnuts left.

He was sorry now that he had asked Ann Frank about trying to put the pressure on that guy Kane. He might better have called Molly and hired a call girl to take Kane to bed. It was just possible that Kane would sign more orders flat on his face than he would standing up straight. But it was too late to make any such changes. He had asked Ann and some of the other girls and the whole thing was set. He had to ride with it.

He lit a cigarette and thought about that Ann Frank again. Man, she had been something! Pure sex. Pure, simple, direct sex. And passion. That was the most important thing—well, one of the most important—that passion business.

Slade started to sweat. Maybe he was falling in love. Maybe that was it. He had never felt this way about a girl before.

Eleven twenty-five.

Well, to hell with them.

He closed his eyes and tried to think about it. First he thought about how it would be to have her every night, to share the same bed with her, and that part of it was fine. Then he thought about what went beyond that—a house, children, bills, responsibilities. Strangely enough, even that didn't seem frightening or so bad. When he thought of these things he remembered her skin, how smooth and soft it was, the hungry movement of her lips under the pressure of his mouth. He started to fill up inside, almost choking, and he knew that he had to have her again and again. He thought if he could have her he wouldn't care about anything else.

It was a terrible driving, haunting force. It was something that was in his blood, way down deep, and he just couldn't shake it. Why, all he had to do was think about her, and . . .

The door opened and Jefferies came in, carrying a brown bag that was wet from spilled coffee.

"Nobody here yet, Slade?"

"No, not yet. Sit down."

Jefferies was a young man in his middle twenties. He was college stuff, out of Cornell, and he looked like a college boy. His bow tie, very conservative and subdued, was just as right as the cut of his coat and the fit of the trousers over his long legs. He sat down.

"You give Betty any coffee?" Slade wanted to know.

"She said one was for her."

"That's right."

Slade stared at the paper bag but made no move to open it. He liked to talk when he drank coffee and there was nothing to talk to Jefferies about. Jefferies wasn't interested in Sales particularly and all Slade had to do was mention Promotion and he'd be up to his neck in theory for hours.

"The old man's late," Jefferies said.

Nobody called Willouby the old man except some of the newer department heads, such as Jefferies and a couple of the others.

"How come Advertising wasn't counted in on this confab?" Jefferies inquired. "I was talking to Sloane on the way up, and he felt pretty hurt."

"Advertising's shot its bolt," Slade said. "They've got nothing to do with this."

"Maybe some heads are going to roll."

"Maybe."

There wasn't much chance of that happening, not at this late date, but if it made Jefferies happy to speculate about it that was all right with Slade. Slade had been around Willouby long enough to know how people got fired at All-Channel. Accounting put a pink slip in the pay envelope and then Willouby ran like a thief for the golf course. Willouby claimed he always shot in the low nineties whenever he fired anybody so he seldom took such a bold step. Willouby was a par shooter, coming in a couple under par sometimes, and he liked to keep his game that way.

The door opened again and Thomas entered. Thomas was in his forties, with a touch of gray in his hair, and he always went around with his shirtsleeves rolled up. Slade liked Thomas. He was down to earth and regular though he was one of the best engineers in the business.

"Ah, coffee," he said, opening the paper bag. "Didn't have time for it this morning at home. Would've missed the train."

Thomas worked late every night and he took the last train home. He lived at Croton, about twelve miles up the valley, and since his wife insisted she needed the car all the time, he rode the Erie. His older daughter, Ellen, also drove, and the year before she'd taken the car out of the garage once too often. She'd started out with a neighborhood boy for the beach only they hadn't gone to the beach. They'd driven up into the mountains and the neighborhood boy had given her something she hadn't known about until a couple of months later. Then it had been too late—the boy and his parents had moved out to St. Louis—and now the girl was just hanging around the house waiting for her kid to be born.

"I was up half the night," Thomas explained, yawning, sitting on the edge of Slade's desk, swinging one foot back and forth. "With Ellen. That poor kid gets so sick sometimes that I swear she's going to die."

"Maybe she'll lose the baby," Slade said.

"You think so?"

Slade shrugged. "How do I know? But you can't be sick all of the time, the way she is, and keep a thing like that inside of you."

"It's a hell of a thing to say," Thomas said, "but it might be better if she lost it."

Jefferies nodded. "How old is your daughter?"

"Eighteen, going on nineteen."

"And the father?"

"Sixteen. Sixteen. Just a kid. If he'd been older I'd have made him marry her."

"Sixteen," Slade repeated. "Old enough, it looks."

Thomas drank his coffee and said nothing. Jefferies crossed his legs, again adjusting the crease in his pants, and looked uncomfortable.

"You've got the darndest way of saying what you think," Jefferies told Slade.

"I make it short and to the point."

"I guess you do."

Eleven-thirty. Thomas finished his coffee, wadded the container into a ball and slammed it into Slade's wastebasket. Jefferies crossed and uncrossed his legs and looked bored.

"Well, hell," Thomas said, "Willouby must be trying to shoot down a duck with a golf ball. I've known him to be late before but not this late."

"He's the boss," Slade said.

"And he don't let you forget it. He don't let you breathe around here unless he pushes a button first."

"Nuts to him," Slade said, with feeling.

Ten minutes later Willouby arrived. He didn't look as though he'd been within ten miles of a golf course. He wore a dark blue business suit and his diamond-studded cuff links sparkled.

"Well, gentlemen," he said, "are we ready?"

Slade cocked one eye at the clock.

"I've been ready for forty-five minutes," Slade said, drily. "The world could have been destroyed in that time."

Willouby ignored the remark and pulled a chair up close to Slade's desk. Jefferies did the same thing with his chair, getting as close to Willouby as he dared. Thomas stayed right where he was, foot still dangling.

"I made two stops," Willouby said, "one at the hotel and the other at the bank. I'll tell you about the hotel first. It's more pleasant." His eyes found Slade's face. "There are nearly four hundred dealers and distributors registered at the hotel."

"The hotel told me three hundred and ten," Slade said.

"Well."

"There's a difference. A big difference." He arose from his chair and walked to the window, not turning as he spoke. "Almost twenty-five percent. That's the trouble around here. Everybody uses round figures and they always use the next highest round figure."

"All right," Willouby admitted a little impatiently. "So it isn't four hundred. It's closer to three hundred. But that's pretty good."

"Out of twelve hundred potential?"

"What?"

"That's the number we mail to every month. Twelve hundred dealers and distributors, plus how many small ones I don't know. Last year we had a little over five hundred here, the year before that seven hundred. This year we've got three. It means we drop two hundred a year. Next year we'll have a hundred and the year after that—nobody. So it isn't good. It's lousy. Know what I mean?"

"You don't have to remind me about it all the time," Cyrus Willouby said. "Can't you let me feel good once in a while?"

Slade swung around. "That's one of the troubles," he said. "You feel good too much of the time. You feel good when you're on the golf course and you feel good when you're drinking whizzers. You even feel good when we aren't doing any business. I don't get it. I swear to hell I don't."

"I have a right to do some of the things around here," Willouby protested. "I'm the boss. Or have you forgotten?"

Slade could see the look of fear in Jefferies' eyes. He wanted to laugh. What Jefferies had learned about human beings in college you could stick in a thimble and lose. Thomas, however, was smiling. He seemed happy to find that somebody had the guts to stick it into Willouby.

"I don't care if you're the boss or not," Slade said. "And I don't care whether you like what I say or not. This is your business but it is also my job. If I do my job good you're going to have a business. If I don't do my job good you aren't going to have any business. It's as simple as that."

"Go on," Willouby said, restraining his temper.

"You said you were at the bank. What did the bank tell you, Cyrus?"

"That was personal."

"Like so much it was personal. Nothing is personal. When what you do affects somebody else it's not—"

"Look here, Slade, if you think—"

"—personal. It becomes part of the great big pot, a part of the heap. That's why I asked for this conference, why I wanted to get everybody together. We've got to know where we're going with this convention and how we're going to get there."

"I agree on that," Willouby said.

"I'm glad you do, but it wouldn't change it any if you didn't." Slade walked back and forth, like a hungry bear seeking a meal. "Here's how she shapes up. Tonight we have the dinner, to get the thing rolling. Cyrus, you give the opening speech, welcoming everybody to the show."

"I've got it worked up. I did it yesterday morning. My wife even helped me with it. She had a pretty good joke, too, and I wrote it down. It goes something like—"

"Keep it short," Slade said. "The speech, I mean. The joke is okay, as long as it's a little dirty. Get them in the mood of it. Make them accept you and All-Channel and make them happy. Mood is important. If you don't think you can do it, I'll do it."

"What makes you better than me?" Willouby wanted to know.

"All right, then, you do it. But remember what I said. Tell them at the hotel to make the cocktails a little strong and this will open the gates for you more than you can imagine. Thomas?"

"Yeah, Slade?"

"You follow Mr. Willouby. We didn't use you last year but we're using you this year. Bear down on the chassis. Give it to them in plain, direct language and let them know we've got a better set than anybody else. Don't invite questions; they'll jump all over you about self-tuning if you do. Cover the topic yourself. Get technical on this one so they don't know what you're talking about. Use electronic phrases they've never heard of but make them think that self-tuning is just a gimmick, that it's a trouble maker and that it isn't practical. Tell them everything you can that's wrong about self-tuning. Make it complicated. Make them wish to hell they'd never thought of buying a set with it on. Then—and don't forget this—cap it off by making self-tuning optional on all our sets."

Thomas stopped swinging his leg.

"But we don't have it," he said.

"So what if we don't have it? They won't want it, anyway. And, if they do, we'll back order it. You could turn out such a device, couldn't you?"

"Why, yes, I guess we could."

"I don't like cutting corners," Willouby broke in. "I don't like selling something that we haven't got."

Slade's laugh lacked any trace of humor. "You want sales, don't you?"

"Naturally, I want sales."

"So stop pussyfooting after them like a mouse being chased by a cat. Go after them like a dog after a coon. Tree the bastards the first chance you get."

"I like that expression," Jefferies said, smiling brightly. "Tree them. That's what we have to do. Tree them."

Slade frowned. He just saw four years of college being wasted on Jefferies. A fellow could be a yes-man without any education at all.

"What do I do?" Jefferies wanted to know. Now that he had found his voice he wouldn't want to shut up for an hour.

"You don't do anything," Slade said. He turned to Willouby. "You made a suggestion the other day that I'm following. Jefferies has some pretty girls in Promotion and I'm pulling every one of them out of there to mix with the dealers."

"Good idea," Willouby said.

"I'm using that cute little blonde, that Ann Frank, on Kane. I've got an idea that she can handle him. If she can and we can get a good order from Kane we'll be in."

"Good idea," Willouby said again.

Jefferies coughed. "I don't know what I'm doing here if there isn't anything I—"

"Here's what you do," Slade said. "You get a photographer down there to the convention and have him cover it day and night. Get as many shots as you can of the girls and the fellows milling around. And get the sets in the background. Don't have them too prominent because they don't look good enough."

"It'll be expensive," Jefferies said.

"Look," Slade asked him, impatiently, "did I ask you if it would cost money or not? I know it'll cost money. And what I have in mind will cost a lot more—if this convention goes over. If it's a success well rush out a brochure and shoot it along to the dealers who didn't show. Then, in a month, we'll put on another convention, a real dilly, to suck the other ones in. That will still be before any of the other manufacturers are holding their get-togethers."

"Excellent," Willouby said. "Excellent!"

Thomas nodded and got down from the desk.

"That's clear thinking," Thomas agreed. "You got any further use for me, Slade?"

"No. Just remember what I said about the speech. Drive it into them like nails into a plank."

Thomas opened the door and paused.

"Nails into a plank," he agreed. "Nails into wooden skulls. What's the difference?"

Thomas went out, closing the door after him, and it was suddenly very quiet in the office. Jefferies shuffled his feet and coughed once but Willouby seemed unaware that he even existed.

"You can go, too," Slade said.

"Is that all you wanted me for?"

"All? Promotion is a big job. It's the meat of the business. You know that, Jefferies. I wanted you in on this so you'd know what direction we were heading."

"We're heading right," Willouby said.

Jefferies arose and walked to the door.

"Right down the center, Mr. Willouby," Jefferies said. "Right down the center."

When they were alone Slade sat down behind the desk and looked across at Willouby.

"Now," Slade said, leaning forward on his elbows, "let's stop horsing around. You said you were at the bank. You figure you can come up with enough loot this week to pay me?"

"Let's not joke about it."

"I'm not joking. I'm serious. And you can be serious with me." He reached into his desk and came out with a yellow piece of paper. "I had a Wells and Carter report run on you. It stinks. It's lousy. You haven't got a dime to your name."

Willouby looked uncomfortable. "If this convention—"

"Forget about the convention for a minute, will you? All we've done so far is talk and spend money at the hotel. What if it's a flop? What then?"

"You don't think—"

"I don't think anything. I'm asking you. Supposing it's a failure? Supposing we come out of it with less sales than we could have made with paper work? What then?"

It took Willouby a long time to answer and when he did his voice shook.

"We'd be dead," he admitted. "Dead and broke."

"Then it's all up to Sales?"

"It's up to Sales."

"It's always been up to Sales, hasn't it?"

"Always. There never was a time when I didn't think that, Slade. You know that. I've given you your way because you're smart. I can talk to you. You see things the others don't see."

"I see something you don't see," Slade said, seizing the opening.

"What's that?"

"I see this convention being a success and I see myself moving up into your chair. At five hundred a week. And I see you on some golf course having a ball. That's what I see."

"Slade—"

"Or I see myself going out of this door in the next second. And I see you with a convention on your hands that you wouldn't know what to do with. That's what see."

"You wouldn't!"

"Like hell I wouldn't. Try me."

But Willouby wasn't willing to try him. Willouby was ready to take what he could get and be happy with it.

"You'd make a good general manager," Willouby said. "By George, I think you would."

"At five bills a week?"

"Even at that kind of money."

They discussed it only briefly after that. If the convention was a success and they stayed in business Slade would go up to the top slot. There was no talk of failure. There was no room for failure. The time when they could afford the luxury of failure had long passed.

After Willouby had departed for the golf course Slade stood at the window for a long time, looking down. Dozens of cars. Hundreds of cars. The cars that belonged to the people he had to keep working. The responsibility for them in that instant made him feel small, ineffectual, as though he were facing a mighty hurricane that could destroy him.

He crossed to his desk and asked for the outside line. He lifted the phone and waited for the long, steady buzz. Then he dialed.

His call did no good. Molly didn't have a girl she could spare, no one except that specialist and Slade didn't think that Kane would go for something so obvious.

"I've got a girl who comes in once in a while," Molly said. "Free lance. Just your type. If she shows up I'll give you a ring."

"Thanks."

"You might even want her for yourself."

"Sure. But some other time."

He replaced the phone and returned to the window. Maybe he was wrong and maybe he wasn't. Wednesday would tell. By Wednesday he would know.

He hoped that Ann Frank would be able to handle Kane. So much depended on it. So very, very much depended upon a girl who was so young and innocent.

Yes, indeed.

He was afraid she wouldn't be equal to the job.

8

Mortimer Kane was a big, powerful man in his early fifties. He had iron gray hair and deep blue eyes and, at first glance, was not the kind of a man who stood out in a room full of people. But as time wore on, as the jokes died and the conversations became keener and keener, as sense replaced earlier nonsense, he stood out more and more until, finally, he became the authority, the only worthwhile voice in the room, a leader whom others followed.

When Ann was first introduced to him by Slade she was not impressed. He resembled a banker, or somebody's father, or just an onlooker who had no real interest in what was going on. Or like some of the men who came to Molly's. Yes, like some of the men who came to Molly's; in the final analysis, they were all the same. Flesh and blood. Just a man. It was this, the way she thought about him, that kept her from being unduly afraid of his great height, his reputation, from remembering many of the things others said about him.

"He's a self-made man," Slade had told her. "He's vulgar and rugged but he's honest. His word is better than most people's checks."

Following dinner Monday night, and after meeting Kane only briefly and shaking his huge hand, Ann had spent hours with Slade in a downtown bar, drinking some, but mostly going over the details of the convention, what they were trying to do, what she could expect and, of course, what was expected of her.

"You could have hung around with Kane tonight," he said, "but it wouldn't have done any good. The first night nobody talks much business. They just drink and sit around and get to know each other again. You know, how's things in Walla Walla, old boy, and all that sort of crap. Tomorrow, though, will be different. Tomorrow we'll unveil the sets and then the pressure will be on. That's where you come in, with Kane."

She had thought, knowing Slade, that he would finish off the evening by trying to take her to bed, but he didn't. He was charged up like a car battery with a heavy-duty generator and the only thing he could think of was business.

"We've got to get Kane," he kept saying. "Somehow, we've got to do it. If we don't—oh, hell, don't think about that. I'll handle most of the technical angles with him, Ann, but you turn on the charm and try to keep his mind off our shortcomings. Between the two of us—Ann, we've got to upset him. We've got to!"

They sat side by side, in a booth, and while they drank rye and ginger he covered the basic principles of the All-Channel sets from the assembly line through to the distributor.

"You've got to know something about the business," he said. "You've got to be able to talk intelligently with Kane. That's important."

He gave it to her fast, all of it, and while she realized she would forget much of what he said, especially about the advantages of a welded chassis and things like that, she supposed she would remember enough so that she would be able to discuss the sets with Kane. Besides, if she wore a low-cut dress, one of those form-molding things she had in her closet, why ...

"Kane likes you, Ann. He likes you a lot."

"How can you tell?"

"The way he groped for words when I introduced you. Kane never gropes for words, not unless he's been hitting the bottle—he does that, heavy, on occasion—or if he's excited. And I could see it in the way he looked at you. Only you shouldn't have worn a blouse with all of those frills across the top. It's like—well, putting catsup on mustard. You don't need it. You've got plenty up there all by yourself. Those frills just sort of hide you."

"It was on purpose."

"Really?"

"I never met him before. I wanted to leave an impression. I didn't know how else to do it."

"Well, you did a good job."

"Thank you."

"Ann?"

"What?"

"Look, Ann, I don't mean to exploit your body. I don't mean that at all and I don't want you to think that. You're a nice girl. Stay that way. But we have to get this across to Kane. If we do—I can't tell you how much it means, how much everybody is depending on you."

"I'll do my best," Ann said.

"I know you will."

About midnight he took her home. He was still talking about the convention, about Kane, about the All-Channel sets. It was a jumble of words. She had never seen anybody so excited before, so determined and concerned.

"We've got to do it," he repeated over and over again. "We've got to nail Kane."

He didn't even try to kiss her good night.

She didn't know, as she walked into the foyer of her apartment building, whether she was glad or sorry that he hadn't attempted to kiss her. There was something about Slade Martin that she found frightening and awesome, and yet there was something about him she liked, too. She liked his driving energy, his desire to get ahead, and she respected his interest in the company. He was a good man, a solid man, the kind of a man a woman might marry and never regret it.

She tried to think of herself as being married to Slade, as being his wife. There would be a home, a nice, comfortable house, and the furniture would be modern and good. For some reason, she suspected there would be two bathrooms. Slade had all of the indications of being a two-bathroom man. And there would be a yard with a barbecue grill and where she could stretch out in the sun. Yes, it would be very nice. Nice—up to a point. And then it stopped.

Marriage to Slade would mean sex. And sex, remembering how it had been for them in the car, would mean frustration for her. She would try and try to respond, to become a part of him, and she knew that she would fail. A man like Slade should be able to excite her, but he didn't. Only his good looks excited her, his smooth, masculine exterior, but beyond that there was only a shell of emptiness. No, marriage to Slade would be a fraud, a fraud which she would have endure and create every night she spent in the matrimonial bed. Maybe if she closed her eyes and thought about Eric she could bring about completeness. Maybe. But that was worse than being nothing, worse than being a liar and a cheat. Yes, even worse—say it, say it!—worse than being what she was. It was one thing to sell your body to a man for a few minutes of pleasure or for a whole night of fun, but it was quite another thing to sell yourself to one man for the rest of your life.

No, it was no good. She was no good. Nothing was any good. And she couldn't make it any better by being a fraud. She could never do that You had to draw a line somewhere.

"Miss Frank?"

She halted, part way to the elevator, and turned to the desk. She took an unsteady breath and smiled.

"Oh, hello, Harry," she said. "Forgive me for not speaking. I was thinking of something else."

The elderly man behind the desk nodded and yawned.

"That's all right," he said. "It's just that you had a phone call."

"Phone call?"

"Yes. Here's the number."

She walked to the desk and looked at the slip of paper. She didn't recognize the number. It wasn't Molly's and it wasn't the one at home.

"The fellow said to ask for Eric."

"Oh!"

"He called four or five times. Said it was important."

"Thanks," Ann murmured, moving toward the elevator again. "Thank you, Henry."

She wouldn't call Eric. She wouldn't call him now and she wouldn't ever see him again. He was like a disease in her blood, a crude young man who should mean nothing to her. And yet he did. He meant satisfaction, overwhelming physical satisfaction that swept past the realm of reason. But she didn't need him. She could do without it. She didn't have to *have* him.

In the apartment she began to undress slowly, trying to remember the evening, the things that Slade had said. But she couldn't think, she couldn't concentrate. Her glance drifted to the telephone, then away. It was almost as though she were numb all over, her nerve ends tingling, her whole body lifting up into a raging, mounting turmoil that begged to be pleased.

She wouldn't go to him.

She wouldn't let him come to her.

She wouldn't.

Wouldn't!

She reached for the telephone and picked it up. Her hand shook as she sought the numbers, spun the dial. An eternity of time passed before somebody answered.

"Yeah?"

"May I speak to Eric?"

"Just a minute."

Hang up, she thought. Hang up, you stupid little fool. Hang up while there is still the chance.

"Ann?"

Her tongue felt full and thick and her mouth was as dry as sand in the sun.

"Hello, Eric."

"Boy, am I glad you called," Eric said. "I was beginning to give up hope."

"I just got in."

"Ann, I've got to see you."

She closed her eyes, fighting down the desire which swept through her.

"Not tonight."

"But, Ann, I have to!"

"No."

Eric was silent for a moment. "Ann," he said, "I'm in a jam. You know where Benson's Cigar Store is?"

"No."

"It's on a corner, not far from where you used to live. South and Vine. It's got a red front and some crummy lights in the windows. I got myself into a little fuss. I owe Benson fifty bucks on one of the ponies and he won't let me leave here until I pay up. He says he'll take my car if I don't And it isn't my car. The old man bought it for me. It isn't even in my name. Ann, are you there?"

"Yes, I'm here."

"I didn't know anybody else to call. The old man wouldn't. He just wouldn't, that's all. And none of the guys have that kind of money. I tried to call Kidder but he's away and he won't be back for days yet. Ann, I've gotta get that money to Benson! Before he closes."

She could hang up on Eric and forget about him. He had gotten into this by himself, let him get out of it by himself. It might teach him a lesson. Oh, he'd go to her father and mother with what he knew about her but she wasn't as worried about this as she had been before. Sooner or later they would find out about her, anyway. It would be bad when they did but it wasn't anything she could help. You couldn't go back and undo what had been done.

"Eric."

Her whole body was choked with her need for him. She could recall how she felt in his arms, and it made her head pound just to think about.

"What time does this Benson close?" she wanted to know.

"Two o'clock."

"Isn't that late?"

"Well, they play cards in the back room, too."

Hang up, she thought desperately; hang up and go to bed, alone, like you should. Forget about him. Get drunk. Do anything to kill this thing.

"Wait for me," she said, softly. "I'll be there with the money."

"Ann, honey!"

"Wait for me. And don't worry."

"Baby, you're all right."

All right, she thought. All right. Was that all he could say?

As soon as she was through talking with Eric she dialed Molly's number. Molly answered the phone.

"Molly. Ann Frank."

"Oh, doll, how good of you to call! I was just now thinking about you."

"You were? Anything for me?"

"You can take your pick. The town is running wild tonight. And on Monday, too."

"Anything good?"

"Well, there's this convention at the Hotel Temple. Some guy was just down here and he wanted four girls for four men. I didn't have them. But there's no reason why you couldn't, if you wanted to."

"No," Ann said. "Nobody with the convention. That's out."

"Something personal?"

"Very personal."

"All right. What about—let's see—a salesman?"

"Sounds okay."

"He sounded drunk when he called but I know him and he's a good sort. Funny, but I was thinking of you when I was talking to him. He isn't one of these all night guys. Dare—you know Dare—was with him once before and she said that you could be on your way in five minutes."

"That's for me," Ann said, looking at the clock. It was nearly midnight.

"Good. You'll find him at the Wadsworth. Room two-ten. Just walk in. He'll be expecting you. And Ann?"

"Yes?"

"Let me hear from you again soon. I can use you every night in the week."

"Okay."

"You mean, okay for every night?"

"No, not that. I'll call you. We can talk about it when I drop off your percentage from tonight."

"No hurry," Molly said, and laughed. "I don't need the dough. Business is really holding up."

The salesman was as drunk as a bull that had fallen in some cider pulp. He wobbled all over the room, bumped into chairs and nearly fell, then sat down on the edge of the three-quarter bed.

"You're not just a figment of the scotch?" he inquired, doubtfully.

"No, I'm real enough."

"And I'm drunk."

"I see you are."

He rested his chin against the heels of his hands, elbows on his knees, and stared at her. He was fairly young, maybe in his early thirties, and he had sandy colored hair. She couldn't tell the color of his eyes because he kept blinking them into the light.

"I'm a bra salesman," he said. His eyes blinked more furiously. "But I can see from here that you don't need no damned bra. At least, you don't look like you do."

"I don't."

He shook his head. "I don't believe you," he said. "I got stung once, in Binghampton, and I'm not forgetting that. I think you're a phoney."

Ann was a little tired of him already. She hated drunks. Oh, it was okay if a man had had a few drinks and he felt a little high. But when a man was drunk, really down, he was apt to get nasty or insulting or do or say a million and one things that could cause trouble.

"There's one way you can find out," she told him, standing there in the middle of the room. "Put your hundred dollars on the line and you'll know soon enough."

"Mercenary, aren't you?"

"It's a hard business, Mister."

"You don't look so hard."

"Thanks."

"I'm drunk."

"You said that before."

"You mind being with a drunk?"

Ann shrugged. "This is a business."

"You've got to get that money angle in there, haven't you?"

"That's why I'm here."

"Maybe you're not worth it, sister."

"Maybe you haven't got a hundred dollars, Mister."

The man on the bed reached for his wallet. With a careless movement he placed a hundred dollar bill on the night stand.

"There's your money," he said. "Now let's see if you're worth it."

He lay back on the bed and closed his eyes.

"Aren't you even going to open your eyes?"

"Sure. What's the hurry?"

"None, I guess."

Ann stood very still, watching him and not moving.

"I hate this underwear business," he said, yawning. "All I like is the stuff inside what I sell."

"Well, your interest is way below normal right now."

"Lady, I'm drunk. Drunk as a skunk." He made a face. "How come I got so drunk? How come I got so drunk when there was pretty girl like you waiting . . ."

His speech became slower and stumbling, and he rubbed his hands across his face a couple of times. Finally, he stopped talking altogether. Moments later he was sound asleep and snoring loudly.

Ann picked up the hundred dollar bill from the night stand. She looked at him, shrugged her shoulders again, and left the room.

She felt justified in taking the money.

The merchandise had been there and he just wasn't in any position to buy.

She had the cab drive around the block three times before she told the driver to stop.

"I'm a nuisance," she said. "I just couldn't make up my mind."

"Don't worry, lady; a lot of us can't."

She paid the driver, told him not to wait, and walked across the street.

Benson's was a typical neighborhood hangout. The windows were streaked with grime and the few shelves, covered with faded crepe paper, held dirty cans of tobacco, dusty pipes and some cigarette and coke ads that had curled in the sun. Inside it was hardly better. There was a small soda fountain along one side and opposite this a magazine rack. The magazine stock was divided into two definite categories—the screen and radio things for the girls and a bunch of risque material, featuring a lot of nudes, for the boys. Even at one-fifteen in the morning the place smelled of sour milk, stale tobacco smoke and cheap perfume.

"Help you?" a bald headed man asked her.

"I was looking for Eric."

"He's in the back room." The man turned and raised his voice. "Hey, Eric! There's a doll out here wants to see you."

Eric appeared almost immediately. He wore blue slacks, a matching blue sport shirt open at the collar and white sneakers.

"Jeeze, baby," he said to Ann when he saw the hundred dollar bill. "Jeez!"

It took a few minutes for Eric to pay off Benson. Benson, who was short and skinny and who had a sallow face the color of a corpse, said he didn't like hundred dollar bills. They were sometimes counterfeit, he said. But he had the man at the counter and a couple of fellows in the back room look at it. Everybody said the bill was all right.

"Well, okay," he said, digging into his pocket. "But next time bring me tens."

"There won't be any next time," Eric assured him.

"That's what you said before."

"Yeah, I guess I did."

"But there won't be any credit next time, kid. You have the dough or you stay out of here."

"Sure."

Outside, they walked down the block and got into Eric's car.

"The old bastard," Eric complained, bitterly. "Who does he think he is? I drop plenty of money in there. Plenty."

"Don't you ever win?"

"Yeah, I win." He started the car. "I win more than I lose. That's what gets him sore. He gets a chance to put the screws on me and he won't let up for a second."

The car made a chugging sound as it crossed over the abandoned trolley tracks.

"You didn't give me my change," Ann said.

Eric drove a block before he spoke.

"Could I use it for a couple of weeks? I'll pay you back then. I got a couple of other things on the fire, too."

"Aren't you working?"

"Me? Naw. Not since this morning. I go in and what do you think they want me to do? They said it's slow and they wanted me to come out of the shipping room and help the girls on the lines. Can you tie that? Me, working on the lines with a bunch of old punks? I told them to go to hell."

It was complete now, Ann thought. Complete. She was just like Ruby and Marla and the other girls who had a boy friend on the side. Few of the boy friends worked or even thought about looking for a job. The girls gave them money, got their kicks and everybody was happy.

"Take me home," she said, struggling against it. "Take me home."

"You want to go home?"

"I said, take me home!"

"All right, all right. Jeeze!"

But it was hopeless. He was beside her, very, very close, and she remembered everything. She remembered the touch of his hands, the insistent flames that seemed to shoot out from his fingers. She could close her eyes and feel his lips on her mouth, seeking, finding, pleasing her.

"Eric."

"Yes, baby?"

"Eric, do you want to come up with me?"

He leaned across the seat and kissed her.

"I'd like to come up with you," he said.

It was better this time, better than ever before.

And later, when desire was stilled, Ann said to Eric, "You could—Eric, you could move in here with me."

"They might not like it."

"I'll tell them you're my brother."

"Would it be all right?"

"I pay the rent. Of course it would be all right. Later on we can find another place, something bigger."

He kissed her on the mouth. "You're sweet, Ann."

"I want to be sweet. To you."

And she proved it.

PART TWO

Lunch on Tuesday was a semi-formal affair, with Slade greeting the guests and making a short speech of official welcome, but after that the giant ballroom of the Hotel Temple was thrown open and the distributors and dealers crowded inside.

"Well, they've got it dressed up some this year," Mortimer Kane said. "You see so many pretty girls around that you don't know whether to look at the girls or the television sets."

"I'm sure you'll look at the television sets," Ann said, holding onto his arm and smiling up at him. "Of that I'm positive, Mr. Kane."

"I keep telling you to call me Kane. Everybody does."

"Yes, Kane."

"I like to be called by my last name. I hate Mortimer. If I had the time and I wasn't so busy I'd go into court and get it changed."

"Well, I like Kane," Ann said. "If sounds strong."

"Does it?"

He squeezed her hand, briefly, and led her toward the entrance of the ballroom.

"In business maybe," he said. "But not in other ways." He squeezed her hand again. "In other ways I'm the softest man you ever met."

Once they were in the ballroom she saw very little of Kane. He excused himself and moved from one set to the other, examining it inside and out. The sets had been arranged in banks around the ballroom, six sets to a bank, and a smiling girl from Promotion was stationed at each bank. The girls were dressed in pink and blue gowns with white carnations in their hair. They mingled with the men, joked with them, and in general attempted to make them feel at ease. She noticed, however, that none of the girls had any luck with Kane. He smiled at them, looked at them, but other than that his attention was devoted to the television sets on display.

"Dammit," Slade said, coming up to her, "you ought to be with him."

"He wanted to wander around by himself."

"Sure, he wanted to wander around by himself. That way, he'll make up his mind. And once his mind is made up there isn't a stick of dynamite in the county that can change it."

Ann smiled at Slade, lit a cigarette and inhaled deeply.

"Don't worry," she said. "The race isn't run yet."

"I hope not."

"Don't worry."

"You look very pretty, Ann."

"Thank you."

"Red's a good color for a blonde, a white-blonde." Slade's roving glance lifted from her toes to her eyes. "You look like you were poured into it."

Ann guessed she did. She smiled.

"I might just as well be on the golf course with Willouby," Slade said in disgust. "Nobody will order anything until Kane has made up his mind."

Kane came back while Ann and Slade were still talking.

"You've got a real job on your hands," he said to Slade. "Moving that junk."

"It isn't junk," Slade said, defensively.

"And it isn't new, either. Why don't you people keep up with things? Arm chair controls are the things, boy. Didn't you know that?"

"What about chassis? Aren't they important, too?"

"Well, there's something to be said for that," Kane admitted. "You've got a good chassis. Sound. Solid. There won't be any trouble with that."

"Cuts down on service work," Slade said. "And that's a big factor."

Kane grinned. "I knew you'd say that. It was a trap, boy. I knew you'd come right back with something like that. Good psychology. But it won't work on me. You've got to sell the sets and get them in the homes before you have to service them. So what do you have to look for first? Sales potential. Sales potential is the thing you hunt out. You can have the best product in the world but if you can't sell it it won't do you any more good than a bunion on your foot."

Slade looked unhappy, as though he had just taken a dose of medicine that didn't quite agree with him.

"You look them over again," Slade said. "And think about it. You may feel differently by tomorrow."

"I'll give you an order for a thousand sets right now and let it go at that."

Again Slade had that look of unhappiness.

"I won't settle for that, Kane," he said, forcing a laugh. "You know me better than that."

"And I know what I want."

"Of course you do. But think about it. Let it stew until tomorrow morning. Then we'll talk business."

Kane shrugged. "That's up to you, young fellow. I'll be here anyway."

Somebody started shouting for Slade and he excused himself. As he crossed the ballroom Kane's eyes followed him.

"Good man," he said. "Plenty of gumption. Too bad he's mixed up with such a backward outfit." He shrugged, dismissing the subject and turned to Ann. "How about lunch?" Kane inquired. "I'm so hungry I could eat the hind leg off a live cow."

They ate in the Terrace Room, which was just off the bar. The lights in there were soft and rose colored and they sat at a table way toward the rear.

"I could have ordered those sets by mail," Kane explained. "But it's a chance to get away, to travel a little, and it does a man good to do that. Business, if he lets it, can kill a man. You have to have a little fun on the side, too. You forget about the fun and you die young."

Ann smiled and tasted the shrimp salad. If fun had anything to do with it, the kind Kane so obviously meant, she ought to live past a hundred.

"You want a drink, Ann?"

"Not right now."

"Do you mind if I do?"

"Not at all."

He had four scotch and sodas, all doubles, and by the time he had finished the fourth one he pushed his dinner aside.

"The hell with going back in there," he said. "You want to go back in there?"

"Not particularly."

"But you're supposed to be working the convention?"

"Yes, that's right."

He ordered another drink from the waiter. "You won't get in any trouble as long as you're with me," he assured her. "They don't fool me none. They want to please me. Everybody says the way Kane goes, so goes the convention."

"I've heard that, too."

"From that guy Slade?"

"From everybody. They all respect your judgment."

"Do they?"

"Well, more than anybody else, that's for sure."

He ordered another drink and lit a cigar half as long as his arm. Now, every time he spoke, she could smell the secondhand scotch. If this kept up, she decided, she'd have to start drinking in self-defense.

"My judgement is they've got a line of junk."

"What?"

"Forgive me, but I said junk. All-Channel, makers of the biggest television trash in the world. You don't think I built up a distributorship, serving more than a thousand stores, by selling a lot of junk, do you?"

"No, you couldn't do that."

"You're damned right. I built it on guts. Guts. Did anybody tell you how I started out?"

"No."

"Waiter! Another drink. And bring one for the lady. What'll you have, Ann?"

"Rye," she said. "With a tall ginger."

He was pleased. "Now you're breaking down. I hate girls who don't break down. And don't worry none about what that Slade fellow will say. He won't say nothing to you, long as you're with me. I know. He wants my order. He'd stand on his head to get my order. Stand on his head in the middle of the street and let all the cars run over him."

The bar was now crowded and the noise drifted into the Terrace Room. A few tables distant a couple sat holding hands. They had been there all of ten minutes and they hadn't ordered a thing. The girl looked like one of the girls Ann had seen at Molly's but she couldn't be sure.

"What was I saying, Ann?"

"About how you started out."

The rye was strong but it was better than smelling Kane's scotch. She lit a cigarette and took another drink.

"I bought a second hand radio, fixed it up in the garage and sold it. That's how I got started. The guy who bought the radio sent a friend around and I fixed up an old Atwater-Kent and sold it to him. Pretty soon I was buying new radios and peddling them out of a Model T. Today I've got twenty trucks and a hundred employees."

"You've come a long way."

"Because I haven't bought any junk. Because I know that the other fellow doesn't want something that I don't want myself. That's how I've done it."

The waiter brought two more drinks.

"That makes sense," Ann said.

"A lot of sense. Take All-Channel, for instance. They put out a line of junk and they expect people to buy it."

"It's a good set," Ann said, trying to remember some of the things Slade had told her.

"In what way? I'm willing to listen. You just tell me. In what way?"

"We guarantee the picture tube for two years, not one."

Kane nodded. "That's the only reason I'm buying a thousand sets. We use them in the rural areas, where service is difficult. The sets stand up, that much they do. But they don't have the looks. And they don't have the features."

"There's automatic tuning."

"Everybody has that. Waiter!"

"Yes, sir!"

"Keep 'em coming, will you? Good Lord, a man can't even get rid of his money around here."

The couple got up from the table and departed for the lobby, holding hands. They were now alone in the Terrace Room.

"About All-Channel," Kane said, leaning forward, his elbows on the top of the table. "If they'd put arm chair tuning on their sets they'd have something."

"But that would make the sets cost more."

"Nobody cares any more about what things cost. All they want to know is how much are the monthly payments. That's no excuse. If it were, nobody would sell a five thousand dollar automobile."

The glow of the liquor inside of her brought new confidence to Ann. This man wasn't so big.

He wasn't so big at all.

"We're going to have arm chair tuning," Ann said. "But it's going to be optional. Mr. Willouby thinks that too many people are getting lazy these days. He says a man sits in a chair and tunes his television set, or changes the station, is the same man who sends for a book on how to take exercise and keep in trim."

"Oh, hell," Kane exclaimed, "he should've been a doctor. They'd give him a medal for that thought at Johns Hopkins."

"Well, that's what he says."

"He says wrong, Ann. It's what the public wants that counts. You put out something they don't want and they'll suck you down the drain every time."

The drinks came faster after that. The late afternoon sun began to find the windows of the Terrace Rooms, and splashed irregular designs across the red and gold carpet. Kane excused himself once to go to the men's room, and she noticed that he staggered slightly.

He talked about his business some more, and finally he talked about his home. His business was in Evansville, but he lived in a small town about thirty-five miles away. He hated that town—its little stores, its army camp nearby. But there wasn't much he could do about it.

"My wife was born there," he said. "And she'll die there."

They had two children, a girl who was in college and a boy who had come into the business with Kane.

"I'd have brought him along," Kane said, "but you can't have any fun when you drag any of the family with you."

He went to the men's room again and when he came, back he sat down next to Ann.

This time he staggered more than before.

"What about you?" he wanted to know. "I've been talking about myself all afternoon. What about you?"

"There isn't much to tell."

"Well, how old are you?"

She smiled at him. "It isn't nice to ask a girl that," she said.

"Nineteen?"

"That's close enough."

"You a model or something?"

"No. I work for All-Channel. In Promotion."

"You have a boy friend?"

"I wouldn't be here with you if I did."

"Even if it was part of your job?"

"Not even if it was part of my job."

"How come you're here, then?"

"Because I like you."

"But we just met. Yesterday."

"I know. And I still like you."

"Hey, waiter!"

"Please," Ann said, touching his arm lightly. "Not any more for me."

"Aw, you've only had a few."

"I know, but I feel them."

"You do?"

Actually, she didn't. Her head was clear and she was thinking straight, straighter than she had ever thought before.

"I'm not much of a drinker," she said, putting her hand on his arm and leaving it there. "I do funny things when I drink, like taking my shoes off, or wanting to dance, or getting so darned sleepy I just have to lay down someplace."

She saw a bedroom look creep into his eyes as he turned to her. He stared—and the look wasn't directed at her face. She could tell he wanted to touch her, to hold her, to make love to her. But she knew that he was still afraid of her.

Ann smiled grimly to herself. She also knew perfectly well that he'd muster his courage before very long.

"Oh, hell," he said, "another drink won't hurt you any."

"Well—all right."

"Waiter!"

"Yes, sir!"

"Keep 'em rolling."

They drank until darkness began to invade the room and then Ann put on her act.

She giggled at everything he said. She slumped against him. And when he put his hand down on her leg a little under her dress and past her knee, she left it there.

"Oh, you!" she said.

That small squeal, a mixture of delight and little-girl awe, was the signal for him to try something else. He put his other hand on her neck, rubbed gently (He thinks he's a great love-maker, Ann thought), and began to insinuate his fingers down inside the top of her dress.

"You mustn't do that," she told him, pushing his hand away. "It isn't nice." At the same time she removed his hand from her leg, though she had a little difficulty with that—he had gotten his fingers caught around the top of one stocking. "It isn't nice at all, Mr. Kane." All the bright-eyed but fascinated innocence in the world sounded in Ann's voice.

"Call me Kane."

"Well, Kane. But it isn't nice. I just don't want you to do that. Supposing somebody saw us?"

"Is that the only reason?"

"One of them."

"And the others?"

"I'm not that kind of a girl."

"I know you're not." He tried to kiss her on the cheek but she avoided him. "You're a nice girl," he mumbled. "And beautiful. It's only natural I'd want to—well, you know."

They had another drink and she yawned discreetly. His arm stole around her shoulder and he moved his hand down to where the fullness of her flesh began.

"You're doing it again," she said, but she didn't stop his hand.

"I won't hurt you," he whispered into her ear. "I'll be careful."

"No."

"I'd make it right with you."

"No."

"Why do you keep on saying no?"

She yawned again. "I'm tired."

"How tired?"

"Awfully tired." She stretched and as she arched her body his hand went a little lower. "I could sleep for a week."

Kane seized the opportunity. "Why don't you lie down for a while? Here at the hotel? Maybe we have been drinking too much. We could have dinner later."

"But I don't have any room."

"I have a room."

This time she let him kiss her briefly on the cheek. His lips were cool and a little wet.

"It wouldn't be right for me to go up to your room," she protested, shaking her head slowly as though the liquor were still much in her brain.

"I don't know why not. I'd take you up, see that you got settled, and then come back downstairs. You can lock the door from the inside. Nobody will bother you." He put his hand over the general area of his heart. "And I promise you I won't bother you at all."

"I don't know," Ann said, dubiously. "It still doesn't seem right."

They talked about it some more but in the end Ann consented. Kane, in his haste to help her up to the room, left a fifty dollar bill on the table and didn't wait for his change.

The room was like a hundred others she had entered. There was a double bed, a dresser, a desk and chair, and an easy chair by the open window.

"You stretch out on the bed," Kane told her. "I'll just run the electric razor over my face and be out of the bathroom in a couple of minutes. Then you can sleep all you want."

He went into the bathroom, closing the door behind him, and she lay down on the bed. She was fully dressed but somehow, she felt worse than stripped. She closed her eyes and waited.

She didn't have long to wait.

"Ann?"

She made no reply.

"Ann?"

She could feel him standing there, close to the bed, looking down at her, staring. She couldn't see him but she knew the lust in his eyes, sensed the way he shook when the need swept through him.

"Ann?"

Watch the old guys, Molly had warned. For some reason, every old guy who took a young girl wanted to be a poppa. He'd never see the kid or even know that it had been born, but he wanted to accomplish something. Maybe, Molly said, it was his male vanity wanting to exert itself one last time before the buzzard kicked off. Maybe it was. Ann didn't know.

"Ann."

He was closer now, his breath on her face, and she felt the first searching touch of his lips on her mouth. He kissed her hardly at all, just enough to see if she were awake. Her own lips were part way open in a half pout, and she left them that way.

"Ann!"

With a groan he fell on her and began kissing her. This time he forced her mouth open. His breath came in heavy, irregular gasps. His body began to tremble and his hands became wild, rough, grasping, painful.

She fought against the hurt and lay very still, a toy in his hands.

"Ann?" he called out again. "Ann?"

She did not move or speak.

His hands went lower, lower, and for a moment then he paused.

Then he was after her, all the way. He was after her and nothing would stop him.

And Ann did nothing to stop him.

Later, she sat on the edge of the bed and gave it to him quickly, driving it into him like a bullet from the muzzle of a gun.

"You just raped me," she said softly. "You know that, don't you?"

Kane's face became flushed, then white, then flushed again.

"You were awake?"

"All the time. And I didn't enjoy one bit of it. In fact, I hate you, Kane. You're an animal."

He stood in the middle of the room. The disbelief in his eyes was replaced by fear and, seconds later, by something else which she didn't understand.

"What are you going to do?"

"Go to the police. Report you."

"No!"

She laughed at him brutally, bitterly. "Why not? They might be interested in my story. Big operator brings young girl to hotel room and takes her while she's sleeping."

"You're not drunk," he accused.

"Of course I'm not."

"I'll bet you could drink a dozen women under the table."

"Maybe I could."

He seemed to have difficulty buttoning his shirt.

"Don't go to the police," he said. "That would only make an unholy mess."

"You should have thought of that before."

He looked defeated. "I know, but I couldn't. I saw you lying there and I couldn't think of anything."

"You thought of one thing, all right."

"That was a mistake, Ann." He doubled up his huge fists and looked at them. "I'm sorry. I'm sorry as hell."

"A lot of good that does me. And a lot of good that does you, now."

"Ann—"

"Supposing I had a baby?"

"You won't."

"That's easy enough for you to say." She stood up. "But it's me that would have it, not you."

"I tell you, I was—"

She started for the door. "To hell with you, Kane," she said. "You can tell it to the police."

He stopped her. "Don't do that. Are you out of your mind? A thing like this could ruin me."

Ann's smile was crooked. "What do you suggest?"

"Let's talk it over."

"What good would that do?"

"We might arrive at something." He tugged at her arm.

"You might arrive at something," she corrected him. "But I wouldn't. Talk won't change the fact that you had me the way you did."

"Will you stop saying that?"

"Well, you did. That's what you did. I thought you were a nice man and that I could trust you."

"How come you didn't yell if it upset you so much?"

"I was afraid. I didn't know what you might do. You were out of your mind."

"I'm sorry," he said. "I'm sorry as hell."

"You told me that before."

"I am. I—I don't know what got into me. I—something seemed to snap, something seemed to set me on fire. Ann, be reasonable! Don't go to the police. What can you get from that? It won't change anything that happened here in this room. We can discuss it like two sensible people. I did wrong. I admit that. But I can make it right. Just give me a chance."

"Everybody, everything has a price, is that it?"

"Something like that, yes."

"Mine might be high."

"You've a right to make it high. Anything good in life comes high. And there was no excuse for what I did. Added together, you get a high price."

She watched him as he walked across the room, opened the top drawer of the dresser and removed a checkbook. The only thing which she could feel for him was contempt.

"Make that for five thousand dollars," Ann said.

"What!"

"Five thousand dollars. Not a cent more and not a cent less."

"Now, see here, if you think for one minute—"

"And make it payable to All-Channel Television Corporation. As a deposit on five thousand assorted television sets."

He fought like a bull but she had him. There was nothing he could do. If she went to the police he would be arrested and, even worse, he could be sent to prison. Maybe she was—what she was, but that had little to do with it. What he had done had a price. And in this particular case the price was five thousand All-Channel television sets.

"I think you framed me," Kane said, when he handed her the check.

"You're wrong. You framed yourself."

"Even so."

"You came here to have a little fun away from home and to sneer at us. You've had some of both. Tomorrow morning, though, you won't sneer. Tomorrow morning you'll tell the others at the convention that we've got the best television set on the market and you'll prove it by signing an order for five thousand sets."

"That's a lot of merchandise."

She laughed. "You're a big man. You've got a thousand outlets. That's only five apiece. And you're getting good merchandise. You don't have to worry about that. Slade says it's the best chassis in the field." She laughed again and patted him on the cheek. "You had another chassis that was pretty good too, didn't you?"

"Oh, shut up," Kane growled, slamming his checkbook into the drawer. "I think this was a damned setup, that's what I think it was."

"It doesn't matter what you think," she reminded him sweetly. "You bought, didn't you?"

A few minutes later Ann hurriedly left the hotel. She was wondering as she crossed the street and hailed a taxi if Eric would be waiting for her at the apartment.

She hoped that he would be.

10

Slade moved up to the general managership of All-Channel TV the first of the following week.

"Were going to miss you around here," Betty said as she stood in the doorway and watched Slade packing up his personal things.

"Who's going to miss me?"

"Well, me, for one."

"You won't," Slade said, looking up. "You're going along."

"I am?" Betty's eyes were wet.

"Damned right. You don't think I'd leave something as good as you behind, do you?"

"You make me feel like a tramp when you talk that way."

"Okay, so I like you. Does that make you feel any better?"

"Not the way you say it."

"Close the door, baby, and I'll say it better."

But she made no move to close the door. She just stood there watching him, her eyes still wet.

"Slade, I can't Not now."

He grinned. "What's the matter with you, anyway? You never turned me down in the morning before."

It was Monday and he could use some of what Betty had to offer. He'd spent the week end out at Willouby's, from early Friday night until that morning, and he was behind on his scoring. All Willouby had talked about was business, which was all right but it got on a guy's nerves after a while. And that wife of his—well, she was out of this world. She didn't want anybody to drink or to smoke and if they could have done without breathing, Slade thought, she would have been against that, too. The daughter, Audrey, was only a notch or so above her mother. She looked half-starved, and if a guy had hitched at his pants within a mile of her she'd have run inside the house and jumped into her chastity belt. It had been, as far as Slade was concerned, a hell of a weekend. But the fruit, nevertheless, had fallen from the tree. He was now the general manager and Accounting knew that he was supposed to draw down five hundred a week. A guy, he decided, could go through mud and slime for something like that.

"Slade."

"Yeah?"

"Slade, I've got to talk to you."

He looked around the office to see if there was anything he had forgotten.

"Sure, go ahead."

"Slade, I think I may be pregnant."

The whole world was suddenly cockeyed.

"Give it to me again," he said, turning his head. "I don't hear so well out of my right ear. And make it slower this time."

Her voice trembled. "I think I may be pregnant."

He had the urge to fire the briefcase out of the open window and then beat hell out of her. He did neither one. He reached for a cigarette, held it unlighted in his hand and kicked at one of the legs on the desk a couple of times.

"Who you been running around with, baby?"

She looked hurt. "Nobody. There's just been you, Slade."

"But we've always been—"

"Not one time. One night we weren't. About a month ago. We worked late and we had a few drinks."

He nodded. He remembered the night. It had been raining outside and the fog had been thick in the streets. Even with the windows closed they could hear the whistles on the train going up the mountain, the rythmic grind of the diesels. She had been passionate that night and he had loved her without caring, without fear. He wished now that he hadn't been so hasty. A guy could get a girl into more trouble in a couple of seconds than she could get out of in nine months.

"You sure, Betty?"

She was honest with him. "I'm not sure, not exactly. I went to the doctor's Saturday and he's going to give me a rabbit test."

He made up his mind that they would know after that. She was ninety percent rabbit.

"Well, we'll cross that bridge when we come to it," he said, starting for the door. "Let's get moved."

But even in his new office that morning he couldn't forget about her. Betty pregnant was all that he needed. It didn't fit in with his plans at all. Betty was a nice kid, soft and warm, but she didn't add up to being part of five hundred bucks a week. She just didn't. She had a body that was good when he needed it but that was all. A good, vibrant, responsive body.

Well, he wasn't going to worry about it. If she was caught, she was caught. A lot of girls got caught and a lot of girls didn't have kids. For a couple or three hundred bucks you could get rid of a kid. Of course, it was an expensive bit of fun, looking at it in that light, but it was better than paying out support money and getting yourself all fouled up for more years than you could count.

His phone rang most of the morning—congratulations from the department heads on his new job. However, the call which he wanted to receive didn't come through. A few minutes after twelve he called Ann in Promotion.

"Hi, honey," he said. "How's about lunch?"

"Whatever you say."

Cripes, he thought, she's a cool one; cool and smooth. Like a shiny new car in a showroom, like a new suit that you wanted to try on to see how good you'd look in it.

"Fine. Meet you in ten minutes."

"I'll be ready."

He hung up. For some reason, he felt guilty just talking to her, thinking about her. She was pounding a typewriter for less than sixty a week and she had put him up into the top position. He'd have to do something to make that right. He really would.

He grinned. There was one thing he'd like to do for her. Man, he really would. He remembered that first time, the only time with her, and he'd never forget the wonders of her body, the little things she did, the importance which she had made him feel. Yes, he'd like to do that with her again. Today. Tonight. Any day. Any night.

But there was another side to Ann Frank that he didn't understand. It was almost impossible for him to accept that a girl so lovely could also be smart. Yet she was smart. She had gotten that five thousand unit order from Kane and on a binder, at that. Kane's order had opened the gates and when the flood had stopped All-Channel had orders for fifteen thousand units. The success of the convention would make it possible for Jefferies to get a good solid plug into *Trade* and this would help sell the next convention which was already scheduled for the following month.

"Marvelous job," Willouby had told him. "You came through with the goods, Slade."

Slade had taken full credit. He had mentioned the help which the presence of the girls had given him but he hadn't gone into the details of Ann's deal with Kane. It would only have confused and marred the issue since he didn't understand it himself. And, besides, what Willouby thought of his ability was worth five hundred a week, fifty-two weeks a year.

But the whole thing presented a feeling of guilt, too. He had to do something for Ann. Just what it was he didn't know, but he had to do it.

"Betty?"

"Yes, Slade."

"Would you come in here a minute, please."

She came in, carrying notebook and pencil.

"First letter from the new general manager?" she inquired, brightly.

"No. Sit down. We've got to talk this thing out."

She sat down on the edge of a chair.

"I didn't mean to upset you today," Betty said, almost apologetically. "I know it's your first day up here and all that, but—"

"No," Slade said. "That's all right. We have to face it."

She looked down at the floor. "Yes," she agreed. "I guess we do."

"You could make it hot for me," Slade said, laying it right on the line. "You could hold me up for a bundle of jack or maybe even have me thrown in the can. You know that, don't you?"

Betty nodded, mutely.

"Which do you want to do?"

"Neither."

So here it was, he thought; so here it was. He'd asked for it and here it was. He thought of the dozens of girls he'd been with, the countless number he'd had, and not one of them had ever gotten caught before. Sometimes, when he'd thought about it, he'd almost made up his mind that he was sterile. He'd been trapped in an electrical storm once, when he'd been a kid and, when he'd been running home, scared as all hell, he'd been knocked flat on his can. He'd read that a thing like that could do it; a thing like that could ruin a man, make it possible for him to be the safest love-maker in town.

Generally, he'd been careful. Not infrequently it had been the girl, wise in the ways of the world, who had been careful. Not wanting a kid, not wanting anything except the pleasure from it. But not Betty. No, not Betty. Betty wasn't that kind or, if she were, she hadn't been that way with him. And all of it had been right there in his old office, on the settee, like a customer going to a red light district and getting his licks. Nothing romantic or sincere about it. Nothing. Now she thought she'd had it, that she was going to get big with his kid. That was a hot one; that was rich. It hadn't been anything before, just a few moments of getting his pleasure. And now, suddenly, it was going to be everything. It didn't make sense. It wasn't right. It was lousy.

"What do you want me to do?" he asked, finally.

Her answer was direct, planned.

"Stick by me, Slade. Don't let me down."

His guts twisted. She could mean a lot of things by that. Marry her? Maybe. That would be hell. He couldn't see himself married to her, listening to a screaming kid, coming home to the same woman every night. Oh, Betty was all right in a dark, soft way but she wasn't what he wanted in a woman. Now, if she were only like that girl in Promotion, that Ann Frank, he might be able to get himself interested. Something like that he could buy. Yes, he could. He could see himself tied down to Ann Frank, owning her body, her blonde loveliness, being able to experience all of the wonderful things she had to offer.

"I'll stick by you," Slade said. There wasn't anything else to say. If he said he wouldn't she could go to Willouby and Willouby would shoot a twenty over par on the golf course. Willouby wasn't the kind of a man who would subscribe to having a woman and then kicking her out. "I'll stick by you," Slade said, more to convince himself that he would than anything else.

"Thank you, Slade."

"Sure."

"There'll be doctor's bills and things to buy and—well, you know. I can work for awhile but I won't be able to keep going right up to the end. At least, I don't think I will. Some girls don't show so much and they don't have any trouble and they can work almost until the day it happens."

"You live with your folks?"

It was funny that he hadn't asked her this before, that he hadn't ever bothered to find out anything about her. They'd sent her up from Personnel that one day and he'd hired her without checking on her typing or shorthand, because he'd been busy. He'd made a pass at her a couple of days later and she'd fought him off, not too hard, and the second time he'd tried, about a week later, she'd let him do what he wanted to do. It had been a vicious trap, he thought now; a trap which she had set and which he had stepped into. He was successful in the company, on his way up—hell, now he was almost at the top—and she had been after a man. Most likely she'd wanted to get herself jacked up off the ground, to be able to burn it into him so that he couldn't move.

He looked at her, waiting for her answer, and in that second he hated her. It wasn't his kid. He'd been careful, except that once and possibly one other time, and it wasn't his kid. She'd picked up some guy off the streets, any guy, and she'd let him have her and neither one of them had had sense enough to watch out. Now she had herself pregnant and she wanted to blame Slade for it. Well, he wouldn't let her. He'd be nice to her and all that but he wouldn't take a kicking around for something that wasn't his fault. He could make her go to a doctor, get a blood test, and he could fight it in court if he had to. A lot of fellows fought dames in court. Just because a girl pointed her finger at a man didn't mean that he was all done, not if she was the kind of a girl who stuck her hand on a running buzz saw and got her hand cut. How could she tell which tooth cut her?

"My parents live in Endicott," she said. "That's upstate."

"I know where it is."

"I wouldn't be able to go home, not for a thing like this. My father—well, he's in the church and my mother just wouldn't understand."

"No."

"I've got this apartment and it isn't so bad. The people in the building are nice. There's a shoe salesman and his wife who lives on one side of me and an artist fellow who lives on the other."

"How old is this artist fellow?"

"About thirty, I guess."

"You ever see him?"

"Not often. Only on garbage days and wash days. He does his own washing. He says he can do it cheaper in the basement than he can by sending it out."

"Talk to him much?"

"A little. One day, the first day I met him, he couldn't get the washer going and I talked to him quite a bit then."

"No dates?"

"He asked me but I wouldn't go."

"Why not."

"It didn't seem fair."

She's trying to be coy about the whole thing, Slade thought. She went out with him and he gave it to her and now she's yelling about it. So the guy paints pictures for a living and he doesn't make a dime and she decides to get herself somebody who can afford a kid. A nice arrangement. A fine arrangement. But not for Slade Martin.

"Don't give me that," Slade said.

"It's the truth!"

"I don't believe it."

"Don't you believe anything?" There was a catch in her voice, the hint of a sob, the blunt edge of despair.

"Sure. I believe you're trying to hang me up for something I didn't do."

"No, Slade. Oh, no!"

"I've only got your word for it."

"I don't want to hurt you," she murmured. "I don't want to hurt myself. But I have to. I have to turn to somebody, Slade. I have to turn to you. There just isn't anybody else."

"Go on."

"I shouldn't have let you—in the first place."

"But you did."

She nodded slowly, as though the effort required a great deal of strength.

"Yes, I did," she said. "I let you have me every time you wanted me. And I would again, Slade. Because I love you."

She had said it before, a dozen times, but it hit him hard in that instant. Love! It was something that you looked for, could never quite find—not until you met Ann Frank—and you accepted any substitute that looked like it. But it was a word that had fear in it, too; a word that could destroy you.

"You're nuts," Slade told her. "You don't love me."

"I do. That's why I don't want to hurt you. That's why I came to you the way I did. I don't want marriage from you or anything like that, Slade. I know that you don't love me and I know that it wouldn't work. All I ask for you is to stick by me, to help me over the rough spots. After that I won't bother you any. I promise you I won't!"

He stared at her. What had he been thinking about? There was nothing wrong with this girl. She had some inner strength that was much greater than his own. He wondered where it came from, how she managed to find it, but that didn't matter. It would save him and that was the important thing. Right then he didn't care about much else.

"You can get rid of it."

"I don't want an abortion."

"You don't have to have an abortion, an operation or anything like that. I can get you some pills."

Her eyes were pained. "Have you gotten them for other girls?"

"No."

Well, he had. Back in high school. He'd been a senior and the girl had been a junior and they'd lived in their own private hell until a friend of his, the son of a druggist, had gotten the brown pills. The girl had been sick as a dog, missed two days of school, but after that everything had been all right. It had been then when the druggist's son had told Slade how he could be careful in the future. Slade had been grateful and he had spent a lot of money with drug stores and gas stations since that time.

"I'll have the baby," she said. "I'll have the baby and bring it up. All I need is your help a little, now. After that I'll be all right. I won't bother you any. You won't even know that we're alive."

Slade began to relax. She was using her head and he didn't have anything to be alarmed over. All he had to do now was get rid of her. He didn't want her around him, didn't want to look at her. Once she started to show, once her belly started to get big, it would drive him out of his mind to see her, to know that he had put the seed in there and that it was growing.

"You can't stay around here," Slade said, trying to be gentle about it but realizing that his voice was brutal, that it was final, that the words were ending everything for them.

"I know. That's why I talked to you so soon."

"I'm glad you did."

She smiled at him a little weakly, as though some of her private world had just collapsed.

"Maybe you don't know it," she said, "but every big stomach around here belongs to you, Slade. They kid about it—the girls, the men, everybody. They say you could impregnate half of the factory and still be ready for more."

"That isn't true."

"Well, that's what they say."

Slade began to sweat. She was right. He had fooled around with the girls in the factory much too much. He had to cut it out. Half the time he didn't do anything with them, just kidded, but it could cause the wrong impression. He was concerned, of course, with Willouby's impression and not anybody else's. Willouby, if the stories kept up, might think he was turning out kids faster than All-Channel was turning out television sets. And anyway, there was just one girl in the place that he wanted to make. That Ann Frank. Somehow, even if it meant using force, he had to have her again.

"You've got some vacation," Slade said to Betty. "A week, ten days—I don't know what it is. But take it. And then just don't come back. You give me your address and I'll send you a check, the same as you're getting here. I'll pay for the doctor and I'll pay for the hospital. After that we'll see how the land looks and we'll take it from there."

She was grateful. She cried. She couldn't help crying, she said. He was good and honest and everything she had always thought him to be.

"I'll always love you," she said. "And I'll always be there if you need me. Someday you will, Slade. I know you will."

"Okay."

She walked to the door and stood there looking back at him.

"I'll leave my address on top of the desk," she said, softly. "And I'll wait for you. Somehow, Slade, I guess I'll always be waiting for you."

He watched the door close and then he lit a cigarette. He leaned back in Willouby's old chair and blew a cloud of smoke toward the ceiling.

Life was good.

Damned good.

And some dames didn't know what it was all about.

He got up, suddenly, remembering his date with Ann Frank for lunch.

That afternoon he boosted her up to the post of being his private secretary.

Yeah, life was good.

The best.

11

Ann's five thousand dollar bonus on the Kane thing wasn't paid out all at one time, but in dribs and drabs because of some crazy system they had in Accounting. It went fast, like spilled milk being soaked up with a mop, and by the time she received her last payment, about five hundred dollars, she was broke.

"I ought to send some money to my mother," Ann told Eric. "I promised her."

"Promises are made to be broken."

"Not to your mother."

"Well, your old man's working, isn't he?"

"Just the way you're working—at nothing."

"You bringing that up again?"

"Yes, I'm bringing it up again. I have to bring it up again, Eric. You know how much I make at the office. Eighty-five a week and that's good, more than any of the other girls make. But it isn't enough. If we'd stayed in the other apartment it would have been enough, but we didn't. We moved up here. All right. We both wanted to. It's nice. But it's expensive. And the car. Eric, why did we have to buy a Chrysler, a big car? Why didn't we just get a Ford?"

"The Chrysler'll last longer."

"Not with you putting a couple of hundred miles a day on it, it won't."

"Now you're yelling at me."

"I'm not yelling. I'm just saying that this is the end of the bonus, that it's all we have, and that it's going to be hard for us to manage on my salary. If you got a job, even in a gas station, it'll be a big help."

"No stinking gas station for me," Eric stated, with feeling. "I've been telling you how it's almost set for me to go out to the Berkshire."

The Berkshire was a big private club east of the city, very wealthy, and Eric had been trying to get on as a bartender. Some nights he rode out to talk to the manager and he didn't get home until very late.

"Almost being set and having the job are two different things," Ann reminded him. "We can't pay our bills on being almost set. We have to be completely set."

"Damn the money!" he said.

"Well, don't blame me. I didn't invent it."

"I know you didn't, honey."

"We've got rent tomorrow and that's a hundred and twenty-five. And the car which is almost one-fifty."

"Plus a hundred for that guy out at the Berkshire."

"What?"

"I told you. You have to buy a job out there."

"But I gave you a hundred last week."

"I know. He wants more. As it is, he's giving me a break. He could get five bills, easy, for a job out there."

Everybody had an angle, she thought. Everybody. No matter where you went you had to make a sharp left turn or you didn't get any place.

"I can't do it this week," Ann said. "Maybe next week."

"But I told him. I told him tonight. I knew you were getting your bonus and—"

"Oh, all right."

"You're mad."

"No, I'm not mad, Eric. It's just that—well, we have to be careful."

"But if I can get the job it'll make things a lot easier."

"Yes, it will."

"Those guys out there, tips and all, make about two bills a week. It's almost like getting a job through an employment agency. If you went to an agency you'd have to pay them, wouldn't you?"

"I guess so. Yes."

"So this manager sucks it up himself. You can't blame him none. For all I know it may even go back to the club. Maybe he don't even keep it."

"I'll bet."

"Well, I don't know. I just said."

"Two hundred seems like a lot," Ann said. "He only asked you for a hundred in the first place. Maybe if you went to him and told him—"

"You mean you won't let me have it?"

"I'm scared to be broke, that's all. Scared to death of it."

She was. She hadn't been to Molly's in weeks and she didn't want to go back there ever again. She had sold herself to Kane for five thousand dollars and she didn't want to sell herself to another man. Not for fifty dollars. Not for hundred.

"I told the guy I'd bring him the dough tonight," Eric said. "I promised him."

"No. Not tonight."

"Please!"

"No!"

And then he was coming toward her, smiling, his hands reaching for her, reaching for her the way they always reached.

"I know what you need," he said.

"Not now," she said. "We haven't even had supper."

"Who wants supper?" he demanded.

"I do."

She wanted supper like she wanted a hole in the head. She wanted Eric. She always wanted Eric. During the day, even there in the office, she wanted him. And at night she wanted him even worse. She wanted to feel the fire in her body, the living, probing flame, the glorious weakness that-followed the moments of frantic, urgent ecstasy.

But she had come to a point, a point of decision and she had reached it that afternoon.

She would not be his slave.

She must become his master.

Their life was good; insecure, maybe, but good. But it could remain good only if they worked together to keep it that way. They lived in the best neighborhood and they ate fine food and they dressed in nice clothes. The people to the right of their apartment were a respectable couple, a lawyer and his wife, and the girl on the left drove a Caddy and had money to burn Yes, it was a good neighborhood, a satisfactory life, but she couldn't keep things going all by herself. She had to have help. Eric had to help.

"Baby," he said.

"No," she said, avoiding his hands. "I'm going to the bathroom."

That was the one place she was safe, the only place that he wouldn't follow her.

"Later."

"I've got a headache."

She crossed the living room, the carpet thick and deep under her feet, and entered the bedroom.

Their bedroom.

She smiled reflectively, feeling the tension mount. Even a half-memory was enough.

Ann could stay away from Eric once, maybe two or three times. But there was no doubt at all; she knew—they both knew—that they had to stay together. Their need found an equal and a calm in each other. Only in each other.

And Ann was not going to let what could be her bodily paradise become a tattered mess.

She entered the bathroom and closed the door.

Her head didn't ache, hadn't ached in weeks, but she had to be somewhere by herself and think. She had to sort this mess out, know where she was, where she was going.

She turned on the cold water and doused her face. Then she rubbed herself briskly with a rough towel. Yes, she had to settle this once and for all. She had to think.

Or she had to stop thinking.

But she began remembering the day at work.

It had been rough at the office. There had been two dozen letters, maybe more, and they'd sent up a girl from the typing pool to help. The girl had been inexperienced, new, and she'd been so thrilled at working in the general manager's office that she almost didn't know a typewriter key from a door latch.

"You'll have to work late to catch up, Ann," Slade had said.

"No. I'll get it done in the morning, when you're in conference with Mr. Willouby."

Thursday was conference day and it was the only time that Ann could call her own. Thursday, almost all day long, the door to Slade's office was closed and she didn't have to keep running in there so he could watch the movements of her body beneath the tight skirts.

Why did she wear tight skirts?

She knew why she wore them. She preferred her skirts tight, snug, so that she knew she had something on.

And they were good for Eric. Eric liked them tight so that he could slap her a little, playfully, and so his hand would bounce just as though she were wearing a girdle. And she had so many of them. She couldn't afford to throw them out just because she worked for a man who could spot a stocking seam a mile away.

Slade wanted her again. Slade wanted her so badly that he sometimes stuttered when he was talking to her. She was fully aware of what she was doing to him, that she was driving him slowly out of his mind because she wouldn't let him play again.

"I like you, Ann," he said. "I like you a hell of a lot."

And she let it go at that. Even nights when she worked late, and the couple of times when he had backed her up against the filing cabinet, sort of kidding with her but not exactly kidding either, she hadn't given him any chance to do what he wanted to do.

"You've changed," he'd said.

She had changed. She'd changed a lot.

Eric had changed her.

Eric had taught her what sex meant, what real love could mean. She didn't want any imitations, not ever again. If anything happened between her and Eric, if it became necessary for her to go back to the life she had lived before, she would probably become the biggest female louse the Lord had ever put breath into. And she didn't want that. She wanted to be like other people, to live like other people. Mostly, she just wanted to be happy.

She was happy with Eric, happier than she had ever been before. If only he would get a job, go to work, then maybe later on they could get married.

Only he had never talked of marriage.

He had never once mentioned it.

That was one of the tough things about it.

The other was the money. She couldn't keep on giving out money when she didn't have it. Nobody could. As it was, in spite of all of the money she had made, she had cut down on lunches and walked home at night when she should have ridden the bus, just to save a few dollars. And for what? It made her a little sick when she thought about it.

For what?

For Eric.

And Eric had to have more and more and more. Maybe he was right and maybe she was wrong, but she just couldn't help it. You couldn't clip up a bunch of newspapers and make money out of it; until that day came you had to use your sense.

If she had to, she could get money through Molly. Molly would always be glad to see her and men would always be willing to pay for the false excitement of her body. Men would pay fifty dollars for a few minutes of that. Or a hundred. Or more.

She looked into the mirror over the sink. She was still beautiful and men would be willing to pay. That was now, but what about later? What about the years when she wouldn't be so beautiful, when she would have to wear prison-like foundation garments to keep from sagging all over the place—what about then? Men wouldn't pay for her then. Nobody would. There had to be something definite to look forward to, a positive future that she could see and know and be certain would exist.

Eric was today.

And Eric had to be her future.

She was not trying to compromise that; she was only trying to understand it. Trying, for one of the few times in her life, to do the right and the sensible thing.

"Ann?"

"I'll be out in a minute."

"Ann, I'm going now."

"Going? Where?"

"Up to the club."

"You'll be right back?"

"No. First, I'm going up to Kidder's house to see if I can borrow that hundred from him." There was a moment's silence. "It's too big a thing, Ann, to let a few bucks stand in our way."

"Eric—"

"So long, Ann."

"Eric—"

"I said so long!"

"Eric, don't be angry with me."

"I'm not angry. So long!"

But she could tell by the way he spoke that he was boiling. She leaned back against the wall and closed her eyes, breathing heavily. She couldn't help it. There was nothing she could do.

She heard the front door slam and a dull stillness filled the apartment. Even the water dripping steadily from the hot water faucet didn't seem to make any noise.

"Eric!"

She rushed out of the bathroom, running after him, sobbing, chasing him.

"Eric!"

He caught her as she came out of the bedroom, spinning her around, holding her tight.

"Fooled you," he said, laughing. "Banged the door and you thought I was gone."

"Oh!" she sighed. "Don't ever do that to me again!"

And then he was making love to her, violent love, the only way he knew how to make love, the way she wanted him to love her.

"Baby!"

He tore her clothes, bruised her mouth with his lips, bruised the soft flesh of her body with his hands.

"Oh, Eric!"

And finally the yesterdays and tomorrows were all swept aside by the storm and there was just this day, this hour, this flaming instant that was important. Their love was always like this.

Long after the storm passed she clung to him, trembling, wanting him, needing him, seeking to assure herself of his love.

"Baby, I've gotta go up to that club."

"Yes, I know you do."

"I'm late already. And I've gotta stop and see that Kidder first."

She arose from the bed and walked into the living room. She opened her pocketbook and took out five twenties.

"Good luck," she told him as she pressed the money into his hand.

"Luck," he said, and kissed her.

She showered and dressed. She didn't know why she dressed. She wasn't going anywhere. She didn't have any money, not after she set aside the rent and the car payment, and there wasn't anywhere she wanted to go anyhow.

But she had to go.

She knew she did.

There was no other way.

Eighty-five dollars a week wasn't much and two hundred wasn't enough. There had to be more, a lot more.

She sat in the living room, smoking, thinking about it. She wished she had a drink.

It was midnight when Eric called. He was out at the club, talking to the manager, and something had come up.

"He wants another hundred," Eric said. "Can you imagine that? The crummy bastard!"

"But, Eric—"

"Please, baby. Please! We've gotta do it some way."

She hesitated only an instant. "All right," she said. "We'll do it. Some way."

After he hung up she didn't put the phone down. She just jabbed at the little button, caught the dial tone, and spun Molly's number.

There was nothing else she could do.

And it would only be for a little while.

Until Eric started working.

12

But Eric didn't get a job. After squandering almost five hundred dollars at the club he reported that the bartender who had been going to quit wasn't quitting and that he couldn't make a connection.

"The lousy crumb," he said, referring to the manager of the club. "The dirty, stinking, lousy crumb, you'd think he'd at least give me my dough back."

By this time Ann no longer cared about the money. The money didn't mean anything. She was making plenty of it with Molly and five hundred dollars one way or the other didn't make a great deal of difference. Five night's work, from seven until nine, that's what it meant. Ten hours a week—not much at all.

"Don't worry," she told Eric. "You'll find something."

Actually, she didn't care whether he did or not. He was always home in the apartment waiting for her to come in and that was the important thing.

"Yeah," he said. "But you're working so damned hard, until nine and ten almost every night. It doesn't seem right, baby. It just doesn't."

"Stop complaining and kiss me."

"Like this?"

And then, together, they would find what no one else had ever been able to give either of them.

Love. A sense of need, an unexplainable tenderness ringed with the violence of passion.

Love, that's what they gave each other. Love that lasted into the night, beyond the slow tick of the clock in the darkness, until the morning light when the spinning wheel of frustration would start all over again.

With all the unhappiness and worry she was feeling at the time, something else happened then which made things worse. Her mother returned the money. Ann had made the mistake of sending too much. In a brief, almost unreadable note her mother said that Ann couldn't possibly afford to send so much money, and that she must be getting it in an illegal way.

"Things are better," the note had continued. "Your father has stopped most of his drinking and he goes to work nearly every day. But he doesn't talk. That's the thing that bothers me. He doesn't talk."

After that Ann didn't send any money.

She was doing well at the office. Slade Martin was a dynamo, lining up the new convention, driving his department heads, yelling for increased production from the assembly lines. Many times his demands were unreasonable, but he was well liked throughout the plant and everybody did their best to get the work turned out.

"You tell me," he said to Ann one afternoon. "You tell me if I'm wrong. Willouby gave me a job to do, to put All-Channel on its feet, and I'm doing my level best to accomplish it. But you tell me if I'm doing wrong in driving these people so much."

"No, you're not wrong."

"With these changes, with colored cabinets, we've got a chance to sweep the whole television industry with this next show. Why, even Sam Anderson is coming up from Baltimore and Anderson is one of the biggest distributors in the country. You know how big he is? He must have at least three or four thousand outlets. He could order twenty thousand sets and not even know he'd been here."

"That's good."

"And it all started with Kane."

"It did?"

"Yes. The word gets around, fast. Kane ordered five thousand sets and that was big business for Kane. Not only that, but Kane has done well with them, better than I thought he would. And better than he thought, I'm sure. He's even re-ordered a couple of times. But that's the secret in this business. You load up their floors with one brand and they don't have much choice but to stick with you. Their credit is established, they run out of one model or the other, and they just naturally come back to the same old trough."

Ann said nothing. There were times when Slade liked to talk about himself or the business and during these moments no comment from her was either necessary or expected.

"It all began with you, Ann."

"It did?"

"Yes, you're the one who pushed Kane over the hump. I couldn't have done it. Willouby couldn't have done it. Nobody I know of could have done it. I don't know how you did."

It was something they talked about a lot, more so now than ever before. With the new convention coming up Slade was trying to decide which method was best to upset Anderson so that he would set the pace for this convention as Kane had set the pace for the previous one.

Ann responded with her stock retort. "I just talked with him about the chassis, that's all."

And Slade had a stock reply for that. "Your own or All-Channel's?"

It was fun working for Slade. He was a driver and a perfectionist but he was fun, too. He could laugh at a joke, tell one—most of his were as off-color as the devil—and he knew just when to ease up on the pressure. But as the convention date neared, as correspondence from the salesmen in the field piled up and letters had to be answered, it was almost impossible to relax, to avoid being caught up in the giant claws of a machine that had only one object—to sell television sets.

They sent up two girls from the typing pool but even this didn't help very much. Ann found it increasingly difficult to complete her work by five o'clock and she had to be finished by that time. She would leave the building, hurriedly, and phone Molly from the corner drug store. Molly would give Ann her call and she would dash to the hotel or motel or wherever it was she had to go and get the business taken care of. The men always wanted her to stay, to have a few drinks, but she always put them off. It was the same old thing every evening—get your money, give them what they want, then dress and run like hell for the nearest exit.

Slowly, like a creeping disease, she felt the pressure at the office wearing her down. Once or twice she thought of quitting but she was now getting a hundred dollars a week and she clung to the hope that Eric would get a job, that she could forget about Molly, that she would be able to pick up some of the pieces and start a different life.

Eric was now drinking heavily, especially in the evening, and she drank with him to keep him company. They made love and got drunk and made love again. Sometimes he went out late, racing the motor of the Chrysler, and she would lie on the bed, wondering where he was going, what he was doing.

"Eric, don't drive when you're drunk."

"Shut up."

"But you shouldn't. If you ever had an accident—"

"Oh, for Pete's sake, shut up. Shut up. It's all right for you, because you're outta here all day. But I gotta sit around and look at these walls. You think it ain't driving me nuts?"

"Eric, if you got a job—"

"At forty or fifty bucks a week? Are you outa your mind? Hell, I make more than that playing the ponies."

But he didn't make any money on the horses. One day he would hit a lucky one and he'd buy whiskey and want to take her to dinner but the next day he would be broke and losing, and she would have to give him the money to pay his debt.

They fought about his gambling, his not working, his drinking; but in the end they went to bed and made love. They made love slowly, wonderfully, but when it was over and they lay there side by side reality returned as their bed partner. She would fight with him then, hoping that he would change, knowing that he wouldn't.

"I need fifty, honey."

"But why?"

"Well, it's a long story. But there's a guy and—"

And she would give him the fifty, or the hundred, or whatever else he needed. She would give him the money she made from Molly, from the men who bought her and used her. Not once did Eric ask where she got so much money, not once was he curious about its source. All he did was ask for money, and more money, and what he did with it she didn't know.

She was keeping a man. That much was so. She was keeping a man the way other women like her kept men, men that could please them, men they could own because they were willing to pay the price in hard, cold cash.

There were times when she knew that this could not last, that it would have to end, and end badly. But other men left her only empty and incomplete, and so she would turn to him again, grasping, begging for the brief moments which were the only wholeness she knew.

Yet all of this began to have an effect on her at the office. She made mistakes, she tired and she was very curt with the girls from the pool. The little blonde who frankly admitted that she wanted Slade irritated her particularly.

"Oh, what a lover he must be," the blonde said dreamily. "Honest, guys like that could make you want to be a momma."

"You wouldn't be the first," the brunette said.

"What?"

"I saw his old secretary, Betty, on the street the other day. She's getting a belly."

"His present one won't," the blonde predicted. "She wouldn't let him touch her if he were president and had an act of congress to back him up."

Ann, overhearing the conversation, felt her face flame.

"You shut up," she yelled, hating the blonde. "You shut your filthy mouth."

But it didn't stop there. It went further, into Slade's office. He had heard her shouting at the blonde and her anger surprised him.

"I think you're working too hard," Slade said.

"No, I'm all right."

"These girls from the pool aren't much, I know. But you'll just have to be patient. In another week we'll have the convention lined up and things will began to slow down for you."

"Yes."

"I want you to be fresh and ready for the convention. Your chore is to take care of Anderson the way you took care of Kane."

Ann smiled, a little bitterly, a little wistfully. She could take care of Anderson.

She could take care of any man.

"All right," she said, turning away. "I'll do my best."

"Ann?"

"What?"

"I'm wondering if you'd mind working a little late tonight. Maybe until seven or something like that. We've got the rest of the brochure to get out and if we get it to the printers the first thing in the morning it'll make about three days difference in the time that it's finished. I want to make sure that every dealer gets one in the mail just before the convention."

Working late meant giving up one night for Molly but she guessed she could afford that. Eric hadn't asked for any money the night before and she had slightly more than a hundred dollars in her pocketbook. And tomorrow night was another night. She could always get more where that had come from.

"I'll be glad to help," she said.

At five o'clock the girls left the office and it got very quiet. Slade's door was open and from the direction of his windows, pushed all the way up to let in the cool air, she could hear the sounds of departing cars.

"Ann?"

"Yes."

"We might as well get with it."

"Okay."

But there wasn't much to do. She could see that right away. Most of the brochure was set, lying on his desk, some of it already set up in type. He dictated a paragraph, had her scratch it out, dictated another one.

"I can't think," Slade complained.

You'd do better, she thought, if you stopped looking at the top of my sweater, or my legs, or whatever else it is you might be looking at.

"To hell with it," Slade said, finally. "I've got no interest in this, anyway."

"Maybe you're not in the mood."

"Not for this, I'm not."

She arose to go. It wasn't six o'clock. She could still pick up a call from Molly and be home by nine at the latest.

"Ann, wait a minute. I want to talk to you."

She paused, turned and came back to the desk.

"Sit down, Ann."

She sat down, crossing her legs.

All right, she thought, maybe that's what he wanted to see. Let him have a good look. He hadn't made a pass at her for so long she had forgotten the last time. Well, no, she hadn't forgotten it. They'd been near the water cooler and he'd sort of pushed in against her, rubbing.

"Ann, I don't know if you realize just how I feel about you."

"I'm trying to do a good job," she said. "Maybe I am a little tired. This afternoon—"

"No, I don't mean that. We all blow up once in a while. If we didn't blow up we wouldn't be anybody at all. No, it isn't that. It's something else. And it's personal."

"Yes, Slade."

He looked at her and then away. It was obvious that he was disturbed.

"Can I speak to you frankly, Ann?"

"I hope so."

"I didn't have anything to do tonight. Not a thing. This brochure is all wrapped up. But I wanted to talk to you. Ann, why are you so distant with me?"

"Distant?"

"Yes."

"I'm sorry. I didn't realize that I was."

"Well, you've been busy. I know that. Ann, you know what they say about me. Up to a point some of the stuff has been true, but a lot of it isn't. And it hasn't been true lately." He laughed a little. "I've been pretty much on the go lately. Maybe that's got something to do with it."

This man, she thought, was the man she had wanted, the man she once had, the man who didn't count. This was her boss, good looking, successful, powerful. And yet he didn't matter.

"I could go for you, Ann," Slade said. "I could go for you in a big way. You know that, don't you? I went for you that one night and I've never gotten over it. There have been others—a lot of others—but there was never another one like you, Ann. I wanted you to know that."

So that was why he had asked her to stay—he wanted her again. She had known, of course, that it was bound to happen. Once a man enjoyed a woman—and Slade had enjoyed her that night, deeply—he had to have her again.

"Slade," she said, "let's not talk about it."

She didn't want to talk about it, to think about it. Her life was too confused as it was. She sold herself to men and she maintained a man. But she earned her money at All-Channel; she earned every cent of it. She wasn't going to give her body to her boss for a bonus. He had no right to expect it. It was the one association which she had left in life that was clean and decent. She had to keep it. If she ever let it slip by there would be nothing else.

"But I want to talk about it," he said.

"I don't."

"You're offended."

She stood up, brushing the dress down over her hips.

"No, I'm not offended. It's just how I feel." Finality was in her voice, leaving much unsaid, but leaving nothing to be misunderstood. "If there isn't anything else I'll go."

"There's nothing else," he said. "I'm sorry, Ann."

"I'm sorry, too," she said. "Good night, Slade."

"Good night."

After she left the building she walked down to the drug store at the corner and stood there thinking.

It was crazy but she had the feeling that she was standing at some kind of a crossroads—some kind of a crossroads to her life. There was no reason for her to feel this way, she kept telling herself; there was no sense to it. But she did.

Once inside the drug store, and for a dime, she could call Molly. Molly would give her a name, an address. She would go to the man and earn the money. After that she would go home to the apartment, to Eric, and there would be love and drinks and more love. And tomorrow there would be the office. It would be the same thing all over again—coffee in the morning, then lunch, then the afternoon break, if there was time, then five o'clock and another phone call.

The same thing every day. Never any changes. Just the work at the office changed and the men changed. The work at the office changed more than the men. The men were big or they were small. Some of them were awfully big and some of them were incredibly small. Kids, almost. Fools. Husbands. Lovers. Men. Just men. Different faces but that was about all that was different. Men.

She hated them.

She turned away from the drug store and walked down the street. She didn't have to call Molly, not tonight. She had a little money, enough for Eric, and she could forget about men for just one night.

She felt good, free. Optimistic, maybe. This didn't have to go on. She didn't have to live this way. She didn't have to go on selling herself day after day, loathing every second of it. She could sit down with Eric and have a long, serious talk. She now earned a hundred dollars a week. Eric could get a job. Whether it was fifty or forty dollars a week didn't make any difference; he could get a job. They didn't have to drive a big car, one of the biggest on the market. They didn't have to live on Tom's Hill. And they didn't have to drink so much. They could cut down on all of these things. They could get a smaller car, maybe something secondhand, and they could move to the East End where rents were cheaper. Yes, they could do all of these things and once they had done them they would be able to live like a couple of human beings.

They might even get married.

That was the one thing that shocked her, the one thing that jolted her into a recognition of what she had been doing to herself—and to Eric. Marriage had to be on the level. Marriage without being on the level wasn't any good. You had to be sure. And Ann thought she knew Eric well enough to be sure.

They were two of a kind, she and Eric. She felt this and she wanted it to be so. What had he done with all of that money she had given him? Drinking? Horses? Women? She didn't know. She didn't want to know. Except—no, not women. She couldn't stand that. She was all the woman Eric needed, all he ever had to have. Not women. That was the one thing he hadn't done. She was sure of that. The other things she didn't know about. And it didn't make any difference. They had both been fools, but it didn't need to go on like this. They didn't have to confess, and they didn't have to apologize. All they had to do was make a sensible start to their lives and keep on going.

He would be surprised to see her; this was the earliest she had been home in days. She felt relief as she thought about it. She had been living in dread that he would phone her at the office sometime and find out that she never worked late.

She hastened her steps, then turned to the street and waved for a taxi. She couldn't wait to get to the apartment! It would be so wonderful to spend the evening with him, to talk and plan, to feel his lips on her mouth, his hands on her body, to know that here was something that would last forever.

The cab got caught in the early show traffic and she asked the driver to hurry.

"I'm hurrying, lady," the driver said.

She couldn't wait.

Why hadn't she thought of this before? They didn't need everything. They could settle for less, and a lot less. As long as they had each other, as long as she could creep into his arms when she needed him badly, what else could they need?

She gave the driver a five and told him to keep the change. She couldn't afford it but she felt too good to wait. The car was there in front of the building, big, sleek and long. Well, they could do without that. Love in a Ford could be just as good.

She let herself into the apartment without making a sound. She would surprise him. Maybe he was in the bedroom, sleeping, and she would wake him up with a kiss. She would place her mouth on his lips and force them open, driving him wild until he took her in a moment of frenzy.

She stopped in the living room. The radio must be on. She could hear voices. She smiled. A soap opera. A girl and a boy in love.

"Darling, darling, darling!"

And the boy, his voice muffled, "Oh, baby, baby, baby!"

She stepped into the bedroom.

And stopped.

She stood very still, hardly breathing, unwilling and unable to believe what she saw.

There they were—Eric and the girl from next door.

And they weren't just kissing.

She turned away, and stumbled toward the front door. She made no more noise going out than she had coming in.

She walked the streets for a long time. She hated him. Oh, damn him. Damn him! No wonder he had needed money, no wonder he hadn't wanted to work. There was too much for him to take care of in the apartment. Too much. The animal. Oh, the stinking animal!

She entered a bar and had a drink. Two drinks. Three drinks. Except for the burning sensation in her throat she hardly felt the liquor. After the fourth drink she walked back to the telephone booth and called Molly.

"The Trendwalk," Molly said. "Room four-fourteen. And this guy is a bear. You may not want to take it."

"Fine," Ann said. "I need a bear."

The Trendwalk was a small hotel on the East side of town, along the river. There was no elevator and she had to walk up to the fourth floor. She was breathing heavily when she knocked on the door of four-fourteen.

"Come in."

The man who stood at the dresser fixing a drink was a big, shaggy man in his early forties.

"Molly sent me," Ann said.

The man's eyes took a quick look and registered instant approval.

"Not bad," he said, grinning. "Not bad."

"Come on, mister," Ann said, moving toward him. "Here's one girl who really wants a man."

Her hate was for Eric, for this man, for all men, but when she gave herself to him, this man believed it was honest, unrestrained, violent passion.

He gave her a fifty dollar tip.

"You earned it," he said.

And she had.

13

Slade was disgusted. You couldn't depend on that Molly any more. The girl she had sent the night before cost him fifty bucks and had been worth five. Or two. What kind of a business was Molly running, anyway? And, on top of that, the hotel room had cost him ten. Being careful, he decided, was expensive. He might better grab one of the girls out of the office and forget about Willouby. That blonde, for instance, from the typing pool, the one who looked at him with sheets in her eyes. But he couldn't forget about Willouby. He had to play it smart. Willouby paid him five hundred bucks a week for being smart.

He couldn't fool around with the girls in the plant. Willouby had been explicit about that.

"And keep the women away from your apartment," Willouby had said. "I don't want any scandal about you or have some woman causing you trouble. You're making good money. If you've got to get in your licks get a girl who does it for pay. You shouldn't have any trouble. This town is full of women for cash."

Dames, he thought now; two dollar dames who got a fancy price. Well, the next time he called Molly he'd make sure he got something with some life. He was making good money and he could afford it. He'd offer a hundred next time.

He drank his morning coffee and stared at the reports from Sales. But he wasn't seeing any of the figures on the paper.

Just one figure.

Ann Frank's.

Hell! It was enough to drive a man out of his mind, seeing her around every day, watching her, smelling her.

He had to have her again. He simply had to! If he wasn't the general manager of All-Channel and if she couldn't cause any trouble by yelling her head off, he'd get what he wanted, even if he had to force her.

Slade shook his head and drank some more coffee. He thought of what Willouby had said to him the other day.

"It's none of my business," he had remarked, "but you ought to settle down and get married, Slade. You've got a good job here and it's yours as long as you want it. If this next convention goes over good you'll be in line for the presidency. That will mean more money, greater responsibility. Yes, I'd say it's time for you to settle down."

To that snob of a daughter of his, Slade thought with contempt. Maybe that's what Willouby wanted, somebody to shack up with her permanently. He couldn't blame Willouby. She was a pain in the you-know-where. Nights when Slade went out to Willouby's for dinner sometimes it made him almost sick just to look at her across the room. Flat chest, a belly that wouldn't stay in and hips like a school boy. The worst part of it was she had a rather nice face—sort of stupid, but nice. She'd look at Slade with those big dark eyes and Slade would look right back at her, trying to see something and finding nothing. Yeah, maybe that was what Willouby wanted. Maybe Willouby was getting tired of looking at her himself.

Slade sighed and pushed the coffee cup aside. Thursday. The day that Willouby came into town and hung around the office like a fat cow up to its knees in mud. Thursday was a slow day at the golf course. Thursday was the day when the doctors took trips out of town, the businessmen worried about and planned for the weekend business, the days when the lawyers were in the local court earning fat fees. Yes, Thursday was a slow day at the golf course. Ladies' day. Just women. Once Slade had gone out there for a drink with Willouby and there had been women all over the crazy place. He still remembered the redhead who'd been leaning up against the bar. She smiled at him and he'd smiled back. But nothing had happened beyond that. Just a smile. Sometimes a guy couldn't win.

He started to sweat. Lord, he had to do something. This dame in the office was driving him out of his mind. And that girl last night—oh, what a thief she was! Just wait until the next time. He'd go up to a hundred and wouldn't pay a dime, not a dime, until he found out that it was worth renting a room for.

He thought about Molly some more. Maybe he could work it so he could get a girl for nothing. He hadn't discussed it with Willouby yet but he thought of hiring some call girls and turning them loose on the convention. He couldn't ask the girls from Promotion to do any of the things that he would like them to do. Maybe it was even a mistake to trust Anderson with Ann Frank. Somebody had told him Anderson looked for fun at a convention and he could only expect Ann to go just so far. He still couldn't figure how she'd bulled Kane into that big order but she had and that was what had put him where he was now. Of course, he had run a risk in doing a thing like that, but to have told Willouby the truth would have only stolen some of his thunder. Willouby thought he was a genius. Well, that part was all right. He'd done a good job as general manager and he'd do a better one. If only that Ann Frank . . .

"Ann?"

"Yes, Slade."

"Have Jefferies come up from Promotion. Right away."

"Will do."

Cool, he thought; cool and nice. Clean. Fresh. He wished he could stop thinking about her. A thing like this was crazy. He might be in love with her. But that was equally insane, having such a thought. He wasn't in love with her, any more than he had been in love with Betty. It was her body that he wanted.

Betty. Now there was a one. He sent her a check every week and he never heard from her. It was almost as though she didn't care, as though she wanted the kid. It was fantastic. How do you figure a dame, anyway?

Jefferies came in, leaving the door open.

"Close the door," Slade said.

He was getting sick of Jefferies, of his theories, of his lack of results.

"Sit down," Slade said.

Jefferies sat down, stretching his legs.

"I envy you, Slade," he said, winking. "That blonde out there—she's a number, all right. Funny, but I didn't used to notice her much when she was in Promotion. But now that she's up here in your office she looks mighty good."

"She's a hard worker," Slade said.

"Is that all she is?"

"What else would she be?"

"Well, knowing you—"

"That's the point," Slade cut in. "You don't know me, Jefferies. How long is it going to take you people around here to understand that?"

"I don't get you."

"You will." Slade didn't like to be kept on the hook and he didn't like putting anybody else on it, but with Jefferies it was different. "What about that magazine release, Jefferies?"

"We sent it out."

"You messed it all up, that's what you did. You ruined the whole thing by putting that dame in there."

"Sex will sell anything."

"Sex, yes. A cute little doll would sell axes in a sawmill. I agreed with you, Jefferies. But you didn't use sex. You used a fully dressed dog next to our best set."

"She didn't charge for it," Jefferies said doggedly. "And she gave us a release for nothing."

"Now listen, Jefferies. I had a good deal set up there, and you boffed it. I had Advertising schedule a full page ad in the mag and the editor said sure, he'd run a plug on our new color sets in his New Products Section. A tie-in, sort of. Then you went and sent him this pic that he couldn't use. All he wanted, for Pete's sake, was a shot of the set. So what do you send him? You send him a crummy pic of the set and standing alongside it a girl with a face full of teeth. He threw it out, that's what he did. He threw it out and we lost the best free ride we ever had a chance to take. That mag has got fifteen million circulation. Get that? Fifteen million. And you doused it like a drowning cat."

Jefferies tried to pass it off. "I made a mistake," he ventured.

"I guess you did. Who was the dame?"

"I'm engaged to her."

"And she wanted to get her picture in a magazine? She thinks she's a model, maybe?"

"Something like that," Jefferies admitted.

Slade gave it to him straight. "You botched it," he said, "and it's costing you your job. You're done, Jefferies. Finished. Through." He reached for a scratch pad. "Here. You give this to Accounting and they'll give you two week's salary. You don't have to stick around. I don't want you. You're liable to screw up something else for me before you get out of here."

"But, Slade—"

"I've got nothing more to say, Jefferies. I hate to fire people. I wouldn't want to get fired myself. But I can't have people who are supposed to be doing a job and then run around and wiping their noses for them."

"It was a mistake," Jefferies said. "An error in judgment. I won't do the same thing again."

"Of course you won't. You won't be here."

Jefferies begged for his job, pleaded for it, but Slade stuck to his decision. He'd get somebody else to run Promotion. Or he'd do it himself. It didn't matter much. He simply couldn't afford costly mistakes.

When Jefferies saw it would do him no good to talk, that Slade had made up his mind, he left. He said Slade was a bastard and Slade agreed with him.

"You got to be a bastard in this business," Slade said. "Only the bastards survive."

He sent out for more coffee and studied the sales reports. They weren't good and they weren't bad. Average. He cursed and pushed them aside. They had to be more than that. They had to be the best.

But there was money in the bank and Production was working at near full capacity. Some of the workers who had been laid off had been brought back. The newspaper hailed it as an economic advancement for North Hope. The write-ups in the trade magazines had been generous, referring to Slade as a boy wonder with both feet planted squarely on the ground. All in all, things were good. But they could be better. And Anderson was the key, the big boy.

Strange, Slade thought, how every convention had one man who led the herd. But he supposed conventions were not much different than anything else, as far as that went. There was always a guy at the top, always somebody you had to upset. Once you cut him down to your size you could go anywhere. Until then, you had to mince along like an old lady with a busted leg.

"Slade?" The intercom buzzed. "Slade, are you there?"

"Yes, Ann."

"There's a Mr. Anderson calling you. From Philadelphia."

The palms of Slade's hands were wet. Maybe Anderson wasn't coming to the convention. Maybe the whole thing was ready to blow up.

"Yeah. Sure, Ann."

Anderson came on. He had a deep voice, as though he were in the next room shouting at somebody.

"Got your letter, Mr. Martin," Anderson said. "Thanks for the personal invitation to the convention."

"You're welcome." It was all Slade could think of to say at the moment.

"Sorry I won't be able to be with you but the wife likes Florida this time of the year. You know how women are—pleasure before business."

Slade was stunned. "I see."

"We're leaving tomorrow."

"Well, have a good trip," he mumbled.

"I'd like to get up to your convention."

"I wish you could, too."

"Your new models look pretty good. Catchy. That one that fits into a corner—that's not bad. And the color scheme ideas—not bad, either."

"Thanks."

"I think I could use about fifteen thousand sets, to start."

Slade nearly fell out of the chair.

"What!"

"When I get back from Florida I'll drive up and we can sit down and really talk some business."

Slade reached for a pencil. His hand shook. This was terrific!

"Fifteen thousand sets," he repeated. "In what ratio—in table models and consoles?"

"Well, you know best what sells," Anderson told him. "You mix up the shipment so's I'll have a good line. You know, so's I can get started. Afterward we can fill in the gaps, once we find out what moves fastest."

"Yes, sir."

"I'll send out ten thousand today as a deposit. Bill me for the rest at two percent ten and net in thirty. Okay?"

"Yes, sir!"

"And have a good convention, will you?"

"Thanks. And have a good trip."

After Anderson hung up Slade sat there staring at the phone. They couldn't miss now. Couldn't miss! The convention was a guaranteed success and Production would be swamped.

He thought of sending out for more coffee and decided against it. He was drinking too much coffee. Coffee didn't help him think. And he had to think. He had to figure out, right now, just where he was going.

He was assured now of the presidency, of more money, of being in so solid with Willouby that he couldn't be more solid if his feet were planted in concrete.

What was it Willouby had said? Respectability. A man had to have respectability, Willouby had said. He had to have dignity, poise, he had to have a sense of responsibility to himself and his community. It was part of the price of success. People looked up to a successful man. They looked up to him and respected him. In turn, the man had to measure up to a certain standard. Again it was part of the price of getting ahead.

Slade again thought of sending out for coffee but discarded the idea. He was coming closer to what he had to think about, to making up his mind about what he had to do. And he had to do it now.

Slade knew one thing. He was going on a tear, a great big, giant of a tear to celebrate this victory over Anderson and then he was going to settle down. Maybe he'd even get married; that would really slow him down to a walk.

Marriage. He hadn't dared to think about it before but now it didn't scare him so much. He could afford marriage—a big house, a fast car, all of the things that a woman would want, all of the things that could keep a woman happy. But what kind of a woman? That was the problem. What kind of a woman? And yet, it was no problem. He knew the kind of woman, and more than that, he knew her name.

Ann Frank.

Ann would make a good wife for an executive, the type of wife a man could he proud to display. She had looks, brains and she had class. She also had a wonderful body. All were important factors but especially the body part. He wouldn't want to stray from that gorgeous body. God, no. When he wasn't at the office he'd want to be at home with her, owning her the way a man was supposed to own a woman. Well, he asked himself, what was wrong with that? What was wrong with it? Nothing, that's what was wrong with it. Nothing.

But it wasn't so easy as that. Inside of him there was an emptiness, a void that thinking about her didn't fill, a hollowness that he didn't understand. It was as though there was something being left out, something being overlooked.

"Slade."

"Yeah?"

"Here comes Mr. Willouby."

"Send him in."

He would have to think about it later. He would have to decide about all this after Willouby was gone.

Right now he was still climbing the ladder.

14

Two days after Ann broke up with Eric—she'd called him on the phone and cut it off that way—the police came to the apartment looking for her. She was just getting ready to go out on an early call for Molly and her first thought was that Molly had been raided and that all of her girls were being pulled in.

"Miss Frank? Ann Frank?"

Ann stood in the doorway, hardly breathing, looking out at the two uniformed officers.

"Yes."

"You own a fifty-eight Chrysler?"

"Yes, I do."

"Well, it's smashed up."

"Smashed up?"

"All to pieces." The officer hooked his fingers in his belt and leaned back. "The girl who lived in the apartment next to you was killed and the fellow is in bad shape."

"Eric?"

"That's the name he gave us. Eric Lowen. He's in the hospital, wrapped up like a mummy. But he can talk. He said we'd find you here."

She had been so hurt she had told Eric to take the car, that she never wanted to see him again. And now he was lying in the hospital, hurt. It didn't seem possible.

"Is he bad?"

"Pretty bad; they don't know just how bad yet. He was lucky he wasn't driving. The girl got the steering wheel right in her chest and it snuffed her out like a light."

"And the other car?"

"No other car. They hit a concrete abutment down near the bridge that goes over the river. I guess she was driving so fast that she couldn't make the turn. You insured, lady?"

"Yes, I'm insured."

"You're lucky. There was no damage to the abutment or any city property but the guy has just about had it and there's going to be some big hospital bills. The girl I guess you don't have to worry about none. Far as I can tell she didn't have anybody, just so much money that she didn't know what to do with it."

"Won't do her no good where she is now," the other cop said. The first policeman flipped open a black leather note book and then returned it to his pocket.

"You and this guy married or anything?" he wanted to know.

"No. Just friends."

"He got any folks?"

"A mother and father but I don't know where they live."

The policeman nodded. "We asked him about that but he wouldn't help us none. Said he wanted to keep his people out of it. We checked the address on his driver's license and came up with an old rooming house. The woman there didn't even remember him."

"Well, his folks ought to know," the other policeman said. "A kid like that ought to have somebody. You got any idea how we could find them, lady?"

"My folks would know."

"Where do they live?"

"Uptown."

The policemen glanced at each other and then back at Ann.

"We could drive you up there," the one said. "And then over to the hospital, if you want."

She looked at the clock. She was already late for her appointment, but it would have to wait. Getting in touch with his people was the least she could do for Eric.

On the way uptown, sitting beside the policeman, she tried to think of Eric as being injured and in the hospital but the vision just wouldn't come through. She hated him for having cheated on her, for what he had done, but he did have a marvelous body. It was incredible to think of it lying smashed and broken, helpless in some bed.

Martha Frank opened the door and when she saw the policemen with Ann she let out a little moan.

"What have you done now?" she wanted to know.

"Nothing, Ma. These men just want to get Eric's address."

"Eric?"

"You know, the fellow who's a friend of the fellow who works with Dad."

"The one who said all those things about you?"

"Yes."

"I don't know." Martha Frank turned her head. "Pa, do you know?"

Pete Frank came shuffling out of the kitchen. He had put on some weight and his face looked good and healthy. He barely looked at his daughter.

"They live on Fullmer Street," Pete Frank said, "but I don't know the number."

"We don't need the number," the one cop said. "We can check the city directory. Thanks, folks."

Neither Ann's father or mother said anything as she turned and walked away with the policemen.

"You want to go to the hospital?" the driver asked her as they got into the car.

"No."

"But he wanted to see you."

"He did?"

"Yes. It was the only thing that he asked."

"It might do him a lot of good," the one in back said. "You take a crack-up like that, there's shock and—"

"Well—all right."

But when they reached the hospital Ann wasn't able to see Eric. They had just returned him from the operating room and he was under sedation. He would be groggy for several hours.

"Are you a member of his family?" the doctor asked her.

"No."

"Then I can't discuss with you the extent of his injuries."

"Will he live?"

"Yes, he'll live but he'll be crippled. I'm sorry. That's all I can say."

Crippled. Smashed. Broken. Again it didn't seem possible.

"Thank you," she murmured, turning away.

She took a cab downtown. There wasn't any point to going up to that man's room now and there wasn't any sense to calling Molly. Molly would be furious with her for missing an appointment. She had better talk to Molly face to face.

Molly was angry.

"We've got to get ourselves organized, honey," Molly said. "It's bad enough to be in this business but it's even worse to throw it away after you get it."

"I'm sorry."

"You ought to be. It cost you sixty bucks and it cost me twenty. Know how I figure that? Well, you get a hundred—you could have from this guy—which leaves you sixty and me forty. But the way it turned out I sent Esther and she can only get fifty. That way, I only make twenty. So you lost and I lost. What kind of thing is that?"

"I said I was sorry, didn't I?"

"Sure, but you just try to buy something with being sorry."

"I know."

"And I know something, too. I know that you're messing around with that crummy job for less than you can make in a night. Why don't you give it up?"

"Maybe I will."

"Honest?"

"Yes."

Molly became more friendly. "That's the idea, Ann. You've got too much to offer in this to throw yourself away on a daytime job. Only the suckers do that."

"Only the suckers."

A couple of men came in and Molly stared at them down the long hallway.

"House stuff," she said. "Five, ten bucks, tops." She shrugged. "So they can have Stella. She likes those cheapies. She says the less a guy spends the longer he takes."

"That's not for me," Ann said.

Molly smiled. "I've got something for you, honey. A hot one."

"Fine."

"He spent fifty bucks with Esther the other night and he howled about her not being any good. Right after I had that first call tonight, the one you missed, he phoned in. I said I'd send somebody as soon as I could. Somebody who'll please him."

"Well, I'll try."

"Try? Hell, you'll do it. He gets one look at you, honey, and he'll go off his rocker."

"He want me for all night?"

"He didn't say. But if he does you can stay. I've done business with him before, and I know that he pays for what he gets."

"Where is he?"

"At the Hotel Temple. Room six-ten. He said he'd be there so just go up and knock. He sounded a little high. Don't let it bother you, though. When he gets drunk he isn't nasty like some of them. He's a pretty regular guy."

Outside, she caught a cab over to the hotel. It had started to rain and the night was cool and dark. The tires hissed on the pavement and the windshield wipers made a clacking sound as they worked back and forth.

She lit a cigarette and considered what had happened to Eric. Life was good when you were young and strong but it was terrible, even if you were mad at someone, when it came to a jolting, slamming stop.

Young. That's what she was. Young and beautiful.

But how long would she stay that way? How long?

Ten years? Five years? Or less? Yes, how long?

It was something to think about, something to be afraid of. Oh, she could make good money at it now, much more than she could ever hope to make working for All-Channel or anybody else. And she could accept it on a moral basis though she knew, inside, that it was wrong. Men, she told herself, had to have women. They would have women no matter what they had to do. They would pay or kill but somehow they would get the women. So she was one of them. Just one. One of many, of hundreds, of thousands. Did that make her any better or any worse than others? Did it?

No!

She hated them, that was her trouble.

She hated them all except Eric.

And she mistrusted Eric. He had cheated on her, had gone to another girl.

Now the girl was dead and Eric was in the hospital. It was hell, a twist of fate.

Well, not a twist of fate, not exactly that. Fate was something that you couldn't help happening and they could have stopped this. They could have been honest with each other. There were two sides to it; she admitted that. She had been dishonest with Eric and he, in turn, had been dishonest with her. They had been a couple of fools. What was the matter with them, anyway?

Her body ached for him, ached for him. It was like a great sickness that came over her, moving in tiny, stubborn waves, a sickness that had to be held and cured and loved. She had never responded to any other man. Never. There just wasn't any other. She had tried a lot of them. And it had always failed. Always.

Maybe there was something that she could do. Maybe it wasn't too late. To begin with, she had to forget about Eric. It was over with for them, washed away as suddenly as snow washes away under the impact of a warm rain. But Eric wasn't the only man. He was the only man who pleased her, but aside from that, there was another.

Slade. Slade Martin.

She could have Slade. She knew that. She could tell it by the way he looked at her, the way he spoke to her. And she could have him for more than just a few minutes. She could have him forever. She could marry him.

Marriage to Slade, she decided, wouldn't be so bad. He had a responsible position, he made good money, and he could buy a woman all the things she needed or wanted. There wouldn't be any physical pleasure in the marriage but she could get along without that. She didn't get any pleasure out of being a prostitute, either. Marriage to Slade would be like selling herself to one man for a long, long time. But then, didn't every woman who got married in a way sell herself? She got a home and furniture and clothes, money to spend, and she made love with the guy. She wouldn't marry him if he didn't have a job, couldn't get up the money.

Or would she? Hadn't she done the same thing with Eric?

It was a crazy, mixed-up world, that's what it was. You stuck your hand into the grinder and sometimes you lost a finger or two. You were just lucky you didn't lose your whole hand.

"One-eighty, lady."

She got out of the cab and paid the driver. She tipped him a buck.

"Thanks, lady."

What the hell, she thought walking toward the hotel, another night, another dollar. You had to look at it that way. If you got sick and disgusted with yourself it wasn't any good. You had to think about the money, just the money. That way it wasn't so bad.

She took the elevator to the sixth floor and when she got off it was like the sliding, banging door was shutting out the rest of the world. From here on it was business. Sex business. The business of body against body, for a fee. The highest paying business in the country.

She knocked on the door of six-ten.

"Come in."

She went in.

And she met Slade Martin.

"Well," was all she could say, staring at him. "Well."

He placed his drink on the dresser and rubbed his forehead with one hand.

"Well," he also said.

And then she was trying to get out of it, blindly, hopefully, wildly. She had seen him enter the hotel. She had asked for him at the desk. She wanted to talk to him.

"What about?" he inquired.

"The convention. I was thinking—"

He shook his head.

"You lie," he said. "You're Molly's girl."

"No!"

"You are. You couldn't have found me here. I registered under another name."

Tears came into her eyes. She didn't know what to do. This was terrible. A few minutes ago she had been thinking of him as her husband and now she stood before him revealed as a prostitute.

"I can't believe it," he said, shaking his head again. "I just can't believe it."

Ann said nothing.

"This was to be my last fling," he told her. He tasted his drink, put it down. "I was even going to ask you to marry me. Isn't that something?" He laughed but there was no humor in the laugh. "Can you beat that? I was going to ask you to be my wife!"

"Slade—"

"Respectability, Willouby said. Find a nice girl and get married, he said. Settle down. And I picked you!"

"Slade—"

"Look," he said. "I don't blame you. You have your reasons. Everybody has reasons. It's just so damned funny, that's all. Me, the smart guy—and never knowing! Isn't that a crock?"

"Slade—"

"You make me sick. You really do. Beautiful. Smart. And—and what you are. Why, Ann? Why?"

She began to cry. "I don't know, Slade. I don't know."

"You must know. You're the only one who can know. Ann, there's a lot of things I've been in my life. But, I've never hurt myself, not deliberately. Why should you? You've got everything. No girl could have more. And you're throwing it all away."

In that moment she despised him. He thought he was so clever, so fine, so good. Well, she'd show him that he was no better than she was. He had sent for a girl. She hadn't applied for the job of spending the night with him. Her job at the company would be shot now, anyway. She might as well get his hundred dollars and forget about him.

"You pay in advance," she said, swaying toward him across the room. "You pay on the line then you get your fun."

He hit her, hard, right across the face. His fingers stung, burning into the skin. She backed away from him, shocked that he would do such a thing.

"Get some sense into your head," he said.

She sneered at him. "Who do you think you are? God?"

"No. Maybe before but not now. Seeing you walk through that door did something to me. And for me. Do you understand, Ann? You did something for me, something that I could never have done for myself."

"A guy can do a lot of things for himself," she said, rubbing her face.

"Ann, don't talk that way. It isn't like you. It isn't you. Don't you see? It isn't you. You think it is, maybe, but it isn't. You're a nice kid. You're no dummy. Smarten up, why don't you? You've got a good job. What more do you want?"

The sting began to leave her face. Somehow, he was a different man, changed. And he was sober. She had never seen him more serious, even when he'd been talking to Willouby.

"I thought you wanted me," she said.

"I did. You don't know how much."

"Well, here I am. Molly's girl. Ready, willing and as able as they come."

"Stop selling yourself short," he said. "I don't want you this way. Can't you see that? I couldn't think a lot of a girl and then buy her. I'm a heel in some ways, but not that big of a heel."

"I suppose just because you're the man it makes you better than me?"

"No, it doesn't."

"I'm surprised that you admit it."

"I said you taught me some things when you came through that door. That's one of them."

A long, tense silence invaded the room.

"I'd better go," Ann said.

"Yes."

"I don't suppose I'll see you again, Slade."

He made no reply.

"Goodbye, Slade."

Again he said nothing.

She went out, closing the door behind her. Not until she reached the elevator did she start to cry. She was still crying when she arrived in the lobby.

Her world had fallen apart.

15

The rain had stopped but the moon still lay behind a bank of thick dark clouds and the night was black. Even the few street fights scattered throughout the Lower East section of the city were of little help.

"I don't know where seventeen is," a woman in a faded housecoat said. "This is twenty-four."

"Then it must be on the other side of the street," Slade decided.

"Must be."

"Well, thanks, anyhow."

"One thing, mister," the woman said. "You go around here banging on every door and somebody's gonna slam you in the teeth." Her glance took in Slade's expensive suit. "This ain't no big shot neighborhood, this ain't. It's regular workin' people and they go to bed early."

Slade thanked the woman and moved away, crossing the street to the other side and going toward the river. Maybe they were working people and maybe they weren't but some of them sure didn't worry about going to bed. Sounds of a party drifted through an open window: the high laughter of women and the deep voices of men. From somewhere nearby a baby cried, and when Slade paused before a darkened brick building, a dog barked savagely.

The hell with this, Slade thought hesitating; oh, man, the hell with it. What are you doing here, you stupid fool? What are you doing here?

But he knew. And there was no other way. He had to do this or he would never be able to live with himself.

His belly still ached from where the pain had seized him when she'd opened the door and walked into his room. Ann Frank. Ann Frank, call girl deluxe.

"I love you," he'd said to the empty room after she'd gone. "I love you."

He'd tried it again and again, saying the words over and over, like he was drunk, like he had suddenly gone out of his mind, but he hadn't felt a thing, just the pain there in his belly and the hollow sickness.

He didn't hate her and he didn't love her. He just felt sorry for her. She was so pretty and she had so much to offer and she was throwing it away. It didn't make sense.

He would never be able to look at her and still want her. No, he'd never feel that compulsion again, that rising, clamoring need that said he must have her. That part of it had been swept away. But he wouldn't hurt her, either. If she wanted to come back to work, if she wanted to keep on with her job in the office, he would do everything he could to help her. Perhaps it would be a good thing for him if she did come back. Every time his office door opened he would see that bedroom door swinging wide and he would see her for exactly what she was. He wouldn't lust for her again, for money or for free. But he would help her, in the same way that one person did not want to see another person drown.

He lit a match and saw that the number on the building was seventeen. It was an old building, wooden frame, and there was a jungle of mail boxes to the right of the big double doors. He lit another match and scanned the names on the mail boxes, most of them fastened to the rusted metal with adhesive tape. The newest piece of tape held the name he sought. Apartment 1C.

It was dark in the hallway, and it smelled of disinfectant. Once he stumbled over a broken window screen.

He found Apartment 1C at the extreme end, on the right. His knock seemed to sound through the whole building.

He knocked again and waited.

"Just a minute." Faintly.

Movement inside of the apartment followed the voice. Slade could hear high, hard heels on the linoleum floor.

"Yes?"

"It's Slade, Betty."

"Slade?"

"Slade Martin."

"Oh!"

The door opened and she stood there, waiting. It was dark in the apartment and he could hardly see her. But he could smell her perfume and her cleanliness.

"Slade," she said, faintly, "you didn't have to come here. I've been getting your money every week. Thank you for sending it."

"Betty." Now that he was here, now that he had found her, he didn't know how to say it.

"Betty, I—"

And then he had her in his arms, holding her tight, her body soft and warm against him, his lips not kissing her but moving over her mouth, her face, to the lobe of one ear.

"You said you loved me," he whispered. "And you said I'd need that love someday. I do. I need it tonight."

"Oh, Slade!"

She turned her head and her mouth found his lips, clinging to them, moving gently.

"I'll always need it," Slade told her. "Not just tonight, but always. I've found out just what you mean to me."

"Oh, Slade!"

He kissed her again.

"What time is it?" he wanted to know.

"About midnight. Why?"

"We could be in Baltimore before morning, if we left right away."

"I guess we could."

"There's a man leaving for Florida tomorrow—or is it today?—a big client of ours, and I could say hello to him."

He felt her stiffen.

"Is that all, Slade?"

He kissed her again but her body was still stiff.

"No. There's no waiting period in Maryland and we could be married on the way back."

She relaxed and clung to him.

"Darling," she murmured. "Darling!"

Slade didn't know if they would leave soon enough to catch Anderson before he left for Florida but one thing he did know—they'd get there in plenty of time to find a justice of a peace.

"I'll have to dress," Betty said. "Won't you come in?"

Slade laughed. "You won't be able to keep me out."

He went in, closing the door behind him.

Ann waited a long time before the doctor would permit her to enter the green-walled room and stand by the side of Eric's bed.

"Don't stay too long," the doctor advised her. "He's going to be all right but he is rather weak."

"I'm okay," Eric protested. "I'm okay now."

But his voice was weak, his face white, and when the doctor left the room he didn't even bother to turn his head.

"I'm glad you came," Eric said.

"I wanted to come."

"Did you?"

"Yes."

Ever since those awful moments with Slade she had wanted something, somebody to cling to.

"That's good," he said. "I was afraid you wouldn't."

"Why not?"

"Because of—her."

"She's—"

"Yes. I know. She's dead." He pressed his lips together. "I wanted her to slow down but she wouldn't. I was yelling at her to slow down when we hit. I remember that."

"You'd better not talk too much," Ann said.

He let out a deep breath. "I have to talk." He was silent for a moment. "My mother and father were here. Just before you came. They weren't sore."

"Nobody's sore, Eric."

"You have a right to be."

"But I'm not."

He reached for her hand and held it.

"I'm sore at myself," he said. "Sore at myself because I've been such a fool. I took money from you, and I knew what you were doing to get it."

She bent and kissed him.

"Let's not talk about that now," she said. "We can talk about that later. The main thing for you to do is get well."

"I'll be in here a long time."

"Yes."

"Ann, I have no right to ask this, but—"

"You have a right to ask anything."

His eyes were grateful. "Ann, will you wait for me?"

All the way up from Slade's hotel and while she was sitting out there in the waiting room she had been thinking about it. She had talked to Eric's father and mother. They were poor people, and they were nice people. Eric's father had explained that Ann's insurance policy didn't cover the car's passengers; it paid primarily for damages to the other vehicle. There would be bills, big doctor bills and big hospital bills, and Eric would be laid up for a long time. Ann had said nothing to them about it because she didn't know if she still had a job at All-Channel, but on a hundred dollars a week she could borrow enough money to take care of the expenses and she could pay it back out of her salary. She did not think of Molly except to know that she was finished with her; she would not sell herself for profit again. If Slade threw her out of All-Channel she could always get a job in some factory or as a waitress.

"I'll wait for you," she said, kissing him again. "And don't worry about anything."

"Thanks, Ann."

"I've grown up tonight," she told him. "You don't know how much I've grown up."

The nurse came in and said that Ann had to go.

"He's had a very serious operation, Miss, and he must get his rest. You can see him again tomorrow."

Ann's lips touched Eric's mouth, lingering.

"I love you," she said. "I just now realized it."

"And I love you. But I've known that a long time. It's the thing that drove me wild, loving you and knowing that—"

"You must go," the nurse broke in. "You simply must."

Ann kissed Eric again and then walked to the door. She turned and smiled at him.

"Don't you worry," she promised. "Everything is going to be all right."

Outside in the hall she met the doctor. It was obvious that he had been waiting for her.

"You said you might marry him," he began. "Is it settled?"

"Yes."

"Then there is something you should know, something that he doesn't know yet."

She thought she knew what the doctor was going to say. Eric would be an invalid the rest of his life. It neither shocked nor frightened her. It was simply something to be accepted and faced with a degree of courage which she had never known before.

"He was thrown forward by the impact of the crash," the doctor said. "He struck the heater and there are parts of the heater that are very sharp. Actually, the only purpose of the operation was to stop the flow of blood. Miss Frank, he will never be a man again. It's unfortunate but that's the way it is."

Slowly, she walked around the doctor and continued on down the hall. She held her head high, walking proudly.

Everything, she thought, had a price. And this was hers.

Maybe she deserved it.

And she knew she would pay it until the end of time.

The End

THE SEX CURE

Elaine Dorian

CHAPTER ONE

The end of Justin Riley began, appropriately enough, in another man's bed, a wide and lumpy four-poster which belonged to Sandy Miles.

Sandy was a farmer, horse trader and riding instructor. All three jobs pleased him.

He lay awake, studying his wife's slender back, remembering how he had rubbed that back with small slow circular motions before they had been married. In those days he had loved her very much. He loved her now even more. But lately she was tired a lot of the time. There was plenty for her to be tired about. A big, rambling dump of a farmhouse to keep clean—an eighteen-month-old kid, forty head of horses that she helped him care for and now, in the summertime, the riding day camp.

He was glad that at least before they got married, he had given Marge a ball—the riding, the sex—because now what they shared were bills and being tired. After they were married and before the baby came, Marge had worked at the hospital as Dr. Riley's lab assistant. Her life had been easier then, he was sure. That Justin Riley—now there was a guy, he thought jealously. Sandy and Justin made their living from the same local society people—Sandy by training their horses, Justin Riley by doctoring them. Some said Justin could get any woman patient he wanted. Except, of course, Marge. Sandy had never believed what someone had tried to tell him—that Marge had quit the hospital for more cause than the imminent baby.

But the very thought of another man knowing the swift, warm delights of Marge's lightly suntanned body caused a sudden rage in Sandy. Hot July breezes climbed through the open windows and brought the tantalizing smells of summer into the room—new-mown grass and freshly bedded stock and open country.

A little sound escaped his lips and he could stand no more longing. His hand began its light, soothing, rotating motion against Marge's back.

She said protestingly, "I'm asleep."

The whisper of protest turned to sleepy-sweet complaint as his body searched for hers. She soon made a sound of acceptance and then of urgency. "Wait, dearest," she begged thirstily, while her passion caught up with his. "Wait for me. I love you."

He buried his face in the hollow of her shoulder as he heard the little whimpering music in her throat that she, and she alone of all women, gave with her love.

He echoed, "I love you."

"You'd better—you've probably made me pregnant again. Just when we're having the best season since we bought the farm."

"Shove the riding season. I want you—all of you—even the babies. Tell me again that you love me."

Her whisper was summery with suppressed and joyous laughter. "Love you? After what just happened, how can you doubt it?"

Satisfied, he rolled over, adjusting cheerfully to the lump in the middle of the mattress. He gave her head a final playful push, reveling in the thick silky feel of her hair.

"It would always be like that," he said sleepily, "If you'd let me wake you more often—"

Marge got up. She headed toward the narrow creaky stairs that led down to the bathroom, robe in hand, fumbling for the armholes. Before she had reached either the bedroom door or her bathrobe sleeves, the phone rang loudly from the night table beside the four-poster.

Sandy rolled over and grabbed the instrument. Mike, the baby, was sleeping in the next room.

Had a horse got loose? Why else would anyone call at—he checked the illuminated dial of the clock beside the phone—twelve o'clock? He said softly and briefly, "Yeah?"

"Sandy?" The voice at the other end was gay, female and slightly martini-thickened. "Misty Powers."

"Yeah, Misty. What's up?"

Misty Powers was the area's gayest divorcee—and because she had three presumably well-born children, a potential customer.

"I'm at the Mohawk Inn," she said. In the background Sandy could hear the music of Tubby Oakes and his Twisters. Cultured and drunken voices were raised in celebration of the midsummer weekend. Misty continued amiably, "Is Marge there?"

Sandy glanced at his wife, who still had not found her sleeves. Marge's nakedness was a sliver of earth-bound moonlight. With unashamed eagerness, Marge waited for the latest gossip or scandal in the gossip-and-scandal ridden life of Misty Powers.

Sandy reported, "Of course she's here. Where did you think she'd be at this hour if I'm here to answer the phone?"

"You two lovebirds," scoffed Misty. "And three months from now, she'll be asking me to recommend a good abortionist." She paused, giving Sandy time to forgive her for the remark. "And that's what this call is all about."

"How's that?" Sandy said, with a sudden illogical feeling that Misty had become a witch in every sense of the word. Did she know what he and Marge had just accomplished?

"Abortions," Misty went on, with the gleeful excitement she brought to any gossip, "and Ju Riley. That girl friend of his who took Marge's place at the hospital just had an illegal abortion. Somebody bungled—and she's been brought into the hospital. The big thing is, she named Ju as the father."

Sandy said soberly, "That's going to fix him." But he was ashamed to find that he was not really sorry for Justin Riley any more than Misty was. Justin had always been too successful with women.

"Fix him? The sonofabitch will be run out of town when Olivia and the senator hear it."

Olivia was Justin Riley's wife. The senator was her father. Justin had married well.

Sandy said worriedly, "Maybe the girl was lying. Anyway, Justin will beat the rap the way he's done before."

"Not this rap," said Misty. "Be sure to tell Marge all about it, won't you? And tell her to call me tomorrow."

"Will do." He replaced the phone in its black cradle. Damn that witch. He wished the call had not come. A minute ago, he and Marge had been as close, physically and emotionally, as a man and his wife could be close. Now a third person seemed to have joined them. The oversized shabby room with its planked floors, its hook rugs, its clothes hung on a corner pole, should not have been invaded.

He reached for a cigarette and said, "It seems your old boy friend, Justin Riley, has been keeping busy lately." He told her what Misty had said, adding, "Why couldn't she wait till morning? The story's none of our business—may not even be true—and anyway, how in hell could a doctor be so stupid as not to take precautions?"

Slipping into the robe at last, pulling the belt tightly about her thin little waist, Marge said, "Oh, I don't know. I guess doctors can be as stupid as anyone when they're in love."

"Was Justin in love with the girl?"

"So I heard. Sandy, I like Justin—whatever anyone says. He was a wonderful friend to us when Mike was so sick. And I don't know how we'd have gotten through, two years ago, if I hadn't had that job at the hospital. We haven't always had good seasons."

"That job sure didn't do much for the girl who took your place." He kept studying Marge in the pale light of the moon. He lit a fresh cigarette from the stub of the old one and wished suddenly and unreasonably that he could get hold of Justin Riley's handsome, perfectly tailored body and do it some hard physical damage. But that was stupid. What, after all, had Justin Riley ever done to him? Nothing—he guessed.

Marge lingered at the window. "I'm sorry for all of them," she said. "Justin's in trouble this time."

The use of Dr. Riley's first name still came easily to Marge, although she had once been Justin's lowly lab assistant. When Sandy first met her, Marge had been a New York deb attending a stylish junior college just outside Ridgefield Corners. Sandy had never been anything but what he was tonight—a lanky, handsome, easy-going guy who could make any horse he sat look easy to ride and jump.

"If the gossip is true, the guy deserves to be in trouble, doesn't he?"

Marge seemed not to have heard him. Instead of answering his question, she said, "Olivia Riley might be able to boss it around town as though she were queen bee with all her money and her servants and her senator father, but I wouldn't be Justin Riley's wife for anything in the world."

Sandy hoped she meant it. She was his world. She had had a hard time having Mike and the doctors down at the hospital had thought, for a while, that she was not going to make it. He could not bear to recall the pain of that time. When Marge died some day, the sun would not rise again.

He said, "Why don't you do what you set out to do and hurry back to bed? We've got a big day ahead. Twenty kids coming to ride."

"All our days are big days," said Marge, still not moving from the window. "You know something, Sandy? Justin will probably ask me to come back to the hospital now and help out for a while."

"That's crazy. Where would you find the time?"

She agreed, "You're right. I don't have that kind of time." She started for the door at last. "As I said—I'm sorry for all of them."

She went down the stairs. While she was gone, Sandy heard the big, echoing silence of the house and was frightened.

Before Marge returned, the silence ended in an ear-splitting scream. Mike had awakened from some nightmare world in which he saw bad things.

There was a funny kind of reassurance in hearing Marge soothe the frightened child. Silence returned as Mike dropped off to sleep again. Her light, barefoot step approached their bedroom door on the ancient, creaking oak.

Sandy, wide awake, was seeing bad things too. He was glad she would soon be with him.

He had an overwhelming urge to put an arm about her shoulders, to say, Look, I know how maybe you're feeling. I know you were hit pretty hard by that guy for a while. But you and I are really on the way now, honey. Don't walk out on me now, when we've finally got it made.

But when she got back into the warm, mussy, fresh-linen-smelling bed, he pretended to be asleep.

There were some questions better unasked.

CHAPTER TWO

The township covered a series of rolling hills. Whenever you topped a ridge, a whole new view crashed into your line of vision. Ridgefield Corners was bordered by the humpbacked shadow of the Adirondacks.

Stretching toward that shadow as far as the eye could reach were the houses, farmlands, stud farms and dairy farms that in one way or another belonged to old Cyrus Stevens. Ridgefield Corners was Cy's town and he ruled it with a tyrant's hand. Stevens also owned the hospital, and would have it within his power after tonight, to see Justin Riley driven out of the medical profession.

Justin flipped open his glove compartment with shaking fingers, took out and lit a cigarette. He drew a couple of deep, steadying breaths. The fragrance of the summer night was heady and yet fragile—the ghost fragrance of love. On a night like this last summer Betty Hogan had told him how much she loved him.

"I want to be the one who never asks anything of you," she had whispered as they lay side by side in a cool narrow bed. She had unbuttoned his shirt with slow, somehow sensuous fingers, and when he tried to preempt the job she had not allowed him to do so. The small, cool hands had touched him in an act of submission and service. *This one,* he had thought, *is different. All she wants is to give.* Well, she had given everything—she had damned near given her life—and he was rushing to the hospital to watch his colleague, Stu Everett, try to save Betty from that useless and ultimate gift.

Now she too had to ask and take, whether or not she liked it, whether or not she loved him. To be human, he thought, was to be poor, a beggar.

He drove the lake shore road alone tonight—last year he had been with Betty. Silent black forests bordered the road. Nearby waters lapped the shores with the soft hunger a man feels for a woman whose body is known to him too well.

She had explained urgently, like a child wanting approval, "I figured out our date tonight so that neither one of us would have to use anything."

"You don't mean that rhythm crap? Just one little emotional upset and you're in trouble."

"I won't be. I promise. It's just the right number of days since my last period."

With her face a white blur against the bigger white blur of the pillow and the bright moon throwing its light through the high rustic window, Justin Riley had reached for her, wordlessly, his desire mounting with the things she had whispered to him, the things she had told him about what he was doing to her and how and why. There was the familiar, short, sharp cry, and silence, and her murmuring little voice saying, "Umm. Yes. All warm and wonderful and you."

He guessed he had never possessed a girl quite so inclusively before—she gave, she yielded, she wanted to prove only that she loved him. Nothing like that night had ever happened again, though. The next time, he found her insipid, had not had the heart to tell her so. But the love affair had been just about washed up, he had just about had it with Betty Hogan when, meeting him in his car behind the hospital, she had given him the bad news that she was pregnant.

"That's rough," he had said.

"No, it's not. Not really. I so want to have this baby, Justin—your baby."

"Then have it."

"How can I? Unless you marry me?"

He had thought briefly, he hardly knew why, of Marge Miles, who had done Betty's job at the hospital before Betty did. He had said merely, "Look, baby. I'm a doctor and all that, and I know when I've been had. But I'm not going to divorce my wife and marry you."

"Why not?"

"Just one reason—I don't want to. Besides, I signed a contract when I got married and I intend to keep it."

"You're lying," Betty accused him. "You don't care for your wife—it's Marge Miles you're thinking of. She's the one you're crazy about."

"That's not a rational thing to say."

"No," the girl had agreed, removing herself to the far side of the front seat. "It's not, is it?" Then, with a new, whimpering note in her voice that crushed the last of his desire for her voluptuous, overripe body, her empty mind, her frightened soul, she had said, "But what'll I do? My pa will beat the hell out of me when I tell him."

"Then don't tell him. I know someone in New Hampshire—very good—I'll take care of the expenses."

That had been a month ago. He had given her five hundred dollars in cash.

He did not know what she had done with the money or whether her old man had found it and stolen it or what. He knew only that an ambulance had found her tonight in a motel only twenty-five miles from Ridgefield Corners. Stu Everett had called Justin at the Mohawk. "You'd better get your ass over her fast, man," Stu had said. "Your girl friend was just brought in hemorrhaging from an illegal abortion and she's naming you as the father."

Justin's car hit the hospital parking lot at fifty miles an hour. He switched off the ignition and vaulted the low-slung door of the Thunderbird all in one quick motion. He half-walked, half-ran up the path to the hospital door, banged in and turned sharp right into Emergency and Minor Surgery. Most nights the emergency room was quiet. There were no through highways near Ridgefield Corners and few automobile accidents. During the day, the room was kept busy with farm accidents or a waitress cutting her hand half off as she pushed some trash into a garbage can. Tractors sometimes messed up their operators.

The high, narrow emergency bed, with its white sheets and folded-over blanket, had a look of aseptic comfort.

Gail Bennett was on Emergency that week. As he entered, she was on the phone. "Emergency. Bennett. We're sending up a patient for OR. Severe hemorrhaging. Illegal abortion. Type O blood—get set for transfusions. Dr. Everett's operating right away."

She hung up and turned to meet Justin's white face and questioning eyes.

"Oh," she said, "it's you. They've already questioned her—in case she doesn't survive the operation. A man from the sheriff's office was here. I thought the poor kid would bleed to death while they—"

"Where is she?"

"Private Five, north wing. There's no use trying to see her, Justin. She's in a coma. Anyway, I doubt you're anyone she'd want to see."

The words were underlined with contempt. Gail Bennett was an indifferent nurse with a sullen, sloe-eyed beauty that had appealed to Justin years ago, when he had first come here for his internship. He and Gail had had, he thought, a fine affair until she began to talk about getting married. Then he had laid it on the line, exactly as he had done with that kid upstairs. He had definite plans for his future, he had told Gail. She had known his plans from the start. He would not marry into the trap of a four-room apartment with two or three kids and five thousand a year from the hospital when he got his residency.

He had almost forgotten those months when his heart would start to pound as he watched Gail Bennett's long slender legs moving beneath the sheer white nylon of her uniform. She had been married and divorced since then. But tonight, meeting that contemptuous, dark-eyed stare, Justin knew that Gail had not forgotten and that she hated him. And yet she had asked for it—just as Betty Hogan had asked for it.

Last night he would not have minded the look on Gail Bennett's face. Last night others had loved him. Tonight, for the first time in thirty-five years, he was afraid of being hated. He had seen no compassion tonight in his wife Olivia's eyes, nor in the senator's sharp pale face with its craggy white brows. No matter which way he looked, all he seemed to see was hate—perhaps in some new reflection of some old hate of his own.

He loosened his tie, unbuttoned a collar which felt suddenly tight, as though it might choke him. A passage from Emergency led to the small, rather dingy staff elevator. He punched the button for the second floor and listened to the creaking of venerable cables. Too bad, Justin thought remotely, that Cyrus Stevens could not spare a few million from his prize cattle and race horses to modernize his hospital. Maybe Cy had no desire to modernize the hospital, or the town. The town was his, a small, almost eighteenth-century world divorced from the larger world without.

The elevator cage smelled of food trays and formaldehyde, though neither were in evidence at the moment. The cage creaked to a stop. The second-floor door stuck for a moment. Justin pushed it back. He stepped out into the midnight quiet of the corridor. Three nurses sat at a wide table writing reports. They all glanced up but none of them spoke as he hurried past their nylon-covered backs.

Would they say, later, That Justin Riley. Serves him right. With all his playing around, I knew he'd get caught some day ...

What of the girl in Private Five? He hoped no one would say it served her right for playing around with a married man. Sin was dealt with sternly in Ridgefield Corners—when sin made itself conspicuous. Tonight he hoped people would think of Betty as a patient.

The sign said, NO VISITORS. Nevertheless he pushed the door softly and saw her lying limply in the high, white bed. She was in deep sleep. She wore a rumpled hospital gown and her glorious red-gold hair was smothered in a sterile cap. He did not know whether she slept in coma or as the result of a preoperative hypo. He picked up her hand and found it cold and clammy, the pulse thready. Were her eyes beginning to sink? There was a faint, bluish tinge around her temples. Saving her life would be a fight.

He had not loved her enough—but he had loved her. And tonight she had his undivided attention—not only because he had loved her but because she was a patient and he was Justin Riley.

She was curiously beautiful, like a cold white marble sculpture. Her face was almost as pale as the pillow where she rested and the high-rising breasts were motionless under the covering.

He said, "I'm sorry, darling—"

Stu Everett's clipped Harvard-accented voice echoed at his elbow, "You damn well should be."

Justin put the girl's hand gently back on the white bedspread before turning to consider Stu's pink-and-white, snub-nosed face carefully, as though he had never seen Stu before and wanted to be sure he knew with whom he dealt.

"When did they bring her in?"

Stu moved the chart from under his arm and consulted the record. "Twelve-five. Her parents were with her. Seems she panicked when the bleeding got really bad and called her mother. They rode with her in the ambulance."

"That's when she pinned it on me."

It was stated as a fact, not a question.

Stu nodded his crinkly blond crewcut. "That's right. She kept calling for you, as a matter of fact. When we had her in Emergency, the man from Ed Haley's office was there and got the facts before she passed out cold."

Justin said, "I told her where to go, Stu—she'd have been safe there a month ago. She waited—why? And she went to someone who bungled. Who was it?"

"We don't know."

"She's got a chance." Justin reminded his colleague. "You do a good job."

As he spoke, the door opened and a nurse and intern brought in a stretcher. Stu helped them move the slight form and draw a white cotton blanket beneath her chin.

The stretcher rolled noiselessly out of the room. The eyes of the two men met again across the empty bed.

Stu said, almost casually, "I talked to the girl's father alone for a minute. After all, you're not in this mess alone, you know. You have Olivia and your son to think about. And the senator's up for re-election this year. Maybe a governor can ride out a personal scandal, but the senator sure in hell can't. Not with Cy Stevens on his tail. So I tried to make a deal with the parents."

"And?"

"They say that if the girl lives, they'll talk to her, take her away from here—if you pony up twenty thousand bucks."

"You know I haven't got that kind of money."

"No, but Olivia has."

With all his heart, Justin Riley wanted to say, *What in hell kind of man do you think I am? I don't take money from women.* But all his life, in one way and another, he had taken money from women. All he could say now was, "You don't think I'd borrow from Olivia for a thing like that, do you?"

"I don't see why not. Olivia knew what she was buying when she married you. She knew it's not in you to be faithful."

"Since when do you have the right to be so holier-than-thou?"

"I'm just stating a few cold facts. One, you've got to think of Olivia. Two, you've got to think of your son. Three, you've got to think of the senator—who, one way or another, Justin, has done one helluva lot for you."

"I'm aware of that." Justin turned to the black night at the window. The distant mountains were out there, although he could not see them. "But even if I agreed to pay, you know it would never end there. They'd be back for more."

Stu shrugged again. "Well, it's your party. This is one no one can help you with. Just hope Olivia sticks with you and that the girl lives, or you might find yourself not only drummed out of town, but drummed out of the medical profession as well."

Justin said briefly, "You see that she lives."

Stu Everett's expression changed. He looked ashamed. He glanced at his watch. "They ought to have her ready by now. Care to watch?"

"I want to."

Justin sat in the dimness of the operating theater and watched Stu, in his green OR cap and gown, mark the exact site of the incision. In addition to Stu, who was the OB resident, there were an intern, a nurse-anesthetist, two OR nurses and an orderly standing by. The green glareless light of the operating lamp seemed wholesome and normal to Justin Riley. The eyes of those present were fixed alternately on surgeon and patient.

Justin saw that Stu was using hypothermia, the reduction of body temperature to lessen blood flow, a fairly new technique.

The intern said, "Total hysterectomy?" and Stu nodded. The OR nurse made a notation on Betty's chart.

Everything was proceeding routinely. Betty was in good hands at last. And after tonight, she would never again have to worry about bearing children, whether unwanted or wanted.

Justin rose and left. No one looked up.

Perhaps not many people in the Mary Stevens Memorial Hospital would look up at him after tonight.

In the hospital lobby, he paused at the switchboard. If Mrs. Riley called, Dodie Mears was to tell her that Justin had been delayed.

"Tell her," he said, "that I don't know when I'll be home."

CHAPTER THREE

As long as he had lived in Ridgefield Corners, Justin Riley had found his car heading for Misty Powers' square, yellow-brick house when his thoughts were troubled. He was willing to concede, as the Thunderbird rolled into Misty's driveway, that the trouble always had something to do with women.

There were the social, outdoorsy women who were his patients—the women in white he worked with, like Gail Bennett—and the tall, passionless beautiful woman to whom he was married.

What he really wanted was someone who believed in him—someone like Marge Miles. Someone young and eager and exciting who believed that Justin Riley was primarily the best doctor on earth.

Well, Marge was not available—and so he turned to Misty, who would at least not blame him the way Olivia did.

"I suppose it's all some childish idea of revenge," Olivia had said to him, the last time someone had brought her word of one of her husband's missteps. "My money and my father's influence got you where you are. Now you hate me for not letting you make it on your own."

"No," Justin had told her as they sat together at dinner. "That's not what splits us, Olivia. What about Stu Everett? You knew you were a fool for Stu. You married me to save yourself from being a bigger fool. I wasn't a lover, a husband. I was a damned rescue squad."

"Don't be vulgar." Olivia had turned her face away, giving him the benefit of her narrow patrician profile. The polished mahogany table had been soft and pretty with candlelight. "I thought I took you out of the gutter when I married you."

"I'm tired," he had said. "And it's only in the gutter that I seem to find human warmth. Can't we be kind to each other? If for nothing else—for our kid's sake?"

"You're the one who has shown all the unkindness," Olivia persisted unassailably.

Lonely—how lonely a man could be in the bosom of his family, Justin thought, as he stood at Misty's doorstep, waiting for her to answer the softly chiming bell. From here on in, he decided, he would not pretend any more. He would not pretend to love women whom he wanted only to sleep with. He would not pretend that his marriage was respectable and good. Well, maybe for his son's sake ...

The door swung inward. Misty's home was furnished in the blended style and tastes of her several former husbands. Surprisingly, the result was warm and relaxed. Misty, a small woman with a dark-blonde pageboy bob was also warm and relaxed. She slid her arms about his neck and offered her mouth for a kiss.

She said, "Hi. I knew you'd head here tonight."

"You a friend of mine, Misty. I need a friend."

"Sure, Justin. You know I'm always your friend—whatever that's worth. I knew you'd need a drink before you faced Olivia and her father."

"A drink will help." He dropped into the armchair beside the fireplace. Nothing in this room matched anything else, but neither did any item here war with any other. The place was a cozy museum for Misty's dead loves and marriages—and only the living make war.

When Sam Powers and Misty had been divorced for the second time and Sam and his new wife went to live in New York, the twenty-room Powers mansion and surrounding five hundred acres had been sold to Cy Stevens. This comparative cottage had once been Misty's guesthouse. The land speculators of whom Cy Stevens lived in constant dread would never get their hands on the one-time Powers estate. The Powers family still took care of Misty and her three children. They supplied her with a thousand dollars a month in addition to the cottage. That income, Justin thought, might be one of the reasons for the coziness of the cottage. But money alone was not enough to warm a cold heart. As he well knew.

She placed a scotch and soda in his hand. With the first gulp, he almost finished the drink. He put the glass on the end table beside him and remarked, "There. That feels better. Everything here is better. I wish I could stay tonight instead of going home."

"Is it pretty bad, Justin?"

He nodded. "It's pretty bad."

"Funny," she commented slowly. "You're still the best-looking man I've ever known. In a tall, quiet way, of course. You broke up my last marriage—you know that, don't you? Maybe I go for your hands—you're the only surgeon I ever saw with hands that look like a surgeon's."

Justin reached for her wrist and pulled her into his lap.

She sat there easily. She was a small girl, given to curves which, so far, her vanity controlled. Like most of the women in town above a certain income level, she had been Justin's patient through the normal disaffections—virus in winter, blues in the fall—before they became lovers. Her beauty had a quality which, Justin had long ago concluded, was simply the result of wealth. His own background—many years behind him now—was slum-tenement and Irish-saloon.

Justin and his wealthy patients, like Justin and his wealthy wife, spoke in the same tongue and remained forever strangers.

He reached up a hand and massaged the back of her neck with strong, gentle fingers while he took another sip of scotch and she fit a cigarette and placed it between his lips.

She asked, "What made you do such a crazy thing—get mixed up with a kid like Betty Hogan?"

"What's crazy about a man wanting a girl—when all he gets at home is sarcasm and criticism?"

"If that were the whole problem you would have divorced Olivia long ago and married someone else. Your trouble is, I think, that you're really in love with your wife."

He smiled. "Then, in this case at least, the husband is the last to know."

"Then why don't you marry someone who really loves you?"

"Such as you?"

Misty returned his smile. "Such as me. I really am crazy about you, Justin."

He did not bother telling her *I happen to have a son.* Instead he said gallantly, "Don't love me. I'm not worth loving. I'm just a cheating, lying, sonofabitch who doesn't care who picks up the tab as long as he gets what he wants."

She turned to him beseechingly, hands on his shoulders. "I'd pick up the tab for you, Justin—any time. Instead of alimony, Sammy would settle a lump sum if he thought I was marrying someone who would really take care of me."

"And take you off the booze?"

She nodded. "And take me off the booze. I wouldn't touch a drop, darling, not a drop, if I were married to you."

He stroked her hand that was cold from its contact with the highball glass. Less than an hour ago he had picked up another cold hand, Betty Hogan's. *All the weak, lovely women,* he thought. *My patients ...*

"Misty, every alcoholic in the world has used that line at one time or another. If they could find a man who loved them or a job they liked or if their kids would be kinder to them—the only thing that will get you off the booze is what gets anyone off it—hitting rock bottom. Coming up against a tragedy so big that something in life will matter more to you than a bottle."

"That's what Phil Sheffers says. I promise him I won't drink, and then, every time he calls, it's a time when I've had one martini too many. He says it scares him."

"Phil is right. He's a nice, decent guy who will bore the hell out of you if you ever marry him, but he's right about the drinking. You'll have to lick it yourself. Betty tried to use me to lick her problem, Misty. She wanted to get away from home, from the farm, from her old man beating the hell out of her every time he came home with a load on. I suppose," he said, suddenly realizing the probable truth, "that's what she did with the money."

"What money?"

"The five hundred bucks I gave her, to go to a guy who was once a fine OB man until he got on drugs. She must have found some local to do the job for peanuts—thinking she'd use the rest of the money to get away from here." The thought made him violently, recklessly unhappy. He continued talking, suggesting without prelude, "Let's take our clothes off and go upstairs to bed."

She stared at him, glass halfway to her lips. "You don't mean that."

"Of course I mean it. Why not? We have before."

"Tonight is different—I mean—how can you, with Betty maybe dying because of your going to bed with her?"

"Betty won't die. But you and I are half dead already. With you, it's not just the booze—it's men. You can't let men alone any more than I can let women alone. A fine pair."

"Justin," she said, the brightness of simple lust coming into her eyes, "are you using me as an escape?"

He rose, made her stand beside him. He put his arms about her almost casually, and let her press herself against him while her mouth sought out his. Misty had a need to be the aggressor in love. She had confessed to Justin that he was one of the few men who did not object to her attitude. Justin had said with compassion, "As long as it's good, clean sex, darling, I can function any way and in any place—"

And now Misty was urging as he had done seconds before, "Let's go to bed, darling."

"Where are the kids?"

"At Dieterle's. I knew it would be that kind of night."

For a moment Justin forgot his own emotional starvation. He frowned. "That woman's not good with kids. You're a fool to leave your children there. If you had any interest—"

"Right now," said Misty, "I'm interested in you. Let's take our drinks upstairs."

She reached behind him and switched off the lights. She picked up their drinks and he picked up Misty.

He entered the familiar bedroom and placed her on the bed, while her hands clung to his neck, keeping his mouth against hers.

"Darling," she whimpered in her need, "I love you so." After that, they did not speak for a long time.

Misty Powers was a lost soul and no one knew her better than Justin Riley, her doctor and occasional lover. She had failed as a wife—she was failing as a mother—and yet she was indestructible in just one way.

She was well-born. There was style, grace and assurance even in her lust. In her bed, in her lust, she managed to flatter Justin into feeling graciously entertained. He guessed that she gossiped about him as virulently as anyone else, but when they were alone, she could charm him.

Justin, who was not well-born, was grateful—he had always been essentially grateful for the friendship of mannerly women and grateful for their scented bodies.

In the darkness he served her need, and she his.

Misty was asleep when he rose and left her. Dawn was streaking the mountain tops. Olivia, he thought, trying to enjoy some minimal defiance, would really let him have it for tonight.

Somehow he found no pleasure in the thought.

What would his son say? What did the kid think? Justin could not reach the boy who was better-born than his father.

CHAPTER FOUR

Olivia Riley knew what it was to be frightened. She had learned, though, not to show fear. She had thought, when she was much younger, that no one else was frightened except herself.

She knew otherwise now. For the past two years, she had watched Justin trying frantically to destroy everything he loved. As though, she suspected, he were secretly afraid he might lose out anyway and the losing would be easier if he could pretend, to himself or to someone else, that he had only relieved himself of a wearisome burden.

She had glimpsed the fear in his tired, bloodshot eyes when he drank too much. She had heard the fear in his voice when he commanded her to submit herself on the increasingly rare occasions when they were lovers. She had yearned to ease and soothe him, not because she loved him any more, because she did not, but because she wished she were capable of love. She had come to terms with her fears but she could no longer love.

Had last night completed Justin's work of destruction?

When Olivia heard—at the Mohawk Inn, of all places, on a Saturday night—of Betty Hogan and her accusations, her hidden inward fears had seemed to cease. She had thought quietly that the end of the world had come. There was nothing left to be afraid of.

Sitting at the breakfast table, waiting for Justin to join her, she knew why he had stopped at Misty's house last night. Misty had called early this morning to make sure Olivia knew. "Be good to him, Livvy," Misty had begged.

But kindness to Justin would come too late, although he might not know it. He had stopped at Misty's because he still was frightened, still was afraid of losing out.

He had already lost. Once he faced that fact, he would be, like Olivia, unafraid.

Of course, Justin had not wanted Misty any more than he had wanted any of the others—the hypochondriac patients and the cute little nurses and his former lab assistant. Insulting, for Misty to have called like that, trying to give Olivia the gift of her husband's love by insisting, "He just stopped by for a drink, Livvy."

From upstairs, she heard the rapping sound of the houseman's knuckles on Justin's bedroom door. Brooks' rumbling voice drifted down the stairwell. "Miz Riley says to tell you it's almost eleven, Doctor Riley. And you're due at the senator's house for lunch at one."

She heard Justin's muffled reply and then his footsteps across the bedroom floor, the rushing sound of the hot-and-cold shower. She could imagine him setting out his shaving things, lathering the lightly tanned face with its narrow mouth that was sometimes tender and sometimes cruel. His black hair had started to frost at the temples—rather beautifully, she thought.

He was still the most attractive man in the world, and she still wished, as she had wished before they were married, that he were hers.

She wondered if he were anyone's.

"Oh, he's a bastard, all right," Misty Powers had hiccuped and wept that long-ago spring day when she had come here to drink martinis and to plead her love for Justin. "But he's an exciting bastard, and a woman always thinks what a terrific guy he'd be if he really loved her."

Olivia had received the drunken thrust in silence. She was that much ahead of Misty—she had the gift of silence.

"My dear," the senator had told his daughter last night, returning the stares of friend and foe with cold eyes that dared them to make a comment, "surely you are used to this sort of thing by now. But you asked for it and you have no choice but to hold your head high and hope the wretched story will die before it destroys us all."

She saw Justin's shoes on the staircase, then the slacks, the tweed jacket. He came toward her across the big Oriental rugs that made a kind of indoor flower bed on the polished, wide-boarded floors. Olivia felt a queer little ache, as though in memory of love. Silhouetted briefly before the leaded windows and the formal gardens beyond the arch of green-and-white draperies, Justin seemed as alone as a person could be. Alone with his fears, his confusion, and whatever remorse he might feel toward the girl or toward his wife—but perhaps he would always have been alone, in victory or defeat.

In the sunny dining room with its pallid green wainscoting and hand-blocked, green-and-pink wallpaper, Justin paused beside Olivia's chair and kissed her cheek. His hand lingered on her shoulder. "Am I still allowed to say good morning?" he asked.

"Of course. Good morning, Justin."

He moved toward his own chair. "Isn't Johnny home?"

"Fortunately, no. Jimmy Hennessy's father is taking them fishing this morning after church and then they're having a picnic in the woods. Later, there's a small horse show down at Sandy Miles' place—just a couple of classes—and I promised Johnny I'd ride over with him this afternoon."

"You're doing a wonderful job of keeping him away from me, aren't you? When I get home from the hospital, he's usually in bed."

"You mean," corrected Olivia soberly, "when you get home from wherever you happen to be. It's just as well he isn't here this morning. We need a little time to decide what to do about Betty Hogan. Of course we both know better—but for all our sakes, you'll have to deny her charges."

Justin slammed his orange juice glass on the table. "Look," he said, "I'll have to take enough crap from your father today, so let's not start in now. I know I have it coming. I just don't want to get it—yet. Especially from you."

"What am I supposed to do? Sit here in virtuous silence and pretend you don't exist? We'll have to agree on a story. We have to face people. We even have to face our son."

Justin did not answer but she saw cords swell in his throat. He was angry—and frightened—and alone.

She reassured him sadly, "This—incident—won't cost you any doting patients. If anything, they'll want you more than ever."

Brooks' wife appeared with a silver pot of fresh black coffee.

"I made plenty," Amelia told Justin. "I knew you'd want a lot of good hot coffee this morning, Dr. Riley."

Justin said, "That was good of you. Please skip the bacon and eggs, though. I got on the scales this morning and I've put on a couple of pounds, thanks to all those terrific desserts of yours."

A flush of pleasure surged on Amelia's light-brown cheeks. A word of praise or a smile from Justin always seemed to make her feel like someone special.

"Yes sir, Dr. Riley. I'll tell Brooks not to fix anything except, maybe, one of those nice, hot corn muffins you like so much?"

Justin gave her round backside a fond pat. "There you go," he said, "tempting me again. No, thanks. Coffee and orange juice will do it."

She repeated, "Yes, sir," somewhat regretfully and pushed back through the white swinging door to the pantry.

Olivia observed, "I imagine Amelia and Brooks heard you come home at half-past five this morning. Misty phoned, you know—before you were awake. She asked me to treat you kindly."

Justin poured himself coffee from the monogrammed silver pot. "Here we go. Speech number three."

"No, Justin. Here we don't go and it's not speech number anything. I'm never again going to mention what happened last night. Oh," she said, at his startled, unbelieving look, "don't worry—it's not over yet, by any means. My father's already found out that the girl's parents want money."

"Who told him that? My good friend—and yours—Stu Everett?"

Olivia said wearily, "Please shut up about my friendship with Stu. That was all over years ago."

A friendship like that, Justin thought, was never over—not as far as the husband was concerned. But who was he to complain?

He stared at Olivia across the lake of polished mahogany, the yellow roses in their low, silver bowl, the tall, white candles in their heavy heirloom holders that had been Stu Everett's wedding gift.

This morning, for many reasons—one being that Stu could keep life under control whereas Justin apparently could not—Justin wanted to clobber Stu with one of those heavy candlesticks.

Marriage. An alarming, uncivilized mess. He had gone to bed last night with a woman who was Olivia's best friend before he destroyed their friendship—and he still felt hurt by her long-ago romance with Stu. And here he sat at the breakfast table, trying to defend himself about that poor, stupid broad who would not take his advice and money and get the thing done right—

He said, "To hell with it."

"With what?"

"With the whole damn show. If they want to throw me out of the hospital, let them. I still have a license. I can go practice in Podunk, Iowa. Or I can sell shoes."

"That's childish."

"Damn it to hell, Olivia, will you stop telling me, twenty times a day, how childish I am? How unrealistic? All right. I'm childish. I'm unrealistic.

I like the good life and I don't want to pay for it by conforming. But once I loved my wife, and when I found out she didn't love me, I kicked back."

"But you didn't kick me. I could have understood that. The person you keep downgrading is Justin Riley."

"I like it that way," he said. "I'm not judging anyone. I don't want anyone to judge me."

In the mirror that ran the entire length of the silver-laden mahogany buffet, he could see the reflection of the two people they had become.

Olivia's finely drawn mouth was mean with frustration. Maybe money could buy a husband, but it could not make him perform afterwards. She was not paying as much attention to the little parts of her looks, either, as she should. A girl like Olivia—a tall, spare girl who suggested the Wellesley campus and walks in the rain and soap rather than perfume—could age early if she were not careful. She could come to look like Betty Hogan's mother, a thin wraith in a black dress, with grey-and-black hair, looking fifty before she was forty because no man challenged her any more to stay young.

Tight lips, quiet dark eyes, suntanned hand toying with a string of pearls, her reflection faced his. For all these years, had she missed the warm secret knowledge that she was loved and desired by another man, and for another reason?

"Stu wouldn't marry me for the same reason you would," Olivia had once told Justin coldly. "He's too proud—too much man—to marry a woman with money. He wants to earn the money he makes."

That had been the first and last time Justin had ever hit his wife—a light slap, across one cheek, with the back of his hand. She had flown at him like a tigress, raking his cheeks with her nails.

He had taken her forcibly to bed—"I'll teach you to scratch me, you bitch, you—" and she had loved it, even though she had lain there like a wooden Indian, flat and hard and rigid.

At the end she had asked, "Are you quite through?"

In almost the same tone, she now was saying quietly, "I wish I believed that some lovely gesture of faith would help you survive this tragedy, maybe even bring us together again. I guess it's too late for that. I guess it was always too late."

He said, "Yes. It's too late for any of that."

Brooks showed his face at the swinging door. Olivia had schooled Brooks as perfectly as she schooled her Irish hunters and her chows and, in the early days of their marriage, her diamond-in-the-rough husband.

Brooks said, "Pardon me for the interruption, Mrs. Riley, but it's getting late and you know how your father is if people gets there late to lunch."

Olivia smiled with instant kindness and warmth. Justin had to admire, even applaud her. Breeding counted, all right. No one would think the young woman at the opposite end of the table had any more on her mind than what to wear to the imminent lunch. Instead, she was facing a family scandal that might change her life before the last accusation had been flung, the last headline printed.

"Thank you, Brooks. We'll be on our way in a minute. Would you check the gas gauge in the Thunderbird, please? Dr. Riley did a lot of driving last night." She added brightly, "Isn't Sunday a funny day? Rushing from one table to another."

Silence followed the departure of Brooks. After a moment Justin said quietly, "I appreciate the fact that you're willing to stick by me, Olivia. I doubt it will do any good."

"So do I."

"If you had any sense, you'd divorce me."

"If I ever get any sense, where you're concerned, I'll let you know."

The summer day awaited outside. The kind of day on which families would get together for picnics. Kids still young enough to believe in love would go swimming together and later try to make out in their parked cars, still believing in the goodness, the bounty of love. State troopers would send out warnings to motorists to drive carefully. The emergency room at the hospital would treat cases of near-drowning and of sunburn and at least one heart attack. A lot of older guys, when they had a day at home, tried to make it with their wives two or three times instead of one. With luck, they managed to get away with a mild coronary. Someone like himself would tell them, "Look, let's face it—you're too sick to be careless. Keep the excitement in reason or your wife will find herself giving a party to a dead guy."

All those things, large and small, fine or mean, happy or sad, would be happening in the kind of world he had once hoped to share with Olivia. The normal world where people did what was right because doing right was easier than not.

All about him was wealth and comfort and ease. Why could he find no ease in his heart, in his life?

"I'm ready to leave, if you are," Olivia said. "If you don't mind, I'll drive."

Justin said, "I don't mind at all."

When you married five million bucks, he thought sourly, you got used to your wife driving.

But why had she never liked him?

She had wanted him, once, even loved him—but liking was something she saved, he thought, for her own well-born kind.

CHAPTER FIVE

Senator John Adams Turner, a direct descendant of the American president for whom he was named, lived in more times than his own. The past and future were alike important to Olivia Riley's father. He had a code which applied to all generations. The code, among other things stated that when a man was guilty of wrongdoing, he had better pay for it in his own lifetime. Otherwise his son would in one way or another have to foot the bill.

The senator's own son had rebelled against the code and was no longer in communication with the senator. Olivia's older brother, a lawyer, had been indicted years ago on charges of bribing a jury in favor of his client. The client had been young, beautiful, and accused of murdering her husband.

The senator had personally led the fight to have his son disbarred. Cleared of the charges against him but embittered toward his father, Olivia's brother had made a new life elsewhere. No one heard from him any more.

"When a man sins against the moral code," the senator had told his wife Emily, "you may be certain that he carries some sickness within him. If Henry is ever healed, he will return."

The senator's wife had privately thought that her husband had driven their son away less for trying to bribe a jury, than for the sin of adultery. She had agreed that Henry had been emotionally sick … but she had harbored a woman's compassion for sickness and longed hopelessly to see Henry again.

And on that hot July Sunday, pacing before the cold fireplace of his study, the senator could find no more mercy in his heart toward his son-in-law than he had found for his son.

"Where does it get a man?" he had demanded of his wife. "All the self-indulgence, all the philandering for which, sooner or later, some decent person must pay—where's the profit?"

"There is none," Emily had concurred. But now he could hear Emily in the kitchen consulting with cook about Sunday lunch. Olivia and Justin would soon arrive. Without warmth, he was still trying to understand a man like Justin. But all he could grasp was that the more beds a man invaded, the less he had to bring to each of them. Emotions were a form of moral currency. If you went on spending more than you should, you became an emotional bankrupt, a person unable to care deeply any more about anything. The senator saw this emotional profligacy all about him, destroying this once-peaceful town as in time it might destroy the nation.

He had spotted the fatal weakness in Justin Riley long ago.

"A man like that," he had warned his daughter, "will break your heart twenty times over. Stu Everett—there's the boy you should stick with—fine family, sense of responsibility, good schools, good clubs. A man like Justin Riley ought never to make a promise—he has nothing to back one with."

His troubled thoughts turned to his daughter. He wondered whether she had gone to her husband as she should have gone to him—untouched and virginal. There had been a pregnancy just a few months after her marriage, a fact which the senator thought somehow indecent, as though Olivia and Justin had permitted the entire town to glimpse their marital life.

Emily had said, "Heavens, John, thousands of young women become pregnant on the wedding night. And I must say, Justin does look like—well—a rather virile young man."

The senator had accepted Emily's explanation as preferable to his own. But the knowledge that he had a grandson who was named for him did not warm him as it should have done.

The Dalmatians set up an uproar outside the wide windows. Emily, hurrying down the front hall to welcome the guests, called over her shoulder, "Oh, dear. Olivia's driving and Justin's glaring so I suppose they've been quarreling again. I do hope we won't have a divorce in the family. Really, the disgrace of a divorce—"

"Hard to know which is worse," the senator grunted, refilling his glass from the silver-topped decanter on the sideboard, "the disgrace of a divorce or the disgrace of that marriage."

"Now, John, please," his wife urged nervously. "Don't start right off making Justin angry. We're all in this dreadful business together and—"

Then the bell was chiming and Emily Turner, soft and pink-cheeked with well-dressed, purple-hued white hair, was opening the heavy door of this house where Olivia had been born.

Justin and his father-in-law began exchanging insults almost before Olivia had tossed her purse on the black leather sofa and kissed her father's cheek. The senator opened his conversation with Justin by remarking, "The girl's parents want money. That means lawyers, headlines, scandal. Have you thought what you're going to do about it, Justin?"

Justin had not, until then. Somewhere, a grandfather clock chimed one. Justin said calmly, "Yes. Nothing."

Olivia interrupted quickly, dropping onto the sofa beside her mother, "The girl was lying, Father. She accused Justin falsely. But of course he's going to have to do something—"

All his life, Justin had been told he had to do something in a crisis—seldom anything to his own advantage. Olivia's phrase dragged him back to the tenements of New York's lower East Side where everyone had told him what to do—his old man, his mother, his teacher, the social workers who had tried in vain to get his old man off boozing and beating the family every Saturday night. The cop on the beat—the priest—"I'm sorry, but this is something you have to do." Now he had it made even without Olivia's vast wealth to back him up. He had the authority of a profession—at least, so far. Now it was Justin Riley who told people what they had to do.

"The only thing I'm going to do," Justin stated, "is see that girl back to health. At whatever cost."

"To whom?" snapped the senator.

"To anyone involved. If it makes for scandal, I guess you'll just have to put up with scandal."

The silence fell like a stone. Even the Dalmatians closed their mouths and stopped panting.

Olivia leaned forward wearily. "Justin means," she tried to explain, "that Stu Everett is the surgeon, but Justin has a personal interest in Betty Hogan. She worked for him, you see."

"Is that what I mean?" Justin queried Olivia. "Because that's not what I told you. I had an affair with the girl. I wasn't in love with her—unless I'm the kind of man who can love a lot of women, which may damned well be the case. She's in trouble, sick. I'm involved. I happen to be a doctor."

Emily Turner leaped to her feet as though her bottom had been scorched by the sofa. "Why don't we all have a cocktail? Lunch is almost ready. It's roast beef, and you know how roast beef is." This last appeal was made to Olivia who could not boil water. "It's the one meat that, as I tell cook, just won't keep—"

"Whereas, I surmise," remarked the senator, "Justin's problem will." His narrow remote face, much like his daughter's face, seemed suddenly very tired.

"What'll it be, Justin?" Emily Turner gushed on, as though this were the single most important item in her life. "Scotch? Bourbon?"

The senator said, "He'll drink anything."

Olivia said, "We'll both have martinis, please. Extra dry. Really," she observed, to no one in particular, "the way Francis tries to save the gin and make a martini with pure vermouth is just too awful. It made me sick the last time—all that vermouth," she murmured weakly.

"I like Francis," retorted her father stiffly. "Only a damn fool or a knave feels free with another man's money. Like the country. Damned welfare state—rob the rich and give to the poor. Well, let the poor make their own just as the rich did once."

Justin felt the cords swelling in his neck again. He knew the observation was aimed straight at himself.

During cocktails the conversation grew hotly political as though to skirt the one subject none of them was yet ready to face. Justin did not know that he had crushed the stem of his cocktail glass until his mother-in-law cried out, "Justin, you've cut yourself. What on earth—"

Following her startled gaze to the pale rug at his feet, he saw the driblets of blood.

"Sorry," he murmured. "I was carried away."

He picked bits of glass from his hand, while Olivia ran for a wet cloth. As she sponged his hand she tried to hold on for a moment and catch his gaze. He pulled away quietly, manipulating the fingers as though to see whether there was something wrong with them.

"No harm done," he said. "At least, not to me—have I ruined the rug?"

Emily assured him that Francis could sponge the blood from the rug while the family ate its roast beef.

The lunch was over by three. Parting was on an inconclusive note, but Justin drove the car on the way home.

Before their door, he waited for Olivia to leave the Thunderbird, but made no move to join her.

She asked, "Where are you going?"

He stared at her for a thoughtful minute. Then he said, "Out to the Miles' farm. Maybe Marge Miles will help me out in the hospital until I find a replacement for Betty—or until Cy Stevens finds a permanent replacement for me."

Olivia stood quietly beside the car. She said, "You haven't seen Johnny today. He's probably home by now and in his room, waiting for you."

"He's not waiting for me," said Justin. "He's waiting for you, Olivia. You're the one he belongs to, counts on. I'll probably see him later. Didn't you say you and he were riding over to the Miles place this afternoon?"

"Yes, at about five."

"I'll see you there," Justin said. "If I'm late you'll know where I am—the hospital."

"With Betty?"

"With Betty and fifteen other patients. Why can't you people understand I have a job?"

He drove away.

CHAPTER SIX

John Justin Riley, aged seven, watched his father drive off in the red T-bird. There was no sound of the front door slamming. Johnny knew his mother was standing alone on the terrace, maybe crying. She cried when she was alone. Once he had told her to stop because he loved her and she had been very angry. Crying made her ashamed.

Forehead pressed against the screen, watching and listening, Johnny felt scared. He had felt the same way when, looking back over his shoulder while swimming, he realized he was farther out than he wanted to be. And he had felt the same kind of fear the day he and Jimmy Hennessey took the long way home from school past the lake shore road. Coming out of the shrubbery and preparing to cross the road, they had seen a parked car with a man and woman smooching it up like crazy.

Jimmy had said, tugging at Johnny's sleeve, "A couple of lovebirds. Let's sneak up and scare them." But before they scared anybody, Johnny spotted the MD on the license plate and the fact that the car was red. The only person in town who owned a bright-red T-bird was Justin Riley.

"Hold it," Johnny had said.

Jimmy's hazel eyes were wide behind thick-lensed glasses. "Gosh, Johnny—is that your father?"

"You're crazy," Johnny had said, his heart pounding queerly. "Of course that's not my father."

Never lie, Olivia had told her son. *Be too proud to lie.* Yet it had been Justin Riley in the parked car with the strange lady who reached up her mouth to kiss him.

Jimmy had said awkwardly, "Well, even if it is your father, I guess it doesn't mean anything. Come on," he had challenged. "Race you to the crossroads."

They had raced, leaping over hedges and narrow brooks to pull up finally, panting and heaving, at the corner of the street where Jimmy lived.

Just this morning, talk in the Hennessey kitchen had ceased the minute Johnny entered. All he had heard was Mrs. Hennessey saying, "... which to be sorrier for—that poor girl or his poor wife. Olivia's taken so—" at which point Mr. Hennessey must have kicked his wife under the table because she had turned away from the waffle iron to greet Johnny like a long-lost son instead of an overnight guest.

"Johnny, I'm fixing your favorite dish—waffles and ham—Jimmy told me that's what you like for breakfast."

"It sure is, Mrs. Hennessey, and thanks—thanks a lot."

The Hennesseys lived in a tiny house at the wrong end of town. When they needed a doctor they went to the clinic, and Mrs. Hennessey worked, mornings, at Newberry's, where she sold things. Johnny's mother was puzzled by his close friendship with Jimmy, but Johnny's father had said, "It's a wonder the kid has even one friend the way you hang onto him. The Hennesseys are fine. Jim Hennessey's the only carpenter in town who can make something hold together for more than a week."

Maybe the friendship was over. Johnny had sensed an ending in the way Jimmy had said goodbye earlier today. And when Johnny had said, "I'm riding in two classes over at the Miles' place—why don't you bike over and watch me and I'll treat you to a coke?" Jimmy had averted his gaze.

"Gosh, Johnny, I can't."

Jimmy's mother must have pulled him aside to whisper, I don't want you seeing so much of Johnny Riley for a while.

His own mother had said that to him when some kid's parents had done something especially wrong. The time Billy Hall's father had lost all his friend's money, for instance. Everyone had been angry at the Halls, who had finally moved away.

There were too many people in the world, Johnny thought as he stood at his bedroom window, and they all watched and talked. It made you feel ashamed, as though you had gone downtown with your clothes off, when everyone knew everything about you. He wished without anger that everyone would drop dead—boom—except his parents and himself and Jimmy Hennessey. And maybe his horseback teacher, Sandy Miles. Johnny could talk to Sandy.

He had told Sandy about seeing his father in the car, smooching with Betty Hogan, and Sandy had made him feel better by saying, "Well, kid, just because a guy becomes a father doesn't mean he's become a saint, you know." And Sandy had grinned down at him as they had walked their lathered horses along the bridle trail. "Your old man's okay, Johnny. He's okay in my book. Don't sell him short."

Once Justin had asked Johnny to come to the hospital with him, to see what it was like. Johnny had had to say, "No, thank you—I have a riding lesson this morning."

Justin had been furious. "If it's something your mother wants you to do, fine—if it's something I ask, it stinks."

Olivia's light, sharp rap sounded on the bedroom door. She called, "Johnny? Ready for the ride?"

"Yes," he said, "all ready." He opened the door. Johnny's mother was beautiful.

While he had thought her still downstairs, she had come indoors noiselessly to change into riding clothes. He loved to see her in riding clothes. Her boots ended just under her knees, making her feet look polished and small. In yellow breeches, she seemed friendlier than she did in a dress. Because of the heat, she wore no jacket, just a white button-down shirt and one of his father's ties. He was glad she was wearing the tie. It was as though, somehow, the three of them still all belonged together.

"All set for the show?" she asked lightly as her gaze approved his jodhpurs and hunting cap.

"All set as I'll ever be. Sandy's letting me ride Mint Leaf today. That's the thoroughbred and just about the best horse around."

"You have your own horses to ride, you know," his mother reminded him as they went down the stairs.

"Sandy says you can't learn to ride if you stay with your own horse—you have to have different horses if you're really going to learn."

"Well, I guess Sandy knows. You can take his word about horses."

They went out the back way. Bondy Walker, who cared for the Riley's three horses, was in the graveled driveway. Bondy tipped his hat and muttered his usual half-drunken but always polite, "'Afternoon, ma'am."

Again, Johnny had that too-far-out scary feeling. Bondy knew. Everyone knew the awful thing that Johnny's father had done—except Johnny. But maybe he didn't want to know it. And neither did the horses.

Bondy held Olivia's stirrup while she swung into the saddle. Next Bondy gave Johnny a leg up, too vigorously, so that it seemed to take him minutes to bounce back into the saddle. Bondy must really be drunk, thought Johnny, and Bondy never dared get really drunk when Johnny's father was around. Was Justin leaving them for good? What would become of the three of them now? He would have to stop being scared, Johnny thought, if he had to take care of his mother. If he were scared, they would both have to be ashamed.

"Mother," he asked tentatively as they turned their horses' heads in the direction of the Miles farm, "is something the matter? Is Dad—well—sore at us or something?"

Olivia used her fly-whisk over Mad Hen's withers. She answered, after a pause. "No, Johnny. Not really. Not sore at us. Sore at the world, maybe."

"Did he get in a fight last night?"

Justin Riley had been in some famous fights in Ridgefield Corners.

Saddle leather creaked. Somewhere a bird sang sweetly. Olivia faced her son. Her son, really hers. Her eyes searched the handsome, sensitive face and saw no likeness to anyone but herself. Not even her parents were there. She understood Johnny both as well and as badly as she understood herself. She saw nothing strange in his taste for solitude.

"Why doesn't he play with other kids instead of moping all day?" Justin was apt to complain.

Olivia had tried to explain that Johnny was not moping, had finally cried in exasperation, "Perhaps he doesn't like the things the kids say about his father—or don't you think children gossip? More viciously and brutally than adults dare to do?"

On this late afternoon she said only, "Justin, your father is in trouble. We hope it won't last. No matter what you hear, promise me you won't believe it until you talk to me."

For a few minutes, Johnny rode in silence. The horse beneath him was known as a child's hunter-small, well-built, reliable over fences but too quiet for the show ring. Johnny's nervous reaction to what she had said, however, must automatically have tightened his hands on the reins and his knees against his horse's sides. Candy Man began to dance and skitter, looking suspiciously at the sunlight across the leaf-strewn trail. The reaction troubled Olivia.

Johnny said almost sullenly, a new tone for him, "Okay. I promise." He added in a sudden outburst, "I wish I weren't just a kid. I wish I were a grown-up."

"Why, Johnny?" Gently Olivia spurred Mad Hen to keep her alongside Candy Man just in case of need.

"I don't know. I just wish, that's all."

But Olivia knew why Johnny wished to be a grownup. He wanted to understand the currents and crosscurrents about him, to see the path ahead. Why did children persist in thinking the years brought wisdom?

She said quickly, "Grown-ups are dopes, Johnny. Just trust the ones who love you—and don't ever blame yourself. You're a good boy—a good son."

"I'm scared."

"Don't be scared."

Johnny touched Candy Man's sides with spurs, leaned forward in his saddle. "Let's really let them out, Mother. Let's really let them run."

"Good," shouted Olivia against the rising wind, giving Mad Hen her head.

CHAPTER SEVEN

By the time Olivia Turner was married to Justin Riley, she had disliked him a little and had been more than a little afraid of him. One reason for her fear had been the fact that she had a secret which he might find out some day.

"Outside of medicine, a man totally without scruples," the senator had described Justin shortly after meeting him. "He can be bought. He therefore assumes that others have their price. Unfortunately, most men and women do. Like you," the hard, cold voice went on. "You are marrying this man because for some reason Stu Everett is rejecting you and you are afraid no one else will marry you. You consider Stu's rejection of you a mark of failure and you are willing to sell out to a man like Justin Riley for something any chambermaid or waitress can have—a husband."

"That's not true," Olivia had protested. She had refrained from pointing out her most obvious reason for marrying Justin Riley. He was her second choice, but he had been top candidate for that dubious honor, for reasons the senator would not have liked his daughter to discuss. Sex as a result of marriage was a biological fact which the senator could accept, but marriage as a result of sex was something which, to him, carried with it the taint of the gutter and the harlot.

From the moment she first met him, Olivia had been attracted sexually to Justin. Stu Everett, to whom she had been engaged at the time, had guessed as much when Olivia went into a tirade over Justin's attitude.

"Honestly," she had raged, in a voice not unlike her father's "what gives with that man? Does he think every woman he meets wants him to make a pass? He really is full of himself."

Stu, blue eyes studying her face thoughtfully, had said, "You know, darling, that's always a dead giveaway."

"What is?"

"When a woman meets a man for the first time, decides he's trying to make it with her and begins to sound off about what a rat he is, you can be damned sure, she wants to go to bed with him."

"Don't be ridiculous. Justin Riley—that would be scraping the bottom of the barrel—socially, financially, and every other way. I doubt he ever pays his bills, for one thing."

"I doubt it, too," Stu had agreed in that faintly amused manner in which they were always to discuss Justin's strange attraction for Olivia and vice versa. "But on the other hand, don't underestimate the guy. He's dynamite with women. Also, he's top man in his class. He'll make a damned good thoracic surgeon when his pussy-chasing days are over. As for paying his bills—well, he always manages to come up with someone who'll pay them for him. Last year, it was the mother of one of our classmates."

Olivia had said, "How horrible," but both her voice and her anger had lacked conviction.

Sometime later she had found that she was pregnant. The child—there could be no doubt of it—was Stu's. To Olivia's astonishment, their engagement ended abruptly, not as she had expected, in marriage, but in her alliance with someone else—Justin Riley. Because Stu was who he was, she was unable to think of him as dishonorable—people with Stu's and Olivia's background were never dishonorable. Stu simply broke their engagement.

She had gone to him for one last time the night before her marriage.

She had pleaded, "I don't want to marry Justin—I want to marry you. You're the one I love—and you know I'm carrying your child. How can you let us go to someone else—your child and me?"

He had replied quietly, "No one will ever own you. And you'll probably never share your child. Livvy—I've loved you. And suddenly it's clear that any man you marry will have to fight for his soul, every day of his life. You're so damned rich, Livvy. Too rich for me. Maybe later, after I had a practice, we could have worked it out. Not now. Besides, you don't exactly find Justin repulsive, do you? Listen. Let's all wait a while. If you have any sense, you'll let me send you to someone, get rid of the baby while there's still time—"

But Olivia Turner was not the kind of young woman whom anyone sent to an abortionist. She would have gone ahead and had the child even if Justin had not married her. She might have gone to Greece, for instance, and come back with the baby and a story about adopting a war orphan. Her code, when she was twenty-four, would have permitted that much prevarication.

She was four years out of college by then and Stu Everett, like Justin, had just finished his internship.

"You don't realize it," Stu told her, "but you've never looked at me the way I've seen you looking at Justin—as though you'd like to take his clothes off in public and have him make love to you." By then, Justin had been accepted at the Mary Stevens Memorial Hospital for a residency in thoracic surgery. He and Olivia could settle down magnificently with his profession and her income in Ridgefield Corners.

"The town is dying," the senator had said sadly, "and Cyrus Stevens is killing it. He'd see it dead, without a merchant left, without a bank surviving, in order to keep it as his personal preserve, hunting lodge and playground."

Little by little, Olivia began to feel that she was dying too. "I ought to feel lucky," she had confided to Misty Powers, who was on her second husband by then. "I have everything. Nice house, a beautiful husband, a beautiful kid—but I never feel joy any more." As, she did not add, she had felt during her engagement to Stu. "I worry, I don't know why."

Misty had given characteristic advice. "You mean your love life is under par. I guess it's tough for any man to be married to a woman who has more money than he has—which, of course, is your problem. Or one of them. The other problem is that you take everything too seriously. Sex is just for fun and laughs. If Justin isn't enough for you, remember there are others."

Others?

Well, plenty of men had fallen for her with comforting regularity while she was Olivia Turner. As Olivia Riley, did her code permit her to hunger for other men—specifically for Stu?

She knew she was not the kind of girl for whom Justin Riley would normally have fallen. Never in a million years, she thought, seeing the kind for whom he did fall, and fall regularly. He had fallen for her money and for a sense of belonging somewhere after half a lifetime of belonging nowhere. He had married position and tradition and the kind of family whose sons are registered at St. Lawrence and Lawrenceville on the same day they are christened.

He had married everything he had always wanted only to find he wanted none of it because no man belongs, as the senator was fond of reminding his daughter, in a position he has not carved out himself.

"You can't give a man self-respect. That's something that comes from doing things that make a man like himself. Justin hates you because you permitted him to marry for money. It's a hard way to earn a living, as Justin is learning."

And marriage to a man who did not desire you physically, Olivia was learning, was the hard way to be a wife.

She had weakened and gone to Stu, after three years of marriage, and had begged him to take her, to make love to her. "Let me feel wanted again—as a woman—please, darling."

"Don't tell me," Stu said, brushing the short, dark, pixie-cut hair back from her face, "that Justin doesn't want you. He wants every woman over the age of six and under the age of sixty."

"I know," she had agreed, "and tonight he's with Misty. Or someone. That's just the way he makes love to me—as though I were anyone. He can't wait to get me to bed and then—he can't kiss me, afterwards. That's what really tells me that he doesn't love me—any normal young man can commit the sex act and, I suppose, perform adequately. But they can't be tender afterwards unless they're in love. They want to take a shower or go to sleep or just get away from the girl. Once, Justin got out of bed and got dressed before I realized it was—was over. It was horrible."

"You're always telling me he's horrible, but you always go back to him. It's one of those terrifically strong love-hate attachments, Olivia. You'll never lick it. Some day, you may get strong enough to run away from it."

"I'm running away from it now. I'm here, with you." And then, eyes widening in bewilderment and disbelief as they stood in the center of Stu's tastefully furnished suite in the Mohawk Inn, "Stu—don't you want me?"

"It's not a matter of wanting you or not wanting you, Olivia. It's just that I don't intend to be at stud for Justin Riley. I'm not going to satisfy your body just because he can't—or won't. I can't quite see myself in the role of life-size phallic symbol, Olivia."

"That's not it at all. On the contrary, you're everything I've always wanted in a husband, Stu—you know that. Since we were kids, everyone said we were so right for one another."

"Until you met Justin—and came to my bed to be cured of the fever—and then wanted me to save you by marrying you. But no one can save us, unfortunately. That's one little job each of us has to do for himself. I'm sorry, Olivia, but I don't want you on these—terms." His mouth had moved as though it hurt him to speak the words.

The fever of Justin Riley. The fatal fever.

In her Junior League days after college, even before her engagement to Stu, Olivia had gone to New York. Thanks to the senator's political contacts and influence, she had secured a position for which she was eminently unsuited. She became a social worker. She had no poise or assurance with the people she was supposed to help. In her heart, she felt toward failure exactly as her father did—contemptuous. Like the senator, she did not equate success with money, but with a way of life, and an inner self-esteem. As for the underprivileged children with whom she dealt in New York, there seemed nothing, really, which she or anyone else could do for them, since they aspired to a way of life which they were not prepared to earn. The single exception had been a young boy with curly dark hair that fell over his forehead, a burning ambition to be an actor and a stubborn refusal to address her as anything but, "Hey."

"Hey," he would say, entering welfare headquarters on Fourth Avenue.

To her own annoyance, she replied with "Hey, you, yourself."

She really tried with Tony Arayo. Tony's father who had skipped out years before, had been a circus performer. Tony had inherited his nerve, if nothing more. Olivia had tried to get Tony accepted at an actors' training school. She found him a part-time job with a newspaper and finally, at Brooks Brothers, bought him the first decent suit he had ever owned.

She had gone to the Arayo apartment in Harlem for a long talk with Tony about working his way through more schooling. She felt about him as she was later to feel about Justin Riley—she liked him and she hated him.

She blamed herself for being afraid of him. At her room at the Barbizon for Women which she shared with a girl she had known and liked at Wellesley, she would tell herself and Liz Hamilton that Tony was just a child. A child whose great energy could and ought to be directed into useful channels. He was just a mischievous kid, and he could be salvaged.

On a spring afternoon, armed with note books and recommendations, she had climbed the six flights of stairs to the Arayo apartment, pretending not to see the roaches that swarmed on the buff-colored walls. Her mission was to prove that if society really cared about the underprivileged, they would respond by turning into people worth caring about.

She knocked. Tony called out, "Come in."

She had walked in and Tony had been in the kitchen, standing before an ancient refrigerator without his clothes.

The first thing she had noticed was the hard tightly muscled magnificence of the eighteen-year-old body. Before she could think what to do next, his arms went around her and his body was pressed against her and his voice was muttering thickly, "Come on, you stuck-up bitch—admit this is what you want."

She slapped at him and twisted away in terror, raking his good-looking young punk's face with her manicured nails. He was far stronger than she. She went briefly insane and started to scream and kick with her high-heeled pumps. He forced her. Afterward he slapped her, hard, and pushed her out of the door of the apartment. She heard the lock click into place as she ran down the stairs, too stunned and too ashamed to believe the incident could really have happened to her. She taxied back to her hotel and took a hot shower. Later she became slightly hysterical, trying to tell Liz about it, and was surprised that Liz was not at all surprised.

"One of the few luxuries the poor can afford," Liz had shrugged, "is sex. I lost my virginity to a fifteen-year-old punk I was trying to help kick the drug habit. It doesn't do any good to complain—they'll think it was your fault. All female social workers are supposed to be sex-starved—and maybe we are."

Olivia had turned in her resignation the following day and had left at once for the haven of Ridgefield Corners, but she was haunted by the incident for months afterward. When she asked herself, *'Why did he do it?'* she always came to the same answer—that was what you could expect of men, what she had been brought up to expect of men. She had had many men try to run their hands over her, and there were some with whom she permitted it. Stu Everett, oddly enough, had always held her at arm's length.

Until Stu had said, "When a man is seriously in love with a girl, he doesn't want sex to happen to them in the back seat of a car."

Until that summer, Olivia had taken it for granted that sooner or later she and Stu would be married, decently and properly and elegantly, in the Episcopalian Church on French Street. The senator would give her away, everyone in town would scramble for an invitation, and the bride and groom would honeymoon in Europe. They would return to one of the several homes which the senator owned, since he and Cyrus Stevens more or less owned the town between them.

That summer, Sandy Miles had offered riding lessons to carefully selected students who had shown ring possibilities. Olivia, who had owned her own pony at six and her first show horse at eight, signed up immediately. Sandy had owned a little riding stable out at the edge of town and had not yet met Marge.

That was the first time Olivia found herself aware of the different kinds of attraction a man could hold for a girl. There was the quietly tender kind, such as Stu, who made you feel like a protected little girl. There was, she was to learn later, the swiftly impulsive kind, like Justin Riley, who had your sweater up over your head before you even knew what he had in mind. And there was Sandy Miles, who was all man but without connivance or guile. If she had not been such a snob, Olivia might have married Sandy and been far better off. She knew he had liked her.

Sandy was a westerner who had drifted east with a rodeo when he was just a kid. He had the westerner's quiet ways and hesitant speech and the westerner's code of chivalry toward nice girls. Which was why, Olivia always thought, he had not been the first man to whom she had freely given herself, leaving that honor for Stu who, as it turned out, had not wanted honors at all.

Or hardly at all.

Meanwhile, there had been the long hours of riding on the bridle trails and the soft yet strong feel of Sandy's hand on her arm, or against her leg as he adjusted her grip to the right place against the saddle. That was the summer the senator and his wife spent in Washington, leaving Olivia alone with the servants, who could not have cared less what Olivia did as long as they got off duty early.

On one such summer evening Sandy had come to dinner. He had looked appreciatively at the white-carpeted dining room with its antique furniture and drapes. "A man could really get to like a setup like this," he had remarked. "And a girl like you, too. Not me, maybe—too rich for my blood."

His comment had set her teeth on edge. But later, when they played the latest records and danced, she said, "You dance like a professional, Sandy. I guess all really good horsemen are wonderful dancers—it's all a sense of timing, isn't it?"

She was aware of an intense longing to place her head against his shoulder and her mouth against the lean, hard, sunburnt throat. He read her thoughts accurately and sat her in his lap and just kissed her, without talking, and he could have had her that night, if he had really wanted her. She had moved closer to him and kissed him in return with her lips parted, and run her hands down his back. He had said, "That feels good—don't stop—" but it was he who stopped.

One moment, they were sitting there kissing and touching—and then he pushed her a little, while a flush spread over his thin, high-cheeked face. He had said, "Let's have a cigarette."

She came floating back to the familiar room, to the realization of just how far she had gone, with her skirt up around her waist and her heart pounding as though it wanted freedom. Then she pulled back into herself and said, avoiding his eyes, "Yes, let's have a cigarette—I'm sorry. I didn't mean to—to let myself go like that. You won't tell anyone, will you, Sandy? Ever?"

He had smiled. "Don't be silly. What would I tell them?"

After that, they went out of their way to be casual with one another, and by the following spring, she was married to Justin Riley.

Soon after, Sandy married Marge.

Now on a July Sunday, Olivia rode with her son, John Justin Riley, to Sandy's stable.

Queer to think that all their futures were dependent at last on a stranger—a girl named Betty Hogan who was probably still in deep anesthetic sleep.

Betty, it turned out, had even affected Johnny's afternoon.

Muff, the Miles' hired girl, told Olivia and Johnny that the show had been called off—Mr. and Mrs. Miles, she said had suddenly had to go to the Mohawk Inn with Dr. Riley. "They had a big thing to talk over," Muff reported excitedly. "They were arguing, sort of—I mean in a nice way, not fighting—about Mrs. Miles' going back to work for Dr. Riley. And finally Dr. Riley said they should all go to the Inn where they wouldn't be interrupted. And they went."

Johnny's face fought disappointment.

"We had a nice ride together, anyway," Olivia soothed him. "And we still have our ride back home."

"Will you go to the Inn too, Mother? Later?"

"Why not?" Olivia answered, turning her horse's head.

CHAPTER EIGHT

Marge Miles had never known hatred. That was the thing that Sandy kept wanting to say, as he sat in a booth in the barroom of the inn with Marge and Justin. Marge did not understand the hatred in this world and therefore was not able to protect herself against it.

Justin was saying anxiously, "It's not just me you'll be helping, Marge—it's every patient in the hospital. I know how busy you and Sandy are. I hate imposing on you. But what choice do I have?"

"We'll make out somehow, Sandy and I," Marge reassured Justin. "We won't let you down."

She seemed not to suspect Justin Riley's motives, but Sandy did.

If she made it with another man, Sandy thought, he would kill the guy. But it would just about kill him too. He had never really loved any other girl, never known what sex was all about. Marge had demonstrated that a really nice girl could like sex as much as a man and yet be somebody the man wanted around him afterward. He would not want to go on living if he thought she was putting out for someone else.

He had never seen Marge look prettier. She was all dressed up in her pale-yellow linen sheath and matching hat with a wide brim and a streamer down the back. Her skin was lightly suntanned. She had that quality of freshness that probably stirred all the men who had ever met her. She made you feel she was on her way to some exciting place and you wanted to go there with her. Sandy had felt that special quality in her the minute he had met her. A kid-like quality, and yet she was all woman and she needed someone who was all man to take care of her.

Justin Riley's lips kept talking about the hospital. His eyes, though, were full of Marge. Was the guy nuts? With the whole town talking about him? Where did he get his gall?

Misty Powers had mentioned the problem this morning when she came to take her Palomino out on the bridle trail. "Marge has just begun to get her head above water. If she goes back to work for Justin, she'll be swamped."

"Well," Sandy had said. "I guess you know Marge. If she wants to go back there, I reckon she'll go."

Looking down at him as her small gloved hands picked up the reins, Misty had said, "I know—and I know something else."

"What's that?"

"I know that I hate that beautiful girl you're married to, darling, and the reason I hate her is that you're so in love with her. What I wouldn't give to have a man—any man—love me the way you love her." She had touched a spur to her horse's side and gone galloping off, leaving Sandy to meditate on what bitches women could be. There was Misty Powers, telling everyone she was Marge's friend, when all the while you could see she just hated Marge's guts. And she did not hate Marge simply because Marge had someone to love while Misty did not. She hated Marge for being young and lovable, which Misty was not. Misty did not want to love a man or have a man love her. Misty just wanted to destroy the people in her life, to keep from maybe some day having to destroy herself.

Marge lived among these people, among these hates, totally blind to evil—a child walking a tightrope, who thought herself on solid ground. He lost the conversation, forgot everything but his own thoughts.

Were there many ways in which he failed Marge? He was a farm boy, used to going for days without a bath in winter or changing his underwear. Could she stand the fact that he wanted her after a long hard day's work, climbing on top of her, wearing his shorts and his undershirt, and just having to have her? Marge had been used to eastern boys, to men he still thought of as dudes, who romanced a girl with sweet talk and candlelight and flowers. To Sandy, sex was just a simple, beautiful, biological act engaged in by two people who were lucky enough to want one another.

And yet, to Sandy, sex could never be purely physical. People just kidded themselves when they said it could be. From the first time he had been with Marge, in the grass back of the school she attended, Sandy Miles had known otherwise. He had come away from that encounter dazed and delighted. He had said to her, "You're terrific. I've never known a girl like you. I didn't know there were girls like you."

She had said, "Now you know—and what are you going to do about it?" She had been laughing at him lovingly, sitting in the warm, sweet-smelling summer grass and pulling a stalk of it through her small, white, even teeth. "I'm going to marry you," he had said, "and make you laugh like that the rest of your life. Try to get away from me and you'll be in trouble."

She had said, "Do you call that trouble?" and her eyes had laughed again and her body had been warm again and soft and yielding beneath his own.

And after that there had been just the noise of the cicadas and the whirring of a tractor somewhere and the whining noise of a buzz saw, and his own heart. The blue sky stretched above him and he was in love.

Later he learned other things about her—how afraid she was, for instance, of hurting someone who liked her.

And yet, for his sake, she had hurt her mother. Sandy would never forget the ripping quality of Judith Harris' voice across the width of her Park Avenue apartment that Christmas. "Marge's sister and I have pink mink jackets for Christmas and Marge has to present the family with a cowboy husband. I never want to see her, to speak to her, again—"

And Judith Harris never had. It had come as a shock to Sandy that two members of the same family could be so unlike. He had vowed that no one would ever again hurt Marge the way her mother had hurt her. As Justin Riley might hurt her.

He remembered the time they had told him, while Marge was working for Justin, that she had been in Justin's arms. "That's right," she had admitted. "I was crying. A patient had just been in and when I read the chart, I knew he had only a few more months to live. Justin had his arms around me, comforting me, trying to tell me that we're all under sentence of death, and either one of us might be dead before Les Franck died."

He felt restless, rose from the table, wandered to the bar.

"Hi," said a female voice.

He looked down at Misty Powers. "Hi," he answered.

He pointed to the table he just had left. "They're having a job conference."

Misty must have had an early start on the bottle. She whispered brightly, "The bitch—the dirty, rotten, two-timing little bitch. And pretending to be such a goody-goody that butter wouldn't melt in her mouth."

"Misty," Sandy said mildly, taking the glass from her hand. "I've never hit a woman in my life and I don't aim to, but if you ever say anything against Marge again, so help me, I'll knock you right on your ass."

The glassy light-blue eyes regarded him sullenly before Misty said, "You're a fool, Sandy Miles. It will serve you right to play the role of cuckold."

Sunday night in the taproom, Sandy thought worriedly, suddenly promised to be far from dull.

CHAPTER NINE

They were all at the bar by nightfall just as Justin had known they would be—the Art Peevers and the John Logans and the Ted Halloways, Ridgefield Corners' gay young marrieds. They were here to talk about horses and each other's business deals and sometimes each other's wives.

They were not rich as they would like to be or as they pretended to be, and the cash register of Harry Kyle's Tavern always held its share of bum checks. These would later be passed back to the owner discreetly.

The checks were always made good. Harry Kyle had lived in Ridgefield Corners for twenty-nine years. He was a New Yorker who had come upstate for his wife's health. Once he had been a waiter at the Stork Club and the taproom of the Mohawk Inn in Ridgefield Corners, under Harry's management, had the same gossipy anybody-who-is-anybody quality which, on a larger scale, had made the New York place famous.

Tonight the small town's smart set had its juiciest gossip in years. People seemed surprised at seeing Justin still among them. He could hear the thoughts that were hidden in silence. *His father-in-law will lose that election sure. Riley'll lose his license. Are the Miles still bothering with him? Why?*

Harry heard the noisy silence too, and went out of his way to leave a party of eight before the dead fireplace to shake Justin's hand in front of the whole damned crew.

"What'll it be, Justin? Have one on the house."

Harry was not in the habit of buying drinks on the house. For some crazy reason, though, he credited Justin with saving Molly Kyle's life during her last asthma attack. Any doctor could have done as much, Justin had insisted, but Harry was a dope of an ex-waiter who clung to oddball emotions like gratitude.

"Bourbon and branch," Justin acknowledged. "And thanks." He had already begun to feel slightly better.

Marge said, "You see, Justin? You can lick this thing if Olivia stands by you and Betty pulls through. I think the ones who don't like you are all jealous of you because you stand for something. And any one of them would have liked going to bed with Betty Hogan, but they couldn't get to first base. She was really crazy in love with you, Justin. She told me so one day when I dropped by the lab to see how she was making out."

Justin said, "Oh, my God. Why? Why do women fall in love with men who can only hurt them? I didn't kid her, Marge. She knew it wasn't for keeps. But that's not your worry."

"You think she'll pull through?"

"Stu is a good surgeon—he's doing his best." Justin realized he was repeating himself. "Yes, I think she'll make it. I told you, I dropped by the hospital earlier. They've got her pretty heavily sedated, and they're giving her transfusions. But I don't trust those nurses. She broke the rules and they've got it in for her. I wish there were someone near her who really cared about her."

"That could be me, Justin."

Justin frowned. He wished Sandy Miles would return to their table—he could not help but feel that Marge's promise, unless Sandy backed her, might have to fall through.

Ed Haley, county sheriff, was sitting at the far end of the bar, his gun prominently exposed in the hand-tooled leather holster. Ed Haley liked the power of that gun and liked the way women's eyes went to it with a kind of fascination. "A gun," he had observed in his dry, flat voice, "is a real phallic symbol, boy. It's the image of power, the power of a male. Never underestimate it."

Stories had leaked out of the little red-painted jailhouse. They said Ed usually made it with any prostitute picked up on a vagrancy charge by his boys. Tonight Ed's eyes were sleepy and unblinking, and they moved deliberately from time to time toward Justin's face—and then to the outline of Marge's clean young breasts beneath the yellow sheath.

Some day, Justin thought, he must remember to slug Ed Haley. Justin was not impressed by the gun. And yet, he felt about sex the way he guessed Ed Haley felt. He could not look at a girl without thinking, *There's something I'd like to knock off*—or, conversely, *That looks like something that even a husband would kick out of bed.*

As a kid growing up in the tenements, walking the streets at night alone, always alone, he had thought that way of women—with a swift, compulsive desire which was nearly always satisfied. There had been no real love in any of it, but there had been release and relaxation, letting him get his mind back on his work again and on the fierce ambition that was stronger within him than sex.

He had always had a compulsive need for many women, for different women, and he picked them up, even now, in almost every city he visited on medical conventions. Whether he did this to make himself more than he was or to make women less, he did not know, nor did he think it important—or any of Olivia's or anyone else's business.

Fidelity was not for Justin Riley, apparently.

He wondered if he would have been faithful to a girl like Marge Miles, who deserved fidelity because she gave it, and in more than physical ways. He found himself wanting her—not only with his body, but with whatever passed within him for a soul. The feeling frightened him badly.

Misty Powers seemed to have arrived at some point with her beau, Phil Sheffers. At the moment, Misty was throwing greetings all around the room as though she were tossing bouquets to an army of admirers. But the greeting and her gaze went mostly to Justin and stayed there for a minute, while the angry look on Phil's middle-aged, ruddy face told Justin that Misty and Phil had been fighting again. Phil said they only fought because of Misty's drinking, to which Misty usually retorted that she drank because they fought. She had certainly been hitting it today. Her eyes were fogged-out. Her greetings had an ominous note of belligerence under the camaraderie.

Some of the most magnificent brawls ever witnessed at the taproom had been brought on by that belligerence in Misty. Twice Harry had had to ask her to leave, the last time threatening not to let her in again unless she stayed comparatively sober.

When she headed toward the empty seat beside Justin, Phil grabbed her arm and pulled her down beside him at their table near the fireplace.

The music started in the other room. Justin called to Harry Kyle, "Why louse up the place with those corny bands from Oneonta? If you can't give decent music, what's wrong with peace and quiet?"

"Peace and quiet," Harry retorted affably, "ain't popular this year." The twist might be finished in larger cities but it still had a hold in Ridgefield Corners the way sex had. By ten o'clock tonight, every hotel and summer resort in the area would have a little bit of dance space blocked off and middle-aged women would be on the floor in their bare feet, twisting and dipping and rotating everything that would rotate, giving the men they were dancing with ideas that they hoped would last until they got home.

As a fashionable small-town doctor, there was little Justin did not know about the health and sex habits of everyone in the room. If he were to go bad—really bad, betraying his profession rather than getting involved with a foolish girl—he could blow the town wide open by telling half he knew.

Sheriff Ed Haley strolled over and sat beside Justin. He asked softly, "How's that girl coming, Ju?"

Justin did not like Ed Haley to call him Ju. He said, "What girl, Ed?"

"Now, Ju, you know damn well what girl." Ed's voice was low, conspiratorial and even friendly. "One of my boys will be there as soon as she regains consciousness to take down anything she says. I'm on your side, I guess you know that, but I've got to uphold the law, too. While we're at it, why not come down to the office and talk the whole thing over?"

Ed Haley's big, thick hand was caressing the gun butt as though it were the silky-soft skin of a girl's thigh, and Justin could read the vicarious sex images that were passing across the screen of Ed's mind. Yes, he'd like to get all the details, all right. He could imagine Ed's questions. *How many times did you have intercourse with this girl? Is there any chance some other guy is responsible and you're getting stuck with this? What did she tell you about her sex life? Any other men in town been with her, do you know?*

He could imagine the questions and the soft, ingratiating voice with which Ed would ask them. Justin had sat in on the questioning of a young farm boy charged with raping a student nurse, and the kid had become hysterical under the sexual probing of the sheriff's voice.

He wondered, since Ed was Cy's man, how much of this was really aimed at Senator John Turner rather than Doctor Riley.

"There's nothing to talk over, Ed. The girl worked with me. I took her to dinner a few times."

"Well." The sheriff stretched and yawned, extending his enormous stomach which some day would kill him with hepatic coma. "If you change your mind, get in touch with me, Ju. And let's just hope the girl makes it. She's got a good chance, with Stu Everett in charge. They tell me he's probably the best gynecological surgeon from here to New York."

Justin nodded. "So they say. Good night, sheriff." When he had gone, Justin asked Marge, "See what I mean? The last thing he thought of was the fact that Betty's sick—and that's how everyone feels. Except maybe you and me and good old Stu Everett."

"She's going to be all right—"

"She'll never be all right. A kid of nineteen with a total hysterectomy. I hate somebody, Marge—somebody whose name I don't know."

"You don't mean that. Who's the person?"

"Whoever did the abortion—the bungling lousy abortion that landed her on an operating table. What beats me is why nobody gives a damn about finding out who it was."

Misty Powers came over to rest her arm heavily on Justin's shoulder.

"What are you being so highhat about tonight, Doctor?" she taunted him. "Just because you're sober for once, and I'm a little tiddly?"

"You're always a little tiddly," Justin said. "Now be a good girl and go sit somewhere else. Marge and I are talking business."

"Oh," said Misty with the lofty affectedness of the far-gone female drunk, "Pah-don—I—" She staggered back to the table where Phil waited for her, looking bored and angry and disgusted. Phil barely drank at all, which made Misty's sprees even more intolerable to him. Also, he happened to be devoted to Misty's three children, especially Martha, the five-year-old. When Misty drank, the children were farmed out, sometimes for days at a time, to the town's baby sitter, Jane Dieterle, who had a heavy hand. When the children became too much to handle, a little chloral hydrate extended their afternoon naps into the next day.

People at the hospital, including Justin and Marge, knew about the situation at the Dieterle place, but no one could prevent it, and women like Misty went on leaving their children in Jane Dieterele's care. The essential problem, Justin thought, was some inner decay in the town. People here felt trapped, with nowhere to go except, occasionally, the bed of someone else's wife or husband. Drinking and fornication were the two local pastimes and Justin, who had availed himself of both, felt no desire to pass judgment. The town, he knew, was not returning his charity.

He would have given a lot tonight, he thought, for a look of friendship, from others in this room besides the tavernkeeper. But nowhere except in Marge's eyes was there any kindness. In return, would he corrupt her, make her as bad as himself?

Marge was saying, "If it's all right with Sandy, Justin—I'll show up tomorrow morning at the lab. Just as early as I can make it."

Sandy rejoined them at last. Evidently he had heard Marge's commitment. His voice sounded the way it always sounded, no matter how he might be feeling. Sandy's voice was soft and easy, the way it needed to be when he moved through the stalls at night, talking to the nervous horses.

"Anything Marge says is okay with me, Doc. We can even use the money. Cy Stevens' closing off his land to the hackers has made it pretty rough—if it weren't for the day camp, we'd have to close up."

Justin said, "Cyrus Stevens is a stupid sonofabitch and this town won't begin to live until that bastard's six feet under."

Everyone in the room heard him—Art Peevers, who managed the Cy Stevens estates and bought up land for himself, on the side, with the old man's money. Gladys Summit, whose husband had prostate trouble and who presented herself at Justin's heart clinic regularly for a totally unnecessary examination just for the thrill of his lifting her heavy breasts as he applied the stethoscope to her heart. And Misty and Phil and the Logans, who, like the Stevenses lived on inherited wealth and needed to keep the town broke if they were to live here like millionaires on a comparatively small income. They all heard it and made a mental note of it and Art Peevers even made a written note, to be sure to pass the information on to the old man in the morning.

The twist music, brassy and ugly, was getting up steam in the big main dining room. Justin realized he was beginning to feel the several bourbons. He ought to eat something. Besides, before the night was over, he wanted to go to the hospital again to see Betty Hogan.

He said to Sandy, "Be my dinner guests. Thought we'd take a table in the other room where it's quiet."

The other room was a small private dining room usually sacred to the weekly meetings of the Kiwanis, the Elks and the local chapter of the American Legion. Sandy hesitated, then said, "Fine, Doc. Marge could stand a blowout, I guess. Looks like a picked chicken these days, the way I'm working her."

At last a hint of pain touched Sandy's voice and mouth. Justin shifted his gaze away from the other man's eyes and the entreaty in them. *You've got so much*, that look said clearly. *Don't take her, too, because she's all I've got ...*

As they rose, Misty Powers threw her glass, carefully emptied, at Marge's head. The glass missed by half an inch and crashed into the bar mirror.

Justin turned furiously, somehow missed slapping Misty's drunken face. "You stupid bitch, what do you think you're doing?" he asked.

"I think I'm throwing a glass at your girl friend, that's what I think I'm doing. And you didn't think Misty was a stupid, drunken bitch last night, did you, darling? You thought Misty was pretty damn' good last night, as I remember."

Purely by chance the music paused just then to underline the silence that fell. Justin Riley felt, for the first time in his life, that he was an object of contempt. He read disgust in the little eyes and in the big eyes—on the ruddy faces of the men and the made-up faces of their wives or their girls. Turning his head, he saw even Marge staring at him in stunned disbelief.

Misty declaimed slowly, "A girl he got knocked up is maybe dying down at the hospital and this sonofabitch is crawling into Misty Powers' drawers the same night."

The party of eight at the fireplace rose as one, and the host said to Harry, "I think we'd prefer to be served in the other room, Harry, if it's all right with you."

Justin asked Sandy politely, "Care to reconsider having dinner with me?"

"Of course not." Marge answered for both of them. They went into the other room.

Justin did not realize that he kept getting drunker. The first time he realized it, his dinner had gone back untouched and Sandy was trying, without success, to pour black coffee into him. Harry Kyle was saying, "Justin, take it easy—Olivia and Stu Everett are here to take you home."

In the depths of his somnolence, Justin heard Olivia say, "It's a shame to wake the poor darling up, but I suppose we'll have to, to get the keys to the car."

Marge shook him lightly. "Wake up, Justin. Olivia's here."

"Don't want go home," protested Justin. "Shove home. Shove Olivia. Stu Everett. Where's that bastard of a Stu Everett who's supposed by my friend and makes it regularly with my wife? Has anybody here seen Stu—" he began to sing to the tune of, *Has anybody here seen Kelly* and heard Stu say firmly, "For Pete's sake, shut up, Justin, and don't make things worse than they are. You're embarrassing the hell out of Olivia."

With a monumental effort, Justin sat upright to face Stu's no-nonsense competence. "I am sorry," he said loftily, "if I am embarrassing my wife, but has anyone ever told you that my wife is a pain in the ass?"

Olivia reached across the table and slapped him, hard, before turning on her heel and walking out. Stu must have followed her, because the next thing Justin was clearly conscious of was the back seat of Sandy's car, with the sound of summer rain pelting the car roof. Marge and Sandy were driving him home in silence. When they pulled up in front of Justins house, Sandy said, "Need some help getting upstairs, Justin?"

"No, thanks. I'm okay now. Thanks for the lift. 'Night."

He made his unsteady way up the narrow flagstone path, up the four short steps to the wide front terrace. He groped for the door handle, glad to find the latch unlocked. He made his way to his own room without switching on the lights.

He was not surprised to find the light on beside his bed or the bed turned down. He collapsed without taking off his clothes. Olivia, of course, was in the guest room and this time would probably stay there. Lost in the fog of liquor, beginning to be dimly aware of the pounding in his head that would be tomorrow's hangover, Justin felt the rising excitement that comes to one who has asked for and received some terrible, final punishment.

He knew now that he was in for it. But good.

He remembered saying a wild drunken thing about Olivia and Stu. Were his words what he really believed—that Olivia and Stu were having an affair? No—his self-esteem could not have sunk so low. Olivia had once been engaged to Stu—Justin was the boy who had taken her away, not the other way around.

Nobody took women, unfortunately, off Justin Riley's hands.

CHAPTER TEN

Misty Powers, wearing only her slip, lay curled on the unmade bed. She fitfully dozed. Gradually, the part of her that was still conscious was penetrated by the singsong bar of melody. The hideous melody persisted, and for a while she thought it was that awful twist music she had been dancing to last night before she had been ordered, finally and forever, from the taproom of the Mohawk Inn. She opened her eyes, rolled flat on her back and listened. At last she realized that what she heard was the doorbell.

She sat up. Her head felt apart from and extremely far above her body, like a toy balloon attached to a string. The cleft between her breasts felt sticky, and her slip clung to her. From years of knowledge, she told herself, *Alcoholic sweat, sweetie, alcoholic sweat.*

That was to remind herself that the sweat had nothing to do with heart trouble or tuberculosis or any of the other things she might wish were causing the sweat. This was nothing for which Justin Riley or Stu Everett could treat her. No one in this world could treat her for this sickness but Misty Powers.

"Coming, coming," she called out thickly as the doorbell continued its insistent chiming.

Propped on an elbow, she looked about her at the familiar room as though she had never seen it before—and, indeed, it seemed like days, weeks, months, since Phil had dumped her here, telling her, she recalled dully and dimly, that he never wanted to see her again.

"I wouldn't have put up with you this long," he had said, "If it weren't for those kids. I'd have dropped you a long time ago, except for that."

Remembering, she began to cry. Since when did Phil or any other man have the right to talk to her that way? She was no tramp like that girl Justin had got into trouble. She was Misty Powers, and Samson Powers, her second husband, had once owned five hundred acres of this town. Powerstown. That's who she was. Misty Powers, of Powerstown, and just because she took a drink too many once in a while was no reason why any man should tell her he would have kicked her out of his life a long time ago if he had not been so sorry for her children.

Her children. Yes, she reminded herself, she must remember them too. She was a mother. That was what Sammy had said, the last time he had come out here and found them, practically unconscious, at Jane Dieterle's.

"You might try to remember once in a while," he had threatened her, "that you're a mother. If you don't shape up, Misty, I'm going to take those kids away from you, so help me."

So help me. Help was what Misty Powers wanted this hot, burning morning when the doorbell would not stop ringing while she fumbled for a robe. She wanted someone to try to understand that she could not help drinking any more than she could avoid the other thing. In fact, drinking helped the other thing. No one seemed to understand how the drinking was a cure. If she drank enough, she could forget about wanting a man for as long as two or three weeks at a time which, for her, was something of a record.

Hurry up. That was what she must do now. Hurry up and stop that doorbell from ringing. Maybe it was Sammy, coming to check up on her. Or Phil, coming to help her. Or Justin, coming to say he was sorry he had been so mean.

She had the heavy satin negligee on now, and she left her room gropingly, reminding herself, "Don't let whoever it is know you're still half-loaded—"

"Who is it?" she called as she made her cautious, precarious way down the carpeted stairs. Reaching the front door, she worked the chain free, marveling that she had been sober enough, the night before, to put it in place. No, she could not have done it. Phil must have put the chain on, then left through the back. She pulled the door open, shutting her eyes and averting her face from the explosion of sunlight and the blast of hot air.

A tall, thin young man in T-shirt, faded blue jeans and sneakers was leaving across the lawn.

"Hi," she called out. "Did you want me?"

He halted and turned. His face was unfamiliar. He must be one of the hundreds of summer visitors who descended on the town in search of fresh air and summer jobs.

"You Miss Powers?" he asked in a voice slightly thickened by a southern accent.

"Mrs. Powers," Misty corrected him.

His face was ugly and striking. His chestnut-colored hair was shaggy and in need of a trim. Maybe he was one of the boys up here with the summer stock company. He had narrow, tip-tilted eyes set in deep sockets, and a kind of fresh way about him. Pausing, he had placed his hands on the bony, narrow hips and swayed backward a little, as he regarded her.

"Mrs. Powers," he corrected himself, with a slight bow. She saw now that the blue jeans were really stretched taut across his loins and she could see what he had in them. She found herself thinking, *He ought to wear a jock strap or something. That's disgusting.*

He was speaking, his lips barely moving, like someone out of a jail or a reform school or something, "—that prescription you ordered—" he was saying.

"What? I'm sorry. I'm still not awake. What prescription?"

"Well, I don't know. Some kind of sleeping pill, I guess. Anyway, the doc down there at the hospital wouldn't okay it for a renewal and said for you to call him—but I've got the other thing you ordered."

"What other thing?" Oh, God, she felt so vague and funny and frightened. She was shaking. She needed a drink, and needed it bad.

The boy gave her a lipless smile, came back across the close-cropped lawn to hand her a small package. Memory began to return. A diaphragm. She had not stayed dumped after Phil left. Last night, she had called the drug store emergency number, rousing the pharmacist from a sound sleep. She had wanted only to renew the nembutal prescription, she began to remember, so that she could take a few too many, but not altogether too many, and call Phil, and tell him that if he did not marry her, she would take them all. Then, to reassure Bill Scott, who was familiar with Misty Powers getting drunk and taking too many sleeping pills, she had ordered a new diaphragm, thinking fuzzily that no woman who intended committing suicide would be ordering a new contraceptive at the same time. So now the new diaphragm was here, wrapped in its plain green wrapper, reminding her of the time when she was a young bride, ashamed to go into the drugstore and order a thing like that. Now, she was sort of proud of it, and would usually call it out in a fairly loud voice, wanting everyone to know that Misty Powers was still too young for the menopause.

"Oh," she said, accepting the package, "yes, I remember. Come, in won't you?"

He followed her into the wide cool hall with its early-morning stillness and neatness. She climbed the stairs slowly, still not entirely sober, but sober enough to know that her credit was no good at the drugstore any more than it was elsewhere in town. She always got drunk, sooner or later, and began handing out bad checks. Both the local banks had refused to handle her account. Now she always had to keep enough cash on hand to take care of any deliveries. She searched for the cash, groping about blindly in first one purse and then another as the young man watched her. She said finally, "I'm sorry, I can't remember which purse—"

The bedroom was untidy, with her clothes in a heap on the floor. There was a half-finished drink on the night-table and an ash tray heaped with lipstick-stained cigarettes. The young man's flat, dark eyes moved over the room and then over her. "That's okay, honey," he said, "take it easy. I've got lots of time."

She dropped onto the bed, a hand to her aching head. "That's good," she said, "because I need a drink. I never in my life ever took a drink in the morning, but this is one morning—what did you say your name was?"

"I didn't, but it's Duke, Duke Dillon. Want I should fix you a drink, baby?"

"Would you? A shot of scotch over some ice—maybe then, I can think."

He came back with the drink and she remembered that she said to him, "What about you?" and he gave her that same strange, lipless smile.

"Never touch the stuff."

She lifted the glass to her lips, and by the time she realized he had done something to the drink, it was too late. This time her head seemed to have left her body for good. There were two of him and three of him and two again and one. He was holding her with one arm and the other hand was unbuckling his belt. His mouth was wet against her own but for a minute she automatically returned the pressure. What roused her was not the kiss, but the pressure against her sore breasts. She was still at an age when around period time, her breasts swelled and felt sore the way they used to feel during pregnancy. There was something good about the pain of his body pressed so hard against her aching breasts.

"I knew it the minute I laid eyes on you," he said. "I thought, 'There's a real hungry broad.'"

"No," she said, but she said it vaguely. Her speech, like his face, like the room, seemed a long, long way off. "No."

Behind the dizziness in her temples there was a struggle toward sobriety, toward consciousness. She did not want this thing to happen to her that had almost happened to her on countless other occasions. Pete, down at Danny's Market, had almost accomplished it, and a pimply-faced kid at the supermarket, and Red, who delivered her laundry, and always made hick jokes about this being the day they had a special on whatever the customers had on that they'd take off. Almost, almost, and always before, sober enough to be saved, but this time she felt herself lean against the boy even as her brain gave the signal to draw from him.

His clothing was off now and he was there before her, naked and taut and ready, and somehow, there had been so many, that one more was not going to matter. She heard him say impatiently, "Come on, baby, let's go."

She said, "Wait—" but impatient hands were tearing at the heavy satin negligee, ripping the slip in half to expose the swollen breasts that seemed to burst free. She heard him draw breath sharply, heard him say, "Boy, do you ever have a pair—"

She tried to ask him to wait, she tried to explain the matter of the diaphragm and to say that if he would only wait …

His arm fell like a crowbar across her throat and her head slammed against the leather headboard of the bed. His teeth bit into her breasts and then into her buttocks and it hurt and she moaned with the pain and tried to rise again.

"Don't hurt me," she said, but his fingers found the places in her body with a viciousness that felt like being stabbed. "Your fingernails—" she moaned again, but she was way down in the darkness by then, and even while her voice asked him to be careful, her body gave the automatic response it had given to so many men through so many copulations and so many years. She closed her eyes, sinking into the darkness where there would no longer be any pain or anything but sensation, willingly offering her flesh so that pain might be sooner ended.

To keep one's eyes closed, that was the trick, closed hard, and just imagine it was someone she liked, like Justin, that time, last night, no a hundred years ago, and yet, like this, now bounded, now limited, now known, her body recoiling and recoiling again from the rhythmical beat and thinking *Now—now, please. I have so many times. Now, you, please,* now—and then the final, searing agony, the hot wetness, the animal smell, and then silence.

She wakened slowly, coming back from a long way off, coming back to the sound of the kitchen door slamming and the sound of running feet and the final sound of a motorcycle starting up. She thought that a minute later she staggered to her feet until she caught sight of the electric clock beside her bed and saw that it was almost noon. Three hours. She had been out, out like a light, for almost three hours.

"Sonofabitch," she said aloud to the room. When she moved, her thighs ached. Everything ached. He must really have worked her over, she thought dully, after she had passed out altogether. She crawled, on all fours, over to the table beside the window where the big alligator purse she had carried last night lay open. That was where her money was. She remembered, now. She remembered having said to Phil, "I've got two hundred dollars in cash in here, don't let me lose it—" but she knew before she investigated the leather-lined interior of the purse that she had lost it. That Duke Dillon had stolen it, and by now, he would be halfway to Oneonta or New York or—or maybe he'd just stay here, daring her to report him.

It did no good to cry. It did no good to be sorry. But just the same she sat on the floor and cried. She cried very softly while the phone rang and rang.

"Go on and ring," she told it, sobbing out the words. "You sons of bitches—all of you—Justin, Phil, Sammy—I hate you, hate you—"

She remembered nothing else until she woke up in the hospital.

Justin Riley tried to tell her, ever so gently, that she was there because she had walked downtown without any clothes on, shouting obscenities. After some hours, Justin told her the rest. Misty's daughter Martha was also in the hospital in a coma as the result of one of Jane Dieterle's chloral-hydrate-induced naps.

"As a rule," Justin explained, "chloral hydrate is a fairly mild barbiturate. In Martha's case, it entered the blood stream and caused toxic poisoning."

"Oh, God," Misty moaned. She did not say the word, Justin knew, as profanity but as prayer. He recognized the difference, because by then, he had used the word in a similar context several times, himself.

CHAPTER ELEVEN

On Wednesday morning, Justin's third clinic patient was a short woman in her early forties or late thirties who was, medically speaking, well-nourished. Ten more pounds would have made her obese. He raised his glance from his study of her figure and recognized her face.

"Well, Nancy Hennessy," he greeted her. "Don't tell me you're sick. You look too happy to be sick."

Jimmy Hennessy's mother rewarded the greeting with an awkward smile. "I guess I'm happy enough," she admitted. "With my two nice men and all."

Two. Her husband and her seven-year-old son. That was Olivia's situation. Justin wondered what Olivia would say if he reminded her to be happy because she had two nice men.

"Sit down," he continued. "Tell me what's wrong."

She sighed. "I bet I'm imagining things. Sometimes I get a pain here—" she indicated her breast—"when I'm lifting the wash or running upstairs, that's so bad I have to stop. It hurts—sharp. Jim takes it more seriously than I do. That's why I'm here. He made me promise I'd come."

Justin said reassuringly. "Never any harm in a check-up."

A small number of Justin's female patients, he had found, were embarrassed by routine examinations. Most of these were either very young or well past middle age. Women in their thirties who had borne children were seldom bashful with doctors, and a good many were the opposite, to Justin's occasional wry amusement.

Nancy Hennessy blushed faintly, a blush that spread to the armpits, as she lay back on the examining table with her soft breasts bared to a strange man. Justin used his stethoscope quickly. "You can button up now," he said. "Everything sounds normal."

She closed her blouse with obvious relief and sat up. As she made to rise, Justin shook his head slightly.

"Let's take a minute," he suggested. "You're not a foolish person. You're not making up this pain."

"You're busy," she said uneasily.

"Not too busy to visit for five minutes. Are you?" She looked surprised. "Well, to tell the truth, I am kind of rushed. I promised the manager at Newberry's I'd be back before eleven."

"You like working, Nancy? It gets you out of the rut of housework—gets you out where you can see people, this standing behind the counter at Newberry's every morning."

"That's right." Nancy Hennessy stopped looking embarrassed. Some part of her spirit responded to his words. He was quoting her defense and she felt secure. "Keeps me from getting stale. And it's nice for a woman to have a paycheck of her own. She can buy herself little things she might not be able to afford otherwise."

"I understand. I guess you've got a schedule pretty well worked out. You get up a few minutes earlier than your two men do, you've got their food ready by the time they're washed—it all works out fine."

"Why, that's exactly right. That's just how it is."

"And there's plenty of time for you to take care of the cleaning and cooking and washing after you get home. No time to waste, but plenty of time to do what you have to do."

Her full, plain, good-tempered face was beginning to show puzzlement. "'That's how it is, sure."

She was wondering, he knew, both why he discussed her working pattern and how he knew about it. He answered the unasked questions. "I know all about it," he said. "My mother did the same things when I was seven, the age Jimmy is now. She died when I was twelve. She died because she was tired, Nancy. There was nothing wrong with her heart. There was something wrong with my father. I don't think the same thing is wrong with Jim Hennessy. You quit that job, Nancy."

She stared at him as though he had hit her. Tears formed in her guileless eyes. "You can't—I can't—"

"You're right, I can't. I'm not the law around here, I'm only a doctor. Why do you need the money, Nancy? Jim's the best carpenter in the county."

He had hit the guarded spot at last, the softness behind the defenses. She cried softly yet bitterly, "Sure he is. But he charges less than anybody else. It's too late for him to change that. It's the way he is. Scared somebody will underbid him. And people don't pay their bills, sometimes, for months and months. I mean, people that can afford it, people that think nothing of having two in help and giving dinners for ten and taking trips south as soon as there's a snow flurry. You take that Mrs. Powers. She owes for a whole new bedroom floor—except you can hardly call it new any more. She's had that floor for eighteen months, and I make up the bills winter and summer, the twenty-fifth of every month and there's that same two hundred fifty dollars, never paid—not even the lumber is paid for, that's been out of our pocket all this while—"

"I see," Justin said. "Mrs. Powers is a good friend of mine. She won't mind my mentioning two hundred fifty dollars."

Nancy Hennessy looked terrified. "Jim will be furious. He doesn't like threatening people." She reached for her purse. "I have to go now. I really must." She hesitated nevertheless, balancing herself on the edge of the examining table. "Dr. Riley, you talked straight to me, and maybe you won't mind if I talk straight to you."

"Let's have it," Justin said.

"That's a real nice boy you have. Quiet and smart—always polite. People can be terrible, the way they gossip. I think he's heard things—a child hears a lot, you'd be surprised. I think it hurts him more than he shows. I wish—"

Justin was surprised at his own reaction. Helpful suggestions from his wife or father-in-law, to the effect that he ought to mend his ways, usually inspired him to look up the nearest friendly female who was willing to share his alleged gutter.

Jimmy Hennessy's mother made him briefly wish that there never had been a Misty Powers, or a Betty Hogan, or a Gail Bennett in his life. "I know what you wish," he said. "But I guess I'm Johnny's tough luck." He looked at the clock on the wall. "How late does your stint at Newberry's run?"

"Just till two. Then I go home for lunch."

Justin wrote a prescription. "This will help the pain," he explained, handing her the paper. "The only place I want you to get it filled is the French Street drugstore. Chances are they'll need an hour or two. You're not to go back to work without those pills. So you might as well stop in town and buy yourself a glass of wine and a salad—too bad you won't get to work until nearly quitting time, but it can't be helped."

She left with a troubled look on her face.

Before seeing his next clinic patient, Justin made two phone calls. The first was to the French Street drugstore, alerting the pharmacist there to delay filling Nancy Hennessy's prescription for placebos at least until one-thirty. The second call was to Jim Hennessy's carpenter shop.

Jim was harder to handle. Before Justin had given him all the reasons for Nancy's quitting her job, Jim Hennessy had relieved himself of some home truths about Justin's private life and possible ancestry, using less tact than his wife had done. "And besides," Jim wound it up, "no kid of yours, even if he's a kid like Johnny, is going to hang around any more with any kid of mine. How do you like that?"

"The hell with you," Justin said. "So I'm a lousy father. You're a flop as a husband and provider. I hope you're keeping up payments on Nancy's life insurance. You'll be cashing in mighty soon."

Jim Hennessy had already run out of profanity. Justin heard his sharp inward breath. The carpenter asked in audible misery, "What can I do?"

"You can bring me a list of your deadbeats. I'll make sure you're paid forty-eight hours from now. This town hates me anyway, for reasons you've stated with admirable clarity. I might as well be your collection agent—what have I to lose?"

Jimmy Hennessy said that Justin was joking.

"I never joke in the clinic," Justin said. "I save it for the carriage trade. You might try my system. Can I have that list in an hour?"

"You can have it in twenty minutes. And listen, doc—"

"Speak up, I'm listening."

"I didn't mean what I said about your kid. Maybe I meant it yesterday. I don't mean it now."

"You never meant it," Justin said, which he knew was a lie. "You'd never have come between a couple of kids like that. Johnny doesn't have lots of friends. He needs a friend like Jimmy."

"I get it. Thanks, doc. See you."

"Drop dead," Justin told him. "But get here first with the list."

He was ready for his next patient.

All about him, in the sunless, humid July day, he sensed the town's contempt like a duplication of weather. He hated them all in return but their lives were safe in his hands. He had no hatred for life.

CHAPTER TWELVE

Senator Turner said, "I realize how busy you are, Justin. I appreciate your stopping by."

He had meant the words to sound sarcastic, Justin thought. But they had not come out that way. The senator had sounded old and tired—and grateful.

They were in the senator's study on the second floor of the rambling magnificent house. The room was high-ceilinged and had its own fireplace. Emily Turner had once remarked that her husband would want a fireplace if he found himself in hell. On this Tuesday in July, the hearth was cold and the Dalmations lay there quietly, chins on the cool stones. Sitting across from the older man, Justin had the same annoyed feeling that his father-in-law always gave him, of being somehow a job-seeker, a childish feeling. The senator was actually the job-seeker now. He had an election to face in the fall, for his seat in the legislature in Albany.

Justin said, "I don't know what to report except that we're still waiting. When Betty comes out of the coma, she'll probably say I gave her the money to help her out. I still won't deny that I would have been the child's father."

"Ed Haley tells me she hasn't regained consciousness, except for a few minutes at a time, since they operated."

"That's true—and also ominous. As a result of long coma, there's always a chance of brain damage, which is one reason I've got Marge Miles in the room. She's to take down whatever the girl says whenever she says it. I wouldn't trust Ed Haley's boys—they're Cy Stevens' boys, too, you know."

"I'm well aware of that."

The senator spoke the words with the distaste he felt toward most other politicians. Senator John Turner should, Justin had always thought, have been born into a less amoral world—the world of Daniel Webster and John C. Calhoun.

"Why in hell," Justin asked, "don't you take those invisible gloves off and dirty your hands for once? For my part, I mean to stick with the truth, if it ruins you and me both. What I'm after is more truth—specifically, who did that operation on Betty—and why he's getting away with it. Senator, I'm a maverick. To me, no operation is illegal if it's successful, if it doesn't impair the patient's well-being and health. Why not fight my way for a change? You just might happen to win."

"I have summoned that girl's parents here," Senator Turner said. "I have decided to meet their demands."

Justin half-rose from his chair. "You're out of your mind. Do you realize the spot you're putting me in? You're selling me out—and you're selling yourself out too."

"You sold us out," said the senator. "I see no reason why the entire family and, indeed, the electorate of this county, have to be sold out along with you. I suppose Olivia has told you that I have urged her to leave you?"

"Olivia and I are no longer on speaking terms, thank you."

"Just as well. From what I have heard of the words that were exchanged between you Sunday evening at the taproom—"

"That was my fault. I got drunk. Like my old man before me. He had one virtue, though. He stuck with his family. We were nothing—but I've seen people since who were less."

"I trust you will be equally generous, Justin, in your final verdict on sober members of society."

"Is there anything else, sir?"

"Yes. I want you here when those people come—I want you to face your accusers. I feel certain that if you are here, and there is profit in sight, they will back down on their charges."

Justin said quietly, "What a scared old man you are. No wonder your son left home."

The senator pressed a button for his occasional secretary, a thin, pale young man who was studying law in the senator's Albany office.

"You can send those people in, Adam," the senator instructed.

The Hogans materialized in the study before Adam had time to turn and relay the instructions. They must have been just outside listening to everything. Betty's parents had made no previous attempt to communicate with Justin directly.

Betty's mother still had traces of loveliness and passion but only a doctor, and one who understood women, would have detected those vestigial qualities. Poverty had done to her what it did to most people, made her mean and cold and sly. She was leathery and gaunt, and all she had on her mind was how much she could get for her daughter's body. All the husband cared about, probably, was getting enough money to get away from his wife.

The senator rose as a signal to them not to be seated. The senator did not seat people like the Hogans either in his home or his office.

He said, pointing to Justin, "This is Doctor Riley. You've seen him before, have you?"

"Oh," Betty's mother smirked, "we've seen him all right. We'd watch from the bedroom window when he'd bring Betty home and my he sure did take a long time kissing her good night. When she told me she was pregnant, it never occurred to me he would refuse to marry her."

Justin said, "But I already had a wife—as everyone knows. By the way your present husband was the first man who ever had relations with Betty, or didn't he bother to tell you?"

Color climbed in Ralph Hogan's sunken cheeks. He did not look at his wife as she turned to him, her voice trembling. "Ralph Hogan, that's a lie. Tell this bastard he's lying about my daughter."

Ralph Hogan looked frightened. "Now, Ma," he said, "take it easy. It wasn't anything like what he's tryin' to say it is—you know Betty always had it in for me since the whippin' I gave her the time she ran away. But," turning to point an accusing finger at Justin, "he's the man what got her knocked up. That's what she told us, when that other doctor was in the room with her, and that's the God's honest truth."

"Let us," murmured the senator, "leave God out of this particular discussion."

Justin said, "I gave her five hundred dollars to have an abortion performed by a capable man because I felt sorry for the kid. What did she do with the money? Whoever operated on her couldn't have charged more than fifty bucks."

"I don't know anything about any five hundred dollars," the girl's mother whined. "I only know my daughter is maybe dying and you're the one who killed her. That's what I know, and that's what I'll say."

"And what," asked the senator gently, "did you say your price was for not saying it, Mrs. Hogan?"

Her husband spoke for her. "Ten thousand dollars. In cash. And we'll say there was so many, we don't know who it might have been. With the money," he thought to say, "we can take her away from here when she's better—if she lives—give her a new start somewhere."

"Yes," said the senator. He motioned to his secretary who placed the ten crisp, new, thousand-dollar bills on the desk. "If you will both sign here—"

When the pair had left the office, the senator remained standing, a signal to Justin that he had served his purpose here and was now dismissed.

Justin said bitterly, "It's your money, I guess. But you just made a contribution to corruption and malpractice. Was that really the price for getting rid of the Hogans?"

"No," said the old man slowly. "That was our family's price, Justin, for getting rid of Dr. Riley. If Olivia wants to be generous, I suppose she'll donate more directly to your account."

Justin had learned since childhood not to hit old men—their hearts might be weak.

He reached for his hat and left.

CHAPTER THIRTEEN

Three hundred acres of rich rolling farmland separated the Cyrus Stevens main house from the ramshackle buildings of the Miles farm. However, with the powerful telescope which helped him to check on most of the people who worked for him, Cy Stevens could also keep a fairly accurate check on Marge Miles and her husband. He had discovered this convenience by accident one day, after sending his foreman to inform Sandy Miles that the Stevens' property was no longer open to hack riders.

"One of your kids got dumped last week," the man had apologized to Sandy, "and the horse tore the hell out of some newly planted acreage. I'm sorry, Sandy."

Cy had learned the conversation at second hand, but had seen the meeting through his telescope while spying on the foreman. Cy had been annoyed when Sandy Miles took the bad news calmly. He had wanted the younger man to curse him out or threaten his barns. Cy would then have had reason to ask Ed Haley to put Sandy under a peace warrant—the first step toward getting Sandy off the property altogether.

Could Sandy have learned that the telephone company wanted to move into Ridgefield Corners with a whole new technical setup as their part of the missile program? Sandy would certainly be tempted to sell out when he found out how much they were ready to offer for his property, which stood squarely on land their surveyors had chosen. All the other wanted land save the Miles farm belonged, fortunately, to a Stevens relative or employee, held for Cy in the employee's name. Senator Turner and other crackpots like him could not charge Cyrus Stevens with keeping a stranglehold on the town for his own profit and convenience—there were lots of other landowners, at least on the town records.

Best to get rid of Sandy Miles by endless harassment and then, finally, by forcing whoever held his two mortgages to foreclose when Sandy was too worn down to fight any more.

All Sandy had said to the foreman was, "Heck, Jim, it's no fault of yours if we can't teach our kids to stay in the saddle. I'm damned sorry about that mare getting loose. Tell Mr. Stevens so, will you?"

"Sure," Jim Edwards had promised. He had relayed the message to Cy, whose tempers were almost as famous, locally, as his capacity for bourbon.

In a combination of bourbon and temper, raging up and down his room which was also his office since a recent mild coronary, Cy conceived the idea of spying further on Miles. Maybe he could get something personal which would make the townsfolk feel right about seeing Sandy run off the property. The house wasn't good for much but burning, as far as Cy Stevens was concerned, although he had to admit Sandy had done a good job of repairing his barns and fences.

One day, telescope in one hand and bourbon in the other, Stevens had watched Marge Miles walking around her room without any clothes on. After a few minutes of that, like something in a silent movie, he had watched her husband come into the room. Later his nurse had chided him for getting upset about something.

"Your pulse is racing like a horse, Mr. Stevens," she had scolded, "and you know what the doctors have told you about not getting upset."

"The doctors at that hospital," Clark Stevens had informed her, "are all a bunch of horses' asses. When I want a doctor, I'll get my doctors from New York. I just keep that hospital for the peasants."

In the days that followed, he found time every morning to train his telescope on the neighbors' bedroom. A new craving was born in him gradually. Although he was an old man of seventy, for whom sex had ceased to have meaning, he wanted a toy of his own. He wanted a woman, and he wanted one bad, to fondle and possess and look at. Often he had longed to put his arms about that slender body of Marge's, and kiss it in all the places he had watched her husband kiss it.

This town, Stevens decided parenthetically, was being taken over by riffraff. People had all but forgotten the iron hand of Cyrus Stevens that could crack down whenever he felt so minded. Money protects and millions of dollars protects absolutely, and yet for years, Cyrus Stevens had let himself be pushed around by his half-assed family. Taking care of his heart, his blood pressure, while they took care of themselves and their women.

"You're an old man," his son-in-law had said after the last coronary, "why don't you do as the doctors say and quit horsing around?"

So he had quit the girls, not minding too much as long as he could sneak all the bourbon he needed. But now he needed a woman, to look at, to touch, to appreciate.

He picked up the phone and called Art Peevers. "Art," he said, "this nurse they've sent me is an old fart. Get down to the hospital. Find something good to look at who'd like to come up and take care of me."

There was a pause of a few seconds at the other end of the wire. Then Art said, "Sure thing, C. S. I'll get right on it."

"Never mind getting on it," Cy Stevens said. "Just get with it."

Art laughed as he always laughed at the old man's cracks. Laughing was what he was paid for.

In an hour there was a light knock on the door.

Stevens called irascibly, "Come in, damn it, don't just stand there hammering."

Art had his uses, after all. He might steal Cyrus blind and not think Cy knew, but Cy Stevens had always been willing to pay for what he wanted. He needed Art for protection and for spying and phony real estate deals. Today, for other reasons, he needed the girl whom Art had sent up.

He did not worry too much about her coming from the hospital. Art would have checked her out pretty carefully, and in this town, there was not much to choose from. The girl was pretty in an overripe, voluptuous way that would turn to fat in ten years. Today, however, Cy Stevens could appreciate the way her breasts seemed ready to explode from the white nylon uniform, and the soft roundness of the thighs. He wondered where else she had dimples as she said, "Mr. Peevers said you needed a special to relieve Miss Crowley."

"That's right. I need someone to talk to. How about a drink?"

"Oh, Mr. Stevens, I couldn't have a drink when I'm on duty." And then she met his eyes.

He said, "There's a hundred dollars in the top drawer of the dresser— I'm all right—I won't hurt you. I'd just like you to take your clothes off for a while."

A shadow of fear came into her wise dark eyes. He heard a threshing machine in one of the distant pastures and saw Sandy Miles ride along the road on one of his horses. Cy Stevens recalled how he had liked to ride, himself, when he was a young man, how all that rocking motion would stir him up. He wanted the girl to sit in his lap and just let him rock her. That was it, that was what he wanted to do. Hold her in his lap and rock back and forth, back and forth.

The girl's fingers were already reaching for the top button of her uniform and she had tucked the hundred-dollar bill into her purse.

Beyond the windows, the summer sky was hot and blue and a breeze blew in from the lake. Cy filled his glass with bourbon and ice and settled himself in the rocking chair and drew the girl down on top of him. Obligingly, she put an arm about his old man's neck and smiled. "Since I have my clothes off, shouldn't you have your clothes off?"

She helped him get out of his clothes, and then she helped him with a lot of things. She was a nice, motherly girl, although she panicked and fled, when she realized the elderly man lying on the bed without any clothes on was not just passing out from drink but from a coronary occlusion. Before she fled the room, she reached back into the drawer for another hundred-dollar bill. She figured she had really earned that money, especially since this day's work would cost her her steady job—if Art Peevers told anyone it was she whom he had sent here.

CHAPTER FOURTEEN

In the movies, Marge Miles thought, everything would have worked out differently. In the movies, Justin Riley would have been played by someone like Gregory Peck, who, everyone knew, would turn out to be a good guy no matter how much of a bad guy he might have seemed. And old Cy Stevens would have been played by someone like the late Lionel Barrymore, and when the young doctor saved his life, Lionel-Cyrus would change and soften and agree to let in new business, like that telephone company setup, and give the merchants downtown somebody to sell things to beside one another.

Mary Stevens Memorial Hospital was not in Hollywood, California, however, but in Ridgefield Corners. From the time the news about Stevens' coronary occlusion started racing through the hospital corridors, Marge felt that same depressed sense of doom about Justin she had experienced that night at the taproom. He had known then how few people were with him.

She knew she was staying in the hospital, after a week had passed, more for Justin's morale than because she was otherwise needed. She knew Sandy needed her too—and hoped things would work out somehow, that no one would get hurt too much. Betty Hogan had come out of her coma only to go into a kind of melancholia. She ate a little, slept a good deal and talked not at all.

They were not yet sure her mind was unimpaired.

Marge was always sorry these days. She could not hurt Sandy and not suffer with him. All she could do, the hours she and Justin worked together, and the other hours she sat beside Betty Hogan's bed and watched the oxygen pump or a new container of blood or of glucose being attached to the iron stand, was to keep thinking, *Look at the mess it got that poor kid into—and Justin. His marriage is really smashed now, and for what? For just one crazy roll in the hay.*

She wondered why she felt constrained to preach at herself that way.

She was not even sure, the day Justin operated on old Cyrus, that Justin would be successful.

She was transcribing a tape recording of a lecture Justin had given to the third-year nursing students when Dr. Harrison came to tell Justin, "It couldn't have happened at a worse time—as serious a heart operation as this when you're under so much personal stress—but unfortunately, Justin, there isn't another thoracic surgeon between here and Utica and there certainly isn't time to wait. In fact, they're prepping him now. He'll be ready for you in the OR in twenty minutes."

"How is he?"

"I doubt that he'll make it—but do the best you can."

It gave Marge a feeling of totally useless omniscience to realize that Cyrus Stevens had been dying for a long time. He had a heart disease called aortic stenosis and now, some final enormous strain had closed the left valve entirely. He would have an oxygen mask, she thought, and the little cardiac massage kit would be ready in the operating room. She knew Justin meant it when he said, "Send up a prayer, kid—that guy's got to make it."

He spoke lightly as he headed toward the elevator but Marge knew he meant it. A doctor, like a lawyer, can be run out of town not because he has done wrong but because he seems a loser.

He still might lose Betty Hogan. Technically, she was Stu Everett's patient. But Stu would not be blamed if Betty remained a ghostly shell of a girl.

"What she needs now," Stu Everett had said this morning, looking down at Betty's face, "is something to live for. God knows how anyone is going to give her that. Her parents packed up and left town last night."

"Why, that's awful. How could they leave her at a time like this?"

"I guess," Stu Everett had said in his quick, rather cold voice, "that people can do anything if they get scared enough. That's the only reason people get mean—they get scared. That even goes for Justin Riley—" He had almost smiled when he said Justin's name. Lately, Stu Everett and Justin Riley had seemed less than bosom friends.

Automatically, Marge checked her watch at four o'clock. Justin ought to be out of the OR by six. She would call Sandy, tell him she would be late. He would understand her wanting to wait here, at a time like this, just in case she was needed. She took out old charts and records and studied the calcification around Cyrus Stevens' stubborn heart. She knew that this operation was a last resort. The valve had closed down tight, and open-heart surgery was a last desperate hope. Probably Cyrus would die. The people in Ridgefield Corners, whose sympathies were all with Betty Hogan and her fight to live, and with Olivia Riley, who had taken so much from Justin and who now, they hoped, was deciding not to take any more, would see in Cyrus' death a new failure of Justin's—further evidence that he was a bad doctor as well as an unprincipled heel—which was what most of the men had decided.

"Copper-riveted heel," Wade Johnson, one of the trustees, had denounced Justin angrily behind the closed doors of Dr. Harrison's office. "We'll give him a fair hearing when the girl is able to make a deposition, but I say, right or wrong, a man like that is wrong for this hospital, this town."

A little before six, Marge left her desk and went down to the hospitality shop for coffee. On the way, she paused to glance through the small windows on the swinging doors of the OR suite.

There was a quick passing back and forth of green-clad bodies and green-clad heads which always meant emergency surgery was under way. A nurse hurried out of the room with bloodstained sheets that told their own story. Marge decided to wait a little longer. Soon Justin pushed through the door, white-faced, exhausted. He seemed glad to see her.

He said, "Wait around—I'll buy you a cup of coffee."

She said, "I'm sorry, Justin."

"Don't be sorry. He made it, the old stinker." Even through his exhaustion, she could hear Justin's delight in the stamina of a patient, whom, as a man, he despised. He patted her hand and headed toward the doctors' lounge to change into cleaner clothes.

She stood there for a minute, knowing an exultation so uncluttered and pure she could have wept—simply because a man whom she loathed had not died under the knife. Why should she be glad?

She knew why. She had caught the feeling from Justin. In some way that no one outside the hospital would understand, she was closer to Justin now than she ever had been to anyone in her life.

The closeness seemed not to conflict with her faithfulness to Sandy.

While she waited in the corridor, an intern rushed past, then back-tracked. He asked her breathlessly, "Dr. Riley—where is he?"

"Gone to wash up," she said. "He's coming back for coffee."

"Coffee? Oh, my God—"

Justin appeared, handsome and pale and glowing. The intern told him, "He's sinking. Suddenly—we thought we had it made."

The proud look left Justin's face. Marge knew and shared the agony of his disappointment. He said to her only, "Wait for me in my office," before he rushed away.

Damn Cy Stevens, *she thought.* He had no right to die when Justin told him to live ... no right to hurt Justin ...

Justin came back to his office to find Marge waiting for him, sitting on the edge of his desk. Wordlessly, he went to her and put his arms about her and she laid her cheek against his now steady shoulder. His hands caressed her hair and held her face. He still had not spoken when he tipped her head back and tried to kiss her.

Marge stiffened to his touch. She moved away from him, her back to the desk, her face wearing an expression he had seen on other faces, but never before on hers. Like the others in Ridgefield Corners, she had just learned to hate him.

"Is this why you asked me to come back and work for you?" Her murmur had shock in it and another quality as well—disgust. "I thought you needed me for poor Betty Hogan's sake. I guess I'm dumb."

"Don't hate me," he said, appalled at her reaction. "You're the one person I can't hate back."

Her eyes turned bright with angry tears. She rubbed her mouth with the back of her hand, as though to get rid of his unsuccessful kiss. "Why did you want to make me feel like dirt, Justin? You think it was easy for Sandy and me to spare my time? I guess you do. I guess you have no idea what it means for a man and woman really to need each other, in every way, and depend on each other. I used to argue with people who said you couldn't be trusted. I said you were our friend. You're not our friend any more."

He had never felt more totally defeated. *Every woman I touch,* he thought, *turns into a whore.* And Marge refused to be touched.

He did not say he was sorry—the word would have been a further insult at this point. "Marge, when I said I needed your work, I meant it. You've been invaluable with Betty."

"You're probably right. But she doesn't need me now and you know it. She's past the crucial stage and so am I. I'm going home to my husband and baby. And I hope none of us will ever be sick for the rest of our lives because suddenly I feel that doctor is a bad word." He had not said he was sorry and Marge was the one to say it. "I'm sorry, Justin. I don't like to be mean. We'll try to forget this happened."

Then he was alone. The solitude was unbearable. There was nothing more he could do for Cyrus Stevens, but he had to do something for someone, and at once.

He left his office and took the elevator to Betty Hogan's floor.

The man from the sheriff's office was on a wooden chair outside the small room. He had the chair tipped back and was reading the local paper. He looked up to say, "Too bad about old man Stevens. One of the docs just told me."

Justin said, "Yeah. Rough."

"Nice break for your father-in-law, though. The old man was out to lick him in the fall. Funny thing to say, but I'm glad for the senator's sake."

Justin said, "That's right." At the moment, he was glad of nothing for anyone's sake.

He opened the door of Betty's room and quietly went in. The oxygen tank gave off a steady little pumping sound. He checked the mechanism automatically. The therapy was a desperate effort to supply needed oxygen to Betty's brain to combat the effects of a long coma.

Gail Bennett was in the room behind him before he became aware of her. He said, "Hi, there," very softly.

To his surprise, he saw tears in her eyes. She said, "I'm sorry about old man Stevens, Justin. I know you did the best you could, and everyone in the hospital says your surgery was spectacular. I'll bet, though, before tomorrow morning, all Main Street will probably have it that you were drunk when you operated. Justin, if you decide to go away—will you take me with you?"

"All right," he said. "But not for long. And not far. Gail, I need a woman—for tonight, for half an hour. I'm nobody's dream. I'm a zombie, too dead to be scared. Will you come with me tonight?"

Gail's look was incredulous. "Are you out of your mind? What do you take me for?"

"Of course I'm out of my mind," he said. "Skip it. See you around." He started to leave.

She whispered fiercely. "Justin—please wait." When he turned, she continued, "I'm off duty in twenty minutes. I'll meet you at your car."

A little later, they stopped at a motel and Gail clung to him hungrily. "It's been so long," she told him. "And no one is like you, Justin. I guess you're a louse—but you're wonderful to love."

She was too voluptuous, too heady—she answered Judson's need as a dish of buttered taffy would have answered a man who starved for bread and meat. His nervous lust probed her thighs, searching for either oblivion or ecstasy. He found neither. Gail was flesh, perishable and familiar, an easy brunette, a broad, another stack of anatomy throbbing from breast to pelvis. His head ached with monotony as he forced his male energy, trying for exhaustion if nothing else.

She suddenly came alive in his arms, her body pressed cloyingly to his. "You're good," she whispered. "You're a good doctor, Justin. This is for being good."

For an instant, he knew companionship and release—they struggled silently in an effort to be one and almost succeeded.

And then in what should have been his reward, Justin lost the sense of Gail's uniqueness. Her lush breasts, crushed against him, reminded him of all the women who had wanted him and whom he had possessed—each possession leaving him with nothing.

Absent-mindedly, he kissed her good night. "Thanks," he said. "I'll drive you home. After that I have things to face."

Gail seemed to understand.

CHAPTER FIFTEEN

On his way home, Justin stopped at the Glimmer Glass Restaurant for a couple of scotches. Roughly translated, Glimmer Glass was a name the Indians had given one of the local lakes. A century or two ago this had been wild country where bear and bobcat prowled. A big summer tourist attraction here was still the graveyard where the last members of an Iroquois tribe were buried.

Lifting his glass to his lips and watching his own reflection in the bar mirror, Justin silently told himself, *I have news for you, kid—to all intents and purposes after tonight you are probably buried here, too.*

When he first had come to town at the insistence of Stu Everett—The *hospital is small but it's the best cardiology research clinic in the east— an internship there will mean something...* Justin had not intended to stay. He had been afraid even then of being buried here. But once he was seriously involved with Olivia, life in Ridgefield Corners had stopped seeming a trap. He had thought of himself for a while as safe, secure.

Back in the womb. Hidden away from the world, from temptations that he both feared and welcomed—and Olivia had been getting, he thought, what she had bargained for.

He was a man who had always been successful with women, and Olivia's lack of responsiveness had amused him at first. He had joked with Stu Everett about maybe arming himself with a marriage manual. Stu had looked at him as though he were an animal.

The well-born people. They liked changing the rules, felt free to change as they pleased, without remorse.

Laborers, farmers from the nearby fields and home-going merchants crowded into the small bar of the Glimmer Glass.

Had he been right the other night about Olivia and Stu?

He was thinking wildly, he told himself. Olivia was basically too thin-blooded to make a husband jealous. But what she had for Stu was liking—and she had none for Justin. In a world full of women who loved him, he had had to go and marry the one woman on earth who did not even like him.

At least, he thought, he still could like himself if for only one reason—he had kicked Marge Miles out of his life. Or she had kicked him out of hers. The thought of her brought an agony of longing and loneliness. Gail Bennett's body had not dulled that agony for more than minutes—the hurt was with him still.

On this particular evening, when he had the feeling he was not to enjoy many more homecomings, he suddenly needed to make peace with his wife. If Olivia wanted a divorce he supposed he would let her have it—but he was tired of being hated. All these characters crowded around the bar, taking little covert looks at him, not speaking to him—what in hell right did the town have to single him out for its venom and spitefulness? At one time or another, he had saved half their lives—and had had half their wives.

They had come to him in fear, not always because of illness. There were also men who had asked him to recommend an abortionist—women who had wanted to be possessed right on the damn examining table, as though he were at stud. The town was full of sinners, if they were looking for someone to throw rocks at.

He still wanted the other sinners to stop hating him.

Why were people unable to come to terms with sex? Sex was the biggest thing in the world. You were born because of it, you lived because of sex, and sometimes sex killed you. Take old Cy Stevens, whose attack had been brought on by something that raised his blood pressure and pulse rate so sharply that it had to have something to do with sex. With whom, for Pete's sake? Maybe no one would ever know.

Maybe her sex life would still kill Betty Hogan. Maybe, after he knew what Betty would be after her convalescence, Justin Riley too would die because of his sex life. He had damned little left to go on for.

What would he tell his kid if he and Olivia got a divorce? We brought you into the world, Johnny, but we needed two worlds afterward, one for your mother and one for me. Maybe you can find a third world of your own.

How did you go about saying that to a kid?

And what did you say to kids like Misty's, who virtually had neither father nor mother—except that Misty's former husband had come up to take the kids back to New York with him. There was another problem—Sam Powers was beginning to insist that Misty was pretty sick and ought to be sent to a state hospital for a few weeks, at least. Which would probably finish Misty.

"I should have helped her a long time ago," Samson Powers had admitted. "Now I mean to do the right thing."

Justin decided against another drink.

Someone whose name he did not know paused to say it was too bad about old Cy Stevens. "Now Senator Turner will have a clear field," the man added savagely. "Crackpot—that's what the senator is. He'll have the whole county on welfare with all the city rabble pouring in. Now that old Cy is gone, the town will be another big city, like Oneonta, crowding the farmers out of here same as they've been crowded out of every place. Rabble," the unknown man repeated. He moved down the bar to order rye and ginger ale.

Justin dropped a dollar on the wet counter and picked up his black case. He went out into the warm night, climbed into his red car and continued down Main Street until it darkened into narrow roads.

When he came in sight of his home, he saw that a guest was waiting. Stu's car was in the driveway.

Before Justin was close enough to hail them or, evidently, to be seen, Stu and Olivia came out of the house, got into Stu Everett's car and drove away.

"To hell with it," Justin said aloud. "To hell with everyone. They can all wait till tomorrow."

CHAPTER SIXTEEN

The summer air of the mountains seemed peculiarly sweet and fragrant in Stu Everett's suite at the Mohawk Inn. Elsewhere the night was humid, unfriendly, with a threat of breaking weather, Olivia thought. But not here.

Stu Everett was saying, "I think you're doing all the right things for all the wrong reasons, Olivia."

She frowned, sitting beside him on the narrow black leather love seat. She said, feeling curiously older than she was, "The story of my life." She let him hold her hand lightly—as though, she thought suddenly, they had been lovers for a long time and had managed a degree of friendship as well.

Stu continued, "To tell Justin the boy is mine is just to open a whole new Pandora's box, when God knows we have enough of those in the family now with their lids flying open."

"But if I don't tell him, and then I leave him for good, he's apt to want at least partial custody."

"What's so wrong with that? He's very fond of Johnny, although he's hardly the father type. But then, neither am I."

"No," she said slowly. "You're not. But there's a vindictiveness in Justin that's scary. One of the reasons sex was never any good between us, I think, is that he may have been a little suspicious about Johnny—for instance, he allowed me to christen him Justin John but insisted we call him John, not Justin. And till nearly the end of my pregnancy, he insisted on coming to me three, even four times a night."

Stu's thin mouth smiled. The mouth was not a thin, sexually exciting one like Justin's, but the kind of thin mouth that men have who are basically unyielding. Some day, Stu's mouth would be like the senator's, the lips clamping together like a steel trap.

And yet, Olivia thought, she felt at home with Stu. He was her kind—he knew her secret. Although he had let her down in the biggest way that man can let a woman down, he had not let her down in the small ways, as Justin had. For some strange reason, Stu never had damaged her pride.

"Justin loved you," Stu said.

"No," she said. "It wasn't love, or even desire. It was just that ugly streak of vindictiveness. He couldn't bear to think that someone else counted more, not even an unborn child. He didn't want me, as he put it, making a fool of him."

"Which you were doing."

"Was I, really? He wanted a rich wife, I wanted a husband. I tried—you know that. I wonder—maybe he thinks that you and I have been lovers for years. If that's true, he'd never believe there were just those two occasions—once, here, when I tried to be your lover but you wouldn't—"

"I couldn't. I tried—I couldn't. A woman has only to receive, the man has to perform. Livvy, I still have a code of sorts. Justin, whatever he is, thinks of me as a friend."

"Then the time at the house," she went on, staring straight ahead implacably. "That rainy day, remember? When you dropped by and found me crying because Misty had just broken up her marriage over Justin. What an idiot. I told her he wouldn't marry her even if I divorced him. With me, he had the perfect setup."

"So did you. You had two husbands. I was always there if you needed me."

"I need you now."

"As what?" He smiled. "Lover? Friend?"

"As everything." The air in this room, Olivia thought, was like air she had breathed in childhood. She stroked his wrist, wanting to touch more of him, to make sure he was near. "I haven't been with Justin now in—oh, weeks."

"That's good."

"Why?"

"Because I love you—in my selfish way that doesn't want to give up my free-wheeling bachelor habits to get married. If you could divorce Justin and not want to marry again—"

"No," she said. "I was Olivia Turner."

He said, "I know. All women want the men they love to give up something for them."

"Women equate love with marriage. Men equate it with sex. When a man says, 'I love you,' he means, 'I want to sleep with you.' When a woman says it, she means, 'I want to marry you.'"

"Of course she does. Besides, I want more children. Justin won't give them to me. He wouldn't even trust me to take precautions. He insisted on taking them himself."

"Are you sure you're thinking straight, Olivia? Can't you let well enough alone—let Justin go on assuming that Johnny is his? If the truth comes out in the open, the damage will be terrible—even to Johnny, even to the senator. Do you think your father can handle a scandal of those proportions? You would just about kill him. Besides, he worships you. He hates watching you be hurt—and so do I, even though I was the cause of it."

She smiled. "You refused to marry me. Why don't I hate you, Stu?"

"Because you understand me, Livvy. The money was a big thing with me. I couldn't marry a woman who had so much more than I did and you respected that. It's different now, of course. I'm successful on my own. Next year, I'll probably move into New York, get a big hospital appointment, set myself up in private practice. I've run away long enough."

"I didn't know you were running away." She felt frightened. She wanted him closer.

"It's always running away when people hide in a town like this, a town that's dying, that's had it. Maybe things will be a little better, now that Stevens is gone."

"Are you glad, too, that he died?"

"Of course. He was over seventy, a lecherous old bastard, without a decent bone in his body."

He rose and went to the teakwood bar to fix a highball for each of them. Returning, he bent and kissed her.

When he drew his mouth away, Olivia cried softly, "That's what Justin was doing to Marge Miles this evening. I went down to the hospital with some wifely idea of forgiving and standing by him, when I heard about Cy Stevens. When I got out of my car, I looked up at his office window. He was trying to kiss Marge Miles—Marge of all people. That good little hausfrau—I mean, is he just an animal? I got back in the car and cried like an idiot. Then I went home and asked you to come for me."

"And cried some more."

"Am I anything, Stu—anything at all that a man wants, that life can use? You didn't want me as a wife—and neither does my husband. Maybe I'm just no good at love. All I have is my illegitimate son, whom nobody knows to be illegitimate—and my money. I'm rich—no man, no love."

Stu said, "You're a wonderful sweetheart. You're great in bed—in case you wondered."

"Then take me there." She begged with sudden fierceness.

"Darling," he said maddeningly, "will you stop trying to prove yourself? Sex is only one part of love—you ought to know that by now. Almost any girl can make a man happy in bed, but damned few make them happy out of bed."

"Am I one of the few?"

"As far as I'm concerned—one of the very few."

"If I divorce Justin will you marry me?"

"No—because I don't want you to divorce him because of me. I won't honestly know how I feel about marriage until you're free. If you're through with Justin, divorce him. Don't do it for my sake, Livvy."

"And you don't want me to tell him Johnny is your son."

"I have no right to give orders. It's you and the boy and your father who'll be hurt, not I."

"Well," she said distractedly, "I won't tell him unless I have to—unless he does another of those crazy, destructive things that make me want to be finished with him—forever."

"Maybe," Stu said, "you ought to warn him."

Instead of replying she leaned forward and kissed Stu's warm, pulsing, sun-tanned neck. Then her fingers began to unbutton his shirt.

"You certainly are persistent, aren't you?" He smiled, but she sensed some flicker of emotion in his eyes—worry, concern, though for what or for whom, she could not have said.

She closed her eyes against that disturbing look and he kissed her, lightly at first, then hard, almost angrily, almost the way Justin sometimes kissed her. Her breasts strained against his chest. She wished in some restless part of her mind that her breasts were more voluptuous, so that Stu would want to tear off her blouse. But she did not seem to madden him with desire.

Instead, he rose deliberately, and picked her up in his arms and asked, "Where? On the carpet?"

"Of course not. In your bed."

He smiled. "You're getting conservative in your old age."

"Don't talk," she said. "Just make love to me, darling. Give me your love—all of you."

"Yes," he said, "all of me."

In Stu's bed, in the clean cool fragrant dark, Olivia turned exultantly wanton. She probed with a married woman's knowingness at the nerve ends that would bring ecstasy to her lover, surprise him out of his smug self-possession that was so much like her own.

He moaned—in spite of himself, she knew—and his strong body convulsed half in joy, half in a kind of indignation. Let him be shocked, *she thought wildly.* Let him be shocked and overwhelmed and bewildered until I become a habit with him, until he becomes a fool for me, as I once was for him ...

She stirred violently against him, and his thighs ground against her, punishingly, so that now it was she who cried out softly. And they were one.

This was how it always should have been between them, a violence and a contentment in their pure native air, in the headiness of the fleeting northern summer.

At last they were side by side, flesh still touching, hand grasping for hand. "Livvy," Stu whispered, "are you like that with him?"

"Never. I'd never—well, lower myself to be like that for Justin."

For a while, Stu was silent, and she found herself murmuring, searching for the truth within her, "I'm not really sorry I married him, Stu. When you're young—very young—the boy next door just doesn't answer your curiosity. You want to know about the other kind, even the ones from the slums—like Justin. And then, when you've learned to long for your own land again—you come home. I want to come home to you, Stu. I want to come home with our boy."

"And the hell with Justin?"

"The hell with Justin," she echoed in a reckless whisper, touching him with erotically-aimed fingers.

He kissed her. Once more, his body possessed hers, perfectly and rhythmically as though they had practiced the dance measures of love from earliest youth.

Then he rose suddenly and switched on the lights. "Snap into your clothes," he ordered. "I've got to make one last call tonight and drop you home on the way."

She smiled delightedly. "Why, Dr. Everett—do your patients come before your sweetheart?"

He grinned. "Get dressed. You've had your turn. And now it's Betty Hogan's."

She made a face, obeying him nevertheless and dressing herself. "That little Hogan bum gets all the attention, doesn't she?"

"Know something, Livvy sweet? You're a bum too, honey. A well-mannered well-born beautiful bum—and so am I. And I love you for it. Poor old Justin Riley."

She started to protest, then changed her mind. Probably Stu was right.

It was rather delicious, she thought, to find yourself being loved for being a bum.

After the strait-laced years.

CHAPTER SEVENTEEN

Justin moved restlessly in his sleep. The night was warm, even with a stirring breeze. He pushed the sheets down, struggling to hang onto a sleep that had finally come, with another stiff drink and two pills. Tomorrow might be the worst day of his life. The paper would carry the story of Cyrus Stevens' death with some clincher of a closing paragraph such as *The surgery was performed by Dr. Justin Riley who was recently questioned in connection with a criminal abortion ...*

Every time they had a news item about him, even one about his treating a citizen for poison ivy since Betty had been brought in, they had printed that little song and dance all over again, as he should have expected the local press, which was Stevens controlled, would do.

"Nuts." The word exploded in his head and he gave up trying to sleep and reached for a cigarette. As he did so, he sensed that he was not alone. He switched on a bed lamp. Olivia was sitting in a chair beside the bed, watching him.

"Well," he said, "welcome home. What brought you back to my bedroom? Couldn't your lover perform?"

She gave him a curiously excited look. "You're just saying that to be nasty," she said. "You don't really believe that anyone is my lover."

Her eyes were too bright. Maybe he had gone too far. "That's true," he admitted. "I feel too licked to give a damn. Of course I'm just being nasty. I know you're through with me, Livvy. Maybe we'd better stay out of each other's way. Unless—" He struggled into a sitting position and wished he could say nice things though nothing but bad things were coming out. He needed Olivia, needed her as he had never needed anyone or anything in his life, and yet he was pushing her away from him. He managed, "I'm in real trouble—big trouble—please stick by me. I need a friend."

s_seew Sex Cure**

er eyes retained that too-bright look. "Justin," she said, "you were
right the first time. I have a lover, all right. I've just been with Stu. I was
passionate—for Stu. Not like I am with you."

He waited for her to explain that she was talking about three other
people, not about Stu and Livvy and Justin. He heard himself say, "I don't
believe you." Sure, he had suspected—but he had hardly realized until this
minute how little credence he had given those suspicions. They had just
been his private way of losing his temper with his well-born ladylike wife.

But she did not explain—she simply said, "Well, you'd better believe
me. What are you trying to tell me—that no man would want me? What a
laugh—I had him half crazy, Justin. I was terrific—great."

Every woman I touch, he had said to Marge Miles only scant hours ago,
turns into a whore.

"Justin," she was saying in a more normal voice, "I didn't come back to
fight with you. Stu and I want to help you."

Stu and I ... The words in her normal tone convinced him at last that
she had been unfaithful—this marble woman.

He flung back the covers and stood up, wearing just the bottoms of his
pajamas.

He said, "I suppose you told him I wasn't able to satisfy your lovely white
body? That you didn't really get what you paid for?"

"Oh, Justin, stop it. Why hurl insults at me when I only want to help
you. You're being crude and vulgar."

He reached for her wrist. Wordlessly, he pulled her into his bed and set
about ripping her clothes off. Just as wordlessly one part of her was fighting
him, scratching and biting in a silent terrible battle, while another part,
which had never seemed roused by his lovemaking before, was tigerish in
response. She seemed cool and clean under the loveless lust—she had
probably showered Stu's sweat from her body as soon as she got home. She
had cheated him out of the final degradation he despairingly longed to
inflict upon their wedded state.

In the single most violent sex act of their marriage, on the bed naked
and together, they were joined and his body, a treacherous thing, betrayed
the indignation in his mind. His body enjoyed Olivia's body, its human
closeness and warmth—and when the act was finished, he heard himself
say, as he rarely had before to Olivia, "Darling." He added, very politely,
"Please don't go away for a moment."

Then he got up and went to the bathroom and showered. When he
returned, wearing a terry-cloth robe, she studied him with a curious new
interest.

"I liked that," she said lazily. She was still naked. "Maybe we can go on
together after all."

He told her, "I never want to sleep with you again."

She picked up his empty whisky glass and hurled it but he ducked. She threw an ashtray but that missed, too.

"Olivia," he said tiredly, "do you want a tranquilizer? If you don't calm down, you'll sure as hell wake the kid. I won't have you driving him nuts."

Her thin straight patrician nose flared ever so slightly with a kind of indignation. He had never before realized, Justin thought remotely, that his wife was beautiful in the same way that a thoroughbred mare is beautiful.

"Let me tell you something," she said, her white body tensing with what he supposed was hatred. "What you will or won't have has nothing to do with Johnny. He isn't yours. He's mine—mine and Stu Everett's."

Justin stared at her, grasping what she had said, and thinking how strange it was that she still had a womb. Unlike Betty Hogan, she could bear another child. "I understand," he said. "Instead of doing what Betty did, when your lover refused to marry you, you found a sucker who would give your bastard a name. So I was the one who saved the kid's life—and now his name is Riley. Do you hear, you whore? Riley. He's mine. You won't get him."

He knew he was more than a little out of his head. He heard Olivia cry out in fright, "Don't take it out on Johnny—" as he ran to the boy's room.

His small dark-haired son—Justin could not abruptly think of the child as not his son—woke in startlement.

"Dad?" Johnny said. "Are we on fire?"

"No, not on fire. But we have to go away. This house has been condemned. It's going to fall down, Johnny. I'm going to take you with me."

Johnny sat up in the dark. "Daddy, where is mother?" he asked in a voice that tried to be brave.

In the queer black blaze that seemed to have burst in his brain, Justin was sure he was acting in the only logical way. "Listen, Johnny," he said one arm across the tense tiny shoulders, "you're old enough now to know the truth. You don't really have a mother. Kid, there's just you and me and we're going away—"

Light flooded the room as Olivia, a robe belted about her, turned on the switch at the doorway. Johnny lifted his arms. "Mother," he greeted her, relief and terror and total love all sounding in the word.

Olivia ran to him. The child and the woman clung to one another and Justin stepped aside.

Sanity came back to him, bitter and ugly and worthless-seeming. He left Olivia with the child who had no father, the child he would have to forget. He dressed and left the house, hoping he would forget the house also, as soon as he possibly could.

In the hospital, in Betty Hogan's room, he found Stu Everett. For an instant he felt outraged all over again—then he recalled that Stu, of course, was the surgeon who had taken away Betty's power to be a mother.

Stu's square face was emotionless, though excitement showed in his voice.

"I'm hanging around," he said, "because this may be the night she wakes up—I mean for real. Look at that chart."

But Justin had only to look at the small face on the pillow to realize that the miracle would probably occur before dawn. Betty had been awake almost daily for nearly a week, but for brief periods only during which she seemed in a trance.

Tonight, her color was different. She was coming back—how? As a harmless vegetable, memory gone—or as a pilgrim climbing from one plateau of hell to a lonelier plateau in the same place?

"You should have married her, Stu," Justin said to the surgeon, "before she had the abortion. Married her and raised my kid—because I did as much for you. I married your pregnant girl friend. I taught your son not to cry when the game didn't go his way."

"So Livvy told you." Stu barely shifted his gaze, then turned his eyes once more to the girl in the bed.

"She told me. Stu, how could you do it? I don't mean to Livvy—she's durable, she's tough—but how could you do it to Johnny? He'll always be partly mine now. I'm the one he'll remember when he thinks of the word father—but I don't belong to him. How can a kid be so damned poor that he even loses me? I've belonged to bums, to beggars, to patients who didn't have fifty cents to pay a clinic fee—but I'm too good for Johnny. Five million bucks—and he can't have Justin Riley."

"Shut up," Stu told him. "You're only hurting yourself. I told her not to tell you. You must have been rotten to her, Justin, to make her hate you that much."

From the bed, a soft little cry sounded. Both men turned and waited.

Betty opened her eyes. She looked at all the apparatus around her bed with a kind of fear. She saw Justin. Her smile wavered, steadied, turned serene and joyous.

"Dearest," she said in a low clear voice. "I knew you wouldn't leave me."

He stood beside her, letting her hand find his. She had made it—all of them had made it, who had worked and agonized over her. He must have been crazy, he thought, ever to let her go, this girl who had carried his child—his very own child. Now it was too late for children. "I'll never leave you," he promised.

She sighed and went back to sleep—a different kind of sleep, though—still holding his hand.

She was exhausted. The climb out of hell had been steep and long.

Soon Stu left them. Justin stayed beside Betty's bed till dawn.

When the day shift came on, he went to his own office. For the immediate future, he supposed he might as well live at the hospital. When he could think ahead, he would make other plans.

CHAPTER EIGHTEEN

Justin Riley felt at home in the hospital and in his white-walled private office with its two Utrillo street scenes which Olivia had bought from Paris. He meant to keep the Utrillos. He was fond of them. He had earned them.

In spite of himself, he found he was remembering a time when he and Olivia had been almost happy together—when they had thought Johnny would one day have a baby sister or a baby brother. He wondered if she had been faithful to him for at least a few years and decided she probably had been—whatever that was worth.

Because in those days there had been instants when he felt he could reach out and draw her to him spiritually as he had drawn her to him physically. He remembered the week in Europe when she had given him those paintings. In an open car, his arm taut about her shoulders, he had driven with one hand along the wide new speedway from Milan.

On this humid July morning whose sky was grey with threatened rain, he remembered the Alps in the distance and ninety miles an hour and Olivia's dark hair blowing. Her beseeching voice had fought the wind ... *Darling, slow down ...*

"Hell with slowing down." He had laughed at her. "I want to get to the hotel and take your clothes off. I want to spend the afternoon making love. Would you like that?"

"I'd love it," she had said, long ago, in another country, another life.

He looked up. Gail Bennett stood in his doorway, a curiously compassionate look on her face and a tray of food in her hands. "I had a few minutes," she said, "so I brought you some toast and coffee. Justin, about last night—" Her voice trailed off.

"That's right," he recalled absently. "We were lovers, weren't we? You're very kind. Just put the tray down some place."

"Justin, are you all right?"

"Why wouldn't I be all right?"

"You sound so gentle, Dr. Riley. Not like yourself at all."

"Well, we all have to change as time goes by. Besides the coffee, you didn't happen also to bring a message, did you?"

"As a matter of fact, I did," she said, making a large business of finding a place for the tray. "Dr. Harrison wants to see you as soon as possible, in his office." Dr. Harrison was chief of staff.

"I'm a very busy man, you know. Lots of patients need me. Dr. Harrison knows that, does he?"

"Yes, Justin. I think you'd better see him. But please drink some coffee first."

For a man his size in other ways, Douglas Harrison was physically small. He had young blue-gray eyes in a wise and weathered face, a pepper-and-salt goatee and no hair whatever on his shining bony pate. "Sit down, Justin," he said in a friendly voice. "How is your world wagging?"

"Not too well, thanks," Justin answered, nervously seating himself. "I presume I'm on the carpet."

"You may presume that, yes. You've been brought up on charges before the county medical association. There's a likelihood of your losing your license to practice—at least in New York State."

Justin stared at the shiny bald pate. Gray light came in at the window. Outside there were people who one day or another would die but who would pause, en route, if a doctor delayed the final day.

"I could have wished," Harrison continued, frowning, "that old Cy had pulled through. Even county medical associations can decide on the basis of emotion rather than reason—and a miracle like saving Cy would have saved you too."

"I tried. But miracles? How many have you seen?"

Harrison ignored the question.

"Of course you tried. You did a damned good job. Cy didn't die of surgery. He died of having lived. This Betty Hogan episode, though—it's too unsavory."

"What are the charges? If it's malpractice—"

"Don't be absurd. You're a hell of a good doctor. You're charged with conduct unbecoming a member of our profession. You'll have to admit, Justin, that your private life has been far from orthodox. Trouble is, this latest scandal won't alienate your patients. If anything, they'll be drawn to you more than ever. But their reasons won't be medical. You're not good for the profession, Justin, in what I'll concede are nonessential ways."

"Granted," Justin said. "By the way, may I ask just which sonofabitch brought the charges against me?"

"I did," Harrison said, still sounding friendly. "Someone was bound to think of kicking you out, and I wanted the charges minimal. I could have made things worse. There's such a thing as complicity in an illegal operation—and you've made no secret of having given the Hogan girl the money to have one. Also your affair with Misty Powers is no secret. She's a helpless alcoholic—perhaps you've taken advantage."

Justin looked at his hands "Sure," he said. "Who else bothered with her except Phil Sheffers and maybe one or two ex-husbands. Not one of them gave a damn that she farmed her kids out to a baby farm where they induced naps with chloral hydrate—a dangerous drug. Perhaps when you're finished with me, the county medical association might like to investigate the Dieterle place."

"Maybe, now that old Cy is dead, we'll get at a lot of things. He was quite a force for the status quo, you know. And a lot of status quo, no matter where or why, is a stinking mess if it lasts. Don't be too bitter, Justin. Lord knows we need you here. Until the end of the hearing, I'm asking you to stay and work your damned head off, as you've always done. You won't be easy to replace."

"Thanks for nothing, Doctor."

"I'm giving you time to plan, can't you realize that? Face it—you've got your gifts—you're a damned good doctor but in some ways you're hardly civilized. You lack the common sense to keep your sins a secret as the rest of us do. You have no respect for hypocrisy like other decent members of society. You like pretty girls."

"These are crimes?"

"I'm afraid they are, Justin, in your situation. Hell, I'm rooting for you. Know what I'd do if I were you? I'd go out somewhere and find a simpler place where a good doctor was needed, no matter how little it paid. I'd take along a woman who thought I was the world. Maybe your wife—"

"My wife," Justin explained, "is about to divorce me, I believe. She shares your views on my conduct."

Harrison said, "Sorry to hear that. You and Olivia."

"The image," Justin said, "was distorted." He rose. "So you want me to stay on till you find a replacement. It sounds like a great deal."

"It's a rotten deal, Justin. You'll always get rotten deals unless you find your own kind of place. I've seen a lot and I ought to be cynical by now. I'm not, though. I'm usually glad to be alive. Which makes me a suitable citizen of Ridgefield Corners—something you'll never be, something nature never intended you to be."

They shook hands—why, Justin could not imagine—and he left the chief of staff to face his hospital day.

He took the stairs rather than the elevator and made his way via the back door from the administration wing of the building to the hospital proper. He nodded to the linen-room lady who was always sorting linens and to the one who sat eternally in front of her sewing machines, repairing linens and surgical gowns and lab coats. He went to the second floor.

The corridor was alive with early-morning clatter. Justin always wondered why anyone thought a hospital a good place for a rest. The PA system constantly called, "Doctor Harrison, Number three—Doctor Everett, Number two—" The huge steel food carts were being wheeled away with shelves full of breakfast dishes and trays, steered by the kitchenmen in their white hats and checkered pants.

The kitchenmen always found something to quarrel about. Justin supposed they had to, or go out of their minds with the boredom of their jobs. It was only in the movies and on TV that hospital corridors and emergency rooms were taut with drama and tragedy. In real life the corridors were cluttered with food trays and gossiping nurses and sloppy aides and quarreling kitchen help. The Emergency Room was as likely to be busy with an intern trying to make it with a student nurse, as with a dramatic medical emergency.

In his cubicle off the clinic, he checked his diary for the day's patients. Art Peevers' wife had come in last week complaining of a chest pain. She had cardiac asthma in an advanced form. Well, Art would be glad. The two had not spoken a civil word to one another in years. Terry Maule had survived a fifty-ton tractor falling on him three months ago. That he had lived had been a major miracle, but now, of course, he was complaining about the bill since the farmer who employed him was not covered by compensation.

There were three routine patients, all suffering from some form of hypochondria or lack of adequate sex life. You could not tell them that—simpler to give them a harmless pill and a lot of sympathy and send them on their way.

Ann Summers, R.N., looked up from typing a chart. "Doctor Riley, Les Green's chart is marked, 'Advise his wife to sell their herd of cows.' Does that mean Les is going to die?"

"Who isn't?" Justin gave his routine response. "But remember kid, that information is confidential—don't go spilling it at the sandwich shop."

"Why, Dr. Riley, what a thing to say. Of course I won't."

But of course she would. The hell of a small one-hundred-bed hospital such as this one, and of small-town hospitals anywhere, was that everyone knew everything about everyone else.

By this time tomorrow, everyone in town would know that Les Green was dying of myocarditis, that one day soon Les would topple over on his way to the barn and that would be that.

"I'm on my way to OR to do that catheterization on the Anderson boy. Then I've got an arterial puncture on Doctor Harrison's mother. Call me on the PA if there's any word on Betty Hogan's condition."

"Yes, Dr. Riley."

And don't, *thought Justin, a familiar rage beginning to tighten the muscles of his stomach,* look so damn sweet and sanctimonious when I know damned well you've shot your big mouth off to everyone about everything you know about me.

He pushed open the familiar doors of the OR. The Anderson kid was resting quietly, sedated but not unconscious, Gail Bennett was ready and

waiting in surgical green. Gail got busy handing him sterile towels with
sterile forceps.

In the delicate business of a heart catheterization there was always a
chance of losing the patient. By passing a narrow plastic tube through the
boy's arm vein into the right side of his heart, a surgeon could tell what was
wrong with the heart and if there was any hope of surgical repair.

Gail's eyes were on the electro-cardiogram, alert for any deviation from
pattern. Justin caught one or two downward blips of the tracings as the
catheterization proceeded. Suddenly he was aware of a whole string of
irregular blips, indicating that the boy had begun to fibrillate. Instantly, he
withdrew the plastic tubing from the boy's arm. His own heart came close
to stopping as he watched the screen and waited for the rhythm to return to
normal.

"Butch?" he asked the boy gently. "You all right?"

"Hmmm?" murmured Butch Anderson through the heavy sedation.
"Huh?"

"Okay," Justin said to Gail. "Have the floor nurse come for him and take
him back to his room. The heart damage is irreparable. To close a defect
like that, the boy would have to withstand a six-hour operation. He'd never
make it."

He thought of John Justin Riley and how it would feel to learn that
Johnny had months to live. You take them so for granted, he thought,
drawing off the rubber gloves. It's only when you lose them that you think
how the years have gone while you frittered away the time on other things.

How sweet and just the revenge, if only he had had wit enough to make
himself first with the kid. He would have liked nothing better than taking
her son from Olivia. Maybe Harrison was right. He would find a woman, a
real woman like Marge, though God knew where he could find another
Marge—he would steal Johnny away from the Turner family and Stu—he
would go with them to some better place and live a good life. His reverie
ended when Gail told him that Butch's parents were waiting in the office.

Justin said, "Okay." He added "I want to talk to you, too. If I hadn't
caught those blips on the screen, that kid would be dead now. What in hell
is the matter with you?"

"Don't talk to me like that. We've all been through a lot. I'm sorry,
Justin."

"Don't be so damned sorry. Just remember you're a nurse, will you?"

The full mouth trembled and the dark eyes grew even darker. Gail said,
"Sometimes I'm sorry for that too."

He broke the news to the Andersons as quietly as he could. They had
been close to middle-aged when Butch was born.

"We didn't feel like we could afford a kid until we had the farm paid for," said Butch's father, "and maybe a few dollars in the bank. We're proud people. We didn't want to take no help from nobody. But now it's too late for Shirley to have any more—Doc Everett told her that, the last time we was in here." Justin let him talk. Shirley Anderson sat staring straight ahead. Maybe she too was recalling years that had passed in the blink of an eye— years when she might have had other children or enjoyed this child more.

"Well, Doc," Anderson concluded, rising, "I guess we can't keep you here like this. You've got other patients to tend to." He told his wife, "Come, Shirley, we'd better be getting home. We can't see Butch until this afternoon."

Justin stood beside his desk, watching them go, trying to accept the fact that this case was hopeless, that nothing more could be done.

Any more than he could find a woman like Marge Miles—or a son like John Justin Riley—or a place where he belonged.

CHAPTER NINETEEN

Betty Hogan at nineteen had resembled a painted baby. She had an immature small face, large eyes and fine red-gold hair that curled into ringlets. Despite Justin's intermittent efforts to change some of her habits, she had persisted in the use of heavy make-up and exotic perfume, purchased at Newberry's, a different scent every week. She had had fingernails like lethal weapons until the hospital nurses clipped them off before taking her to the operating room. In a possible post-operative convulsion, those nails might have had Betty damaging herself. Ordinarily, the claw-like nails had been dyed with what Justin thought of as gore. She had had an intimate little speaking voice, copied from Marilyn Monroe.

She had dressed unbecomingly in clothes which she described to Justin as, "Cute. Don't you think this is cute, Justin?" Invariably, he did not.

Their acquaintance had started at the taproom of the Mohawk Inn where unattached females could wait to be picked up. There were not many extra men in Ridgefield Corners, but the telephone company had sent in a crew of land surveyors and emergency linemen last year, turning the taproom into a better hunting ground than usual. Betty had been sitting there, brooding at her sweet martini when Justin dropped by for a drink after seeing a patient out near Fly Creek. Harry Kyle had introduced them, if the exchange of a few words could be called an introduction.

"Justin, I want you to meet a friend of mine, Betty Hogan. Justin works down at the hospital—oh, pardon me—Doc Justin Riley, I should have said. I keep forgetting Justin's a doctor. Probably because he's still got his hair and the girls fall for him hard."

"I don't blame them," Betty had said. "He's cute." She had turned to repeat to Justin, "You're cute. You really are. You've got funny, strange-colored eyes. Sort of like a panther's."

"How many panthers' eyes have you seen, Betty?"

"Well, none, really, but they're the way I imagine a panther's eyes would look—sort of gloomy and broody and all."

"You certainly have some quaint expressions." Justin had smiled. "Meanwhile, how about letting me buy you a drink?"

"Ummm—I'd like that." Justin had known then that there was something else she would like and at which, unless he missed his guess, she would be extremely talented.

But from the beginning, it had been her childlike quality that had amused and, on occasion, actually delighted him. The quality was one which Marge Miles also had, although in any other way the two young women could hardly be compared.

Betty reacted to the smallest gift, the slightest kindness, with the enthralled rapture of a child on Christmas morning. Unfortunately, in the end she bored him.

Harry Kyle had said, "Betty may come to work for me when the tourists start in Jane and I put on extra help."

"Where do you work now, Betty?" Justin had asked her.

"At Newberry's. It's the only place that'll hire a girl who hasn't been through high school. I wait on table there. The job stinks. Those fanners. They leave a ten-cent tip and think it's a big deal. Besides, the food isn't very good. I've always wanted to sit down to really good food—like a thick steak or something. But the boys around here, they never ask a girl to dinner. How can they, with maybe two dollars in their pockets, if they're lucky?"

Justin had watched the painted baby-face switch its moods in a fascinated way. One minute her face would be as old as the Adirondacks, suggesting a practiced prostitute—the next it would be a child's, grotesque in make-up. When she spoke of the town, the face was sullen.

"In this dump," she had said on the second drink he bought her, "you're either in or you're out, and I've always been out."

"So have I," Justin had told her with a smile she did not understand. That was when he decided to give her the job that Marge had left. He wanted to give her the job, wash the make-up off her face, get the hard, farmer-like "g's" out of her speech, possibly ready her for a better job in a bigger town after a year or so.

Also, he supposed, he had wanted to give her the job because he knew Olivia and the senator would be annoyed.

On their second date, they had made it together at a motel. After that, she had come to work for him and they found more congenial places, such as the cottage he had rented out by the lake.

The lake was a constant in her dreams now. She would swim up slowly from the soft black depths and find herself in a hospital bed. Then she would sleep again before she quite remembered how she had gotten here.

One day she remembered.

"What time is it?" she asked someone sitting beside her bed. The nurse said, "Twelve o'clock, exactly. Noontime."

"That's what time it was before," said Betty vaguely. "I remember looking at the clock and seeing it was twelve and calling Ma to come and get me."

"That was weeks ago," said the nurse. "You've been sick, but you're all right now."

"The baby," Betty said. "I lost the baby, didn't I?"

"Yes. You lost the baby."

How had she lost it? Events were coming back to her in snatches.

The motel neon lights blinking on and off, and laughter in the next cabin and a juke box playing an Eddie Fisher recording, *Arrivederci Roma.* The night had been very hot and there had been blood … blood …

The baby's blood. Justin's baby.

But Justin had sent her to the doctor in New Hampshire who had said, "I'm sorry, but you waited too long. The fetus is too big. No one in his right mind would terminate a pregnancy that's four months along."

The girl she once had worked with at Newberry's had said, "You poor kid, you. I know. I went through one last year. Never again."

"What will you do if you get pregnant again?"

"I know a midwife. She took care of me twice. She's okay. She charges two hundred bucks. Have you got the dough?"

She had had the money. Justin—but Justin was somewhere near, wasn't he? He had been here, in this room. He had promised never to leave her alone again.

But that had been nighttime—maybe she had seen him only in a dream. Now the sun was shining.

Wearing a starched white coat, he walked into her room. "I'm right here, Betty," he said.

She had wanted to say so much, but the words floated away when she tried to pin them down. She was very tired. She was happy just to keep holding Justin's hand. But he kept asking her questions.

"Why didn't you go to the man in New Hampshire, Betty?"

"I did."

"What happened?"

"He said the baby was too big. I waited too long. My baby. Yours and mine. I waited—"

"Why didn't you tell me?"

"What good would it do? You were married."

"Yes, I was married. Betty, who finally did it? You've got to tell me."

"She said if I told you, I'd go to jail."

"You won't go to jail. Who did it?"

"Jane Dieterle. You won't tell her I told?"

"I won't tell her."

"Justin?"

"What is it, baby?"

"I've made a lot of trouble for you. I'm sorry. Do you love me a little, Justin?"

"A little," he said and kissed her. "If you'll be a good girl and get strong again, I'll love you a lot more. Will you try to get strong for me, Betty?"

"I promise," she said in her childlike voice.

He kissed her lips and left.

CHAPTER TWENTY

It seemed to Jane Dieterle that all her life, there had been someone she had to take care of. First, there had been her mother, a cardiac invalid, her voice whining down the stairs, "Janey—is that you?"

Jane had wanted to shout back, Of course it's me. Who else would come into this stinking hellhole of a house?

But you did not shout at an invalid, especially when the invalid was your mother. Instead, you said, "Yes, Mama, it's me."

And then, after her mother's death, there had been the three younger children to care for. One of them was always sick, and another always had wet pants, and the third pushed her food away, refusing to eat, until Jane sometimes wanted to choke her. They were all girls. Jane's father had said contemptuously, "Your mother wasn't capable of having a son."

Her father's second wife had a son—had three sons, in fact—and refused to have anything to do with the first Dieterle children. Jane had found a job as a practical nurse down at the hospital. She had rented a room and tried to take care of her younger sisters. But after a few months, she had had to give up and place them in an orphanage. She never saw them again, and maybe it was because she felt guilty about them that she hated children.

Sometimes, she would be sitting in her darkened living room, watching TV, when some child who was to stay with her for anywhere from one night to two weeks, would sob out on her front porch, "All right, but please tell Mrs. Dieterle I don't have to take a nap."

"All right, darling, all right," the mother would soothe the frightened child, but Jane saw to it that they had a nap, anyway.

"I'd never have a minute to myself," Jane had complained to Al Harkness, who owned the local taxi service, "if I let those brats tear in and out of the house all day."

She had known all about chloral-hydrate from her work at the hospital, and Cy Stevens had seen to it that she got all the prescriptions she needed. Cy had been good to her in his rough, brusque way.

"I'll not keep you," he had told her, "because I'm not going to have any whore making claims against my estate after I'm gone. But I'll protect you, and if you ever need anything, I'll see that you get it."

The promise was not much to salvage from a love affair that had promised marriage. Jane Dieterle had been young then—twenty-five, in fact—when Cy Stevens, on an inspection tour of the hospital, had spotted her buxom good looks. A few days later, his secretary had called her and said Mr. Stevens wanted her to take a private case. The private case had been Cy Stevens, already sexually impotent, but needing a woman's body just the same.

He had said, reaching for his bottle of bourbon as he sat at his wide cluttered desk, "I'll be good to you—at least with me you won't have to worry about getting knocked up."

At first she had hated having an old man touch her. Then she had found herself acquiring a taste for Cy's curious kind of love.

Cy had to give her up after his first coronary occlusion when his family tried to take over his care. He had suggested that she run a baby farm.

"There's no place in this town," Cy had said, "where you can hire a decent maid or even a nurse, since the nurses would rather work at the hospital, where there's a chance of maybe getting one of the doctors. I'll buy the house for you and furnish it but I won't be big-daddy. You'll have to make your own way, same as you've always done. And if you ever open your peeper about us, I'll run you out of town on a rail. Is that clear?"

It had been very clear. It had also been clear sailing.

"You'd never think," she used to confide to Al, "how many women in this town have to leave their kids with me while they spend a few nights with the wrong man. Of course, sometimes they have to work."

Jane had never permitted her baby farming, however, to interfere with the infinitely more lucrative practice of illegal abortions, for which she charged up to two hundred dollars. She justified her activities with, "If I don't do it, somebody else will, and at least, with me, they've got somebody clean who knows what she's doing."

She had known what she was doing with that Hogan girl, too, and had known she was a fool to risk it. Betty had waited too long, hoping that Justin Riley would marry her. Imagine a doctor marrying a tramp like that. Nevertheless, because Justin Riley was the father, Jane had gone through with it. Justin was the senator's son-in-law and some day Jane might need political pull.

Cy used to say, "If a girl's not good enough for a man to marry before he's gone to bed with her, she sure in hell isn't good enough for him to marry after he's had it."

Cy was all right. A tight man with a dollar, but while he lived, she had been safe, and even now, if he were alive, he would find some way to protect her. He had ruled this town, and they could say what they wanted about him, but he had been all man.

She remembered and smiled. Her hand went automatically to her hair, to push the dyed stray strands back into place. Ed Haley had always had a sort of crush on her. Even if that girl lost her nerve and ratted, there was still a chance that she could make Ed sort of laugh it off. Why, hadn't his own wife—

The doorbell chimed twice. Through the window where the blinds were always drawn, she saw a small black-and-white police car.

She walked calmly and firmly to the door. Not only Ed Haley but Justin Riley and Misty Powers were standing on her doorstep.

She said courteously, "Won't you come in?"

They came into the spotless front hall with its pretty green-and-white wallpaper and its beige wall-to-wall carpeting. Nobody in town except Jane Dieterle and the really rich had wall-to-wall carpeting.

"Jane," Ed said heavily, "I'm sorry, but I've got a warrant here for your arrest, sworn out by Dr. Riley. It accuses you—among other things—of having performed a criminal abortion on one Elizabeth Hogan. Do you deny the charges?"

Jane looked into Ed's rum-scarred face and his mean little eyes. She saw the gun bulging from its holster. She was aware of Misty, dressed up in a dark silk suit, as though she were going somewhere special. She saw Justin Riley, and remembered how hard that girl had cried for him, all the while Jane was taking from her the baby she so wanted.

"No," she said, "I don't deny the charges, Ed. If you'll wait till I get my coat, I'll be with you."

Cy used to say that when you did not have the guts to confess, it was always a relief to be found out

CHAPTER TWENTY-ONE

Justin Riley knew the road to Misty's house from anywhere in town, as he knew the back of his hand. As well as he knew the meaning of every systolic and diastolic murmur in a patient's heart. Tonight, the road seemed long and strange. Perhaps, he thought, because this was the start of a far longer trip than the one across the township. Queer, that now as he really learned the full meaning of his profession, that profession was getting ready to kick him out.

Many people seemed to ride with him on this night late in July, though only Misty was physically present. He said, "All these years, Misty, I've been excusing the things I did by saying to myself, 'All right, so I'm a doctor, but I'm also a man.' Today, in that girl's room, I had to say to myself, 'I'm a doctor—' and take it from there."

"Meaning," Misty said, "that I've got to stop saying to myself, 'I'm a mother, but I'm a woman, too—' and take it from there."

"Meaning just that. You can't have it both ways, Misty. You can't have the kids and the lovers and the booze and the abortions, too. Martha almost died the day you were sleeping it off."

"I know." She had been thoughtful after they left the sheriff's office, where Jane had been put under bond and Justin had signed the complaint warrant. "Since that night in the taproom," she said, "Phil won't even speak to me. I advertised to the whole world that night how much I loved you, darling."

"No," Justin contradicted her. "You advertised to the whole world how drunk you were and how jealous you were of Marge. I don't blame you. I feel the same way about Sandy. We hate them because they're two of the very few people who happen to like what they've got—namely, each other."

"Justin, now that you and Olivia are really through—is there a chance for you and me?"

"Not a chance, honey."

"I've got money too. I'd be good, Justin."

He patted her hand. "We both need some steadying. We wouldn't be good for each other."

"What do you want me to do, Justin?"

"You'll never live this thing down, Misty, so don't try. Before the Dieterle trial is over, everyone in town on whom she has performed an abortion or whose kid has told her that Mommy left me here because Mommy is spending a week-end with Phil, will be exposed. Call Sammy. He loved you once. He'll help you. Sell your house. It's too full of memories anyway. It helps you to live in the past, Misty, and the past is done and finished. You're not twenty years old any more. You're forty."

"Thirty-seven," she said.

"Thirty-nine."

"All right. So I'm thirty-nine. Does that mean I'm supposed to give up sex, live like a nun?"

Justin winced. He had seen so much of the cruelty of sex, he felt, when sex had no love in it, no sense of emotional responsibility toward the beloved, that he wondered if he would ever want a woman again.

"No," he told Misty. "All I mean is you'd better shape up into someone your kids can respect instead of a run-down, would-be, middle-aged glamor girl."

"That's really letting me have it."

"That's really letting you have it. And since I won't be seeing you again, try to remember that I'm probably the last man in your life, except maybe Sammy, who will tell you the truth. So long."

He left her on her doorstep and drove toward the house where he had lived with Olivia. He had things there and now it was time for the tired ignoble gesture of clearing them out.

He saw Olivia's white luggage stacked in the front hall. The labels read, "RENO, NEVADA." He could not have cared less.

He had seen that painting of Johnny every day for the past two years. But today, he saw it for the first time as the artist must have seen it. He crossed the hall for a closer look. There were zinnias, he noticed, in a gold vase on the table between the windows. The zinnias were red. His Irish grandmother used to say that bad luck comes to a house that has red flowers in it.

He walked to the painting that was hung above the sofa, and stood there a little while, saying goodbye to an image. The boy's hair had been ruffled by wind. He was wearing a dark-blue Eton suit. The socks ended below the knees, and the tie was wide—too wide, Justin decided now. The narrow face seemed distant, like Olivia's face, but the eyes were not distant.

Deep in those dark eyes he saw truculence like his own. Some day when that lonely kid was a man, he would have to fight or run at some crossroads of his own. Stu Everett, Johnny's father, had been one of those who ran. Johnny's mother—why not face it—was only a well-heeled bum. But Johnny would be different. Johnny would stand and fight, never knowing who had taught him courage.

Olivia said behind him, "I've been waiting for you. I didn't want to leave without saying goodbye."

He turned to look at the strange woman beside him. There were probably dozens of people who knew his wife better than he did. At the moment, he seemed to know her not at all.

He said, "That was kind of you."

"Not at all."

The well-ordered house lay about them, silent and echoing. Justin was newly aware of the exquisite pattern of the wallpaper, the depth and quality of the carpeting at his feet, the serenity of the world which was Olivia's world and where he did not belong.

He asked, "Where's Johnny?"

She looked exquisite in the black dress that had so much style it seemed beyond any style.

"Johnny is at my mother's. He'll stay there until I return. Father's lawyers are handling the divorce. When you decide on your own attorney, you're to let him know."

"Thanks."

"Amelia and Brooks have the evening off. However, you may use the house and the servants until I get back, if you wish. Johnny, in any case, will remain with my parents."

"Look," he said, and took a step toward her, and halted. "All right. You hold the cards. I've stopped giving a damn. But I wanted to see the kid."

Fear came into her eyes. "You wouldn't hurt him? He's only a little boy."

"I wouldn't hurt him. Listen, Livvy. For years I've thought of him as mine. You don't just wipe out a feeling like that."

"I suppose not. I'm sorry, Justin. But it might be best, all things considered, if you didn't try to see him. Why mix him up?"

Why indeed?

Outside there were summer noises of cicadas and singing birds and kids playing baseball in some distant yard.

She straightened the slim shoulders and glanced at her watch. "Will you drive me to the airport?"

"No."

"Will you call a taxi to drive me there?"

"No."

She walked into the hall. He heard the phone dial spin, heard her say, "Oh, Al. This is Olivia Riley. I'm making a six-ten plane from Mr. Tillepaugh's airfield—can you come and pick me up? Thank you."

Justin was in the book-lined den, selecting volumes he had brought here in the first place, when he heard the door of Al's brand-new station wagon, a gift from Jane Dieterle for many services rendered. The taxi door slammed shut.

Out at the Miles' farm, Marge said to her husband, "Look, Sandy—there goes Olivia Riley in Al's taxi. She's headed toward the airport. Poor Justin. Remember the night you told me that Betty Hogan was in the hospital?"

Sandy, standing beside her, said, "I remember. I thought that night I was going to lose you, honey."

"Don't you know," said his wife, "that no man loses his wife if he makes her happy in bed?"

"I guess," Sandy said with a chuckle, "that, and riding horses, are where I'll always win out."

There is a white hour in hospitals between the last change of shift and dawn. At that hour, post-operatives wake and ask for morphine if they have learned its deceptive blessings. Young mothers awake, look at their watches, and fret for sunrise and breakfast and a sight of their newborn babies.

At that hour the corridors are comparatively quiet. Justin nodded to the third-shift floor nurse who was looking at him with wonder.

"Don't you ever sleep?" she asked.

"How's Betty Hogan?"

"Glad you asked. Restless. She's all slept out, I guess—slept out for years, if you ask me."

Someone had brought Betty a magazine. Her thin hands held it tentatively but Justin could tell she still lacked the strength to concentrate.

"Hello," he greeted her briskly.

"Justin. At this hour. You're being so good to me." She let the magazine drop. The easy tears of physical weakness made her eyes big. With her face washed, with only the trace of lipstick which one of the nurses might have suggested, Betty was beautiful.

He sat beside her. "I want you to be better. Feel like talking? You can sleep all day tomorrow."

"How long will I have to stay here?"

"Maybe no more than another week, if you take good care of yourself."

"And then where will I go?"

"You'll go with me," he said.

The tears spilled over and her small hands hugged his.

"My wife is getting a divorce," he explained quietly. "And then you and I will get married."

Some of the old sullenness came back to her face. "You can't mean that. What man would want me—with everything gone that made me a woman?"

I'll have to find out, Justin thought, *which idiot told her so early about the hysterectomy.* Meantime, there was explaining to do. "You're still a woman. A lovely and very desirable woman. Having kids is important, sure—but it isn't everything. There are kids without parents. One of them might need us."

The small hands were alternately hot and cold, he noticed. "But why would you marry me, really? I'm dumb and we both know it. I'm nobody. You're an educated man, a somebody—"

"That's right. I'm somebody. I may lose my license, Betty. I'll need somebody with me on a kind of uphill road."

"Why me, Justin?"

"Because," he said simply, "you're the one who loves me. That's real rare, Betty. I'd be the world's biggest fool to pass that up."

Her features illuminated. Justin had seen people walking in light and darkness—the Andersons learning their son must die, and other parents learning that another child would live. He had tasted the sweet lust on the lips of more beautiful women than he cared to remember. He could not remember a face that looked as Betty's did, in this quiet instant.

Soon she started to talk and plan, excitedly, not quite coherently. "We'll go away. Anywhere you want. West, do you think? South? We could go to Africa. I'll learn to help you. I'll learn and learn."

She fell back to sleep as the window lightened and Justin stayed with her. He had another hour before his office required his presence. He touched the red-gold hair.

Maybe he was foolish. Everything had been taken from him—house, kid, wife, professional security—but he would not have changed places, as the new day broke, with anyone in the world.

THE END

Bibliographies

Robert Campbell Bragg
(1918-1955)

As N. R. de Mexico
Madman on a Drum (1944)
Marijuana Girl (1951)
Strange Pursuit (1951)
Private Chauffeur (1952)

Isabel Moore
(1911-1989)

The Other Woman (Farrar & Rinehart, 1942)
I'll Never Let You Go (Farrar & Rinehart, 1942)
It is Time to Say Goodbye (Farrar & Rinehart, 1944)
The Day the Communists Took Over America (Wisdom House, 1961)
A Challenge for Nurse Melanie (Ace, 1963)
Women of the Green Café (Dell, 1969)
That Summer In Connecticut (Prestige Books, 1970)
Chateau Sinister (Lancer, 1971)

As Elaine Dorian
Love Now—Pay Later (Beacon, 1961)
Suburbia: Jungle of Sex (Beacon, 1962)
Second-Time Woman (Beacon, 1962)
The Infidelity Game (Beacon, 1962)
Suburban Affair (Beacon, 1962)
The Sex Cure (Beacon, 1962)
Double Trouble (Beacon, 1962)
The Country Club Set (Beacon, 1962)
The Pain of Loving (Wyndham, 1976)

As William Hurley
Young Man on the Make (Lancer, 1969)

As Marc Weston
My Search for Manhood (Lancer, 1969)

As Grace Walker
Elaine Moore Moffat, Blue Ribbon Horsewoman (T. Nelson, 1965)

Orrie Hitt
(1916-1975)

Love in the Arctic (Red Lantern HC, 1953)
I'll Call Every Monday (Red Lantern HC, 1953; Beacon, 1954)
Cabin Fever (Uni-Book, 1954; Beacon, 1959 As Tawny; Softcover Library, 1964, as Lovers by Night)
She Got What She Wanted (Beacon, 1954)
Shabby Street (Beacon, 1954)
Leased w/Jack Woodford (Signature HC, 1954; revised by Hitt & retitled Trapped)
Unfaithful Wives (Beacon, 1956)
The Sucker (Beacon, 1957)
Nudist Camp (Beacon, 1957)
Pushover (Beacon, 1957)
The Promoter (Beacon, 1957)
Ladies' Man (Beacon, 1957)
Dolls and Dues (Beacon, 1957)
Trailer Tramp (Beacon, 1957)
Teaser (Woodford HC, 1956; Beacon, 1957; Lancer, 1963)
Devil in the Flesh (Valentine HC, 1957; Kozy, 1957, as Sins of Flesh)
Ellie's Shack (Beacon, 1958)
Suburban Wife (Beacon, 1958)
Summer Hotel (Beacon, 1958)
Wild Oats (Beacon, 1958)
Affairs of a Beauty Queen (Beacon, 1958)
Call South 3300: Ask for Molly! (Beacon, 1958)
Burlesque Girl (Beacon, 1958)
Trapped (Beacon, 1958)
Girl's Dormitory (Beacon, 1958)
Woman Hunt (Beacon, 1958)
Hot Cargo (Beacon, 1958)
The Cheat (Beacon, 1958)
Rotten to the Core (Beacon, 1958)
Love Princess (Saber, 1958)
Hotel Women (Vantage HC, 1958)
Hotel Confidential (Vantage HC, 1958)
Sheba (Beacon, 1959)
The Widow (Beacon, 1959)
Add Flesh to the Fire (Beacon, 1959)
Private Club (Beacon, 1959)
Carnival Girl (Beacon, 1959)
The Peeper (Beacon, 1959; Softcover Library, 1973, as Twisted Passion)

Too Hot to Handle (Beacon, 1959)

Sin Doll (Beacon, 1959; Softcover Library UK, 1973, as The Excesses of Cherry)

Ex-Virgin (Beacon, 1959; Softcover Library UK, 1969, as Made for Men)

Suburban Sin (Beacon, 1959)

Pleasure Ground (Bedside, 1959; Kozy, 1961)

Affair With Lucy (Midwood, 1959; Midwood, 1961, as Married Mistress)

Girl of the Streets (Midwood, 1959)

Summer Romance (Midwood, 1959)

As Bad as They Come (Midwood, 1959; Midwood, 1962, as Mail Order Sex)

Hotel Woman (Valentine HC, 1959; Kozy, 1960, as Hotel Hostess)

Wayward Girl (Beacon, 1960)

The Torrid Teens (Beacon, 1960)

From Door to Door (Beacon, 1960)

Motel Girls (Beacon, 1960)

Tell Them Anything (Beacon, 1960)

Call Me Bad (Beacon, 1960)

Untamed Lust (Beacon, 1960)

Never Cheat Alone (Beacon, 1960)

The Lady is a Lush (Beacon, 1960)

Sexurbia County (Beacon, 1960)

Tramp Wife (Chariot, 1960)

Hotel Girl (Chariot, 1960)

Lonely Flesh (Chariot, 1960; reprinted 1963 as Lola)

Suburban Interlude (Kozy, 1960)

The Cheaters (Midwood, 1960)

A Doctor and His Mistress (Midwood, 1960)

Two of a Kind (Midwood, 1960)

I Prowl by Night (Beacon, 1961)

Dirt Farm (Beacon, 1961; Softcover Library UK, 1968, as The Hired Man)

Summer of Sin (Beacon, 1961)

Four Women (Beacon, 1961)

The Love Season (Beacon, 1961)

Frigid Wife (Beacon, 1961)

Virgins No More (Beacon, 1961)

Party Doll (Chariot, 1961; reprinted 1963 as Strange Longing)

Man's Nurse (Chariot, 1961)

Hot Blood (Chariot, 1961)

Diploma Dolls (Kozy, 1961)

Dark Passions (Kozy, 1961)

Twisted Lovers (Kozy, 1961)

Suburban Trap (Kozy, 1961)

Carnival Honey (Kozy, 1961)

Wild Lovers (Kozy, 1961)

Easy Women! (Novel, 1961; reprinted 1963 as Inflamed Dames, 1964 as Love Seekers, 1965 as Jenkins' Lovers)

Shocking Mistress! (Novel, 1961)

Peeping Tom (Wisdom House, 1961)

Love Thief (Beacon, 1962)

Dial "M" for Man (Beacon, 1962)

Torrid Cheat (Chariot, 1962)

Twin Beds (Chariot, 1962)

Naked Model (Chariot, 1962)

Libby Sin (Chariot, 1962)

Passion Street (Chariot, 1962)

Bad Wife (Chariot, 1962)

Passion Hostess (Chariot, 1962)

Bold Affair (Kozy, 1962)

Campus Tramp (Kozy, 1962)

The Naked Flesh (Kozy, 1962)

Violent Sinners (Kozy, 1962)

Love Slave (Kozy, 1962)

Frustrated Females! (Novel, 1962; reprinted 1963 as I Need a Man!)

Warped Woman (Novel, 1962; reprinted 1963 as Taboo Thrills, 1964 as Wilma's Wants)

Abnormal Norma (Novel, 1962)

Bed Crazy (Novel, 1962; reprinted as Perverted Doctors)

Man-Hungry Female (Novel, 1962; reprinted 1964 as More! More! More!)

Carnival Sin/Playpet (Vest-Pocket, 1962)

Torrid Wench (Kozy, 1963)

Strip Alley (Kozy, 1963)

Nude Doll (Kozy, 1963)

Loose Women (Lancer Domino, 1963)

An American Sodom (Novel, 1963)

Male Lover (Gaslight, 1964)

Passion Pool (Lancer Domino, 1964)

The Color of Lust (Lancer Domino, 1964)

The Passion Hunters (Lancer Domino, 1964; Domino, 1966 as This Wild Desire)

Lust Prowl (Lancer Domino, 1964)

The Love Seekers (Novel, 1964)

The Tavern (Softcover Library, 1966)

Woman's Ward (Softcover Library, 1966)

While the City Sins (Ember Library, 1967)

The Sex Pros (Softcover Library, 1968)

Panda Bear Passion (P.E.C., 1968)

Nude Model (MacFadden, 1970)

As by Kay Addams
Queer Patterns (Beacon, 1959)
Warped Desire (Beacon, 1960; UK as Night of Desire, 1975)
Lucy (Beacon, 1960)
Three Strange Women (Beacon, 1960)
The Strangest Sin (Beacon, 1961)
Autobiography of Kay Addams, as told to Hitt (Novel, 1962)
My Secret Perversions (Novel, 1962; reprinted as Hidden Hungers)
My Wild Nights With Nine Nudists! (Novel, 1963; reprinted as Nocturnal
    Nudists)
My Two Strangest Lovers (Novel, 1963; reprinted 1964 as Beyond Love)
Cherry (Novel, 1963)

As by Joe Black (as told to Hitt)
Unnatural Urge (Midwood, 1962)

As by Roger Normandie
(co-authored with Joe Weiss)
Run for Cover (Key HC, 1957; as Race With Lust, Kozy, 1959)
Web of Evil (Key HC, 1957)
The Lion's Den (Key HC, 1957; as Tormented Passions, Kozy, 1959)

As by Charles Verne
(co-authored with Joe Weiss)
Mr. Hot Rod (Key HC, 1957)
The Wheel of Passion (Key HC, 1957)

As by Fred Martin
Hired Lover (Midwood, 1959)

As by Nicky Weaver
Love, Blood and Tears (Kozy, 1963)
Love or Kill Them All (Kozy, 1963)

CPSIA information can be obtained
at www.ICGtesting.com
Printed in the USA
LVHW021202071019
633402LV00001B/199/P